CITIZEN

— OF —

EARTH

JOSEPH KASSABIAN

KYANITE
Publishing

Paperback ISBN: 978-1-949645-29-3
eBook ISBN: 978-1-949645-30-9
Hardcover ISBN: 978-1-949645-34-7

Cover design by Sophia LeRoux

Editing by Sam Hendricks

Cover image © depositphotos.com

www.kyanitepublishing.com

CHAPTER ONE

The door flew open and slammed into the wall with a crash. Vincent Solaris looked over to see his father standing in his bedroom doorway.

"How are you still asleep?!" his father screamed. "It's nearly time to get ready for your Citizens' Day ceremony!" He picked up a wrinkled grey uniform off the floor and threw it at Vincent. "I remember when I was your age. This was one of the happiest days of my life. Youth these days. Bless the Chairman, I swear you are useless." His father turned around and marched back out of the room. He muttered something about how he wished Vincent was more like his younger brother as he walked down the hallway.

Vincent rubbed the sleep from his dehydrated eyes. Unbeknownst to his father, he had been out all night drinking with his friends and had only snuck back in a few hours before. His father had warned him a dozen times not to sneak out at night without a permit or the State Ethics Police would, as his father said, "beat the immoral behavior out of him or kill him in the effort."

Vincent rolled over and gulped from a stale glass of water on his bedside table. He sat up in his bed and glanced around the room. Piles of dirty clothes and pieces of unfinished schoolwork littered the hard tile floor. He walked on top of it to the desk, fumbled around underneath it for a second, and dislodged a pack of hidden cigarettes. Then he slid open his small bedroom window, placed a crinkled cigarette between his dry lips, and lit it.

Several groups of his classmates wearing their grey Citizens' Day uniforms were walking on the street below toward the school. Their heads were held high and their chests were puffed out. The creases in their uniforms were as sharp as knives.

"Assholes," Vincent muttered. "I bet most of them are already sitting on university acceptance letters or job offers." He frowned. Vincent wasn't as lucky. He had barely passed his senior year, though it wasn't like he tried very hard either. If skipping school wouldn't have gotten him assigned to hard labor, he probably wouldn't have gone in the first place.

Vincent tossed his cigarette butt out the window and stood up. He walked over to where his dad had thrown his uniform and began to get dressed. Compared to those of the other students, Vincent's uniform was in shambles. It still smelled of a long night of smoking and drinking cheap booze. He wasn't entirely sure, but he thought it smelled a little like vomit.

Vincent looked at himself in the long mirror that hung over his small desk. His wrinkled grey uniform swallowed his thin frame. The eagle and star badge he wore over his heart was dull and scratched. He was under strict orders to keep it shined and flawless. Vincent reached behind his back and pulled a grey wedged cap from his belt line. He brushed back his thick brown hair, placed the cap on his head, exited his room, and walked out of his family's house. He stood on the landing and was greeted by his two friends.

"Man, you look like shit!" bellowed Roy, a hearty grin on his face. Roy was a tall, thick kid Vincent had known since they were both in elementary school together. Vincent had always thought of him as a little slow.

"And you still look fat," Vincent sneered, lighting another cigarette.

"Bless the Chairman, you didn't even iron your uniform? The headmaster is going to beat you again, Vincent." Chester shook his head. Chester was a short, mousy kid with thick glasses. For someone who was as easily scared as Chester, it always surprised Vincent that he wanted anything to do with Roy and him.

"Why do you say shit like that? Just use swear words like normal people, would you?" Vincent said as he exhaled smoke. "You sound like my dad."

The three turned and started walking down the crowded streets. Throngs of grey-uniformed kids pushed their way down the flawlessly clean road. The featureless forms of the Detroit Area Six family housing units framed the road on either side of them. Aero cars zipped around in the sky overhead, filling the air with the dull hum of their engines.

"So did you guys get accepted into any universities?" Chester asked.

"I know you're dying to tell us, so why don't you just go ahead," Vincent said, waving his hand forward sarcastically.

"Well, if you insist." Chester pushed up his glasses. "I was accepted into the Medical University of Vienna." He looked very pleased with himself.

"Holy shit, really?" Roy exclaimed. "Can't believe you're going to be going to school in the British Providence!"

Vincent shook his head. "Vienna is in the Austrian Providence, you idiot."

"How about you, Vinny?" Chester asked.

"I wish you wouldn't call me that."

"Sorry, Vincent."

"I sent out some packets . . . but no."

"Not a single acceptance? Damn, man. That's rough. What are you going to do?"

"Be a miserable failure to my family, apparently." Vincent tossed his cigarette butt onto someone's overly manicured lawn.

"So same as always then?" asked Roy.

The group came to the steps of the Area Six School of Ethics and Citizenship. Two professors waited on either side of the large double doors.

"Mr. Solaris!" barked the older-looking professor standing to the left. The professor was tall and bent in half by some unknown malady. He was wearing the same grey uniform as Vincent, though he had several more badges of varying shapes and sizes on his chest. Vincent couldn't help but notice that his eagle and star badge were far shinier than his own.

"Yes, sir?" Vincent answered. Suddenly he was all too aware that he probably stank like a pack of cigarettes. Smoking was strictly prohibited for anyone who wasn't a citizen.

"Look at yourself!" the professor snipped. "Your uniform is a disgrace to this school, your family, and most importantly the Chairman! Go sit in the back of the auditorium so no one else sees you. And take your two idiot friends with you!"

"Of course, sir," Vincent droned. Chester let out a disappointed whimper.

The large double doors opened to a massive auditorium filled with students. The three made their way up a flight of stairs all the way to the top. They were so high that they could barely make out the now tiny podium in the center of the stage.

"Great. Thanks a lot, Vincent," Chester scolded.

"What? Are you really upset about having bad seats for the headmaster's speech?" Vincent asked.

"Yes!" Chester frowned.

"Why? You know exactly what he's going to say." Vincent stood up in their row of seats. He turned and faced his two friends and threw his arms out to his sides, faking authority. "Students of Area Six! You came to us as annoying kids from the worst area of Detroit, and today you leave us as citizens! Your duty from this day forth will be to work shitty, meaningless jobs just like your parents, to please the Chairman until you eventually die and get incinerated by some other asshole working another shitty, meaningless job." Vincent bowed deeply in faux reverence. "Praise be to the glorious Chairman!"

"Are you high?" Chester sputtered in total shock. "What if the professors hear you?" Roy rocked back and forth in laughter. The kids around them shot Vincent disgusting looks. Some of them placed their hands over their eagle and star badges, almost like they were protecting them from the filth of Vincent's fake speech.

"Oh, screw them." Vincent laughed. "After today, they have no power over us."

The headmaster appeared on stage. The old man stood for a moment in front of a large eagle and star flag that hung behind the stage. He stood tall and ramrod straight, bringing his heels together and his fist to his heart in the traditional salute. The students of the auditorium stood and copied his motion. The headmaster walked to the podium and motioned for everyone to be seated once again.

"Pupils of Area Six," he began. "This day will become the most important of your entire life, for today, your service to our glorious and most merciful Chairman truly begins." The grey-uniformed crowd erupted into applause. "On your first day here, you came through those doors nothing but whelps. Today, you will leave as citizens of Earth. Now rise and recite with me our sacred oath of citizenship." The students in the audience rose to their feet and, in the same rigid fashion as the headmaster, brought their fists to their chests.

"I swear I will be faithful and obedient to the our most glorious Chairman, the leader of all humanity, to observe and obey the law, and to conscientiously fulfill my duties to the Chairman and to all people." A chorus of voices repeated what the headmaster said.

When they finished, the headmaster spoke the most important line: "Until death," then he turned and saluted the flag once again, and the students of the auditorium again followed suit and sat back down. Then the headmaster exited the stage. Another professor, a short, fat woman whose uniform was straining to hold together, walked to the podium.

"You will now be presented with your Book of Ethics. This booklet, which must be carried on your persons at all times, signifies that you are a true citizen of Earth. It is to be your most cherished and prized possession from this day until the day your oath ends. Please come forward."

Slowly, the rows of students stood up and began milling down the walkways toward the front of the auditorium.

"You're into this kind of stuff, Chester," Vincent began. "Do you feel any different now? Has the Chairman smiled upon you on this day?" He grinned.

"Oh, shut up." Chester nudged him. "Hey, Roy, you never told us if you got into any schools. What's up?"

"Oh yeah! I got into the mechanics institute over in Area Four!" Roy beamed.

Vincent groaned. "You got accepted somewhere? Damn, I really messed up." He feigned shooting himself in the head as the three moved further down the stairs in the slowly moving line.

"Clearly," said Chester. "Ever think about enlisting in the Defense Forces?"

"Hell no. So I can get stuck out in some godforsaken hellhole on Mars or the Moon policing the damn hillbillies?" Vincent made a disgusted face. "I hear they bang their cousins up there."

"Well, you're going to have to find something or the area leader is going to assign you to the working crews. What's worse? Sitting in some hole on the Moon or picking up trash off the side of the roads?" Chester asked.

The working crews were a real sign of shame. They consisted of citizens who managed to stumble their way through school with grades so bad they weren't accepted to any universities. The crews picked up trash, worked as landscapers, and were generally looked down upon by everyone in an area.

"Ugh, I don't even know anymore. I need a drink. You guys want to join me in the spot after we get the most important book of our lives?" Vincent said, mocking the professor's tone of voice.

"Might as well. Probably be the last time I can before I move over to the European Sector."

"Of course!" chimed in Roy.

The three were soon in front of the podium. Roy stood in front of the fat professor. She bowed deeply and extended both of her hands, presenting Roy with the small Book of Ethics. Roy took the book and returned the professor's bow. Then he slowly walked off without saying a word.

Vincent stepped in front of the professor, who again bowed deeply with the book extended out in front of her. Vincent glanced down at it. It was a small brown book with decorative script that read "Ethics" on the top and "The Central Committee of Earth" on the bottom. In the middle was the massive eagle and star stamp. Vincent took the book, stuffed it in his pocket, and walked off without bothering to return the professor's bow.

The three went their separate ways after receiving their books. Vincent walked down the road home, staring down at the small brown book that was supposed to be the most important thing he would ever own. He flipped it open and looked at its pages.

"Service to the Central Committee is the cornerstone of citizenship" said one line. "All citizens must think of how their actions further the cause of the citizens of Earth and the human race," said another passage.

Bored with the book, Vincent stuffed it back into his pocket. Just before leaving the campus grounds, a bright light caught his attention. As he got closer, he saw that it was the Area Six announcement board. The board in front of the school was lit up in bright green letters. The letters scrolled by slowly at face level.

"Help the traitorous humans of Mars learn the peace and grace of our glorious Chairman!" The text scrolled through the air. "Volunteer today for the Rehabilitation Project Force!" The texts faded away one letter at a time before cycling back through the message, this time with the contact information of a recruiter.

The last thing Vincent wanted to do was pack up his life and move to Mars. He remembered from one of the few classes he had paid attention to that Mars was still suffering from severe starvation and drought stemming from a failed revolution nearly a decade before. To restore faith in the Central Committee, Earth had been sending thousands of volunteers to the planet in a rebuilding effort.

Joining the Rehabilitation Project Force would allow Vincent to save face with his family. Rather than pick up trash on the side of the road or burn bodies at the end-of-life facilities, he would—or at least his family would think—be serving the Chairman. He rummaged through his pockets for a piece of paper but couldn't find one, so he quickly pulled out his Book of Ethics and scribbled down the recruiter's office number.

Vincent stuffed the book back into his pocket as he walked through the front door of his family's housing unit.

"Hello, brother!" called out the cheerful voice of Vincent's younger brother, Austin. Austin, as always, had a pile of school books in front of him and was busy taking notes on a data sheet.

"Hey," Vincent answered, trying to walk by him.

"Did you receive your Book of Ethics?" Austin asked, putting his study material down.

"Yeah, check it out." Vincent pulled the book out of his pocket and tossed it onto the kitchen table where Austin was sitting. Austin jumped back.

"You know non-citizens can't touch an ethics book, brother!" Austin had a look of concern on his face. Vincent reached over and picked the book up.

"Oh right, of course." Vincent feigned surprise. He walked upstairs, threw his wrinkled uniform back on the floor, and put on a hooded sweatshirt and a pair of jeans. From under his mattress, he pulled out a clear plastic bottle with no label. Inside sloshed around a clear liquid.

Roy's dad, a mechanic for the Central Area Committee, had built a small liquor still and routinely distilled the stuff. It tasted like paint thinner, but it was the only booze the kids could get their hands on. Only fully employed citizens were allowed to buy alcohol at the area's general store.

Vincent pocketed his pack of cigarettes, put the unlabeled bottle of booze in a backpack, and threw the backpack over his shoulder. When he walked downstairs, his father was waiting for him in the kitchen.

"Where are you off to?" he growled.

"Oh, Chester said he would help me prepare for university before he goes off to the European Sector," Vincent answered. He never told his father that he hadn't been accepted anywhere. His father thought badly enough of him already, and he couldn't imagine what he would do if he found out that Vincent was going to end up on one of the area working crews.

"Hm," his father grunted. "What school eventually let your stupid ass in anyway?"

Vincent thought quickly for a name. "The . . . uh . . . Ontario School of the Arts in the Canadian Providence," he answered, fumbling over his words, as he wasn't actually sure if a school by that name even existed.

"Well, it's something. I thought for sure you'd end up on the working crews with that retarded Roy kid you always hang out with. Well, get on with it then." His father waved him off. Vincent escaped before he was roped into further conversation and his lie was discovered.

He was supposed to be meeting Roy and Chester at the spot—an ominous sounding name they had given to an abandoned family housing unit. Vincent had found it one day while skipping class with a girl, and immediately told his friends. Ever since then, they had used it to hide out and drink the kitchen-brewed, rot-gut booze from Roy's dad and bring girls whenever one of them happened to have a girlfriend—which wasn't very often.

Vincent walked several blocks down the empty streets. He passed rows and rows of identical family housing units until he finally got to unit number four sixty-five. That was the spot. The State Ethics Police had posted a sign on the front door that read, "Family Housing Unit Number Four Sixty-Five is unassigned until further notice. Any entry into the unit is hereby considered trespassing and violators will be prosecuted to the fullest extent of the law."

The sign had been there for months, though Vincent and his friends had never seen a single officer come near the house, so he had always just ignored it. He pulled a small knife out of his pocket and jimmied open the front door's lock. They always made sure to lock it again when they left, just in case some bored officer thought to check on the house. The door swung open. Inside, Roy and Chester were sitting on the floor of the empty living room.

"Hey! We thought your dad finally killed you or something. What happened?" Chester asked. He held his own unlabeled bottle and his speech was slightly slurred.

"Not yet, but he is asking a few too many questions for my liking. I think he's on to me." Vincent sat down next to them on the hard tile floor. The house was exactly like his—all the family housing units were.

Roy laughed. "You mean on to the fact you are totally and completely screwed?"

"Yeah, that's the one." Vincent opened his bottle and took a swig. The liquid burned the whole way down his throat and he coughed.

"He's going to find out eventually, you know," Chester said. "What are you going to do?"

"I don't know. I was thinking of just running off to another area or sector or something."

"Without travel documents? I swear it's like you're trying to mess your life up even more," Chester laughed, taking another drink from his bottle.

"I saw something about a work program on Mars," Vincent said. "It's pretty much the same as the working crews, but everyone says it's considered honorable to further the people of Earth. Plus, it'll get me away from here."

"That is true. My cousin works on Mars and likes it—you know, now that the war is over," Chester said.

"Isn't he a doctor, though?" Roy asked.

Vincent smiled. "Of course he is. He's Chester's family, isn't he?" He lit a cigarette and took a deep pull. "And since both of you two assholes are leaving, I might as well, too."

Roy stood up, swaying back and forth. He had obviously been drinking for a while.

"Fuckin' right!" he boasted. "We are getting out of this hellhole and we're gonna see the whole damn universe!" Chester and Vincent laughed and raised their bottles to toast their drunk friend. Roy whooped loudly and spiked his plastic bottle into the floor in celebration. Everyone laughed as it exploded and sent booze everywhere.

"I'm going to miss you guys," Vincent said, trying to catch his breath from laughing so hard.

"Yeah, me too," Chester said as he cleaned Roy's splashed booze from his glasses.

Suddenly, the three heard footsteps outside. They all slowly turned toward the door in horror.

"Did you guys hear that?" Roy whispered, his eyes wide.

The door's handle jiggled and then started turning. Roy and Chester turned to look at Vincent, who had forgotten to relock the door when he came in. He didn't have time to curse himself before the door flew open, revealing two State Ethics Police officers. Their black uniforms and tall peaked hats made them look like angry shadows.

"You three!" one of them barked. Vincent jumped to his feet and took off through the back of the unit without another word.

"Stop! In the name of the Chairman!" an officer screamed. Vincent could hear the officer's heavy boots slamming against the tile with every step. Vincent rushed through the unit's empty kitchen and launched himself through the back door. He smashed through it and landed in a heap in the small back yard.

The officer ran out after him. Vincent rolled and got back to his feet. With the officer doubled over and panting from their short chase, Vincent knew that this was his chance. All those years of his father forcing him to compete in the area's track club were about to pay off. Vincent turned on his heel and ran down the darkened streets. This time he couldn't hear the officer behind him anymore. He laughed to himself. He was home free.

CHAPTER TWO

Vincent leaned against the kitchen counter and drank a glass of water. As talented of a sprinter as he was, drinking half a bottle of booze had made things a little more taxing for him. That had hardly been the first time he had to outrun the local Ethics Police, though it was the first time anyone had stumbled on the spot.

Vincent was curious if Roy and Chester had managed to get away. He assumed not. Roy was one of the strongest men Vincent had ever met, but he was slow, and Chester would surrender at the first sign of authority. He thought about how bad of an influence he and Roy had been on poor Chester.

Vincent wasn't worried. Drinking without a permit wasn't a serious offence. Someone like Chester probably wouldn't even get a fine. The Committee would see how successful his family was and give Chester a pass. Vincent or Roy would never be given the same allowance for misbehavior. Vincent sat down in a kitchen chair and lit a cigarette as the unit's front door burst open and spotlights blinded him.

"Get on the ground! Hands out in front of you!" screamed an angry voice. Vincent quickly complied. Once he was on the ground, he could see that the spotlights were actually flashlights attached to the barrels of rifles belonging to Ethics Police officers, and all of them were pointed directly at Vincent. His heart slammed in his chest and he couldn't think straight.

"ID and ethics book!" the voice screamed again. "Now!" Vincent tried to fumble with his words and explain to the officer that he didn't have either of those things on him. The officer didn't wait for an answer and started searching through Vincent's pockets. He flipped Vincent over and felt around.

"No ethics book?" the officer delivered a kick to Vincent's midsection, and Vincent coughed with the impact.

"Search the house!" ordered another officer. Two officers stormed upstairs, pushing aside Vincent's father, who dared not intervene, and his brother, who watched in horror.

Vincent lay pinned to the ground by the third officer. He tried to avoid the gaze of his father and brother as they looked on. Vincent used to think his father thought of him as a failure. The look that Vincent caught in his eye as he stood cowed in the stairwell was no longer one of pity. It was a look of absolute hatred.

The two officers stomped back down the steps. Vincent could see the shape of a small brown book in one of their hands.

"Cuff him," ordered the oldest-looking officer. He had a look of disgust on his face. Vincent's eyes widened in terror. He had been in trouble plenty of times in his life, but he had never been arrested before.

"What?" he finally got out, the panic evident in his voice. "What did I do?"

"Unpatriotic conduct unbecoming of a citizen," growled the oldest officer. He looked familiar, and it dawned on Vincent that it was the same officer that he had run away from at the spot. The officer who had been pinning him down clamped a pair of metal handcuffs around his wrists. He winced in pain as the cold metal edge cut into his skin. He was pulled to his feet by his arms and pushed out of the unit.

The older officer opened the door to the jet-black police aero car and shoved Vincent into the back seat. The door slammed shut, and the two officers got into the front seats. The aero car hummed and vibrated as they took off through the air. Vincent glanced out of the barred windows and watched as his family unit grew smaller and smaller as the aero car flew higher.

After a few minutes, the car swung down and came to a stop on a platform high up in the air on the side of a tall, featureless grey building. The back door opened and Vincent was pulled out. Below, the expanse of Area Six spread out as far as Vincent could see. Other jet-black Ethics Police aero cars zipped around the building, landing and taking off from other similar-looking platforms.

An officer pushed Vincent forward and a door silently slid out of their way. Inside the room, another bored-looking officer sat at a desk. Behind him was a huge eagle and star flag hanging from the wall. He didn't glance up from what he was doing on his computer.

"Name?" he asked.

"Vincent Solaris. Area Six," answered the older officer for him.

"Charge?"

"Unpatriotic conduct unbecoming of a citizen, resisting arrest, unpermitted drinking of illegal alcohol, and vandalism of state property," the officer listed.

"Throw him in," ordered the desk officer. The older officer unlocked Vincent's handcuffs. Vincent rubbed his wrists soothingly where the handcuffs had left deep red marks. A small door to the left of the desk slid open. The older officer shoved Vincent through the door without another word, and the door slammed shut behind him.

Vincent found himself standing in a gleaming white room. A massive flat data display was on the opposite wall with a row of simple white chairs lined up in front of it. An animated eagle and star flag flapped in a faux wind on the display. Crowds of people milled around in the room, some wearing little more than dirty rags. Several people were curled up on the floor in the fetal position. A few of them were sobbing into their arms. He wondered if they were all there for the same kind of thing he was.

The display flickered and the flag vanished from view, and it was replaced by a list of rules. In plain white text it said, "No speaking unless spoken to by an officer from the Ethics Committee. No questioning your charges until brought to the Committee; you know why you are here. No personal effects are allowed in the holding area. You will proceed without pause to the door at the rear of the holding facility when your name is called. Any violation of these rules will be considered an affront to the Chairman. The display flickered again and the flag returned.

Vincent sat down in one of the chairs facing the display and put his head in his hands. He tried to remember when he took a criminology course in school and what some of the sentences were for the charges the ethics officer listed off. None of them sounded promising.

The flag vanished from the display once again. It was replaced by a recording of an ethics officer sitting behind a giant gun-metal-grey desk. Vincent assumed that, based on all the medals and stars on his uniform, he was someone important. The officer had deep wrinkles and a white mustache. His eyes were piercing.

"You are currently interned at the Area Six Central Ethics Violators Holding Facility. Shortly, you will be brought before the Area Ethics Committee and sentenced for your crimes against the Chairman and your fellow citizens. No correspondence is authorized with anyone outside of these walls." The officer said, without any change of tone or inflection in his voice. The screen quickly switched back to the flapping eagle and star flag, and an orchestra version of "Hail to the Chairman" played in the background. Several of the men in the room bowed their heads and placed their hands over their hearts—as was the law when the song was played. Vincent stayed in his seat.

A door on the opposite side of the room slid open and two ethics officers marched in. Everyone in the room, Vincent included, jumped to their feet. One of the officers looked down at a piece of paper in his black gloved hand.

"Miller, Johnas, come forward," he ordered. An older man who had been sitting on one of the beds stepped forward. He was openly weeping.

"No!" the man cried out. "I beg the Chairman for forgiveness! I did nothing!" He didn't resist the officers as they marched forward and grabbed him by the shoulders. The man went limp and sobbed as he was pulled away. The door slid shut behind them.

Once the door shut, everyone who had stood up sunk back into their seats. They looked like Vincent felt: hopeless. Eventually, the door would slide open again, and one by one, they would be pulled away to learn their fate.

Over the next few hours, that was exactly what happened. The door would slide open, and the officers would march in and call a name. Someone would break down crying, though no one would ever resist being dragged off through the doors with their feet dangling beneath them. No one ever came back.

Vincent's father, his professors, and even his younger brother had always told him if he didn't get his act together, he would one day be staring down the Ethics Committee. Vincent always brushed them off as up-tight losers who always had their noses buried in their school work or ethics booklets. He always thought they never really lived.

A lifetime of devotion to the Chairman had gotten Vincent's father a factory job that barely made enough money to feed the family. He was constantly unhappy and had driven his mother away with his attitude and closet drinking problem. Vincent had made a choice early in school that no matter where he ended up, he refused to be like his father. Sitting in that flawless white room and watching people get dragged away made him think that he had gotten about as far from his father as he ever could.

The door slid open again, and the same two jackbooted ethics officers stomped into the room. One of them glanced down at a piece of paper.

"Solaris, Vincent," he grunted. Vincent meant to stand up, but his legs wouldn't let him. He stayed glued to his seat, unable to move. The rest of the prisoners looked around the room and waited for someone to move.

"Solaris, Vincent!" The officer yelled this time. Harnessing his feelings of fear, Vincent commanded his body to function. His mouth went bone dry, and he was shaking so badly he nearly fell over once he finally stood up. The two officers marched over and grabbed him. "You fuckin' deaf, boy?" asked the officer who had called Vincent's name. For the first time in his life, Vincent found himself unable to think of something sarcastic to say.

The officers didn't wait for Vincent to walk—they dragged him by the armpits, his feet trailing behind him. They exited the holding area, and the door slid closed behind them. The officers dropped Vincent, and he landed on his hands and knees. Vincent looked up and saw he was in a waiting room. The room was as gleaming white as the holding area. In the seats against the far wall sat Chester, Roy, and his father. They had solemn looks on their faces and refused to make eye contact with Vincent.

An officer hauled Vincent back to his feet and clamped on a set of handcuffs. He pushed Vincent forward, past his waiting friends and family and through another sliding door. It was there that the Area Ethics Committee was waiting for him.

Four men wearing black uniforms sat behind a long desk. Behind them on the wall hung a large eagle and star flag. All of them were looking at Vincent with disgust and making no attempt to hide it. Everything else in the room was featureless to ensure all eyes remained fixed on the Committee.

The Area Ethics Committee was the governing, judicial, and moral body of appointed judges who were in charge of all aspects of life within an area. They were said to be appointed by the Chairman himself for life, so no fault could be legally found in their rulings or sentences. Vincent remembered in school when a professor told him the word of the Committee was to be considered the word of the Chairman.

"Are you Vincent Solaris?" asked the judge to the far left. He peered down at Vincent over a hooked nose and a pair of glasses. He reminded Vincent of some kind of bird.

"Yes, sir."

"What are the charges?" asked the same judge. An officer marched forward with paperwork in his hand, stopped in front of the Committee's desk, and handed the paperwork over to the judge on the far right. He looked down at the paperwork and grunted.

"Unpatriotic conduct? Destruction of state property? These are very serious crimes. What evidence do you have of unpatriotic conduct, officer?" Another officer marched forward and handed the same judge a small brown book; it was Vincent's ethics book.

"Sir, when we were searching the violator's room, we found his assigned ethics book not in his possession. Also . . ." The Officer turned to the back page of the book. "He had written inside of his book with an ink pen, sir."

Vincent's heart sank. He knew the officer was pointing to the Rehabilitation Project Force recruiter's contact information he had found at school . He couldn't believe that the officers had found something so small.

"Bless the Chairman!" cried the judge looking at Vincent's book. "This is a grave crime, young man!"

"The crime of unpatriotic conduct comes with a sentence of death," the judge on the far left said deliberately. Vincent shook violently and fell to his knees. He started panicking. His eyes darted all around the room, which suddenly felt four times smaller as the walls closed in around him. He could have sworn the judges had grown three times larger.

A fat judge leaned forward heavily on his desk. "Do any of you in the gallery have anything to say in support of this man?" Vincent wanted to scream for them to help him. To his surprise, Chester stood up.

"I do, sir."

"State your name, boy," the fat judge ordered.

"Chester Brent, sir." His voice waivered.

The bird-looking judge leaned forward over the desk and stared down at Chester over his glasses. "You may speak."

"Well, sir, the day he was arrested, Vincent, I mean Mr. Solaris, talked about going to Mars to help with the rehabilitation projects going on there." His voice faded away quickly. "He was accepted into several schools but turned them down to help Mars recover from the war and to show them the true grace of our dear Chairman," Chester said. Chester, who no doubt was the one who told the Ethics Police where Vincent had lived, had just lied for him. Vincent smiled.

"Hm. The backward Reds might benefit from someone with such drive to serve his Chairman," the fat judge pondered.

"Even with such blatant disregard for our Chairman's book?" asked the bird-looking judge.

The fourth judge, who had been silent until this point, nodded. "We could show those treasonous Reds that our beloved Chairman is truly merciful."

"Yes, but are we sending the right message by shipping disloyal criminals to them?" the bird-looking judge asked. "There are other ways to serve." He glanced at the other judges. Vincent swallowed deeply. He had a feeling he knew what that comment meant.

"We have wondered enough about this particular boy," growled the fat judge. "I believe it is time to deliberate." The judges nodded to one another, then bowed to the eagle and star flag before exiting the room through a door behind their desk.

Their absence left a deathly silence in the room. Two ethics officers stood at the ends of the judge's desk, their eyes boring holes into Vincent. He didn't dare glance at his friends and family. They were watching what might soon be the final moments of Vincent's life.

The door behind the desk slid open and the judges re-entered. They sat down behind the desk silently and glared down at Vincent. There was no emotion on any of their faces. Vincent wondered how many times that was the last thing someone had seen.

"The charges against you are very grave, Mr. Solaris, and they carry an equally grave punishment," grumbled the fat judge. Vincent began to panic again. Tears began flowing freely from his eyes. He felt his throat tighten.

"You are a slightly different case, however. Due to your clean record, you will escape the gallows, but you cannot and will not escape punishment for your unpatriotic conduct." Vincent lifted his head up.

"We see how badly you wish to serve our merciful Chairman. We sentence you to three years' service in the Earth Defense Forces, to be served immediately and without break," ordered the bird-looking judge.

He hoisted a gavel up high and slammed it on the desk.

CHAPTER THREE

After the judgment was passed, Vincent had no time to say goodbye to his friends and family. The two ethics officers who had been staring him down since the beginning of the trial simply marched forward and grabbed him. He was pulled back through the door and dragged down a hallway. His father never once looked up from the floor.

The hallway was white and featureless. Vincent was flanked by nondescript doors on either side. The officers pushed Vincent by so quickly he couldn't see where any of them led. His mind was still racing as he struggled to process everything that had just happened during the trial.

Chester, who had presumably been the one to rat Vincent out, had seemingly saved him from a far worse punishment. He knew that just because the Committee wasn't executing him, didn't mean it wouldn't banish him to some mining camp on the Moon and work him to death. From his history classes, Vincent knew of a kid who was sent there for two years for punching an ethics officer after a night of drinking. The day after that class, when he was walking back from school, he saw the kid's family being escorted out of its housing unit. No one ever saw the kid or his family again.

Vincent wondered what the Defense Forces were like. He knew they generally sat around in bases at outposts in the far reaches of Earth-controlled space, but little else. When he was young, Mars declared independence and the Defense Forces were sent there to crush the rebellion, but that was over within a few weeks.

Then there was the Alliance, a group of alien races that sat in their little empire beyond human space. Vincent's professors constantly said they were some kind of disgusting barbarian collective that couldn't wait for the day it would sweep through human space and enslave everyone. Vincent had never seen an alien before—they were banned from human space—but his professors always showed horribly ugly pictures of them in class.

Finally, the ethics officers stopped dragging him. They were standing in front of a white door, next to which was a sign that read, "Colonel Rostov, EDF." The door slid open, revealing an old man seated at a desk. He wore a grey uniform that was heavy with colorful medals. He typed away at a holo-keyboard, his fingertips tapping away on the top of the desk as they passed through the blue light.

"Sir, per the Committee's judgment, this man is in your charge now," the ethics officer standing to Vincent's right said, then saluted. The old man looked up from his work, eyeing Vincent up and down.

"And what am I to do with him?" he asked.

"Er, he was sentenced to three years' service in the Defense Forces. You are to process him and send him on his way, sir," stumbled the officer. The old man stood up slowly from his desk.

"Another one? Ugh, fine. You can leave him here." He waived off the officers. The officers saluted the old man, a salute he did not return. They turned and walked out of the office.

"What's your name?" the old man asked.

"Vincent . . . Sol—" Before the words were all the way out of his mouth, the old man slapped Vincent across the face. Vincent was nearly knocked off his feet. Pain seared across his face. He stumbled and caught himself on the wall.

"Sir," the old man demanded.

"Vincent Solaris, sir," Vincent corrected himself. His face felt like it was on fire. The old man was deceptively strong.

"I am Colonel Rostov, commander of the recruiting office in Area Six. Due to circumstances that I'm sure neither of us wanted, I will be processing you into the Defense Forces." He clasped his hands behind his back and walked a little circle around Vincent, eyeing him up and down. "I'd rather my Defense Forces weren't full of criminals and malcontents like you. It used to be a thing of honor. But I am just an instrument of the

Chairman." A little smile crossed his face. "Just like you now, boy."

Rostov locked Vincent in an empty room in the back and gave him a stack of paperwork to fill out. The room was full of posters depicting soldiers fighting aliens while victoriously holding an eagle and star flag overhead.

"Forward toward victory!" proclaimed the caption above it.

"For the Chairman, for humanity!" screamed the words from another poster. That one showed the black boot of a soldier stomping some ugly green alien into the ground.

Vincent flipped through the pile of paperwork, signing it absent-mindedly. He did try to read the first few pages but quickly grew bored of it. He did notice a few pages extolling the fact that breaking any part of the enlistment contract was to be met with death by firing squad.

He stopped and wondered how often that punishment was actually carried out; then decided he didn't really want to know. He read a passage about life insurance in the event that he died, only to see a bullet point clarifying that those sentenced to service were offered no benefits or pay whatsoever. Vincent signed it anyway.

When Vincent finished with the stack of paperwork, he set it aside on a small table. As if he had been waiting the whole time, Rostov slid open the door and entered, picking up the paperwork.

"When an officer enters the room you are sitting in, you get on your feet, boy," he growled. Vincent leapt to his feet.

"Sir?" Vincent asked.

"Hm?"

"What happens next?"

"I give you to the local muster garrison. You'll be stored there until they find a place to stick you," he said. "You'll be with all of the true patriots who want to serve their people—and a few pieces of garbage like yourself." Rostov turned and started walking out of the room. "Well then, let's go." He motioned with the stack of papers in his hand.

He dropped the papers onto his desk and walked back out into the hallway with Vincent at his heels. Rostov walked with a pronounced limp. His right leg moved harshly, almost stuttering a few seconds behind his left.

"Sir?" Vincent began.

"What, boy?"

"If you don't mind me asking, what happened to your leg? Is it service-related?" Vincent didn't care about the man's health; he mostly wanted to know what kind of threats he would be facing shortly.

Rostov cackled. "Oh that?" He stopped walking, bent down, and lifted his pant leg. A gun-metal-grey prosthetic was attached to his knee, and a shined black leather boot was on his metal foot. "One of the goddamn Reds blew it off with a rocket on Mars. The Chairman blessed me enough to replace it with this so I could keep stacking bodies in his name. It hasn't aged well, but back in the day I could still keep up with everyone else." He tucked his pant leg back into his boot and walked on.

"Do they serve in the Defense Forces?" Vincent asked. "The . . . Reds."

Rostov nodded. "Oh yes." "Due to their continued disloyalty, every family is ordered to turn a child over for conscription. It has slowly turned them placid over the years." His laugh gave Vincent the chills.

They exited the Area Ethics Committee building and walked out onto a sidewalk. The smell of the fresh air rushed Vincent's senses. Just a few hours ago, he was certain he would never smell it again. Even the dull line of grey featureless buildings that made up Area Six were a welcome sight.

"Are you from Area Six, sir?" Vincent asked.

"No." Rostov shook his head. "Russian Providence, Muscovy Area."

"Why come here of all places?" Vincent couldn't help but to blurt out the question.

He glared down at Vincent. "I go where the Chairman commands me. Trust me, boy. There are far worse places in this universe than your Area Six." It was almost like he knew that Vincent couldn't stand his hometown. The two ended up in front of another large grey building. A star and eagle flag hung on either side of a large main door.

A Defense Forces soldier stood at the gate. His uniform was grey like Rostov's, but it had no medals. The soldier wore a thick black vest covered in various pouches. He had a black helmet on his head that nearly covered his eyes. Vincent couldn't help but stare at the rifle slung across the soldier's back; it was the same kind the ethics officers had shoved in his face.

When the soldier noticed Rostov and Vincent approaching, he snapped his heels together and raised his hand to his helmet in a crisp salute.

"Good morning, sir!" the soldier called out.

"Good morning, Private," Rostov growled, not returning the salute. The front door slid open and the two entered the building. The inside of the building looked a lot like the holding area Vincent had just come from. It was a massive open space with several rows of bunk beds lined up in the middle of the room. The requisite star and eagle flag, with several other smaller flags underneath it, covered most of the back wall. They depicted things like screaming eagles, a knight fighting a dragon, and a valiant horse rearing its head.

"What are those?" Vincent asked, pointing at the flags.

"Unit insignia. They are worn by various units of the Defense Forces. They're the only symbols allowed to exist outside of the Chairman's flag, through his grace of course." Rostov pointed to a patch he wore on his left shoulder. The insignia was an armored knight's gauntlet crushing a demon.

Vincent nodded. "Of course."

The two walked past the rows of bunk beds. They all had perfectly uniform sheets and blankets. In stark contrast to Vincent's trashed bedroom back home, not a thing was out of place. Rostov marched up to a door in the back of the room. A title next to it read, "Sergeant Major Ladd, Area Six Replacements."

Rostov walked right in without knocking. An older, gaunt-looking man shot to his feet and rendered a crisp salute. This time, Rostov actually returned it, though slowly.

"Good to see you, Ladd. Bad news. I have another one of the Committee's charity cases for you." Rostov pointed back to Vincent.

"Another one?" grunted Ladd. The man was stooped at the waist, his back bent somewhere between his shoulder blades. He still managed to puff his chest out as he walked over to look at Vincent. His face was sunken in and his eyes bulged slightly. "Bless the Chairman, but why on Earth are so many of these little bastards being sentenced to service? It seems like we are getting a hundred a day now. Just take them out back and shoot them. Save us the time." Ladd and Rostov both laughed.

"I wouldn't question what the Chairman is thinking, but I have to agree. Maybe he thinks those disgusting Alliance creatures are going to attack," Rostov muttered.

Ladd laughed. "I hope they are that foolish. You can leave the boy here with me. I'll billet him over with the rest of his kind."

"Good luck, boy," Rostov said as he turned and walked away.

"Alright, kid. Your kind is over on the right side of the building. Find a bunk. Your uniform will be issued to you when it's ready. Chow is in one hour. You miss it, you don't eat. Any questions?" Ladd rattled off the information so quickly Vincent barely had time to take it all in.

"Um, yes, sir," Vincent answered. Ladd responded by slapping him across the face. "I am a sergeant major and you'll address me as such! Now get your ass over to your bunk before I smack the goddamn taste out of your mouth!" he barked.

Vincent didn't give him another chance—he was running over to the bunks as soon as Ladd was done talking. He didn't know much about the Defense Forces, but he hoped in the long run he would be slapped far less than he had been in the past few hours. His face was throbbing.

Vincent passed by row after row of neat and orderly bunks. He assumed he was in the right place when he came to a row of bunks that looked different than the others. Instead of uniform green blankets and white sheets, the beds were covered with torn and ratty-looking blankets. Several soldiers sat on the bunks, and they too looked much different. Instead of buzz cuts and cleanly shaven faces, they had shaggy hair and days of beard growth.

A large guy with a bushy beard and curly hair grunted, "Another one?" He had thick ropes of muscle for arms and was wearing a grey tank top that was ratted and torn and looked several sizes too small.

"So what did you do?" asked a skinny guy with poufy hair and glasses.

"I . . . drew in my ethics book, drank booze, and ran away from the ethics officers," Vincent mumbled.

The big guy laughed. "Impressive!" "My name is Richardson. I got five years for punching an ethics officer in the face."

"I'm Collins," piped up the skinny guy. "Ten years. I was stealing people's credit chip numbers."

"Ten years?!" Vincent exclaimed.

"Yeah, one of the guys I stole from ended up being the brother of that fat bastard who sits on the Committee. No mercy." Collins laughed.

"So they separate us because we didn't enlist?" asked Vincent.

Richardson shrugged. "Technically, they aren't allowed to separate us. It ends up happening, because when we get marched in here looking like beaten dogs, everyone knows where we came from. They ostracize us accordingly."

"Pretty messed up, eh?" asked Collins. "Don't worry. Once we get to our actual units, no one will know any better, unless you're dumb enough to speak up."

Vincent nodded. "Noted. So what do we do around here?"

"We pretty much just wait," Richardson said. "Until a unit makes a personnel request and then we are sent off to wherever."

"Jeez, how long does that take?"

"I haven't seen anyone get stuck here for more than a week," Collins answered. "A few hours ago, a ship came for pretty much everyone but us. Took them to Fort Triumph on the Moon."

Vincent was in awe. "Wow, they landed a ship here?" He had heard stories of the Earth Defense Forces' massive space navy. Vincent heard of ships so big they would darken the entire sky when they came back to Earth. He had never actually seen one, though.

Collins shook his head, "Nah. They're so big they can't land on the planet. They just hover and send down transport ships to ferry soldiers back and forth."

Suddenly, it had dawned on Vincent that he hadn't eaten anything since he was arrested. His stomach gnawed at him.

"So when do we get something to eat?" he asked, holding his stomach.

"In a few minutes, the regulars get to eat." Richardson said. Seeing the puzzled look on Vincent's face, he continued, "The guys who enlisted. We get to eat after they're done."

Vincent was shocked. "We have to eat the scraps?"

"To be fair we aren't missing anything. The food is terrible regardless of the pecking order." Richardson laughed. A bell rung throughout the building, and in unison all the soldiers stood up and started making their way to the back of the building.

A food cart was wheeled out and two other soldiers started doling out a ladleful of something Vincent couldn't make out. Just like Richardson had said, Vincent and the rest of the sentenced soldiers stayed seated on their beds. As Vincent sat, elbows on his knees and head in his hands trying to not think about food, a young female soldier approached them.

"Are you Private Solaris?" she asked.

"Yeah, I guess so," Vincent said. The soldier dropped a bag on the floor next to him.

"That is your uniform. If anything doesn't fit, you will have to bring it up with your unit once you get there." Without another word, she turned around and walked off. Vincent reached down and unzipped the bag. Inside was a pair of black leather boots and a grey uniform.

"So where can I change?" asked Vincent.

"You're looking at it." Richardson waved his hand around in a little circle. "If you were going to get privacy, they would have issued it to you." He laughed.

Vincent frowned. "Wonderful." He stripped down nervously, looking around to see if anyone was paying attention. He wasn't the most masculine-looking guy and being surrounded by uniformed soldiers suddenly made him feel self-conscious. He wished he had spent more time in the gym with Roy. Most of the soldiers stood motionless in line waiting for their food; Vincent might as well have been invisible.

He was surprised to find that his uniform fit him perfectly, though the boots were painfully stiff and heavy. He felt like he had two weights attached to his feet. He smiled a little to himself when he saw the exact same kind of hat that he had to wear with his school uniform. Vincent was about to sit back down on his bed when he heard the loud voice of Sergeant Major Ladd.

"Hey, shitbirds! Your turn!"

"I'm assuming that's us." Vincent smiled sarcastically.

Collins nodded. "You assume correctly."

The three stood up and walked over to the food carts. The two soldiers who'd been serving everyone else had abandoned it. Inside two brown tubs was a thin soup-like substance that reminded Vincent of bad oatmeal. Richardson spooned some of the slop into a bowl and started carrying it back toward their bunks. Vincent picked up the ladle next.

"Where's the spoons?" he asked.

"Oh, the enlisted guys think it's funny to steal them all so we have to drink this garbage straight from the bowl." Collins motioned toward a crowd of enlisted soldiers who were laughing to themselves as they watched the three scrape the bottom of the tubs.

Vincent frowned. "I'm starting to think those guys might be assholes."

"You're very perceptive." Collins patted him on the shoulder and they walked back over to their bunks.

Vincent sat down on his bunk and drank his meal from the chipped and dirty bowl. It tasted exactly as Richardson had said: like nothing. He wondered if they had had gone out of their way to ensure the food was tasteless. He felt the mostly liquid meal slosh around in his empty stomach. Instead of feeling hungry, now he just felt sick.

"I seriously hope the regular forces have better food than this," he said, holding his stomach.

"Doubt it. Probably not a lot of gourmet cooking going on in a metal box flying through space for a few months," Collins said.

"At least we won't have to wait for everyone else to finish," Richardson retorted optimistically.

Vincent lay back and slipped off into a nap. The next several days passed much like the first one. Vincent and the other sentenced soldiers sat around on their bunks waiting for their turn to eat. Occasionally, Sergeant Major Ladd would scream at them to mop the floor. Other than that, they were left to do as they wanted. It wasn't exactly exciting, but if that was what the Defense Forces were like, Vincent thought he might be okay after all.

*****

During one of his many naps, Vincent was kicked awake by Collins. Vincent shot up in his bed.

"Movie time, dude!" Collins announced.

Vincent was still half-asleep. "What?"

"Once a week they let us go to the movies. I hear they mostly suck, but they're better than sitting around doing nothing." He smiled.

"Oh." Vincent rubbed his eyes and stood up.

Crowds of soldiers made their way out of the building. Sergeant Major Ladd stood by the exit, inspecting soldiers' uniforms before they stepped outside. He stopped one soldier who was in line.

"Did you even bother to shine your goddamn boots?" Ladd screamed in the soldier's face. The soldier tried to stand ramrod straight with his hands clasped behind his back but kept pulling away as Ladd spit at him. "Pass revoked! Go back to your bunk!" The soldier turned and walked away from the line looking dejected.

Vincent smiled to himself. He had been so bored he had shined his boots several times the day before. Vincent stepped in front of Ladd, who eyed him up and down.

"For being a low life piece of shit, you know how to keep a uniform, boy." . Ladd seemed mad he couldn't find any reason to stop Vincent from going out on pass.

"Thank you, Sergeant Major!"

"Don't thank me! Thank your dad, who didn't know how to raise you right! Get out of my face!" Ladd snarled. Vincent ran through the door like he was being chased. Outside, he met up with Richardson and Collins.

They walked toward the movie theater with the rest of the soldier population of the replacement unit. Civilians going about their daily business stopped and bowed deeply as they walked by.

"What are they doing?" Vincent asked.

"Did you even bother to read your ethics book before you got locked up?" Collins laughed.

"I was too busy getting drunk in an abandoned house actually." Vincent smirked. "Okay, admittedly that sounds bad."

"Well, according to the Book of Ethics, the Defense Forces are an extension of the Chairman's will to protect and further the human race," Collins said. At that moment, Vincent thought Collins was the spitting image of Chester.

Richardson shook his head. "That sounds dumb as hell. Most of these kids enlisted because they wanted to get out of this sprawling grey shit hole and knew they were never going to get into a school or get a job that would take them anywhere else."

"That's very enlightened of you, Richardson," Vincent said sarcastically.

"And you see where being so enlightened got us." Collins motioned down at his uniform.

The movie theater came into view. The tall grey storefront was decorated with movie posters. The windows at the front, which normally took money and gave out tickets, were closed. A sign across all the windows uniformly said, "Theater closed for weekly Defense Forces Appreciation Day."

"Which one do you want to watch?" Vincent asked. He eyed the posters on the wall. "The Battle of Hellas Basin" read one. Its poster was a Defense Forces soldier with a lantern jaw and pointed officer's cap slashing at someone with a sword. "Raising the Flag at Olympus Mons" read another, accompanied by a squad of Defense Forces soldiers raising an eagle and star flag.

"What about that one?" Richardson pointed at a poster that had a beautiful blonde embracing a Defense Forces soldier, the grey landscape of the Moon behind them. "It might have a sex scene at least."

The three walked inside the theater, where throngs of soldiers helped themselves to popcorn, drinks, and other snacks. The popcorn machine had been left open and unlocked, so there was hardly enough left to fill Vincent's bag. Collins took an entire box of a candy, ignoring the "please take one" sign posted over it.

The three headed down the hallway to where their movie was playing. Red curtains were draped across walls and cardboard cutouts of action stars were propped up against them.

Vincent noticed he and his group were the only ones heading that way.

"Think we picked the right movie?" Vincent asked, looking around.

"There is just a difference between us and them," Collins answered.

Vincent raised his eyebrows. "Oh yeah?"

"They wanted a porn that would make them feel better about what they really want: to be some kind of war hero. We wanted a porn that might show us what we really want: boobs," Collins explained.

"War porn?" Vincent laughed.

"Absolutely!" Collins exclaimed. "It gets them all excited and shit. When they leave, they're all smiles and talking about how they wish there was a Martian rebellion or an alien invasion or something for them to go charging into. We are the normal ones. We just want to look at boobs."

Vincent shook his head. "I'm actually baffled about how much sense that makes."

"Don't encourage him." Richardson laughed.

Vincent pushed open the door to their theater, past a poster that said, "Two Hearts, One Duty." Vincent glanced around the theater and saw that not a single seat was filled. They walked up the theater stairs and sat in the last row of seats against the back wall.

The movie started. It showed a pale blonde girl who fastidiously studied medicine and fell in love with a soldier she had met on a weekend out. They got together at a community gathering on All Patriots' Day, and the soldier fell for her after he was amazed by her devotion to the Chairman.

"If that's how my parents met, I swear to God I would punch them so hard in the face I would feel it in the womb," Collins sighed.

"Is this how people find girlfriends?" Vincent made a face. "If that is the case, I'm going to die alone."

"Oh, Viiiiincent!" Richardson screamed in a mock woman's voice. "Even though you're pale, skinny, and weird, your knowledge and loyalty to the Chairman just make my heart go crazy!"

Vincent frowned. "Hey! I'm not weird."

On the screen, the soldier was kissing the blonde girl, sweeping her off her feet. They barged through double swinging doors that led to a master bedroom. Vincent had never seen anything like it before. It was a massive four-post bed with curtains that hung down on the sides.

The soldier dropped the girl on her back and onto the bed. He pounced on top of her, kissing her hungrily.

"Wooo! It's finally going to happen!" Collins cheered, his clapping sent the rest of the popcorn falling onto the floor.

Richardson laughed. "I bet they don't even show anything. Citizens as loyal and upright as those two probably have sex strictly in the dark under the sheets with their shirts on."

"Why do you have to crush my dreams like that?" asked Vincent, getting caught up in Collins's excitement.

The girl ripped the soldier's shirt off. Under it, he had a sculpted, chiseled body unlike any Vincent had seen on Defense Forces soldiers so far. She felt all over his chest and abs. The soldier started to reach down and take her shirt off. Her pink shirt was just above her belly button when the screen went dark.

"Hey!" Collins screamed, his voice a mixture of anger and pain.

"Don't tell me they edited this crap!" Vincent said, exasperated.

The black, dead screen flickered, and an eagle and star flag appeared. It had a caption under it: "Stand by for an official announcement from the Central Committee of Earth."

"What the hell?" Vincent asked. In seventeen years, most of which he spent being lazy in front of an entertainment screen rather than studying, he had never seen anything like this before.

"If they aren't announcing something to do with that blonde chick's boobs, I'm going to be pissed." Collins frowned and crossed his arms like an angry child.

The screen flickered again, and footage from what looked like a war zone came onto the screen. Skyscrapers were on fire and people covered in soot and blood were running through the streets. Sirens wailed as State Ethics Police officers tried to evacuate a terrified crowd.

The screen changed to a news anchor. A woman with dark skin and slicked-back hair appeared. She wore a blue tunic with a small eagle and star pin on her raised collar. She glanced down at a stack of notes and read carefully from them.

"Citizens of Earth, that footage is live from Lunar City, the capital of our Moon. One hour ago, an unknown weapon detonated above the city, causing untold death and destruction. Evidence shows that the weapon was fired from Alliance-controlled space. Such barbarity, violence, and aggression cannot and will not be tolerated against the citizens of Earth or our race. The Chairman has declared total war against these vile creatures. Our glorious Defense Forces have already begun their march and will avenge the people of Lunar City one hundred times over!" She pounded her desk in anger. "Fire will rain from the sky! Our soldiers will slay the Alliance's ungodly hordes and cast them aside! Our glorious Chairman will not rest until every single one of them is dead!"

Then the screen cut back to black.

CHAPTER FOUR

The rush of soldiers out of the movie theater made any voluntary movement impossible. The human wave effect carried Vincent, Collins, and Richardson out of the lobby and into the street. Soldiers were confused and unsure of what to do. The confusion led them to just start making their way back to the replacement unit building.

Vincent looked up into the sky. In the pitch blackness of the night, the Moon shined brightly. Instead of its normal, eerie grey glow, it was glowing red.

"It looks like someone set the Moon on fire," Vincent gasped.

As the other soldiers also looked up, there were gasps as the realization of what had happened dawned on them. The burning sky lit up the soldiers in a flickering shade of red as they piled back into the building. They gathered in a large group in the open bay. Sergeant Major Ladd stood in front of them, his arms clasped behind his back as he paced back and forth.

"Hurry up! Get your asses in here!" he shouted. The last soldier filed in and the room fell deathly silent. "We are at war, gentlemen." A smile crept across his deeply wrinkled face. "Tomorrow, the ESS Victory will dock at the naval station above Earth, and you will board it."

The soldiers shot each other nervous glances. It felt like a weight hit Vincent in the chest. They were being shipped out to fight.

"Onboard that ship, you will be equipped and trained to fight en route to whichever vile planet we are going to burn to the ground first." He continued pacing. "You will be the spear that the Chairman thrusts into the hearts of those barbaric creatures who threaten us. For the glory of Earth!"

"For the glory of Earth!" echoed the crowd of soldiers. Vincent didn't cheer with them. He stood still, frozen in shock.

Collins and Richardson were frozen the same way, unable to keep up with the running emotions of the room.

At Ladd's orders, the entire population of the replacement unit lined up in front of an unmarked door in the rear of the building. No one had come or gone through that door the whole time Vincent had been there. Slowly, the line moved forward. The person at the head of line was issued the same black body armor and black helmet that the guards at the replacement unit building were wearing when Vincent first arrived.

They still weren't being issued weapons, though; Vincent thought that must have been something they did on the ships. Vincent, Collins, or Richardson still hadn't been assigned a job within the Defense Forces, and Vincent wondered if they would end up at the front line or if he would get some cushy support job far away from the danger. If they had access to his test scores, he'd be doomed to the front line for sure.

It was Vincent's turn to be issued gear. The same girl who gave him his uniforms a week before had a helmet and vest on a table in front of him.

"Try it on," she said without looking up from a data screen. She tapped away on it with her free hand. Vincent slipped his arms into the vest. It was heavier than it looked. Thick, hard panels weighed down the front, back, and sides. They felt like they were made of steel. The helmet swallowed his head. The brim nearly covered his eyes, and he had to push it back up so he could see.

"I think this is too big." Vincent shoved the helmet back again.

"You'll have to take that up with your unit once you're aboard the Victory. Sign here." She held out the data screen. Vincent made a bad attempt at signing his name and the screen blinked and accepted it. "Next!" she yelled.

Vincent walked back to his bunk, his helmet sitting almost completely on the back of his head so he could look out from under it. Collins and Richardson laughed when they saw him.

"You look like a developmentally-stunted turtle," Collins teased.

"Shut up," Vincent huffed as he sat down. The heavy vest was already hurting his shoulders and back. "This shit is heavier than it looks," he said, sighing.

Richardson smiled. "I haven't noticed."

"You can make fun of us weaklings all you want," Collins sneered. "But don't come crying to us when they make you a machine gunner or rocketeer or something on the front lines."

Richardson flexed, his grey uniform struggling to contain his bulk. "Muscles like this weren't made to work some stupid support job on the ship, man!" He laughed.

"Neither was your gene pool," snickered Collins.

"Replacement unit!" Ladd shouted over the room full of soldiers excitedly chatting with one another. The room fell deathly silent. "Form up!" At Ladd's command, the soldiers gathered together. Vincent shoved his way into the group next to Collins and Richardson.

"About face!" Ladd growled. The soldiers spun around on their heels. They now all faced the front door through which most had walked for the first time only a week before. "Forward, march!" From the far-right side, the soldiers started filing their way toward the front door.

In the movies, Vincent remembered seeing legions of soldiers marching in lock step, their heels snapping off the ground as one in an intimidating spectacle that the Martian rebels couldn't help but flee from. The replacement soldiers looked nothing of the sort. Each man couldn't stop accidentally kicking the man in front of him, and the whole group was so badly out of step that it sounded more like a herd of animals than a well-trained military unit.

The door opened. The guards on either side of the door were armed, but this time their rifles were in their hands, not slung across their backs. The guards were facing the replacement soldiers, not marching with them. It dawned on Vincent that these soldiers were making sure the replacement troops went outside as ordered. They must have assumed that, faced with the prospect of being sent away to war, many soldiers wanted to turn and run away as fast as their legs would take them.

Vincent didn't feel the pangs of fear he thought he would have—not like when he was standing in front of the Committee or when the ethics officers burst into the spot. He felt pulled forward with everyone else. He glanced around at the guys around him. They were all staring stone-faced, straight ahead. Even Collins, who Vincent had come to like over the last week, had nothing smart-ass to say.

A wall of blistering heat struck Vincent as he stepped through the door. The jet of air was so powerful it forced him into a crouch to keep himself from getting blown away. Through squinted eyes, he saw the large black form of a transport craft flanked on either side by massive, whirling jet engines. The back of the transport craft was open, creating a ramp that led to the front of the replacement unit's door. On either side of the ramp stood soldiers in black jumpsuits and shiny black flight helmets that covered their heads and faces.

Vincent stood in pitch darkness as he moved forward. He glanced up and saw a long black form blocking the sun, casting a massive shadow over the entire city. Collins, who was holding on to Richardson's shoulders to keep himself from being taken away by the transport craft's engines, was trying to yell at Vincent over the din of the craft, but he couldn't hear him; he shook his head and pointed to his ears. Collins leaned in close and grabbed him by his collar, yelling directly into his ear.

He pointed up at the darkened sky. "It's the Victory!"

CHAPTER FIVE

The ramp slammed shut when the soldiers were seated on the transport craft. Once Vincent was seated, a harness automatically slammed down over the top of him, locking him in place. Richardson struggled as the stiff metal bars pinched down on his broad shoulders.

"Oh man, I always get sick when I fly!" Collins cried. Vincent looked over his right shoulder and saw Collins trying to close his eyes and steady himself. His cheeks bulged as he fought back the urge to vomit.

"We aren't even flying yet!" said Vincent.

"But I know it's coming!" Collins whined.

Vincent had never been out of his home district, let alone off the planet. Few people had, unless it was permitted by their job. His father and mother had been to the Moon for their honeymoon long before he and his brother were born. After the Martian Rebellion, the Central Committee had severely restricted interplanetary travel.

"You've been off-world before?" Vincent asked.

"Yeah, a few times," Collins said, his eyes still squeezed shut. "My dad got a permit for travel a couple times. It never makes this any easier, though!" he whimpered.

The transport craft rumbled and shuddered. Vincent could hear the engines winding up. The craft's shaking rattled him to the bone. His knuckles turned white and his fingertips burned with pain as he gripped his harness on either side of his body.

Vincent gritted his teeth as the craft tore away from the Earth's surface. The force made him feel like his insides were trying to rip their way out of him. He swore he was going to somehow warp the metal of the harness as he bore down on it with all his strength. His eyes were forced shut against his will, and no matter how hard he tried, he couldn't make them open.

As fast as the flight started, it ended. The craft shuddered to a halt with a loud metallic clang. The harness unlocked and swung back over Vincent's head. Richardson had to force his harness off and it got stuck on his bulk. The rear ramp opened once again and the two soldiers in jumpsuits motioned for everyone to get off.

Vincent stood up, struggling to steady himself on the craft's bulkheads. The soldiers filed out and found themselves in a massive, cavernous bay. There were at least a half-dozen other formations of soldiers, and there was room for another half-dozen more. The inside of the Victory was gun-metal grey. Wires, hoses, and other unidentifiable cords wrapped around the walls in thick trunks held in place with bolts, tape, and anything else the crew could get its hands on. The air smelled stagnant with a faint wisp of burnt oil. Vincent's ears picked up a constantly dull humming in the background of everything.

Vincent glanced around. "This is not . . . what I expected." The glamorous warships he had seen in the movies looked so much different. They were sleek and elegant; they were brightly lit and spotlessly clean. The Victory was dark and dreary; it looked like it had never been cleaned. It looked like another jail cell.

"Yeah . . ." gasped Richardson, looking around the huge bay. A speaker system crackled to life. The rumbling of what seemed like one thousand soldiers stopped.

A loud voice commanded, "Listen up!" Vincent glanced around to try to find the person who was speaking, but all he saw were black-helmeted heads like his own. "You are now aboard the ESS Victory and will be constituted as a regiment in the Earth Defense Forces. You will be quartered in this wing and not permitted anywhere else on the ship unless otherwise ordered. Please follow the quartermaster; he will lead you to your living quarters." The speaker crackled and died out.

The crowd of soldiers started moving forward. Through the mass of people, Vincent could see a man in an officer's uniform leading the group.

"How many people do you think are on this thing?" Richardson asked.

"Probably hundreds of groups like ours at least," Collins guessed. "Plus the people that they need to fly it. And all the regular soldiers that were already onboard." The thought of all those people onboard the Victory put Vincent at awe. The ship didn't seem crowded at all. Even though he was in a group of what had to be around one thousand people, the ship felt empty and barren.

The group of soldiers followed the quartermaster out of the landing bay and down a connecting hallway. It seemed everywhere they went was badly lit and dingy. More than once, a boot would splash down in a puddle of oil or some other colored fluid that had pooled on the dirty floor. Every few steps, they had to step over a giant metal bulkhead; a few soldiers who weren't paying attention went down with a thud. Eventually, they came to a stop.

"These are your billets," called out the quartermaster. "No more than one hundred soldiers to a bay. That is how you will be divided into troops tomorrow morning. Wake-up is zero-six." When the quartermaster finished speaking, he noticed no one was moving. "Dismissed!" he commanded. The soldiers slowly made their way through one of several doors. Every room was the same—another large bay full of bunk beds. The three of them stayed tightly together to make sure they weren't separated.

Vincent sat down on a bed. Collins took his top bunk and Richardson took the bottom bunk of a bed across from him.

Vincent looked around. "What's a troop?"

"Jeez man," Collins laughed. "You don't even know that? It's a military unit, about a hundred people. Squadrons are made up of a few troops, and regiments are made up of several squadrons for better control on the battlefield."

"How do you know all this stuff?" Richardson asked.

"Haven't either one of you two idiots ever read a book?" Collins answered, laughing to himself.

A soldier climbed on top of Richardson's top bunk, and the group glanced upward. To their surprise, a woman was taking her helmet off and placing it at the foot of the bed. She was pale, and her blonde, nearly-white hair was cropped almost as short as Vincent's. Her blue eyes were so bright that they nearly glowed.

"What are you three slack-jawed idiots staring at?" she spat. Vincent picked up an accent in her speech he had never heard before.

"Nothing much," Collins sneered.

"Shut your dick trap, four-eyes." She jumped off the top bunk to confront Collins. Vincent stood up and got between them.

"Damn, calm down, you two. You're acting like you're still in lock-up or something." Vincent immediately cursed at himself. He had forgotten that no one would've known they had just gotten out of jail—unless one of them had said something stupid.

"Lock-up?" The woman glanced at the three men. "You guys are sentenced, too?" she asked, her brow raised.

"Yep," Vincent nodded. "For one stupid reason or another. How about you?"

She shrugged. "I didn't do anything. I'm from Mars." Vincent remembered what the colonel told him: every Martian family had to give up a child for national service. "Though these assholes think that makes me as bad as you." She gave a slight smirk. "No offense."

"None taken," Collins laughed. Vincent eyed the woman up and down. He'd never met a Martian before. All his books in school just said they were disloyal to the Chairman and shouldn't be trusted. She shot Vincent a look.

"Why are you eyeing me, you skinny prick?"

"Oh . . . I . . . uhh," Vincent stumbled. "I've never met . . . one of you before."

She frowned. "You mean a Red?"

"No," Vincent corrected. "A Martian." He knew Red was an insult, even though the term was used commonly on Earth. She softened a little.

"My name's Fiona." She plopped down on Vincent's bed. "Fiona Olympus."

"I'm Vincent. The four-eyed dick trap is Collins, and that's Richardson," Vincent laughed, while Collins crossed his arms.

"Nice to meet you." Fiona smiled a little. Vincent couldn't help but smile when she did. "Fellow outcasts."

The door to the bay opened and a man wearing a grey uniform stepped in. He was short with a curled-up mustache and a frown plastered on his face. His hands were clasped tightly behind his back, and his black leather boots made a distinctive rapping noise against the metal floor. He had a pistol on his side.

"Troop!" he commanded in a voice that sounded like it came from a much larger man. "Attention!" The soldiers all jumped off their bunks and stood ready. The man slowly walked down the bunk line, looking each soldier up and down.

"I am Sergeant Himmelstoss." He stopped to glance down at a soldier's boots. "I am in charge of your training here aboard the Victory. The Chairman has bestowed upon me the duty to prepare you for planetfall on whichever planet he decides to rain down his almighty vengeance." Himmelstoss paused in front of another soldier, inspecting his uniform. "In my unit, there will be no deviation from the acceptable standard. Is that understood?"

"Yes, Sergeant!" the bay screamed in one voice.

"From this point on, no matter where you came from, you are Charlie Troop, First Squadron, of the Two-Hundred and Forty-Eighth Regiment of the Earth Defense Forces. Tomorrow morning, we begin training, and there will be no excuses!" His voice echoed off the bare metal walls. He turned on his heel and marched back out of the bay.

"My, he sounds like a friendly guy," Collins quipped.

"Can we just feed him to Richie here?" Fiona commented, pointing over to Richardson.

Richardson laughed. "I'm not one to turn down a meal, but I'm going to have to say no thanks on this one."

*****

The night passed with Vincent and most of the bay of soldiers tossing and turning without sleep. The dingy and dirty overhead lights of the bay never turned off, and the smell of oil fumes in the air—not to mention the thoughts of what the Sergeant had in store for them come morning—made it impossible for Vincent to doze off.

The bay door slammed open, startling the few sleeping soldiers awake. Himmelstoss marched in, his boots sounding like gunshots off the metal deck plates.

"Attention!" he screamed. The soldiers all stood up in various stages of undress. Vincent found himself standing at the end of his bunk in a pair of ill-fitting boxers and one sock. Somehow, he had managed to kick the other one off in the middle of the night. He couldn't help but glance over at Fiona. She was wearing a tan shirt and a pair of black underwear that amplified the color of her skin. It was almost alabaster, and covered in a tapestry of twisted scars and black tattoos. The thought dawned on him that this was the first time he had ever seen a woman in her underwear before. She must have felt him staring at her because she shot him a look that was of full of anger.

"You have five minutes to be dressed, shaved, and ready to train. Go!" Himmelstoss commanded. At his word, everyone in the bay franticly began throwing on articles of clothing and lacing up boots. Jumping around on one foot while trying to put on his boot, Vincent tripped and fell over on his back. Just as he was back on his feet and buttoning up his jacket, Himmelstoss looked up from his watch.

"Time's up!" Everyone in line. Now!" He saw a few people fumbling with their remaining clothing items. He marched up to one of them, a young girl who was trying to lace up her one remaining boot, and punched her square in the chest. She crumpled onto the floor and moaned in pain. "I said time's up!" he screamed.

"Because you want to be so slow, how about you go put on your vest and helmet!" They ran back to their bunks and did as ordered. Himmelstoss grinned. "Now let's go for a run."

It didn't take long for the jog down the ship's hallways to start making soldiers collapse left and right. Vincent couldn't blame them for it; he was a great runner and even he wanted to vomit. Vincent's still way-too-large helmet forced his head down, and his heavy vest constricted his chest. The recycled, oil-filled air of the ship made his lungs burn with every breath. The issued black boots made him feel like he was running with weights attached to each of his feet.

Collins was one of the first to go down. Vincent wasn't sure if it was from being out of shape or if he tripped on a bulkhead like so many others. Vincent had to hurdle over him as he fell. Up ahead, at the front of the line of ragged soldiers, was the Sergeant. He was running like he didn't have a care in the world.

As the group ran down hallway after identical and featureless hallway, their numbers became smaller and smaller. Vincent wasn't sure if they had doubled back toward their bay, were going in circles, or if Himmelstoss was leading them somewhere deeper into the ship.

Vincent was impressed that Fiona was still huffing alongside him. Because of her slender build, he hadn't thought she could run for what had become several miles. She didn't seem to notice the several extra pounds of body armor and helmet. She was barely sweating, while he was drenched straight through his vest. Sweat even seeped out of his boots with each step.

Mercifully, Himmelstoss finally came to a stop. Vincent looked around at where he had taken them. It was an obstacle course: tires lay all over the ground, nets hung from the bare metal walls, and ropes dangled from the high ceiling.

Vincent gasped for air. "Ugh. Why do you look like you didn't even do anything?" Fiona didn't answer; she just smirked at him. He looked around and noticed less than half of the group was still with them.

"First two, go!" Himmelstoss ordered. Vincent and Fiona charged forward into the course, her a little faster than him. They ran through the tire portion and heaved themselves up a rope. He climbed a few feet up but fell straight back onto the ground. He didn't even bother trying to get back up.

She didn't fare much better. The weight of her vest and helmet dragged her straight down the rope, and she slammed into the ground next to him.

"Disgraceful! Get your weak asses off my course!" Himmelstoss yelled. They didn't need to be told twice. Both collapsed against a wall, taking their helmets off and brushing the sweat off their faces.

"You okay?" Vincent asked.

"You should be worried about yourself." She looked sideways at him.

"Sorry, just trying to make conversation." He coughed. "Ugh, my lungs are killing me."

She smirked. "The one benefit of growing up on Mars is it makes everywhere else feel like it has the freshest air imaginable."

The two watched the rest of the group go through the course. Few of them fared better than Fiona or Vincent, though after a while, it looked like Himmelstoss had gotten sick of people failing and started hitting them. When he got tired of abusing the exhausted soldiers, he made them all line back up.

"We are going back the same way we got here. Do not quit on me, or so help me, I will beat you within an inch of your life!" he snarled. The soldiers exchanged worried looks.

The run back was much slower and uglier. Vincent had resorted to sliding his heavy boots across the floor and using all that was left of his strength to get over the bulkheads. He wasn't even sure if he was actually running anymore. The only thing that urged him along was the figure of the Sergeant, jogging up ahead like the whole ordeal was routine.

Those who managed to finish the run collapsed into their bay. Vincent lay flat on his back, unbuckling his vest and relieving the pressure on his chest. The thin, polluted air of the ship made him feel like he would never catch his breath. He saw more than a few soldiers vomit onto the floor. Fiona strode past where he was lying and leaned against her bed frame.

"Get some water. Our next training time is in three hours. You had better pick this pace up or I'll kill you before the Alliance ever gets a chance to get its disgusting hands on you!" Himmelstoss barked, and marched out of their bay.

There was a faucet for water in the cramped confines of the bay's bathroom. Vincent was the first one to it. He stuck his entire head under and turned it on. The water was warm and had a tinge of a chemical taste. He spat it out.

"What the hell is wrong with the water?" he asked.

"It's purification chemicals," Fiona answered. "All of the water on Mars is like that." Vincent gagged and spat out another mouthful of water. Fiona laughed. "You don't get used to it."

Vincent forced himself to drink, even though his gag reflex fought the water every step of the way down.

"Ugh," he groaned. "This is awful." He watched Fiona as she drank it down without issue. Collins and Richardson staggered into the bathroom, and without exchanging words, they chugged back the water so fast the acrid taste never hit them.

"What is that asshole going to have us do next?" Collins complained.

Richardson shook his head. "If we're lucky, he'll just shoot us." As they dragged their feet across the ground and back into the bay, a bell sounded over the speaker.

"Finally, some training I'll be good at," Collins weakly joked.

"Attention, Charlie Troop," a voice said over the speaker. The voice was cheerful and struck a contrast with the drab and depressing look of the bay's occupants. "It is now your allotted chow time. Please make your way toward the chow hall located to the east of your bay." The bell tolled again and the voice left.

The group of soldiers struggled to make their way down the hallway. Almost everyone was limping or favoring some kind of injury after the morning's training. Vincent saw one soldier walking bare-footed, his boots chafing his feet so badly he tossed them aside. His feet were bloody and torn.

The chow hall was a bay that looked almost exactly like the one they lived in. Instead of bunk beds, it had rows of long tables with bolted-on stools. A buffet line of food was staffed by a few soldiers wearing crisp white uniforms that were the brightest thing Vincent had seen since coming aboard the ship.

The food was the same gruel that the replacement unit had served. Vincent groaned to himself and doubted that the Victory staff ate like the regular soldiers did. A white-jacketed soldier dolled a huge ladleful of the brown mush onto Vincent's metal tray.

"Man, I was hoping for something with actual flavor this time around," Vincent sighed, poking the gruel with his spoon. Fiona dug into her food hungrily.

"You know what they say: hunger is the best spice," she said in between bites.

Collins frowned. "You make Mars seem like the most depressing place in the entire nation."

"I think my feet are bleeding. These boots are terrible," Richardson complained. Vincent thought the same thing; he was just trying to ignore it. Ever since they had finished their run to the obstacle course, his feet had been burning and sore.

"It wasn't so bad," Fiona said.

Collins laughed. "Not so bad? The air feels like I'm inhaling exhaust fumes!" He dropped a spoonful of mush back into his bowl. "It's thicker than this damn gruel."

"We have dust storms on Mars that make it feel like you're breathing razor blades if you get caught outside during them." She shrugged, and helped herself to another spoonful.

Vincent shook his head. "Is that how this is going to be? Every time we complain about something you are just going to point out how much worse life is on Mars?"

Fiona frowned. "Have you tried not complaining so much?" She reached her spoon across the table and ate from

Vincent's plate. A siren sounded and everyone looked around, trying to figure out what was going on. The door to the chow hall flew open and Himmelstoss walked in.

"On your feet!" he commanded. The tired soldiers of Charlie Troop stood up. "You have five minutes to have your combat gear back on and be in the hallway waiting for me. Go!" The soldiers scrambled, some leaping over the gun-metal-grey chow tables and kicking over bowls and plates. They rushed past Himmelstoss and back into their bay.

They tossed their gear on in various states of correctness and ran back out into the hallway. The Sergeant was standing next to several hovering carts, which were stacked high with battle rifles. Vincent had only seen weapons like those in the movies, never in person. Himmelstoss filed down the line of soldiers and handed a rifle to each of them—uncharacteristically, without saying anything.

Vincent held the weapon in his hands. It was heavy and cumbersome. He figured it would be black like in all the pictures in his history book. They were an ugly unfinished metal color, like the interior of the ship.

"This is the Earth Pattern Rail Gun, or EPRG. It fires these." He held up a small black metal shape in between his fingers. It was about the size of his thumb and curved slightly to a gradual point. "This will be your primary means of taking the fight to the disgusting creatures beyond our system. With this weapon, you will cut them down and raze the holes in which they live." He turned on his heel and faced down the same hallway they had run down earlier.

"March!" he commanded. In no particular order, the soldiers started walking after him. Most of them were still exhausted from the morning run. Holding their weapons high, they dragged their feet across the metal floor plates.

Himmelstoss marched silently in front of the troop, leading the soldiers down hallway after hallway. Vincent couldn't find any markings that indicated directions on the ship. He wondered how the Sergeant knew where he was going and how long he had been on the Victory to memorize all its labyrinthine passageways.

Himmelstoss turned and entered through an unmarked metal door, the soldiers following after him. Inside was a giant open space with a line of metal barriers near the door. There was a control panel staffed by a bored-looking soldier in the far corner. The open space looked like it had a built-in rail system with chains and pullies showing through gaps in the floor.

Himmelstoss walked over and spoke to the soldier manning the control station. The chains and pullies whirled to life and human-shaped targets popped up from the floor. The rail system in the floor allowed the targets to slide from one side of the room to the other. The soldiers stood watching in awe.

Himmelstoss barked from the control panel, "Line up! One soldier per barrier!" Vincent moved to one of the barriers. A pile of three black, curved metal blocks sat on top of it. He picked one up and saw it was hollow. Inside, stacked on top one another, were the same black metal slugs that Himmelstoss had held up a few minutes before.

"Pick up one of the magazines on the barrier!" he ordered. "Insert it into your weapon!"

Vincent slid the magazine in the well at the rear of his weapon in the stock. The weapon made a metallic clicking sound as the magazine locked into place.

"Shoulder your weapon!" Vincent fumbled with the heavy weapon, placing the butt stock against his shoulder. He struggled to find a place where it felt comfortable against his bulky vest.

"Fire!" Himmelstoss ordered.

Vincent wrapped his finger around the trigger and squeezed. The weapon slammed into his shoulder with a crack. He couldn't tell if he hit anything. His arm throbbed with pain as he pulled the trigger again. Crack. He saw a spark on the far wall. Vincent cursed to himself that his shot was so far off target.

He tried to line up the sights on the barrel of the weapon and train them on one of the various targets bouncing around in front of him. He fired again and sparked the slug off the wall. The obtuse human-shaped target danced off back in the other direction unharmed.

A siren sounded and the soldiers behind the barriers stopped shooting.

Himmelstoss scoffed. "I don't think a single one of you hit a target. Congratulations on being completely useless!" Again!" The siren sounded, and the targets started bouncing around on the rails again.

Vincent fired and fired. He thought he managed to clip a few of the targets, but none fell down. He wondered if perhaps the target simply didn't fall. He glanced over at Fiona's position and saw at least three of her targets fall in quick succession.

Vincent sighed, resettled the weapon on his shoulder, and resumed firing. Each crack of his gun created another wildly off-target spark at the back of the room. With the last slug in his magazine, he managed to hit a target, just clipping its shoulder. It fell so slowly to the ground, it seemed like the target felt sorry for him.

The siren sounded again, and the soldiers stepped away from the barriers. Himmelstoss walked down the line of soldiers, looking each of them in the eye.

"Most of you seem to be getting the hang of it. You aren't so depressing to be around after all . . ." He trailed off as he stepped in front of Vincent. "Except you . . ." Vincent's eyes widened.

"M—me, Sergeant?"

The small man screamed at him. "You hit one target. One!" He had to look up to actually yell in Vincent's face. "You wasted one hundred and twenty of the Chairmen's slugs and hit one target!" Vincent tried to look away—he hadn't realized he had fired so many. "Everyone else, back to the bunk room. You . . . what's your name?"

"Solaris, Sergeant," Vincent mumbled.

"Solaris. You stay here with me,." The rest of the soldiers slung their weapons on her backs and slowly trickled out of the gun range. The last few clearly wanted to catch a glimpse at whatever punishment Himmelstoss was going to deliver.

"Start doing push-ups!" the Sergeant screamed. Vincent set his weapon on the ground, got in the position, and started pumping out push-ups.

"Why in the hell is your weapon on the deck?" he spat. He delivered a kick to Vincent's stomach. Even though he was wearing a heavy vest, the force was enough to drop him to the floor. "You better balance that shit on your hands!" Vincent coughed and slid his weapon so it balanced on the backs of his hands while he did push-ups.

He pushed and pushed. With every repetition, his chest bounced off the floor and his chin hit the weapon. Himmelstoss kicked him again. He gasped with pain and fell to his side.

"Get up! On your feet!" the Sergeant screamed at him. "Since you can't shoot to save your life, you better prove to me you can hurt the enemy in some way!" He snatched his weapon away and kicked him in the back, toward the targets on the range. They still bounced back and forth, dodging gunfire that wasn't coming. "Use your damn hands!"

Vincent was on his feet and running toward the targets. His oversized helmet bounced around and slipped to the back of his head. He got to the first target and gave it a two-handed shove. The target swung side to side.

"You going to cuddle that target next? I said use your hands!" he called out from the front of the gun range. Vincent kicked the target, but his foot glanced off the metal frame and pain shot up his leg.

Crack.

A slug sparked off the ground next to Vincent's feet, and he froze in place. Vincent turned to the front of the gun range where the Sergeant was standing. He raised a weapon and pointed it directly at Vincent.

"Do not disobey my orders! I said attack that target with your hands! Now attack!"

Crack.

Vincent heard a snap as the slug passed by his head and slammed into the back wall. Without another word, Vincent turned and punched the target. The hit made a dull thudding noise as his fist bounced uselessly off the sheet of metal. Vincent howled in pain and fell to his knees. Blood trickled from his knuckles and dripped onto the floor.

"Again!" he screamed from the back of the room. Vincent pulled himself to his feet and punched the target. He continued throwing lefts and rights, and bloody outlines of his knuckles formed on the target. Tears welled up in his eyes, and he gritted his teeth.

He could hear Himmelstoss laughing from the back of the room after each blow. His laugh was short and high-pitched. Vincent screamed in rage, kicking the target as hard as he could. It snapped on its hinges and fell over, clattering onto the floor. Blood oozing from his mangled hands covered his now broken target.

Vincent picked the target up over his head, and with a running start, heaved it in the sergeant's direction. It only went a few feet before slamming back to the floor with a loud crash. Flooded with blinding rage and pain, he took off his helmet and started slamming it into the faceless metal head of the target.

The only thing he could see under the repeated blows of his helmet was the smirking face of Himmelstoss. Vincent wanted to bash in his face with what was left of his hands. He wanted to punch that mustache straight through the back of his head.

"Enough!" Himmelstoss yelled. He looked up, his eyes wild with hatred. Himmelstoss gave him a look of disgust, waiving him off. "Go back to your bunk room and clean yourself off." He turned to leave, but stopped before walking through the door and turned back. "And there better not be any blood stains on that uniform." The door slammed.

CHAPTER SIX

Vincent stumbled back into the bunk room. Fiona, Collins, and Richardson were waiting by his bunk.

Collins gasped. "Holy shit, man. What happened?"

Vincent dropped his rifle and helmet on his bunk and forced a weak smile. "I finally killed a target."

Fiona frowned. "What did you do to your hands?"

"You know how I couldn't shoot the targets?"

"Yeah," Richardson nodded.

"He made me take it out with my hands." The soldiers' jaws dropped.

"If those targets are like everything else on this tub, you probably need to clean those cuts out," Fiona said, looking down at his bleeding hands.

Vincent walked over to the bathroom and turned the rusted knob until the chemical-scented water rushed out. He stuck his hands under the faucet but quickly winced away when the ice-cold water hit the fresh cuts.

"Quit being such a wuss," Fiona joked from the doorway. Vincent looked down at his knuckles. The skin had flayed back and torn off. Fiona tossed a cloth over to him, and Vincent gently started wrapping the cloth around his left hand when he saw it was a shirt.

"Is this your shirt?" he asked.

"A civilian one I had with me. I don't think I'll be needing it anymore." She stuck a hand in her pocket and fished out a pack of cigarettes.

"Where did you get those?" Vincent asked in shock.

"I used my feminine wiles of course." She smirked and handed him one. They lit up together.

Vincent blew out a cloud of smoke. "I don't know what feminine wiles are, but damn that's good."

"I wasn't aware they let you pampered Earth types smoke," Fiona joked.

He shrugged. "They don't."

"So what did you do?" she asked, her eyebrows raised.

"Ran from the ethics officers, drank, and wrote in my ethics booklet." He laughed a little. After what he just went through, it all seemed like a joke.

"Hm." She eyed him up and down. "Impressive."

Vincent laughed. "Why's that?"

"You don't seem like the rebellious type. You look more like someone who would be doing the arresting, not the other way around." She tapped the end of her cigarette, sending ash onto the floor.

"What about you?" he asked.

Fiona looked down. "I was my family's firstborn. Not much to it really." She shrugged.

"So you just knew your whole life that one day your parents would send you away?"

"Well, on Mars everyone knows your firstborn is kind of a wash. No matter what they do in school, at home, whatever, when they turn seventeen, they're gone. Normally, parents just abandon them on the streets of Olympus and get on with their lives. Make some more kids that they can actually raise." She took a long drag on her cigarette.

"Fiona, I didn't . . ." he stumbled, not realizing he would bring up something so sensitive.

"It's okay. I'm over it. You know what the really unfair part is? No one in my family even fought for the Resistance." She gave a sardonic laugh.

"So how long are you sentenced for?"

"Oh, you don't know?" Fiona asked curiously. "We serve for life."

CHAPTER SEVEN

The next morning, the soldiers of Charlie Troop were brought to a massive warehouse deep in the bowels of the ship. There were endless rows of unlabeled boxes as far as Vincent could see. Himmelstoss stood next to a desk; he was talking to a soldier who was standing behind it, flipping through countless screens on his data display.

"Line up, idiots!" Himmelstoss ordered. The soldiers gradually fell into a line, still not entirely sure what was going on. "You will be issued the rest of your gear today. Under no circumstances are you to lose any of it. You can ask Solaris what happens to soldiers who do not obey my orders." With this, he shot him a glare.

The line inched forward as the soldiers received their gear from the man at the desk. Eventually, Vincent was led through the shelves by a short, squat soldier who was also scrolling through a data screen.

"Solaris, right here," he said, pointing to a bag on the shelf.

"Can I check to see if it all fits me? You see, they issued me a helmet and—"

"No. Take your bag and go," the soldier barked.

Vincent bent down and grabbed the bag, throwing the straps over his shoulders. The bag pulled his shoulders back so far that he had to stop and regain his balance as the weight of the bag tried to drag him to the floor. He leaned forward and trudged back to where everyone else was waiting.

Collins was sitting on the ground, his bag propping him up into a seated position.

"Guys," said Collins. "How far did we walk here?"

"A few miles probably," Fiona said, as she dug through her bag.

"Aww, man. We have to carry all this shit back," Collins whined. Vincent sighed, dropping his bag. He hadn't thought of that.

"Any bits of Martian wisdom to explain to us how weak we are being?" Vincent asked Fiona jokingly.

"Nope, this is probably going to suck," she said without looking up from the inside of her bag.

Collins shook his head. "Well, now I'm really worried."

The troop began its walk back through the maze of hallways they had taken to get to the warehouse. Slowly but surely, the giant bags started dragging people down, leaving them pronate on the cold metal floor. Some who managed to stay upright tripped on one of the bulkheads and went down hard.

Near the front, Richardson, Fiona, and Vincent marched on. While Vincent was straining hard against the weight of the bag, Richardson didn't seem to notice, and Fiona didn't show any sign of slowing down. Ahead of them was Himmelstoss, who, unencumbered by any bags or weapons, marched forward without a care. Vincent's hatred for the man drove him forward, as if he were chasing him. He didn't want to give the Sergeant the satisfaction of watching him quit.

Finally, the troop made it back to the bunk room. Vincent fell onto his bunk and slipped off the bag. He stretched his shoulders and back, trying in vain to chase away some of the soreness. Collins was the last one through the door; he was nearly doubled over, his uniform soaked clear through with sweat. He wasn't even carrying his weapon anymore; it hung uselessly from its sling and dragged across the floor. He collapsed through the door.

"You!" shouted Himmelstoss. Collins barely peeked his head up from where he had landed on the floor.

"Huh?" he panted.

"You seemed to enjoy the walk so much that you took longer than everyone else. Explain yourself."

"I . . . uhh . . ." He fumbled with his words. "My bag was kinda heavy?" He gave a weak smile.

"I hope you enjoyed it, because you're doing it again. On your feet, soldier."

"What?" Collins coughed. "There's no damn way!" Himmelstoss closed on him quickly. He kicked Collins in the side of the head. When Collins went down, he began punching him, over and over again. In an effort to protect himself, Collins curled up, but that didn't stop Himmelstoss.

The other three watched in horror. Vincent seethed with anger as he watched Collins, one of the only people who had been nice to him since his sentencing, get viciously beaten. He started to step forward but was stopped in his tracks. He looked down to see Fiona grabbing his sleeve. He looked at her, and she slowly shook her head.

Himmelstoss finally seemed to get bored of beating the defenseless form of Collins.

"Are you ready to go now?" he asked without a hint of anger in his voice. Collins pushed himself to his feet. He braced himself on his weapon like it was a walking stick. Without another word, Collins turned and walked back out of the door, his feet sliding across the floor.

"Why did you stop me?" Vincent hissed at Fiona.

"What would getting your ass beat again have done for him?"

"I could—" Vincent started.

"You could take him? You're probably right. The guy is the size of a newborn. But what then? You know what happens to someone who attacks their troop commander? They get taken out back and shot." She shook her head. "And you guys are the only halfway decent pricks here. I can't let you go and get your stupid asses shot."

*****

At dinner that night, Vincent, Richardson, and Fiona were still waiting for Collins to return.

"Can we go looking for him?" Vincent asked.

"They lock us up in between meals. What are we going to do? Sneak out of the window?" Fiona answered. "He'll come back."

"Yeah, we just have to worry about training tomorrow. If he's lucky, he'll miss it," Richardson joked. After he was done beating Collins, Himmelstoss had informed everyone that they had simulation training the next day. A full bay set up to look like a war zone full of attacking enemies would be readied for the soldiers of Charlie Troop.

Vincent frowned. "True, and I'm not really looking forward to it either. One of the other guys said they outfit us with something that shocks the piss out of you if you get shot by the enemy,"

"Well, hopefully you can hold them back with your superior marksmanship," Fiona joked.

"I'm doomed," Vincent said sadly.

"Speaking of which, how the hell can you shoot so well?" Richardson asked Fiona.

Setting her spoon down, she smirked. "A girl doesn't tell secrets," she said, shrugging.

Vincent chuckled. "I think in this case she should,"

The siren sounded and everyone got to their feet. Table by table, they filed out of the chow hall and back to the bunk room to start getting ready for training. Vincent saw Collins lain out on his bunk, snoring away. He gave him a shove. Collins barely opened an eye.

"What the hell, man? Where were you?"

"Oh, you know, walking around this endless damn ship all night."

"What took you so long?"

"I got lost at one point. Wasn't really paying attention where I was going. So I camped out inside someone's office until this morning and hiked back."

"I don't have any food, but here." Vincent handed him one of the cigarettes that Fiona had given him.

"Hell yeah. This is even better." He lit it and took a long drag.

"Don't get too comfortable. Before you were sent off on that death march, we were told we had training, so I'd get ready unless you want to get your ass beat again," Fiona helpfully pointed out. Collins swung his feet over the side of his bed; they were chafed and red with several ugly blisters. He gingerly lowered himself to the ground and whimpered when his battered feet touched the floor.

The door slid open, revealing Himmelstoss.

"Charlie Troop, follow me." He turned without another word and marched off down the hallway. The soldiers followed him, and Richardson and Vincent supported Collins as he limped on his torn feet. Collins never bothered to put his cigarette out.

After what seemed like a few too many miles of marching, they found their way into a bay larger than the landing area from their first day on the ship. It was the first area of the Victory Vincent had seen that wasn't just bare metal, rivets, and bulkheads. Instead, it was a lush field covered in rolling hills; complete with bright green grass and a small forest worth of trees. The soldiers of Charlie Troop stared in awe.

Fiona bent down and ran her hands through the grass. She took in a big lungful of air with a giant smile on her face.

"You okay?" Vincent asked.

"Yeah." Her facial expression quickly hardened. "I've just never seen grass before."

"What?" Vincent gasped. He remembered seeing pictures of Mars in his history books; it had been lush and green. "What about all of the generations of terraforming?"

"It was like that before I was born . . . or at least that's what my friends said. After the war, the machines that kept the ecosystem in check were all destroyed. We manage to survive, though."

Vincent was speechless. He stared at her like an idiot while she picked a few pieces of grass and stuck them in her pocket.

"You know that's not real, right? The air still smells like burning oil and smoke, too." Richardson shook his head.

"Don't go crushing my dreams."

"Listen up!" The shrill voice of Himmelstoss broke up Fiona's moment. "It may not look like it, but you are in the middle of a war zone!" The soldiers all looked around, seeing nothing but a peaceful meadow. "You will be outfitted with these." He held up a small harness. "You will be firing something called simunitions. These slugs travel much slower than real ones. If one hits you it will send a signal to your harness to shock you to unconsciousness. I promise you, it will hurt a lot." A small smile spread across his little face.

"Opposing force?" Vincent whispered. "Who's that?"

Collins shook his head. "No idea."

"Far on the other side of this training area, Bravo Troop is being given these same instructions. There is only one way to achieve this objective: kill your enemy." Himmelstoss grinned. "Before the mission begins, you will be broken up into squads at random. Line up and step forward."

Vincent, Collins, Richardson, and Fiona stepped forward. Vincent could tell from the look of recognition on Himmelstoss's face they were going to be screwed. Even though a few others in the troop had been punished by him, the Sergeant seemed to always bring down the hammer hard on them specifically—or maybe they just couldn't stop screwing up.

"My favorite soldiers," he smiled, glancing around. "And I know why now." Himmelstoss's beady little eyes bore into Vincent. "You're a Red." He pointed at Fiona. "And you three are criminals." He smiled so wide his yellow-stained teeth showed through his thin lips. They exchanged glances with one another.

"You will be my weapons team," he informed them. He bent down and lifted the Earth Pattern Light Machine Gun. It was a huge weapon, both in size and weight. They had trained on the weapon for only one day at the range, and Vincent had not enjoyed it. Unlike their rifles, which used magnetic force to propel slugs, the machine gun used gunpowder. When the gun fired, acrid smoke stung his eyes and nose, and it kicked like a mule.

Vincent strapped on the electronic harness and hefted up the machine gun, placing it on his shoulder. Fiona grabbed a heavy backpack full of ammunition, while Richardson seized the tripod onto which the machine gun would be mounted. Collins was left with nothing to carry, which was probably for the best since he could hardly walk.

"Um, Sergeant, what do I do?" Collins asked weakly.

"You're the spotter." Himmelstoss gave him a set of binoculars. "I don't want to break your weak body before we make planetfall. Hopefully you can at least carry those without incident."

The newly minted weapons team trudged off to find the rest of the troop. Fiona collapsed onto the grass, her backpack pulling her down.

"Do I finally see some weakness in the Martian?" Richardson joked, the tripod held across his shoulders.

"Can't a girl lie in the grass for the first time ever?" She winced as the backpack's straps cut into her shoulders. "Okay, yeah. Maybe a little weakness. Shit, this thing is heavy."

Himmelstoss marched out in front of the troop. Many were still trying to load their magazines into ammunition pouches.

"Soldiers of Charlie Troop! Your position has been compromised and the enemy is coming. Remember your training and work together! Defend yourselves!" Soldiers jumped to their feet, looking around wildly.

"What?" Fiona yelled, flailing around on her back like a turtle, unable to get up. Richardson grabbed her by the arm, and effortlessly pulled her to her feet.

"We have to get out of here or we're are all going to get shot," Collins said calmly. Vincent saw a hill covered in trees off to his right.

"There!" he pointed, throwing the machine gun over his shoulder. The rest of the weapons team chased after him, Collins trying his hardest to keep up.

Vincent heard weapons popping off behind him. The confused masses of the rest of the troop ran around trying to find places to hide. Finally, a few of them saw the weapons team running up the hill and ran after them. The opposing force of Bravo Troop was already shooting at the Charlie Troop soldiers who failed to move. It was clear all previous training escaped the soldiers who were mowed down en masse.

Richardson dropped the tripod, and Vincent fumbled with the machine gun, trying to get it mounted correctly. Fiona dropped the bag of ammunition next to them. Five soldiers who ran from the starting point with them fell into the dirt next to them. They crawled over to the hill ridge and began aiming their weapons.

"Hey!" Fiona whispered harshly. "Don't shoot!" They looked back at her confused. "They don't see us. Wait for them to finish everyone off and think they won!"

Vincent lay down behind his machine gun. He picked up the feed tray and fed in a belt of ammunition. He closed the it as quietly as he could. He stared over the gun and saw the hundred soldiers from Bravo Troop advancing slowly on the few surviving stragglers of Charlie Troop. They ran back and forth, trying to form some kind of defensive line while being methodically gunned down.

Eventually, some of the last soldiers threw down their weapons and tried to surrender and save themselves from getting shocked. The Bravo Troop soldiers laughed and shot them anyway. They twisted at odd angles, screamed, and fell over as the current ripped through their bodies.

"Now?" Vincent asked, looking over at Fiona.

"Start shooting over there." Collins pointed to the rear of the Bravo soldiers. "Drive them into a big group."

Fiona smiled. "Let's do this."

Vincent squeezed the trigger of the machine gun and it roared to life. Even though he was firing training rounds, it felt just like the real thing. The rest of the soldiers on the hill poured fire into the crowd of Bravo soldiers. They jerked awkwardly from surging electrical current and collapsed. Rounds started impacting the hill as they tried firing back. Tree limbs cracked and fell onto Vincent and Fiona as the rounds tore through the trees overhead.

"Give me another belt!" Vincent yelled as his gun ran dry. Fiona dropped her weapon, reached into her bag, and gave him another belt. He fed it into his gun, pulled back the charging handle, and opened fire.

"Arggh!" Howled one of the soldiers who had followed them. He rolled over on his back, twitching and kicking his legs as his body was wrecked by an electrical surge.

"They're trying to flank us!" Collins screamed as a group of Bravo soldiers snuck around the side of the hill.

"Richardson!" Vincent yelled over bursts from his gun. "Cut them off!"

"I got this!" he called out, running towards them. His weapon fired off dozens of rounds in quick succession.

"They're coming up the other side!" Collins screamed, rolling over. He brought his weapon up and shot a Bravo soldier, sending him twitching to the ground. "They've surrounded us!"

"If we stay here, we are going to get shot," Fiona asserted.

"Hey, Richardson! You got that side?" Vincent called out.

In between gun shots, Richardson answered back. "So far!"

"I got an idea," Vincent said. He pulled the machine gun up from the tripod and cradled it under his arm.

"The hell are you doing?" Fiona asked as she shot at the soldiers trying to come up the other side of the hill.

"We're going to get the piss shocked out of us either way. Might as well see how many of them we can take with us." Vincent nodded down at his gun. He stepped over the prone form of Collins and fired the machine gun down the hill at the encroaching invaders.

The gun was far too heavy to aim, and the recoil was too powerful to control. Vincent struggled in vain to try and hit anything with his wild bursts. Faced with a soldier running at them with a machine gun, the Bravo soldiers didn't stick around to find out if he could aim; they turned and ran back down the hill. Fiona shot several of them in the back as they tried to escape.

"Suck it!" she screamed after them. She fired several more times, sending a few more Bravo soldiers to the ground.

Vincent laughed, panting heavily from running. "So what do we do if they come back?"

"Get the piss shocked out of us, no doubt." Fiona smiled, changing out the magazine in her weapon. "You're pretty damn good with that thing." She motioned down at the smoking machine gun.

"Thanks," Vincent said, trying to catch his breath.

"And good call sending us out to the flanks like that." Richardson patted him on the shoulder with a big hand.

"Looks like we finally found something you're good at," Fiona laughed.

A siren sounded and a calm voice came over a loudspeaker.

"Exercise complete. Return to your start areas," The soldiers on the hill made their way back down to the base. The Bravo soldiers they passed gave them dirty looks, angry that the ambush had cost them their victory. Most of the other Charlie soldiers were confused and had no idea that the weapons team had escaped into the hills. With grins on their faces, the troops of the weapons team marched through the field like conquering heroes.

Himmelstoss met them back at the start area. "Used the rest of the troop as bait, eh?" He asked with a raised eyebrow.

"That wasn't our intention," Fiona said. "But it ended up working out that way."

Himmelstoss frowned. "Whose idea was that?"

"Mine, Sergeant," Vincent admitted. He closed his eyes and prepared for a beating.

"Do you know what is more important than the final victory?" Himmelstoss asked.

"No, Sergeant."

"Nothing," he growled. "Absolutely nothing. Our lives are simply a vessel to ensure the Chairman's will is carried through the stars. Weapons team, you have the rest of the night off. Everyone else, you are staying here with me!"

They didn't wait for him to change his mind. Richardson, Collins, Fiona, and Vincent ran out of the training area and back into the hallway. Collins used the wall to brace himself as he escaped.

"This might be the first time I have ever been happy to go to the chow hall," Vincent joked.

"I talked to one of the cooks there. I got us something," Fiona smiled.

Vincent grinned. "Now I'm even happier. What did you get us?"

"It's a surprise. I have to build the suspense, don't I?"

The group walked into the chow hall. With everyone else busy being punished, the whole place was empty. They grabbed bowls and stepped into line. A cook on the other side of the serving counter reached over and handed Fiona a clear, unlabeled bottle. He then doled out the normal colorless gruel to them.

They sat down at their usual table, and Fiona unscrewed the bottle and poured out some shots to the group.

Vincent eyed the clear liquid. "What is it?"

"The guys stationed on the ship brew their own booze a few wings over. I noticed the cook staff always smelled like a bar and figured I'd ask," she answered.

"Man, you are observant. The only thing I can smell in here is oil fumes and farts," Richardson laughed, putting a shot back. His face twisted. "Damn, that's strong."

Vincent knocked his back, and the familiar burning made its way down his throat and into his stomach. "Just like the stuff back home. Awful." He laughed.

"It does the job!" Fiona smiled and poured out more shots. "I wish we had some beer, though. Say what you will about Mars, but we know how to brew." She put back a shot and grimaced.

"I miss . . . food." Vincent shook his head, twirling his spoon around in his food. "Real food."

"I miss not having to use the bathroom in front of other people," Collins sighed.

"I miss my girlfriend," Richardson said, putting his shot glass down.

"You had a girlfriend?" Vincent asked.

"I still do. She said she would wait for my sentence to be over." Richardson smiled. "But that was before this whole war thing."

"I wish I had someone to miss." Vincent laughed. "My dad acted like Himmelstoss, and my little brother was the perfect little student. The people I thought were my friends sold me out to the cops. So yeah, I just miss food."

"No girlfriend for you then?" Fiona asked, filling her glass back up.

"Nope. You have anyone back home?"

She laughed. "No, most people were probably pretty relieved when I was finally dragged off to the draft office."

"How is Richardson the most normal one here?" Collins patted the big man on the shoulder. He was starting to slur his words slightly.

Fiona pointed at Collins. "You seem pretty normal."

Collins shrugged. "I stole from everyone I ever knew. My own dad gave me over to the cops and disowned me." He saw the looks of concern on the group's faces and smiled. "Oh, don't worry. You guys don't have anything I want to steal."

*****

The four stumbled back to their bunks. Fiona was still carrying a half-full bottle of booze and supporting herself on Vincent's shoulder. Vincent was bracing himself on the wall, unable to walk on his own either. The room was empty, with everyone else still trapped in the training bay with Himmelstoss.

Vincent collapsed onto his bed, and Fiona sat down next to him.

"It's not fair," she pouted, her words running together.

"What isn't?" Vincent slurred.

"You guys' sentences are going to be over one day. Not mine!" she spat, swaying back and forth.

"We'll find you a way out," Vincent said, trying to cheer her up but not exactly sure what that meant.

"Maybe, once we hit planetfall, I just run. Take off into the hills or something," she mused.

"What if they kill you? And if the Defense Forces catch you after that, they absolutely will kill you."

"I know. I just can't accept that I was born to do nothing but this." She gestured around the bay with her hands. "I mean my life in Olympus sucked, but this is just shit." She frowned. Vincent wasn't sure what to do. He was never good at dealing with his own emotions, let alone someone else's. He put an arm around her shoulder.

"We'll get out and go get some Martian beer." He forced a smile. She started to laugh. Fiona had a sarcastic smirk on her face most of the time. This had to be the first time he had ever seen her have a genuine and totally off-guard smile.

"I'm going to hold you to that." She pulled away from his arm, slowly getting up to her unsteady feet. "You know, you're not so bad."

CHAPTER EIGHT

The next morning Himmelstoss had them out of their bunks and marching through the hallways yet again. With weapons in their hands and packs strapped onto their backs, the soldiers marched silently, the only sounds being the stomping of tired feet on the metal floor.

Unfortunately, since Fiona, Vincent, Richardson, and Collins had distinguished themselves in training, they were now the permanent weapons team. Vincent had the heavy machine gun across his shoulders, while Fiona struggled on with the pack of ammunition. Richardson and Collins didn't seem to mind their roles.

Vincent was staring down at his feet, so he wasn't paying attention to where they were going. The soldiers came to a stop at an unfamiliar area. In front of them, Himmelstoss stood in front of a large window. It was the first one any of them had seen in a month. Up to that point, Vincent was sure windows didn't exist on the Victory.

The deep black of space stared back at them. All around the window, they could see the gun-metal-grey color of the ESS Victory stretched out in front of them. Long tubes pointed out from its seemingly endless wings. Collins pointed out the Victory's cannons. There were easily hundreds of them. Past that, they could only see black.

"How many people thought they were a part of some armada moving through space?" Himmelstoss questioned. Most of the soldiers raised their hands. Vincent was one of them. "False. We are it. We are the armada." He motioned out the window. "You are among about one million soldiers on this ship. We are the Chairman's spear, and we are going to be driven into the heart of the creatures that lie beyond our system."

"How many of the other soldiers are like us, Sergeant?" asked one of the soldiers in the crowd. "New."

"Only a few thousand. We can't throw waves of you untrained idiots at them and expect to win." Himmelstoss sneered. Somehow, that made Vincent feel better.

"When will we be there?" asked another voice.

"In about another month and a half. When we are closer to planetfall, you will be informed of your troop's mission."

Everyone was speechless. The fact that they would be invading a planet suddenly became very real to everybody. Vincent was nervous.

"Kind of freaky," Fiona said. "There's nothing out there."

"Sure there is." Collins stared ahead. "There's a couple million pissed-off aliens we're going to go fight." He smiled weakly.

"Oh, right," she said, sounding depressed. "Lovely."

"You ever think they'll just surrender?" Vincent asked.

"Doubtful. They blew up half of the damn Moon, didn't they?" Collins pointed out. "Why do that and then just surrender when we come knocking?"

Fiona shrugged. "Or they know we'll come running across the stars after them and they're leading us into a trap."

"Shit," said Vincent. "I didn't think of that."

The soldiers walked away from the window and continued with their march through the ship. Himmelstoss took them to another gun range, where they fired off several hundred more rounds apiece. After a month of practice, they were getting better at using their weapons. Vincent was thankful he had the machine gun now, so he and Fiona would just blast away at the targets without much aiming.

Every morning before breakfast, Himmelstoss would wake them up and drag them out into the hallways for a run. Collins kept limping badly; his feet still hadn't healed from his forced march a few nights prior. Vincent had caught a glimpse of them that morning, and they still looked ripped and raw. Finally, one morning his feet couldn't support him any longer, and he collapsed.

"Are you okay, man?" Vincent stopped to check on his friend. Collins was rolling back and forth on his back.

"I just can't do it anymore! My damn feet! Arrgh!" He gritted his teeth in pain and his eyes slammed shut. Himmelstoss ran back to see what all the fuss was about.

"What happened, soldier?" he asked Collins.

"My feet!" he cried. Himmelstoss eyed Collins with disgust. He bent down and took off one of Collins's boots. He recoiled in horror from what he saw.

Without proper treatment, Collins's feet had become badly infected. They were weeping a clear fluid and were pale white. All his toe nails had fallen out.

"Bless the Chairman, soldier. What happened?" He either didn't remember or didn't care that he was the one who had caused Collins's injuries. Himmelstoss grabbed the radio from his belt and turned it on.

"I have a soldier here in Charlie wing that needs transport to the sick bay." He put the radio back on his belt and walked away. After a few minutes, a medical cart driven by two soldiers wearing white arm bands pulled up to Collins. They unloaded a stretcher and placed it on the ground next to him. Without a word, they loaded him onto the stretcher and set it in the back of the cart. Collins weakly waved goodbye as he floated away down the corridor.

"Anyone else forget that their feet are rotting off?" Himmelstoss asked sardonically. "Then let's go!" he ordered. The soldiers kept on running like nothing happened.

"Those looked bad," Fiona said, huffing slightly.

"Yeah. Maybe they'll just send him home," Vincent mused.

"We're almost two months away from Earth. No way," said Richardson, running along next to Vincent. "They might just transfer him over to serve on the ship. He does have a brain on him after all."

Vincent laughed. "Lucky bastard."

*****

Even though they joked about Collins, they all assumed they'd see him again in the coming days. Weeks passed, and he never came back to the bunk room. Eventually, a soldier came and collected all his personal things, stuffed them into a green cloth bag, and left without a word. After a while, Vincent finally built up the nerve to query Himmelstoss about it.

"Sergeant, what's happening with Collins?"

"Who?" Himmelstoss asked, clearly annoyed.

"The guy with the bad feet."

"Oh, medics say it's going to take a while to recover. Won't be part of the invasion at any rate so he's no longer in my troop," he said shortly. Vincent turned and walked back to his bunk. Richardson thought that the infection in Collins's feet had somehow killed him, which was why they had come to grab his things.

"It's true, isn't it? He's dead!" Richardson moaned. The two had been close since their time together in the replacement unit.

Vincent shook his head. "No, dude. His feet are messed up and they transferred him to the hospital. That's it."

"Told you, you idiot," said Fiona. "People don't die from infected blisters."

"But he's so little!" Richardson said.

Vincent patted Richardson on the shoulder. "Look at it this way. He will be far from the invasion, so he's safe."

Richardson acquiesced. "Yeah, you guys are right."

"Let's be honest. He would have gotten chewed up once the real shit started flying around. He barely shoots his weapon in training," Fiona said harshly. It was mean, but mostly true. They all liked Collins, but his smart-ass comments and sarcastic humor wouldn't count for a lot once they made planetfall. Richardson didn't have anything to say to that.

*****

Charlie Troop ran through another set of training drills in the giant field bay. Slowly but surely, the soldiers started looking like they knew what they were doing. Himmelstoss's beatings became slightly rarer as he ran out of things to nitpick, though he didn't look too pleased about it.

Himmelstoss also started handing out rank to soldiers who had shown some skill. After one training mission, he took the weapons team, now a whole weapons squad, aside.

"Solaris, was it?"

"Yes, Sergeant," Vincent answered, exaggerating how much he had to look down at Himmelstoss.

"You're now the weapons squad's leader."

"Like, for training?"

"No, until you die or get fired. Whichever happens first." Himmelstoss dug in his pocket and handed him two pieces of pin-on rank for the collar of his uniform: corporal's chevrons. "Do not make me regret this, Solaris." Himmelstoss turned and walked away.

"Whoa! Look at you, big shot," Fiona said sarcastically.

"Wait, does that mean we can't hang out anymore?" Richardson asked, concerned.

"No, I don't think so anyway." Vincent scratched his head. Fiona grabbed the pins from his hand and affixed them onto his collar. Whenever she touched him or made eye contact, he would always get ceaselessly nervous. No one had ever done that to him before. He tried his best not to show it, though he had a feeling he was failing at that.

"I'm proud to be in your squad, Corporal," smiled Ikari, a soldier from the Japan Province who had been assigned to the weapons squad the day before. He turned out to be something of a sniper with a rocket launcher.

Vincent laughed. "Oh, shut up. Nothing's changed except apparently now I'll be leading us into a war. It's cool. No pressure." Up until that point, Vincent had always assumed some officers and other sergeants would swoop in and take charge of Charlie Troop before they made planetfall. It turned out that all the training they were doing was part war preparation and part trying to find the unit's leadership. Vincent, and everyone else, was stunned.

"This calls for a celebration." Fiona smiled and slapped Vincent on the shoulder. "I can get more of the good stuff from the cooks and we can turn the bay into a damn bar!"

Richardson laughed. "Is that all you think about?"

"What else are we going to do around this place?" She shrugged. "What do you say there, squad leader?" she asked sarcastically.

Vincent couldn't help but smile. "You know you were going to do it anyway whether I said it was okay or not." Over the past two and a half months, he had grown to feel like he'd known Fiona his entire life.

"Yep, sure would have," she said while digging in her pocket for cigarettes.

"Such a disobedient soldier," Vincent joked, taking one of her cigarettes.

"What are you going to do? Give me the Himmelstoss treatment?" she asked.

"I think we both know you'd win that fight." The rest of the squad laughed.

CHAPTER NINE

That night Fiona made good on her promise to turn the bunk room into a bar. Through the connections she made with the ship's crew, she'd managed to get her hands on a radio, several bottles of booze, and cartons of cigarettes. Vincent stopped wondering how she made the deals weeks before, not that she would have told him.

There were several soldiers playing drinking games and using their weapons as funnels. Various card games sprung up along the bunks. Cigarettes, booze, and candy were being used as currency. A few couples had formed, slowly dancing back and forth in the space between the bunks that had become the night's dance floor. Vincent smiled when he saw Ikari dancing with a girl he'd been crushing on for weeks.

Richardson was running the card table and taking on anyone who tried to arm wrestle him. Somehow he ended up drinking and smoking without a care in the world, wearing nothing but his underwear.

Vincent stood and took it all in. Streamers were taped to the dull grey walls, music was blaring, and soldiers, in various states of dress, were drinking and dancing together.

He smiled at Fiona. "I like what you've done with the place." She was wearing a white tank top and her uniform pants. For some reason, Vincent found that incredibly attractive.

She laughed. "Thanks, as you can tell I really like the color grey." A cigarette dangled between her lips and a canteen cup full of bootlegged booze rested in her hand.

"The Martian in you is really showing," he commented on her appearance with a laugh.

"Nah, if that was the case, I already would have tried to steal your boots at knife point," she chuckled, offering him a drink. He took it.

Vincent coughed. "Man, that's some harsh shit."

"Yeah, I guess they're brewing it extra fast since everyone knows planetfall is so soon. Everyone is just getting hammered on whatever they can find to make themselves feel better." She looked sideways at the cup. "Quality has certainly suffered."

"For such a fine pallet as yours, it must be torture."

"Do you have any idea how hard it is to pair fine cheeses with the liquor brewed from used engine parts in the bowels of a massive starship?" She blew a cloud of smoke in his face.

The song on the radio changed—to a slow song that Vincent had never heard before.

"I love this song!" Fiona declared. "Do you dance?"
He stumbled with his words. He had never danced before in his life. She didn't wait for his answer. Instead, she grabbed him and dragged him out into the middle of the bay. She placed her hands on his hips and locked her bright blue eyes with his.

She grinned. "Never done this before, eh? It's okay. I'll be gentle."

She rested her head on his chest as they swayed back and forth to the music. As much as Vincent wanted to focus on the beautiful girl wrapped around him, he was focused more on not stepping on her feet.

"This song used to play all the time on the radio back home," she said with her eyes closed.

"Dance a lot then?" Vincent asked.

"No," she said quietly. "Not a lot of slow dances happening there."

"Me either, though I'm going to assume it was for different reasons. Can I tell you something?"

"Of course."

"I'm scared. I'm scared shitless," he mumbled. She looked up at him as they twirled around.

"I am, too," she said. "Anyone who isn't is either stupid or lying to themselves."

"We'll get through this together," he said quietly. "All of us. Somehow."

"Worrying about all of that won't get me anywhere. I just want to think about right now." She smiled up at him. Her hands moved from his back to the back of his head, and she pulled him in. Vincent didn't think about anything else; he leaned in and kissed her, half expecting her to punch him for it. Instead, she kissed him back. They stopped dancing, wrapping each other up with their arms, pulling each other in closer.

She pulled away after what seemed like an eternity. She was smiling up at him.

"I didn't think you had it in you," she smirked.

"Had what?"

"The balls to make a move." Her hands slid down and grabbed his butt. He flinched a little.

He laughed nervously. "To be fair, I don't. You did about ninety-nine percent of it."

"Well, I had to. If I waited for you, I'd probably be dead already."

"So what does this mean?" he asked awkwardly.

"Oh, don't start on that. Like I said, I don't want to think about anything other than right now." Her head pressed against his chest again. "I just want to enjoy something before our lives all turn to shit." She reached up and kissed him again. "Can you do that?"

Vincent smiled and stared into her eyes. "Yeah."

The party swirled around them, but they never looked away from one another. They didn't mind the songs changing or being left alone on the dance floor as it emptied out. They didn't want to look at the outside world; they created their own in the small space between them. They had no plans on leaving it that night.

*****

For the first time in as long as Vincent could remember, the soldiers of Charlie Troop woke up without a siren or Himmelstoss screaming at them. Vincent looked over and saw

Fiona still snoring away next to him. He rolled over and put his arm around her. Her skin looked paler than usual against the black blanket. It made him wonder if she had ever seen the sun before. Her eyes opened, and she smiled when she saw him.

"Morning," she said groggily.

He smiled. "Good morning."

"Ugh." She pulled the covers over her head. "Your breath smells like you were gargling garbage. Go brush your teeth." She pushed him away, and he slipped out from under the covers and shuffled towards the bathroom. Soldiers were piled on beds at awkward angles, and after having drank away their shame hours before, many were naked. A raven-haired girl was sleeping in her underwear with a cigarette somehow balanced between her lips. The bay door opened. Himmelstoss stood in the doorway, taking in the scene.

"Give me all of the squad leaders," he said calmly. Vincent and the others made their way over to where he was standing. "You look like you had a night. Celebrating something?"

"The promotions I guess." Vincent scratched his head. He had one hell of a hangover.

"I have something else for you all to celebrate." A smile crept across Himmelstoss's face. "Planetfall is in one week." The news hit Vincent in the gut like a punch. It was really happening. He nervously exchanged glances with the other squad leaders. The fear in their eyes equaled that of his own.

"Is there any training coming up then, Sergeant?" Vincent asked.

"No, we've done all we could. If you haven't learned how to survive on the surface by now, then you're a lost cause," he said curtly. He turned to walk out of the room.

"Sergeant!" called out a burly squad leader. Vincent remembered his name was Burt and that he came from somewhere in the European Sector. "What planet are we landing on?"

"Intelligence is saying the beasts call it Ryklar. The Defense Forces have labeled it Planet Eleven."

Vincent walked back to his bunk where Fiona was still dozing and sat down at the edge of the bed. Never in his life had he felt his emotions go from one such extreme to another. A few minutes earlier, he had woken up next to a beautiful woman for the first time in his life. Now, he had to prepare for war.

Fiona stirred. "What's wrong?"

"Planetfall is in one week," he said quietly. Her eyes widened. The reality dawned on her as well. She slowly sat up in bed, drawing the covers with her.

"One week. Shit." She fumbled around in her discarded pants pocket for her cigarettes, found them, and handed Vincent one. She lit them both. "Well, I'm glad we got to have some fun before being murdered in some alien shit hole." She smiled, leaned forward, and kissed him on the cheek. Vincent wasn't sure what was going on between the two of them, but he liked it.

"You never brushed your teeth." She grimaced and kicked him away.

*****

Vincent was brushing his teeth in the bathroom when Richardson and Ikari walked in.

"Hey there, Mrs. Olympus," Richardson joked.

Vincent spat out his toothpaste. "Oh, go to hell."

"So what's the word?" Ikari asked.

"One week."

"Damn, man. It's going to be real, huh?" said Richardson.

"Well, at least we will get off the ship finally." Ikari tried to be optimistic by forcing a smile. "These walls are starting to close in on me."

"Fight for our lives or live in this floating prison. Our options kind of suck." Vincent shook his head. He forgot that Ikari was enlisted and generally didn't like it when they trash-talked his service.

"So, any more training?" Richardson asked.

"Oddly no. We're being left alone until the day comes." Vincent shrugged and walked back into the bay.

"So no more Himmelstoss then?" Ikari asked cheerfully.

Vincent laughed. "As far as I know."

"Thank the Chairman," Ikari sighed. Himmelstoss had developed a particular hatred for Ikari. He was short and rail thin, which was something Himmelstoss zeroed in on. His hate for the poor guy was probably what landed him in Vincent's squad in the first place. Even though he was the only enlisted soldier in the weapons squad, he managed to fit in—before Fiona would goad him on with jokes about the Chairman until he got angry and walked away. Ikari still hadn't caught on that he was alone in his devotion.

The attitude among the soldiers was anything other than celebratory, even in the enlisted ranks. A few months ago, when they boarded the ship and started training, they all knew they were going to war, but it was some vague and intangible idea that they didn't spend much time thinking about.

Now that it was right in front of them, the patriotic fervor and talks of killing the "beasts beyond our system" faded. The enlisted soldiers suddenly became as dour and introspective as the sentenced ones had been during the whole trip.

That didn't stop the troop from blaring music and drinking, though. Without the heavy hand of Himmelstoss smacking them into line, the soldiers reverted back to being the seventeen-or-eighteen-year-old kids they were. Some of the more mature soldiers still went on morning runs in full gear and did push-ups in the bay. Vincent saw a few others practicing setting up a defensive firing line or rehearsing loading magazines repeatedly.

Richardson taught a group of soldiers how to use their standard-issued knives. Vincent hoped he would never get close enough to one of the Alliance to warrant the use of a piece of steel.

The bay door opened and an unfamiliar older man walked in. Unlike the soldiers of Charlie Troop, he was wearing rank and unit patches.

"Lemme get the non-commissioned officers up front with me," he ordered in a thick, unknown accent. Unlike Himmelstoss, his voice was calm and deliberate. Vincent and the rest of the squad leaders stepped forward. Mostly at Fiona's insistence, Vincent hadn't bothered to dress himself beyond pants for the past several days.

"Not sure if that sergeant of yours talked to you, but your troop is getting split up." Vincent saw by his rank that he was a first sergeant. "Your squads are getting put in with one of our regular units. Is there a Solaris here?"

"That's me, First Sergeant."

He smirked. "You done a lot of killing before?" Vincent read the name "Collier" on his nametag.

"Um, no," Vincent sputtered. "Have you?"

"I did two tours on Mars during the last Rebellion. What do you think? I got plans to do a whole lot more once we hit the planet. You and your rookies better not slow me down."

"Should my squad pack their things and move into your wing, First Sergeant?"

"We'll come get you when it's time. Just make sure you're ready. Here, take this." He handed Vincent a small radio, one like Himmelstoss had. "I don't want to walk my ass across this damn ship every time I want to talk to ya. Keep that on and answer me if I call ya." He turned and walked out the bay. Vincent returned to the rest of the squad, which was playing cards around the bunks. As usual, Richardson was cleaning house and had a pile of cigarettes, bottles, and candy in front of him.

"What's the good word, boss? Ikari asked. He was too honest to effectively lie, even during a card game, and had almost nothing in front of him.

"I met our new boss. He seems . . . lovely." Vincent smirked and sat down next to Fiona.

"How so?" Richardson asked.

"He asked me if I have done a lot of killing," Vincent said, mocking his accent.

"He's a Loon." Fiona commented. "Explains it."

"He didn't seem crazy," Vincent muttered.

"No, idiot, a Loon. As in a Lunar." Fiona saw the lingering confusion on his face. "He's from the Moon, dumbass." She shook her head. "You've never heard a Loon's accent before?"

"Oh, well that explains his bloodlust." Vincent raised his eyebrows.

Richardson slapped down a card on the table and laughed, raking in another few packs of cigarettes.

"I swear you cheat half of the damn time," Fiona complained.

He smiled. "You can't prove a damn thing, Red."

"You don't even smoke!" She screamed as she threw her cards. Richardson giggled and tossed her one of his newly won cigarettes.

"I am a generous winner," he answered.

She changed the subject. "Well, I like our chances better landing with a veteran troop rather than this one here."

"Me too," Vincent agreed. "Or really anything that takes responsibility out of my hands." He gave a little smile.

Fiona groaned. "Our fearless leader."

*****

In the middle of the night, the soldiers in Charlie bay were awoken by the room shaking as if they were caught in the middle of an earthquake. Soldiers fell from their beds and crashed onto the floor as trunks full of gear spilled out around them.

"The hell is going on?" Ikari cried from under the safety of his blanket.

"Shit!" Vincent braced himself on his bunk. The ship rocked again and sent the overhead lights crashing to the floor, which shattered on impact. Sirens started wailing, and even in the middle of all the commotion, Vincent half-expected Himmelstoss to wander through the bay door at that familiar sound.

"Brace for attack," came a calm, accented voice over a loudspeaker. "Brace for attack," it repeated.

"An attack!" Fiona yelled. "What's attacking us?"

"Get your gear on!" Vincent screamed. He wasn't sure what was happening, but he knew he wanted to be as ready as possible for anything. The soldiers of the weapons squad made their way to their gear, some crawling and others being thrown across the bay by explosive jolts. Vincent struggled to pull on his vest and helmet while trying to keep one hand on his bunk rail. He slung his rifle onto his back so he wouldn't lose it.

Since he was the squad leader, he didn't have to tote around the machine gun anymore. That duty fell to the bulk of Richardson, who also managed to carry his own tripod. Over the last few months of training, Fiona had adapted to carrying thousands of rounds of machine gun ammunition on her back.

Richardson was quickly in front of Vincent, down on one knee to stabilize himself. The machine gun strapped across his chest looked like little more than an oversized rifle on him. Fiona stood next to him, and she had one hand on his vest. Ikari slammed to the floor behind Vincent, his rocket launcher strapped across his back and his rifle slung to his chest.

Vincent struggled with the radio he'd been given by First Sergeant Collier. Through the fog of his hangover, he fumbled with the switches and knobs while trying to get ahold of anyone over the headset. Empty static hissed at him uselessly.

"Collier?" he stammered, still messing with dials. He had to cover the headset with his hands and press the ear cups hard against his head trying to drown out the sounds of screaming soldiers in his bay. "Goddammit! Screw this thing!"

"Sounds like operator error, kid," joked a thickly-accented voice on the other side of the radio.

"Collier? It's Solaris. What the hell is going on?" The ship jolted under him and tore out the bolts holding his bunk to the floor.

"Feels like the beasts know we are comin' fer 'em." Collier laughed. "Trying to swat us outta the sky before we even land."

"Well, shit. Are they going to succeed?" Vincent asked with obvious panic in his voice.

"Nah, the Reds tried the same shit against us. Didn't work out so well fer 'em then, did it? Keep your boys in line and I'll check in with you when it's over. Collier out."

Fiona stomped her foot against the deck in anger as Vincent put down the radio. She didn't even seem to notice the gear and people flying around the room.

"What's wrong?" Vincent asked. The question seemed ridiculous in the middle of what he assumed was a space battle with an alliance of alien races that wanted to burn Earth to the ground.

"Reds. He said Reds had tried to shoot him down before." Collier had been part of the Defense Forces army that had invaded and crushed the rebellion on Mars. Vincent had been hoping they could keep that a secret.

"Shit. I'm sorry."

Before he could say anything else, they were all blasted across the bay. His head slammed into the wall at full force and he dropped to the ground. His head rung with pain and his eyesight was blurry, but he was grateful he had put his helmet on. Others weren't as lucky. He saw the limp, bleeding body of another soldier lying on the ground next to the writhing form of Ikari. Ikari looked over and saw the body. He panicked and crawled away from it.

Another jolt sent them skipping across the floor and sprawling across the bay. A few of the soldiers were limp.

"Shit!" he said, straightening his helmet. Suddenly his eyes burned, and when he wiped a hand across his face, it came back stained with blood. He felt a ragged gash on his forehead above his right eye. He cursed his badly-fitting helmet. His forehead seared with pain.

After a few more jolts, it was over. Vincent forced himself onto his unsteady feet. The cut on his forehead hadn't stopped bleeding, and his helmet and vest were covered with blood. The bay in front of him was in a state of chaos. Bunks were torn from the floor and soldiers lay all over. Trunks full of gear were upended and their contents vomited out. In many places, the grey metal was stained bright red with blood.

"Vincent!" Fiona screamed. He turned to face her. Her eyes widened. "Are you okay?"

"Yeah, it's just a little cut." He looked her up and down. "Are you?"

"Yeah."

"Weapons squad, you guys good?" Vincent called out.

"I'm good!" He heard the voice of Richardson.

"Yeah!" chirped Ikari in a shaky voice.

A few panicking soldiers tried to shake the dead in a vain attempt to wake them up. Vincent keyed his radio.

"Hey, Collier, can we get some medics sent to our bay?"

"Yeah, you guys got any dead?" Collier asked. The calmness of his voice told Vincent that this wasn't the first time he'd had to deal with such things.

"No, my squad is good. We have a few in the bay, though."

"Good to hear ya pulled through. Stay strong in there. Collier out."

A few hours passed before the medics made their way to Charlie Troop's bay. Three older-looking soldiers wearing white helmets drove a medical cart through the door. One of them approached Vincent and eyed his forehead wound.

"Do you need assistance?" he asked.

"No, I'm fine. A few guys over there have some broken bones, I think . . . And the dead . . ."

"I need you to gather them for me, Corporal." The medic put his hand on his shoulder before walking off.

Vincent bent over the first body—a boy who didn't look any older than his younger brother. He was lying on his back, and most of his face was caved in from hitting the wall. He had died in his underwear. Vincent hoped he was still asleep when he impacted the wall. He hooked his arms under the boy's armpits and dragged him toward the cart.

Fiona appeared at the boy's feet and lifted them up. Vincent looked up at her, her blue eyes making contact with his. They carried the boy across the bay and loaded his twisted body into the back of one of the carts. They stood together and looked down at his damaged remains.

"I feel like we should say something," he mumbled.

"Like what?" Fiona asked with an edge in her voice.

"I don't know." Vincent shook his head. His eyes started to burn with tears. They started streaming down without warning. "Shit. He looks like my little brother."

Fiona put her hand on his shoulder. "I'm sorry, Vincent." The edge in her voice faltered.

"I didn't even know his name. Is that how this is going to be? A bunch of us dying and no one ever knowing who we were?"

"Yeah." Fiona gave a sarcastic laugh. She put a cigarette in her lips and lit it.

"What?" he said, his voice full of shock. "How could you say that?"

"This war will end eventually, Vincent. They all do." She took a deep drag and blew out a cloud of smoke. "But a whole lot more of us are going to die first."

CHAPTER TEN

The soldiers stood silently in the launch bay. A troop or a squad would be called, and they would walk forward and climb into the dropships lining the walls. Vincent couldn't tell how much room was in each ship, but it looked like a tight fit.

His weapons squad had broken off from the rest of Charlie Troop and pressed into First Sergeant Collier's Delta Troop. The soldiers of Delta Troop called themselves the "Dogs" and had the stern face of a bulldog painted onto their helmets. The weapons squad's helmets were still matte black and featureless, though Vincent's helmet sported several dents from the day he lost his mind and attacked a metal target with it.

The rest of Delta Troop was older and more grizzled-looking. They were lean from years of living on Defense Forces rations on far away planets and moons. Many of them had jagged scars on their faces or crude tattoos on their hands and necks. Such things all but ensured that they'd remain on the fringes of Earth society. Vincent got the feeling that was exactly how they wanted it.

Most of Charlie Troop lined up and climbed into a dropship with a large wolf painted on the outside. Vincent wanted to go with them. After months of living and training together, they almost felt like a second family. He kept telling himself that they were better off with First Sergeant Collier and his men.

Fiona stood next to him, weighed down with thousands of rounds of machine gun ammunition, her rifle, and her armor. She had been chain smoking since they reported to the launch bay and now stood in the middle of a small graveyard of cigarette butts.

"I thought this would be quicker." She tapped her foot while taking another drag.

"Well, I imagine loading up and dropping a million soldiers takes some time," Ikari said. His small frame was loaded to bear with his rocket launcher and its ammunition. It always shocked Vincent that he could hold it all up.

Fiona frowned. "Gives them time to start getting weapons ready to shoot us down." She had a point. It felt like they had been waiting for hours.

"Or time for them to waste all their ammo on those dudes," Richardson laughed. He rested his machine gun on the ground, holding it like a walking stick. It looked so small when he held it that Vincent was pretty sure he could just snap it in half if he wanted to.

"Listen up, Dogs!" called out Collier. "It's our turn. Line up and move out." Delta Troop filed down the launch bay, passing about ten other troops of soldiers. Every soldier Vincent passed looked as nervous and scared as he felt. His stomach turned and his limbs tingled. Weeks ago, he wanted nothing more than to get off the Victory; now, he would have given anything to stay there.

He ducked through the small door of the dropship. It was a cramped, windowless space lined with metal benches. It looked like little more than a shipping crate with an engine slapped on the side. The soldiers smashed themselves together to fit. Vincent turned and contorted himself to squeeze between another Delta soldier and Fiona. There was a harness hanging from the wall behind him, but there was no way he could reach back and grab it. He noticed none of the veteran Delta soldiers bothered hooking into their harnesses.

The dropship shook. Vincent could hear various metallic whirling and clanking noises coming from all around them as the ship was unlocked from the Victory. He closed his eyes and tried to ignore the fact that they were about to be dropped several miles from space onto a hostile alien planet. He looked over to Fiona and Richardson, both of whom had their eyes clamped shut. Richardson looked like he was about to vomit.

Vincent felt suddenly weightless as the ship moved from under him. The pressure in the ship gradually increased as the gravity compensators turned on, pinning him to his seat. The dropship accelerated, hurling Vincent back into the seat. It felt like his chest was being crushed. He gritted his teeth and fought to breathe as the dropship plummeted through the planet's atmosphere.

The ship shook violently as landing jets kicked on. Several soldiers vomited onto one another. Vincent's nose burned with the smell of bile and regurgitated booze. Gear was thrown all over the inside of the ship, slamming into the soldiers pinned against the walls.

The door to the ship opened with a hiss and flooded the inside of the ship with blinding light. The soldiers slumped out of their seats and struggled not to fall over. Vincent couldn't tell if the ship was done falling or not as his limbs had not stopped shaking from their rough descent.

"On your feet!" screamed Collier. Vincent struggled to get up. He hoisted himself up by the pack of another soldier standing next to him. Past Collier, all Vincent could see of the alien planet was brown dirt.

Collier led Delta Troop out of the ship. Most of the soldiers struggled to get their legs back underneath them. Vincent stepped foot onto the planet's surface, and a vast brown, barren plain stretched out as far as he could see.

Black streaks filled the sky as other dropships slammed to the planet's surface. Their doors popped open and each disgorged a troop of soldiers. One ship failed to kick on its landing jets and hit at full velocity, erupting into a fiery cloud of debris.

"Shit!" Richardson called out. "Did you see that?"

"Damn." Vincent shook his head. Fiona whistled and lit a cigarette next to him.

"Sucks to be them," she said through a cloud of smoke.

Delta Troop moved out across the plain and past dozens of other dropships with groups of soldiers milling about around them. Vincent glanced around in every direction nervously, expecting to be assaulted by the alien hordes.

Shouldn't they be trying to kill us or something? he wondered.

"Maybe they had something better to do?" laughed an older-looking soldier walking next to him. Vincent read his nametag: "Stronk."

"I know. I don't like it," growled a soldier whose face was twisted up with thick scar tissue. Vincent remembered someone calling him "Animal." "I Am Become Death" was written on the side of his helmet.

"You don't like anything, Animal," smiled Stronk.

Jets screamed overhead, leaving bright orange streaks in the air. Their boxy, ugly shape with stubby wings on either side reminded Vincent of a bumblebee.

"What are those?" Vincent asked, gawking up at the sky.

"Reapers," replied Stronk. "Think of them as the Victory's kids. She spits them out and they go out and spread hatred on those creatures' heads."

"Nice," Richardson smiled. "How come I couldn't get that job?"

"Because you're a big dumb gorilla person," Fiona commented.

"Oh right," Richardson frowned.

More dropships landed, these ones much larger than the one Delta Troop had flown in on. The doors of one opened, and a fearsome-looking armored vehicle rolled out. Its jet-black armor plating looked freshly painted, and a huge cannon jutted out of the front of a sloped, rotating turret. The armored monster churned up dirt as its metal tracks tore into the soil.

"What the hell is that thing?" Fiona asked.

"It's a Lunar-class battle tank," Collier pointed out from the front of the troop. "Back before I enlisted, I worked in the factory that builds 'em in Lunar City." He spat into the dirt. "Before they blew it up, anyway."

As Delta Troop marched, it passed by the wreckage of the dropship that crashed into the surface. Twisted pieces of metal were embedded in the dirt at the bottom of a small crater. Vincent saw the faded painting of a wolf's head on one of the pieces of burning metal. He tapped Fiona on the shoulder and pointed at the painting.

"Shit," she gasped.

"Everyone we trained with . . ." Vincent began.

"Too bad Himmelstoss wasn't on there." Fiona tossed a cigarette butt into the crater as they walked by.

After several miles of walking, fatigue had replaced the initial nervousness of landing. The air of the planet was thin, and Vincent's lungs burned slightly with every breath. Most of the soldiers coughed sporadically. Fiona never seemed to notice, though. Instead, she hurled insults at the soldiers who seemed to be suffering.

Hours passed, and Vincent noticed the sun hadn't budged in the sky above them. Of all the things he was worried about on the planet, he never actually thought that its day and night cycle would be different than Earth's.

"Anyone know what the day and night cycle is here?" he asked the group.

"There ain't one," Collier answered.

"Wait, what?" Vincent was baffled.

"Didn't you notice that when we landed?" Collier shook his head. "This hellhole has got two suns. It means it's never actually dark." Vincent knew they were going to a different solar system, but he never thought how different it would actually be.

"Well, that explains why it was so bright," Vincent joked, trying to mask his obliviousness.

"Anything else you missed, Corporal?" one of the soldiers in front of him joked. "Do I need to explain we invaded another planet or are you tracking that?" The gathering of soldiers laughed. Vincent slunk behind Richardson, trying to hide from their view.

"Fuck off, you little shit!" Fiona cursed at the soldier. The soldier's eyes grew wide in shock. "No one talks shit about my squad leader!" she growled, looking around. "Except me!"

"Calm your tits, Red." Stronk waved her off. Without missing a beat, Fiona dropped her rifle into the dirt, cocked her arm back, and blasted Stronk in the jaw with a right hook that made the troop of soldiers gasp. Stronk dropped to the ground like a sack of bricks with a thud.

"Don't ever fucking call me that," Fiona spat down at him.

"Holy shit!" Ikari cried. Collier laughed at the head of the troop, and the soldiers moved aside as he walked toward the weapons squad. He patted Fiona on the shoulder, and she flinched at his touch.

"You're alright, girl. You get that one for free," he laughed. "From now on, if anyone calls the girl a Red, she's allowed to knock you on your ass." She directed her hateful gaze at Collier.

"My name is Olympus, not girl."

"Alright, shit. Olympus." Collier smiled at her before walking back to the head of the troop. Stronk struggled to his feet and chased after him without even looking back at Fiona.

"Thanks," Vincent said quietly.

"I didn't do that for you," she sneered.

"I didn't mean punching him—he deserved that. I meant standing up for me."

"If anyone screws with my squad leader, it's going to be me," she said, examining her knuckles for any damage.

"Sometimes literally," joked Richardson, walking alongside them.

"Shut up, dick, or you're next," Fiona snapped at him. Richardson held his hands up in mock surrender and laughed.

"I think that means you earned their respect or something," Ikari smiled.

"Either that or the one you punched wants to kill you now," Vincent said.

Fiona smirked. "I'll consider that a form of respect."

*****

The troop came to a stop in front of a mountain range poking up from an otherwise featureless landscape. It formed a naturally jagged wall across the horizon. Vincent cursed to himself when he realized they would have to cross it. The soldiers, tired from miles of marching, sat down in the dirt. Most took drinks from their canteens or a bite from their ration packs.

A soldier with a large radio on his back kneeled down next to Collier, who held the receiver up to his ear. After a few seconds, he handed the receiver back and turned to the troop.

"Listen up," he started. "Command wants us to camp out here for the night. Those mountains can wait till tomorrow." The crowd sighed with relief. Vincent sloughed off his pack and collapsed down next to it. His uniform was soaked through with sweat. It dripped down from the brim of his helmet and into his eyes.

"How far to you think we walked?" Richardson asked as he wiped his brow.

"No idea. Too damn far," Vincent sighed. "You think they're going to attack us?"

"What kind of military let's a million soldiers just waltz through its front door without a fight?" Richardson asked.

"Cowards," Fiona frowned. "When they landed on Mars, the rebels held them off for weeks."

"Didn't they get crushed?" Richardson raised an eyebrow.

"Shut up," she said dismissively.

Vincent kept hoping that the planet's second sun would set, but Collier was right. As soon as one sun slipped beneath the horizon, the other appeared to replace it. He dug around in his backpack and pulled out his sleeping bag, unfurling it on the dirt. He opened a plastic-wrapped ration and grimaced.

"What the hell is this?" The ration looked like little more than a yellow sponge with red specks showing through it.

"Cheese omelet," Fiona read off the packaging.

"It looks like someone vomited into a machine of some kind and pressed that vomit into a brick," Vincent frowned. Richardson took a bite of his ration.

"It's better than the gruel on the ship," he said as he struggled to swallow. "Kind of."

Vincent took a bite from the yellow brick. "It tastes like feet," he coughed. Stronk and Animal were sitting nearby, eating their rations, and laughing.

"Don't worry, kids. They don't get any better with time!" Animal called out.

*****

An explosion shocked Vincent awake, and his patrol cap fell off his face as he sat up. Another boom and a flash of light from beyond the mountain range tore through the sky and shook the ground. The rest of the Delta Troop soldiers sat up in their sleeping bags.

"What the hell is going on?" sputtered Vincent.

"Those are ours," Collier commented. "The Reapers are bringin' the pain. Some of the Victory's orbital guns, too."

"That's pretty close," Ikari uttered, fear obvious in his voice.

"That's because the creatures are pretty close, dumbass," commented one of the soldiers. Soldiers pulled themselves from their sleeping bags to watch the spectacle. Many of them high-fived one another and whooped and hollered as the Reapers swooped down and lit up the horizon with streaks of bombs and missiles.

After what seemed like only a few minutes, the bombardment ceased as the Reapers retreated into the clouds and back to the Victory. Vincent wasn't sure how far away the enemy was, but he had a feeling they were going to find them soon. Nervously, he lay back down into his sleeping bag and tried to sneak in a few more minutes of sleep.

*****

A bright blue light flashed overhead. It slammed into the ground several hundred feet behind Delta Troop with an explosion that tore the ground apart and sent dirt and debris into the air.

"Incoming!" Collier screamed. "Get down!" Soldiers threw themselves to the ground. A cascade of blue lights cut through the sky and impacted all around the troop. The explosions shook Vincent to his bones.

Another explosion, this one even closer, sent up a plume of dirt and rocks. The violence of the barrage froze Vincent where he was lying. Debris kicked up from the incoming artillery ripped through the air like bullets, and several soldiers fell in its path. The world around Vincent became fuzzy as his eyes shook in their sockets and the ringing in his ears reached a fever pitch.

Reapers screamed overhead toward the source of the lights. One blue light impacted only a few feet from Delta Troop. The explosion showered soldiers with debris and sent them tumbling across the ground. After one more impact further away, the barrage stopped.

"Shit!" Collier cursed. "Leaders! Check on your soldiers and report!"

Vincent sat up, brushing off dirt and trying to find the rest of his squad. The screams of wounded soldiers assaulted his ears and he looked around franticly.

"Weapons squad!" he screamed.

"I'm good!" Fiona coughed. He hadn't noticed, but she ended up face-down in the dirt next to him, having been sent flying by a close impact. Ikari and Richardson appeared through the lingering dust and haze.

"What the hell were those lights?" Ikari brushed the dirt off his head.

"Plasma artillery," Fiona said. "I heard the ship's crew talking about it when I was buying booze from them."

"Medic!" screamed out a voice from out in the distance. Vincent ran past where an artillery shell had nearly landed on top of him. The round had dug a crater into the ground. The dirt inside was scorched by plasma explosions and had been turned to glass.

Further down the line, where the majority of the rounds landed, was a nightmare. Vincent watched as medics pulled the wounded away from the impact craters. Their limbs were melted off, exposing bone and torn muscles. Their uniforms were fused to their skin and were still smoldering. When medics tried to pull away one soldier, his skin sloughed off like a loose sleeve. The chorus of piercing screams from the wounded could be heard above any commands.

"Holy shit," Fiona stuttered. A pair of Reapers swooped down from the sky, passing so close to Vincent and Fiona that their jet wash pushed them off balance. The Reapers hung inches above the ground, throwing open their sliding bay doors. Medics rushed forward with the wounded on litters and passed them onto the Reapers. After a few seconds, the Reapers once again screamed off into the sky toward the Victory.

Fiona snapped back to reality. "We have to help. Come on." She grabbed Vincent by his arm and led him forward.

Medics were rushing from litter to litter to check on the wounded. Several soldiers whose uniforms had burned off wandered around in shock. Many had their faces seared off, their skin blackened with only the pearly white of their bones showing through. Fiona and Vincent pushed through them and found a sergeant screaming over a radio.

"What can we do?" Fiona asked him.

"Huh?" He snapped from his radio to look at the two soldiers standing in front of him. "Grab a litter, and get them lined up over there for evacuation." He went back to screaming over the radio.

Fiona and Vincent grabbed a litter. The soldier lying on it had his face almost entirely burned away. A medic had inserted a tube into his throat so he could breathe. The skin on his exposed chest was scorched and peeling away, showing his ribcage. The nametag from his uniform shirt had been seared to his burnt flesh. A medic stopped them as they begin to lift the litter.

"Don't bother. He's dead," the medic said. Her uniform was soaked in blood and covered in dirt. Her white armband looked ten shades brighter by comparison. "Move him." She pointed to another wounded soldier.

The soldier didn't even have a litter. He was lying on the dirt. His legs below the knees were burned off and wrapped in blood-soaked dressings. His head lolled back and forth as he slipped in and out of shock-induced unconsciousness. Vincent grabbed him from his armpits and Fiona grabbed him at the waist.

A Reaper landed a few feet away and opened its bay doors. A flight medic waved at Vincent and Fiona, and they hurried over to him. They put the soldier down on the Reaper's floor. The medic, peering down through a bulky insect-like flight helmet, looked back at Fiona and Vincent. He shook his head.

"He's not going to make it." His voice came through a speaker in his helmet. The medic rolled the dying soldier off the Reaper and he flopped limply into the ground. "Bring me the next one."

"Why did you do that?" Vincent snapped at the medic. He grabbed the medic by the collar of his flight suit. "Fucking take him!" he snarled.

"It's a waste of time!" the medic fought with Vincent.

Before they could argue any further, another litter team pushed Fiona and Vincent aside, sliding another wounded soldier onto the blood-slicked floor of the Reaper. The medic looked down, nodded and them, and slammed the Reaper's door shut. It quickly retreated to the safety of the Victory, its jets blowing a thick coat of dust onto the watching litter teams.

CHAPTER ELEVEN

The soldiers of Delta Troop slowly made their way down a small mountain ridge. The events of the previous night had everyone on edge. Instead of looking down at their feet and trudging as they had done before, they kept their heads up as they examined every crag and boulder in the mountainous terrain.

Collier gave a long speech before the troop entered the mountains, and he reasoned that the enemy was likely to stage their defense there instead of in the open, where they were vulnerable to Reaper attacks and orbital artillery strikes.

Vincent didn't see any way that they would escape the area alive if the aliens decided to attack. Thanks to their numbers, though, the Defense Forces had most of the area covered.

During the troop's march into the mountains, Reapers cut through the skies overhead to attack far away and unseen targets. Above the surface of the planet, dark yellow clouds obscured the immense form of the Victory. Occasionally, the clouds would flash as the Victory let loose with its orbital weapons. The impact of the shells caused the ground to shake, sending rocks tumbling down the mountain slopes.

Ikari was busy humming some patriotic song when Fiona hit him in the back of the head with a rock.

"Hey!" Ikari complained.

"You have any idea how annoying that damn humming is?"

"I'm just trying to remember the songs from my ethics book!" he whined. Fiona hit him with another rock.

"Ugh, you're even more annoying than I thought." She rolled her eyes. "Your Chairman isn't going to protect you out here."

"Faith in the Chairman is the cornerstone of a good citizen, Fiona!" Ikari said proudly.

"Yeah?" she spat. "Well I'm not a damn citizen."

"Vincent!" Ikari cried. "Are you hearing this?"

"Yep," Vincent answered dismissively.

"Are you going to do something about a non-citizen cursing our Chairman?"

"Nope," Vincent laughed.

"But—" Ikari started before Vincent cut him off.

"I'm not a citizen either. Neither is Richardson." A look of shock appeared on Ikari's face. "They strip you of that when you're found guilty of something, Ikari. Fiona's case is different, though."

"Because I'm a dirty Martian," she shrugged.

"My squad leader isn't a citizen?" Ikari gasped.

"It doesn't change anything, Ikari. Chill out." Vincent patted him on the shoulder. Ikari frantically reached in his pocket, pulled out his ethics book, and started reading a passage. The rest of the soldiers started laughing.

Collier slowed down and started walking next to Ikari.

"What exactly are you doin'?" He looked down on Ikari's small frame.

"I'm reading my ethics book, First Sergeant. For guidance," he beamed. Collier reached down and stole the book out of Ikari's hand. After a few seconds of struggling, Ikari gave up and looked up pitifully at Collier.

"This book is gonna to do nothin' for you out here, boy," Collier frowned. He cocked his arm back and tossed it over the mountain ridge. It flapped in the wind and vanished from view. "Your weapon is your ethics book now."

"No!" Ikari cried. Collier slapped him in the face.

"Your eyes need to be up and scanning this damn mountain for the fuckin' alien horde, boy, not in some goddamn book!" He slapped Ikari again. The rest of the weapons squad watched in silence as Ikari marched on, tears streaming down his face.

Collier, once again at the head of the troop, turned to face the soldiers. "My job is to bring a whole planet's worth of pain and anger down on these monsters. You are my tools for this job. If you stop me from doin' my job, I will shoot you myself. We clear?"

"Yes, First Sergeant!" the troop screamed in unison.

"Damn right, Dogs!" Collier smiled. "Spear of the damn Earth!" He turned and kept marching.

*****

That night—or what the troop had deemed to be night—Vincent and the rest of Delta Troop camped out on a ridge. Sleep was nearly impossible. Most soldiers were sitting on the ridge, chain smoking and watching the Reapers come and go from their bombing runs.

After the bombardment from the night before, most soldiers nestled their sleeping areas under ridges or under rocky overhangs. Collier told everyone to be ready to get hit again, but it never came. Vincent assumed the Victory and the Reaper attacks had destroyed whatever war machines fired those horrible plasma rounds.

"Not a chance." Fiona shook her head. She chewed a mouthful of ration and little specks of it flew out of her mouth as she spoke. "They have the ability to blow up half the damn Moon from a different solar system but get beat down by airstrikes in two days? I don't buy it."

"Yeah," Ikari said. "Or maybe they're going to surrender."

"That makes even less sense," Vincent pointed out. "Like we wouldn't chase them down and fight them after they attacked us first."

"Guys, this Alliance thing spans a ton of planets, right?" Richardson asked. A few of the soldiers shook their heads. "Maybe they just decided this particular planet isn't worth defending," he mused as a Reaper streaked overhead so low some of the soldiers ducked.

"Then what the hell are they bombing?" Vincent pointed up.

*****

Several hours later, the soldiers made their way down off the ridge. Still, no matter how far they marched, they saw no sign of life—nothing that hinted at any kind of civilization.

"Where the hell are all the towns, cities, anything?" Richardson asked.

"There's plenty of places you could wander around on Earth for a few days and not see any sign of life," Vincent pointed out.

"Shit," Fiona smiled. "Outside of Olympus, there is no life on Mars. It could be like that."

"Okay, fine. Maybe I just want to see an alien," Richardson pouted.

"You want to be the first person to see a new life-form and shoot it in the face," Fiona laughed.

"It would make me pretty popular back home," Richardson smiled.

The hike through the mountain range took its toll on the soldiers of Delta Troop. Vincent's feet were torn and bleeding; his boots did little to protect him from the rough terrain. Most soldiers had twisted their ankles at least once and sported limps of various severities. Earlier, they watched a soldier from another unit trip and fall from a ridge. No one bothered to look for his body.

Vincent was happy that Collins was sitting somewhere onboard the Victory without a care in the world. He had little doubt that Collins, always a clumsy one, would have fallen off the mountainside. Even if he managed to survive that, his feet would have failed him miles ago. What would Collier do to a soldier who couldn't march anymore, Vincent asked himself.

Because of the endless daylight, none of the soldiers could sleep for more than a few minutes; even then, sleep was fitful and restless. Vincent's eyes hung heavy, and even while marching, he struggled to keep his head up. No one was actually walking anymore; the soldiers just shuffled their feet, causing them to trip over the rocky terrain time and time again.

Vincent and many others concluded that they had invaded a dead world. Maybe the Alliance had left a few token pieces of resistance behind—those being the plasma artillery—but they must have abandoned the rest of the planet. Or maybe the planet was never populated at all.

Vincent lost track of time. Fiona had been recording how many times they stopped marching and bedded down with a collection of rocks in her pocket. According to her rock calendar, they had been marching for two weeks. Vincent concluded that Collier would march them around in circles until they all finally dropped dead.

"Halt!" Collier called out. The tired soldiers shuffled to a standstill. Collier spoke into his radio for a few seconds before handing it back to his radioman. "Squad leaders, up front with me."

Vincent was so disoriented that he didn't move. He forgot he was one of Collier's squad leaders until Fiona slapped him on the shoulder and pointed to the front of the troop.

Huddled with the rest of them, Vincent took a quick look around. One of the other squad leaders, a guy named Wolfe, didn't even look like he'd been marching at all: he was well-rested and fresh. The medical squad leader, the only other woman in the troop, was a sight. Her uniform was caked with the dry blood of wounded soldiers, and her eyes were sunken and ringed with dark circles. She looked exactly how Vincent felt.

"Good news," Collier smiled. "The Man Above has a mission for us." He pulled out a small data pad and turned it on. During the early phases of the march, Collier spoke of "The Man Above" without offering any explanation. Eventually, Vincent learned that he meant the planetary commander of the mission.

Whenever the Earth Defense Forces were deployed on some far-flung planet to "exercise the Chairman's will," one high-ranking officer was selected to command the entire force. According to some of the Delta soldiers, that officer almost never stepped foot on the planet until Defense Forces could be sure it was safe for him. Instead, he would sit in hulking, armored monsters like the Victory and direct the war from above.

A small electronic map flickered to life. Collier pointed to one of the many mountains in the area; it was simply labeled "Hill 213."

"The Task Force is being sent to take what The Man Above thinks is a hub of what these monsters call civilization. Us and Bravo Troop are being broken off to guard the main column's flank on this hill. We're gonna hike up this hill and set up shop until further notice." He clicked off the data pad and slipped it back into his backpack.

"Is this really a good idea?" Vincent asked.

"I'm afraid I agree with the new kid here." Wolfe shook his head. "We aren't even a full squadron, but we're supposed to hold the flank for the entire task force?"

"Pretty much. They're gonna need all the soldiers they can get to take that strong point, whatever it is," Collier nodded. "We got the Victory overhead. Anyone grows the balls to come for us, we call for an orbital strike right down on their heathen heads." Vincent saw a smile creep over Collier's face. "Let's go get some, boys."

Once Vincent got back to his squad-mates, they quickly started asking him questions.

"Do they think some of those beasts are over there?" Ikari asked giddily.

"No idea. But they found something for the Main Task Force to handle. We're going to sit there and make sure no one sneaks up on them," Vincent answered dismissively. "Only thing I know is once we are on that hill, we aren't going to have to march across this damn planet anymore. At least for a while," he sighed. Ikari looked disappointed.

"I guess your Chairman's great crusade will have to wait, eh?" Fiona joked. Ikari bristled at her calling the Chairman "his" but had learned long ago not to say anything to the fiery Martian.

*****

Delta and Bravo Troops broke away from the long line of tired soldiers that stretched off into the horizon and left behind the small mountain valley they had been marching through for days. The valley led them out into a field littered with boulders and jagged stalagmites that stuck out of the ground at every angle. The field looked like an overgrown forest of rocks. The soldiers carefully picked their way through it by scrambling over boulders and jagged rocks to make any headway across the unforgiving terrain. Vincent was careful not to let the rocks graze him after watching another soldier open a ragged gash across his leg.

Fiona nicknamed the area the "Razor Rocks," a name it earned quickly. Just a glancing blow on the rocks cut through skin like a knife. Vincent tripped and barely caught himself before falling onto the rocks, but a boulder ripped open his backpack and spilled out a flood of ration packs, cigarettes, and his sleeping bag. He watched his sleeping bag tear apart as it slid across the rocks.

"Guess you'll have to share with Richardson now," Fiona smirked. Vincent gave her a nervous smile while trying to keep his balance. Somehow, even in the worst situations, Fiona's sarcastic grin always made Vincent feel a little better.

Before Vincent managed to say anything back, he saw a soldier out of the corner of his eye trip and go down onto the rocks face-first. He didn't even scream. Blood pooled onto the rocks and turned the grey dirt a dark brown.

A medic squatted down next to him, rolled him on his side, and shook his head before reaching down and pulling the soldier's identification tag from his neck. The troop kept marching, leaving the soldier's body where it lay. Vincent wished he would have stopped to take the dead man's sleeping bag.

With every step, Vincent's boots stuck to the rocks, and he had to forcefully pull them up. The soles were being cut into like a hot knife through butter. The thick, heavy boots, which he had hated since the beginning, now became his saving grace. The thick soles flopped around with deep slices taken out of them. He hoped they could hold together for just a little bit longer.

*****

The troops climbed their way out of the jungle of razor rocks. Every soldier sported at least one gash from a wayward rock. Many soldiers had lost their packs and their contents. The main body of Vincent's pack was a lost cause, a large cut rendering it useless. The numerous side pockets still gave it some purpose, though.

Fiona had a cut on her shoulder. A rock just barely grazed her skin, but it cut her backpack strap clean off. She caught it before it hit the ground, and she slung its remaining strap over her midsection like a satchel. Ikari sliced open the palm of his hand and was tended to by a medic. Richardson lost his entire backpack, but he remained mostly undamaged.

The troop sat at the foot of Hill 213—a gentle slope covered in what passed on the planet as grass. It was a slightly thorny stalk plant that looked more like a short species of wheat than grass, and it was a vivid purple. It swayed back and forth in the gentle breeze. It also tore at and stuck to the pant legs of the soldiers as they marched through it. Vincent winced in pain as the thorny grass found purchase against his pants, tore through, and scraped on his bare skin.

Vincent cursed to himself. He swung his rifle back and forth trying to clear out the grass around where he was walking. It felt like the planet itself was trying to fight them. First the meat grinder of the Razor Rocks and now even the grass was trying to lash out at them.

The soldiers crested the hill of their new position. Vincent sighed in relief when he saw the top of the hill was grass-free. It was just another rocky hilltop like so many others they had passed—much like the mountains they'd been climbing through when they left the Main Task Force. He gently touched one of the rocks to make sure it wasn't of the razor-sharp variety; thankfully, he felt the dull, rounded side of a boulder.

The hilltop was a mostly flat, open area. It overlooked an open, purple-grassed field. Its strategic importance to The Man Above was obvious. The Alliance could march an entire army through it and right into the rear of the Main Task Force without being seen. The Defense Forces' weapons could turn such an open area into a killing field.

"Squad leaders!" called out the tired voice of Collier. Vincent made his way over to him, his shredded boots making it a little difficult.

"How are your soldiers?" Collier asked. Vincent was a little shocked he even cared.

"Good," Vincent nodded.

"Down one," Wolfe said. Vincent assumed the soldier that fell in the Razor Rocks was Wolfe's. Vincent shuddered at the thought of how unconcerned all of them looked when they were talking about the death of a soldier. He was little more than a footnote during a meeting.

"Um," Vincent started. "Our gear is shredded. Boots, packs, everything. Any hope of getting new stuff dropped off?" he asked.

Collier turned on his data pad and typed in a few things. The other squad leaders nodded in agreement. "Noted. The Victory can probably send us a Reaper full of supplies tonight." Collier said.

"Medical evacuations?" the medical squad leader asked.

Vincent read her bloodstained nametag as Price. "Some of these guys got torn up pretty bad by those rocks."

"Okay." Collier made another note in his data pad. "I want ya'll to spread out amongst these rocks. Solaris, you get your guns on the highest part overlooking the rest of us. Get it dug in real good."

"Yes, First Sergeant," Vincent answered.

"Turn this hilltop into a fuckin' fortress. Dismissed," Collier ordered and walked away.

Vincent sat down on a rock near Richardson, who was busy trying to clean dust out of his machine gun.

"So what's the deal?" Fiona asked. She was digging in her mangled backpack and trying to fish out a ration pack.

"We're setting up shop here. We're going to deploy our guns on that ridge." Vincent pointed to a rocky ridge that overlooked the rest of the hilltop. "Collier said The Man Above is going to resupply us tonight."

"That's good, otherwise our fearless squad leader might starve to death," Richardson joked. Vincent hadn't thought about that. All his rations had fallen out of his pack with his sleeping bag.

"Whatever are we going to do without him?" Fiona faked a dramatic voice. She tossed him an extra ration pack, and Vincent caught it with a smile.

"I guess Ikari will be leader if I die."

Ikari's head popped up at the sound of his name.

"Over my dead body. I'm not listening to that little worm," Fiona spat. She explained to everyone earlier that "worm" was a derogatory nickname Martians used for Earthlings who worshiped the Chairman. When Ikari said he didn't get it, she explained it was "because they live down in the earth and happily eat shit."

"Who else other than a true citizen?" Ikari smiled.

"Literally anyone else," Fiona frowned. "I'd rather go join the Alliance," she laughed. Ikari gasped.

Vincent broke up the argument. "Calm down, guys. Let's get the guns ready to go. Then we can screw with Ikari."

The squad clambered up a few boulders. Vincent contemplated how he would defend the looking around position. After, he noticed a ring of boulders and rocky outcroppings that effectively turned the small position into a castle-like turret. With the exception of when he was promoted to corporal, this was the first time he felt happy being in the weapons squad.

The other soldiers were busy digging away with their small portable entrenchment tools at the hilltop. They hacked away at the dirt to make foxholes from which to fight an attack. None of the weapons squad had done anything like that before and judging by how much they were huffing and sweating, they wanted no part of it.

Richardson set his hulking gun between two boulders, its barrel barely sticking out on the other side. Fiona made neat stacks of ammunition next to him and lined up several extra barrels. She'd learned to carry extra machine-gun barrels for Richardson, who during training on the Victory developed a tendency to wear out the gun by firing thousands of rounds without a break. She decided that the weight of a few extra barrels was better than waiting for his gun to cool down.

Ikari set up his launcher on its tripod. He attached a laser sight to the side of the launching tube and peered through it. Several dozen small rockets—none larger than the size of his hand—were stacked next to him. Vincent was always curious as to how Ikari would perform when under real stress. He winced and shied away from Fiona whenever she cursed at him, and he cried when Collier had slapped him. At the range, though, Ikari had shown himself to be a real marksman with his rocket launcher.

Vincent had a pair of powerful binoculars and his rifle. While he was comfortable with the machine gun, a skill that eventually earned him a promotion, he never learned to be competent with his rifle. One weapon he'd never used (and he hoped it would stay that way) was his bayonet: a razor-sharp knife issued to him when he got his rifle. It had a small lug nut on it that could slide over his rifle barrel, turning the weapon into a high-tech spear.

Fiona stole Vincent's binoculars. She was sitting cross-legged on a boulder and looking through them into the distance. A cigarette dangled from her lips and her rifle lay across her lap. Vincent climbed on top of the boulder next to her; he made certain that their shoulders touched when he settled in.

She took the cigarette from her mouth and stuck it between Vincent's lips. He took a deep drag and blew out a cloud of smoke. She leaned her head against his shoulder as they watched the planet's two suns pass one another in the sky over their heads.

CHAPTER TWELVE

Two Reapers flew in low toward the hilltop. Vincent and Fiona watched them burst through the dark yellow cloud cover, coming from the Victory far overhead. Soldiers made their way out of their freshly dug foxholes and onto the hilltop to meet them.

The jet-black form of the Reapers floated for a second before gradually lowering onto the hilltop. Collier had ordered a wide swath of the area be left untouched to give the Reapers sufficient space to land. The Reapers' powerful jet engines filled the air with an acrid smell that made Vincent's nose wrinkle.

Price, the medical squad leader, led a train of wounded soldiers toward the Reapers as the personnel onboard the crafts tossed off several metal crates to those waiting below. Soldiers with bandages blood-soaked from the trip through Razor Rocks were loaded onto the Reapers. Most of them, even though they had to be suffering to some degree, had smiles on their faces.

Once the Reapers were filled with their human cargo, their doors slid shut and the crafts lifted off from the hilltop. As they lifted off, the extreme heat of their engines distorted the air and scorched the rocks underneath them.

Hopeful for fresh supplies, the weapons squad made its way down from its position to the landing area. Vincent, who had been struggling with his mangled boots since the Razor Rocks, prayed they had sent something in his size.

As the Reapers made their way into the sky, a bright blue flash erupted from the purple-grassed field. A blue beam tore through the air and slammed into the hovering black body of one of the Reapers. It cut through the Reaper like a welding torch, bursting through the other side. The Reaper exploded in a plume of orange flames and rained debris onto the hilltop. Another blue beam erupted from the field and detonated the second Reaper, blowing it into pieces. The soldiers gawked up into the sky, unsure of what was happening.

"Get to your battle stations, you damn idiots!" Collier screamed. His deep, rumbling voice snapped everyone back to reality. Vincent turned and ran back toward the ridge to meet the rest of his squad. The rocks around him exploded with the impacts of small blue lights. His ears were assaulted with snaps and cracks of near misses. He hurled himself over the last few rocks and back onto the top of the ridgeline.

Vincent rolled onto his stomach and looked out into the field in front of the soldiers' position. The once purple grass was full of brilliant flashing blue lights. He could see masses of brown bodies moving through the field, the finer details of them obscured by the grass. The dirt around the forward entrenchments erupted, sending the soldiers diving into their foxholes for cover. A few soldiers weren't so lucky. They were caught in the open and felled by gunfire, their bodies being left in the open where the Reapers had landed.

"All units, this is Collier!" came Collier's voice over the radio. "We got an unknown number of those beasts at the foot of our damn hill. Hold your damn ground!"

"Roger!" called Vincent over his radio in response. He saw Richardson eating a ration while sitting with his back against the rock that held his machine gun.

"The hell are you doing?" Vincent screamed over the deluge of incoming fire. "Get on that damn gun!" Richardson looked ignorant of the attack. He spun, got to his gun, and pulled back the charging handle. Within seconds, he was pouring an ungodly amount of fire down the hillside.

"Ikari! Canister round!" Vincent screamed over Richardson's gun. Ikari ducked down, grabbed one of the rockets from his neatly stacked pile, and loaded it into the back of his launcher. The canister round was Vincent's favorite. It would explode over an area and fire thousands of tiny metal balls through the air. Ikari, peering through the launcher-mounted sight, fired. Its firing kicked up a thick cloud of dust in front of the position.

The squad watched as the rocket sailed over the heads of the entrenched soldiers below them. The rocket exploded with a dull thump over a patch of thick purple grass. The thousands of flying steel balls cut down the tall grass in a huge swath, like a scythe cut through the overgrowth. Anything nearby was certainly dead.

"Solaris!" the radio screamed at Vincent: it was the name that Collier had given him. "Good shot! Give me more of those!"

"Copy!" Vincent responded. "Ikari! Another one!"

"Yes, Corporal!" Ikari sounded off. He once again reached down to his pile of rockets, selected one, and loaded it. Within a few seconds, he fired off another round, once again clouding the area in dust.

With nothing else to do, Vincent settled in next to Fiona against a boulder, brought his rifle up to his shoulder, and fired. It kicked and sent a badly aimed slug flying into the open field in front of him. Countless blue flashes, looking more like small sparks than gunshots, were still popping all around the field. Vincent squeezed the trigger over and over again.

Richardson's gun fell silent as he reached down to grab another belt of ammunition from Fiona.

Fiona yelled over the gunfire to Richardson, pointing to the east. "I see a lot of muzzle flashes over there!"

"Got it!" Richardson answered back. Her most important job on the gun crew wasn't to just carry Richardson's ammo, but to spot out new targets for him as they fought. Richardson slammed it into place. Before long, his gun was roaring back to life. He was careful to fire small, well-aimed bursts. Vincent had no doubt that every time Richardson pulled the trigger, something was dying out in that field.

Reapers swooped in from the dark yellow sky. They fired off a number of rockets and peppered the area with machine-gun fire with every pass. Another Reaper went down. It spun end over end as it careened into the field and exploded in a ball of flames.

A blue light tore through the sky and impacted on the hilltop where the soldiers were dug in. It hit the ground and exploded with a flash. It covered the area with dirt and debris and sent soldiers flying. Ikari fired a rocket toward the origin of the light. He was rewarded with a massive fireball out in the field on impact.

After a few more Reaper strikes, the firing from the field slackened and died off. Ikari sat back in the dirt and away from the rocket launcher. He blinked his eyes repeatedly to recover from looking through the launcher's sight for so long. Richardson slumped back against the rock and breathed heavily. He was surrounded by thousands of brass shell casings, all crunching under his feet. Fiona dropped an empty magazine from her rifle, grabbed another one from her ammunition belt, and slammed it home. Vincent plopped onto the dirt. He didn't have to reload because he had barely fired, knowing it was mostly a waste.

A deafening silence came over the soldiers on the hilltop. They were all still staring over their weapons and out into the smoking field. The constant rocket fire and Reaper strikes had lit large sections of the field ablaze. A foul, black smoke wafted onto the hilltop as the Reapers turned and jetted back up into the yellow sky.

CHAPTER THIRTEEN

Collier dropped a skinny corpse onto the ground in front of the watching eyes of the soldiers. He had sent scout soldiers down the hillside and into the field to determine how many enemies they had killed. While it wasn't nearly as many as anyone had hoped, the scouts brought back a dead body. Its long, brown legs, clad in something resembling a dress, bent outward. Thick, dark fabric covered the thing from its shoulders to its ankles. Vincent thought it looked like a summer dress the girls back home wore.

The alien's head was covered in a matte black helmet, and a thick cord came down from the back of the helmet and led to what must have been the alien's weapon. The creature didn't wield a gun like what the Defense Forces soldiers carried; instead, its right arm fit into a metallic sleeve that narrowed into a small barrel and opened into a large bore where its hand would be.

Collier grabbed the end of the small cannon-like object and pulled it off. It came off without a struggle, revealing a brown hand with three long fingers. A single ragged hole was punched into the alien's chest. Vincent was surprised to see the wound weeping red blood, just like that of a human.

"Disgusting," Collier cursed, looking down at the body. "Worthless animal." He kicked the alien in the side of the helmet, and it came dislodged. It swung open to reveal a screen on the inside. The screen scrolled a language that none of the soldiers could read. It also had a reticle that peeked out from wherever its right arm was pointed. It would have made them much faster at acquiring and engaging targets.

The alien's head was so skinny that it resembled merely a neck with small slits for eyes. The slits were open, and its eyes were a dull red. The alien's thin, lipless slit for a mouth was slightly agape, with a line of blood leaking out, no doubt due to its chest wound.

Collier fired a shot from his rifle. It slammed into the long, skinny head of the alien. Thick blood seeped heavily into the dirt, turning it a deep copper color. The sight made Vincent sick to his stomach. He quickly made his way back up to his squad's position in the rocks overlooking the hilltop.

"What's Collier think?" Fiona asked. Unlike everyone else, she never bothered to go investigate the alien corpse.

"He thinks they were just feeling us out. Maybe fifty of them." Vincent shook his head. "Scouts maybe."

"Scouts normally . . ." Ikari began.

"Lead the way to a huge assault," Fiona frowned.

"Try not to think about that," Vincent said. "We did good. A few guys died that got caught in the open, but other than that, we escaped untouched." Vincent tried not to think about how he was one of the soldiers who was down there waiting for the Reapers to land. He just happened to be a few seconds faster than those who didn't make it.

"How many Reapers does the Victory have?" Richardson asked. He had his gun stripped into ten different pieces and was cleaning them all intently.

"No idea," Vincent responded. "But Collier wanted me to tell you that you all did a great job."

"I feel so honored," Fiona said.

"Well, not you. Mostly Richardson and Ikari," Vincent joked.

"I am just a tool for the Chairman's will," Ikari smiled.

"Oh, shut up and just accept you're a damn sniper with that launcher of yours," Fiona spat. "You put rockets down those dudes' throats." She took a deep drag from a cigarette and blew a cloud of smoke over the group. "You're annoying as hell, but damn you're good with that thing."

"The Chairman acts through my fingertips," he beamed. The rest of the group groaned in complaint.

"I wish I had some of that good will," Vincent laughed, patting his rifle.

"That's because you are unworthy, Corporal," Ikari said matter-of-factly.

"Not arguing with you there."

Somewhere far off in the distance, the soldiers could hear gunshots and see blue flashes lighting up the horizon. Explosions made the ground shake under their feet.

"Hey, Collier," Vincent began on the radio. "What's going on over there?"

"No idea. I guess they're finally hitting the Main Task Force," Collier answered. The soldiers of the weapons squad watched, legs crossed, as the horizon was lit ablaze by a blue fire. The blue streak of the plasma artillery arched through the air. Vincent fumbled around with a pack of cigarettes, only to find it empty. Fiona reached out and handed him one.

"I don't like the way that shit looks." Richardson shook his head. Blue streaks cut through the dark yellow sky and impacted somewhere beyond the horizon. The ground shook under them again. Fireballs erupted in the sky and fell to the ground below.

"Me either," Vincent said softly.

"Isn't that where the Main Task Force is?" Ikari asked, his voice still beaming.

"Well, they certainly aren't bombing nothing," Fiona countered.

"So, Vincent . . . that alien you saw . . ." Richardson started.

"Yeah, what did the beast look like?" Ikari jumped in.

"Like a skinny brown thing wearing a dress," Vincent shrugged.

"A dress?" Richardson raised his eyebrows.

"Yep, but it was thick, like an armor of some kind. Not sure if it worked, though, since someone shot him straight through the chest."

"Must work as well as ours." Fiona shook her head. "Saw some guys hit right in the vest and drop dead."

"Makes sense," Richardson commented.

"Why?" asked Fiona.

"We've never fought these guys before. Why would they know what kind of weapons we have? We assumed everyone fired guns like ours at each other before these assholes lobbed plasma at us. They probably did the same thing. Our armor only protects us from our own weapons," Richardson shrugged.

"Comforting," Vincent sighed. "Glad I carried it all this way for nothing."

"You mean like Ikari there carried his dick is whole life?" Richardson snorted.

"Yeah, pretty much." Vincent busted out laughing. Ikari fumed and crossed his arms. Even in the most stressful situations, someone in the group could break the tension with a joke. It was normally Richardson and sometimes Fiona, but it was always at the expense of Ikari.

"Don't worry. I'm sure his Chairman will take care of him when he returns home a triumphant hero." Fiona faked an announcer-type voice.

"He will!" Ikari protested.

"Ew." Richardson puckered his lips. "What do you plan on doing with the Chairman?"

"What?" Ikari gasped. "Nothing like that! Imagine if the ethics officers heard what you were saying!"

"You know, I really wish there was an ethics officer here," Richardson smiled, patting his machine gun gently.

"I bet that's a shot even Vincent would hit," Fiona laughed.

"I wouldn't bet on it." Vincent smiled and tapped the ashes off the end of his cigarette. "That's why I have you guys."

*****

Vincent tried not to think about the line of dead soldiers covered with their own sleeping bags. Collier had ordered the surviving soldiers to consolidate the troop's dead near the Reaper landing area. Vincent counted at least twenty twisted, distorted figures obscured by sleeping bags.

Reapers slowly descended from the yellow sky, gliding silently through the clouds. This time the Reapers were different; they were loaded down heavily along their stabilizers with different rockets and machine guns. They flew with more distance between them, swooping back and forth rather than flying straight down to the hilltop. The wash from their engines blew away the sleeping bags covering the dead.

Staring up at them as they circled around the hilltops, Vincent noticed scorch marks up and down the sides of the Reapers. Clearly, whatever was happening with the Main Task Force was not promising. The Reapers floated down and landed in the open area, their doors quickly being pushed open.

First, medics ushered in tens of wounded soldiers, many of whom were being carried by litter. Vincent was surprised to see many soldiers try to convince medics they didn't have to go, jumping off their litters and trying to walk around. They must have been terrified they would be shot out of the sky like the last group of wounded and decided to take their chances on the hilltop.

Their protests didn't last, and most of them quickly fell due to their wounds. After the last of the wounded were loaded, the Reapers lifted off one at a time. When the first one was in the air, it quickly flew in circle, scanning for any threats lurking in the field. When the circle was complete, the second one lifted off. Before long they disappeared unbothered.

Vincent assumed the Reapers were going to shuttle away the troop's dead, but they remained in a rough line near the landing area. Collier motioned for the weapons squad to come down off its perch. The rest of the troop stayed behind.

Based on Collier handing out shovels, Vincent understood what was going on: the dead wouldn't be taken away; they'd be buried in the same fields where they had shot down several enemy soldiers only a few hours before. Vincent had never thought the idea of never going home would become so literal. The soldiers marched off the hilltop and into the barbed purple grass below. As a group, the soldiers hacked away at the hard alien dirt, making one large pit that would hold the remains of their fallen.

The work was tiring, and all the soldiers digging had dropped their helmets and vests onto the dirt. A refreshingly cool wind whipped around them while they dug. Vincent stopped to take the breeze in. After being encased in a cumbersome vest and helmet, the breeze was the best thing he had felt in days.

He stretched his head up, trying to ease the tension in his neck from supporting the heavy helmet for so long. Vincent wondered if he would ever get a helmet that would fit him properly. Before his mind could wander any further, he saw the cross-armed figure of Collier standing on the hilltop staring down at them. The privileges of rank meant Collier simply watched as everyone else did the hard labor. Vincent didn't mind since it kept the man far away from him. Vincent had come to respect Collier as a talented leader but was certain he was just as likely to shoot him as the Alliance.

After finishing the hole, the soldiers made their way back up the hillside. Vincent heard a crack pass by his ear and something that smelled like burning plastic curled up his nostrils. Confused, he looked around and saw another soldier drop to the ground, a smoking hole in his unarmored back. Another blue flash cracked by Vincent's face, and he dove into the stinging grass for cover.

"Sniper!" screamed Wolfe. Vincent's heart slammed in his chest and he started to panic. His armor was on the ground just a few feet away, but those few feet might as well have been a few miles. His rifle was leaning against a rock next to Richardson up on the ridgeline. He was completely helpless.

The soldiers on the hilltop started returning fire. Their bullets snapped and cracked over his head. Another blue flash impacted in the dirt a few inches away from Vincent's right arm, and it puffed a small cloud of dirt into his face. A round slammed into the back of another soldier lying on the ground a few feet away from him. Vincent heard a small grunt as the round punched into the soldier's body. He didn't see him move again.

"We gotta make a run for it!" yelled another soldier who was clearly starting to lose control. The soldier leapt to his feet and took off running but was cut down in a burst of gunfire.

"Stay the hell down!" Wolfe screamed, trying to control the panicking soldiers. His efforts were useless. Soldiers sprung to their feet all around Vincent and tried to desperately sprint up the hillside. They didn't make it far before they were dropped by the impact of a multitude of laser shots.

The telltale streak of one of Ikari's rockets screamed overhead, a bright orange ball of light leading a twisting trail of smoke. It popped over Vincent's head and sent down a cloud of thick white smoke. Although Ikari's shots didn't neutralize the sniper, its aim became erratic thanks to the smoke from the rockets. Vincent knew this was his only chance.

"Now!" Vincent yelled. "Run!" He rose to a crouch, trying to stay as low as possible and run as fast as he could through the cloud of smoke. The chemical smoke burned his lungs, but he refused to slow down; the snaps and cracks tearing past his ears urged him forward, even though his lungs screamed for him to stop. Several forms running along next to him, obscured by the smoke, dropped quickly.

Then it happened. A searing pain cut across his neck, and he screamed in pain. Vincent stumbled as he reached the top of the hill. He tripped over a soldier hunkered down in a fighting position and fell face-first into his hastily dug hole. The soldier spun toward Vincent, rifle at the ready. After recognizing Vincent as a fellow soldier, he lowered it.

Vincent rolled onto his back and raised his hand to his neck. He pulled his dirt-stained hand away to see it tinged red with blood. He reached for his first aide pouch, only to remember it was attached to his vest, which was now lying at the bottom of the hill.

"Hey!" Vincent yelled at the other soldier in the foxhole. The soldier was peaking over the lip of the hole, trying to take a well-aimed shot.

"What?" the soldier turned around.

"I'm hit," Vincent pointed to his neck. Vincent could feel the warmth of his own blood seeping down his neck and chest. The soldier scooted over to Vincent without sticking his head out of the hole. He examined Vincent's neck and smiled.

"You just got grazed!" he yelled over the din of gunfire. He patted Vincent on the shoulder and turned back to his rifle.

Vincent made his way back up the rocky ridge to where his squad was located.

"We thought you were dead!" Fiona's voice sounded angry.

"Me too," Vincent gave a weak smile.

"You're hit!" Ikari shrieked.

"I just got grazed. I'll be fine. Thanks for that smoke round, Ikari. You saved our lives." Vincent smiled at the slight soldier.

"What do you mean ours?" Richardson asked.

"The people on the hillside," Vincent shrugged.

"Dude, you were the only one who made it back."

CHAPTER FOURTEEN

Surrounded by a small graveyard of cigarette butts, Vincent stared off into the distance. Fiona sat down next to him, and, as always, she made sure she sat close enough to touch him.

"Are you sure you're okay?" she asked. For the first time, Vincent thought he heard actual concern in her voice.

"I think so." Vincent gave a weak smile.

"Good." She rested her head on his shoulder. "I would be upset if you died." Vincent looked down and saw a smirk on her face, which by that point was, like everyone else's, smeared with a filth that obscured her pale features. Vincent still thought she was beautiful.

"I'd be upset if you died, too." Vincent couldn't help but laugh. Somehow, after everything that they had been through together, that was the closest they had come about talking about their feelings.

"So what do you think is going to happen next, Corporal?" Ikari asked, interrupting their small moment.

"I don't know, man." Vincent shook his head.

"I overheard one of the other squad leaders say Collier wanted to promote you to sergeant," Richardson smiled.

"What?" Vincent asked shocked. "Why?"

"You might find this hard to believe, but you handled yourself pretty well during those first two attacks." Fiona nudged his shoulder. "When I first met you, I didn't think you'd be able to handle yourself when we got neck-deep in the shit," she said through a cloud of cigarette smoke. "But you took to it like a natural."

"What did you think I was going to do?" Vincent laughed.

"Probably disappoint her worse than you did in bed," Richardson laughed.

"Hey!" Vincent frowned, and the rest of the squad burst into laughter. As they all regained their composure, Fiona raised an eyebrow.

"Have you noticed something?" Fiona asked.

"What?"

"The fighting … I don't hear it anymore," she said, staring off into the horizon. Vincent hadn't been paying attention. She was right, though; the battle had been raging off in the distance for days, but now it was silent. Not even rifle fire could be heard anymore. Only a rising cloud of smoke from beyond the horizon gave any indication that a battle was fought there.

"Do you think we won?" He asked the question everyone had to be thinking.

"If we won, why are we still sitting out here?" Richardson asked.

"If we won, why did they ambush the burying detail?" Vincent retorted.

"Of course we won." Ikari waved them off. He was cleaning out the inside of his launcher tube with an extra sock.

"I hate to rain on your parade, Ikari, but I haven't been seeing any Reapers flying that way. Or anywhere else for that matter." Fiona stubbed out another cigarette in the dirt. Vincent hadn't noticed the lack of Reaper flights.

"Shit," he cursed.

"If the Task Force lost, then . . ." Richardson began.

"We're alone," Fiona muttered.

Streaks of blue cut into the sky. The soldiers on the hilltop sprinted for cover. Vivid memories of their last run-in with the Alliance's plasma artillery had Vincent running faster than he thought possible. He slid under a rocky overhang, which housed the rest of the weapons squad.

They tensed, piled against one another, and waited for the impact. It never came. After a few minutes, Vincent poked his head out and looked around. Several more streaks of blue light were cutting through the murky sky, but they weren't landing— at least not anywhere anyone could see.

"Collier, what's going on?" Vincent asked over his radio.

"No idea. They're attacking something. I just don't know what."

"Any word from the Main Task Force?"

"I'm getting ahold of them now. See if we can't break camp and get the hell off this hill. Stand by to move."

Vincent set his radio in the dirt. He was still waiting for the high arcing blue lights to slam down onto the hilltop, which suddenly felt far too small. He recalled the destruction that the Alliance's artillery brought in the weeks prior and wondered seriously if the few feet of rocks and dirt over his head would do anything other than serve as a ready-made grave.

Ikari poked his head out and recoiled in horror.

"Vincent!" he screamed. "The sky is burning!" Vincent stuck his head out from the cover and looked up. Bright blue flashes of artillery impacts lit up the once dark yellow sky with flickering orange flames.

"What the hell is happening?" Vincent gasped. Fiona and Richardson climbed out from underneath the rocks.

"What in the . . ." Richardson muttered.

Thick curls of black smoke seeped out of the yellow clouds. A dark object trailed after it. Emerging slowly and surging with the bright orange flames, it grew as it dove toward the horizon. To Vincent, it looked like a skyscraper was crashing to the surface of the planet. Then it hit him.

"It's the Victory!" Vincent screamed. The massive flaming form of the ship sparkled with the impacts from distant artillery. As it passed overhead, it cast the entire hilltop and purple fields in a dark shadow, sending flaming debris plummeting down to the surface.

It crossed over the jagged mountain peaks and gradually vanished. The ragged and tired soldiers of the hilltop stood and watched as a bright plume of orange fire erupted into the sky as if the mountains themselves had exploded. The planet shook like it was splitting in half. Dirt, debris, and a thick cloud of choking smoke rolled down from the mountains and cast the once bright field in a haze.

"No fucking way," Fiona sputtered. "No way."

"Chairman help us," Ikari stammered. Vincent climbed down the ridgeline and onto the hilltop. He walked past dozens of frozen soldiers, their eyes locked onto the burning mountain range—a range now covered in the wreckage of the ship they thought was invincible.

Through the billowing smoke, Vincent could see the unmistakable figures of enemy soldiers stalking through the fields in front of the hilltop. Large armored vehicles floated a few inches above the purple grass, and scores of enemies sat atop them. Before he could scream or alert anyone, two silver jets, their wings curved like crescent moons, swooped down over the hilltop and let loose a torrent of rapid fire.

Gunfire tore through the hilltop, ripping several terrified soldiers to pieces. Vincent dove to the ground and made his way back up the ridge to his squad. With long bursts from his machine gun, Richardson was trying to keep the enemy in the field at bay. Fiona was firing well-aimed shots one at a time, while Ikari fumbled with his launcher as he loaded in another rocket with shaking hands.

It wasn't just the skinny, lanky aliens with the strange armored dresses this time. Vincent could see short, muscular aliens wearing what looked like black overlapping plate armor and firing hand-held rifles. They were wearing brightly colored helmets that came down on either side of their faces. What actual skin Vincent could see looked like it was covered in bright paint.

A few massive aliens were scattered about the enemy ranks. They stood twice as tall as an average human and were wearing so much armor they looked like walking tanks. Their armor was covered in intricate carvings and designs. From their mannerisms and small number, Vincent assumed that they were directing the other aliens.

"They're everywhere!" screamed Richardson in between bursts.

"Just don't stop shooting!" Vincent shouted, bringing his rifle up, sighting in on one of the giants, and snapping off a shot. His shot sparked harmlessly off the alien's chest. The floating tank's sides came down like ramps, and more aliens came spilling out. The tank had a small squat turret rotating around and firing at targets on the hilltop.

Instead of a cannon or machine gun, it attacked with an unbroken blue laser beam. The beam cut into the lip of the hilltop, where most of the remaining soldiers were entrenched. It tore through their positions like a piece of paper and burned defending soldiers. The turret spun back and forth, its beam of light never breaking.

Vincent slapped Ikari on the shoulder. "The tank!" he screamed. "Shoot the fucking tank!" Ikari adjusted the controls on his launcher and fired. With a thump and a whoosh, the rocket screamed through the air toward the tank. Its turret immediately swung up and fired a cutting beam up the ridge and toward Ikari.

Ikari's rocket burst through the front of the tank and exploded out the back, creating a small burning hole. The tank shuddered and fell to the dirt. Its beam sliced through the rocks and cut into the box of rockets sitting next to Ikari, detonating them.

The explosion threw Vincent through the air. He flew over Richardson and landed with a crash next to Fiona on the far side. He scrambled to his feet and ran back to Ikari. The launcher position was blown apart, and Ikari was nowhere to be found. The dirt around the scattered wreckage of the twisted launcher tube was littered with blood-stained scraps of a grey uniform.

Vincent collapsed against the ridge and screamed, his pained voice muffled by the deafening sound of the soldiers fighting for their lives on the hilltop.

"They're on the hill!" Fiona screamed. Vincent popped his head over the ridge and saw the short aliens cresting the destroyed defenses and firing into the backs of retreating soldiers. Behind them, the hulking form of the armored giants pumped single blasts from what looked like cannons attached to their arms. One shot hit a man in the waist and tore his torso from his legs. Another shot blew a medic apart as he tended to a screaming soldier.

Just as the panicking soldiers managed to form an improvised defensive line, another silver jet swooped down and strafed them to pieces. The battlefield devolved into chaos. Soldiers began disregarding orders and fleeing in every direction.

Vincent caught a glimpse of Collier, standing fast in the middle of the hilltop and firing at the oncoming horde as his broken soldiers sprinted past him. Several of the short aliens dropped dead at his feet. He rushed forward and stabbed another with his bayonet. He then spun around to club another when he was struck in the back by one of the monstrous cannons of the encroaching armored giants. The first sergeant vanished from view in a cloud of dirt and blood.

Richardson continued firing wildly down onto the incoming enemy. Every time he let loose with a burst of gunfire, another swath of the hilltop was cleared of enemies. Their chewed-up remains began covering the troop's position. No matter how much gunfire Richardson poured down on their heads, they relentlessly pushed forward.

Once the outer perimeter collapsed, the short aliens closed in on the remaining defenders. They were either steadfast in their duty or simply too scared to move. At close range, the stout aliens dropped their rifles and drew large ornately designed handguns that tore gaping holes straight through the soldiers' armor. The few who stood up to them didn't last very long.

The survivors broke and ran for their lives. They sprinted toward the ridgeline where the weapons squad remained hunkered down and firing at the incoming enemy.

"We need to get out of here!" Fiona screamed. She dropped a magazine from her rifle and slammed in a fresh one.

"Where can we go?" Vincent yelled, firing a few badly aimed shots. He grazed a short alien, tearing a scar across its thick leg armor. "We can't run through the Razor Rocks!"

"We stay here, we die!" Richardson screamed without looking up from his unending machine gun burst. A few lucky soldiers hurled themselves over the ridgeline and landed on the other side. They quickly flipped around onto their stomachs and started shooting back down the ridgeline.

Vincent reached down and grabbed a hand grenade from one of Richardson's ammo pouches. He pulled the pin from the baseball-sized bomb and slammed down the arming button on top. He tossed it over the ridge and listened to the dull thump as it detonated. A few seconds later, a long stick topped with a spike-covered ball landed in the dirt next to him. Vincent glanced down and noticed a small trail of smoke curling up from it.

Another soldier picked up the stick and hurled it back over the rocks. Another explosion rang out. An alien hand grenade. Vincent turned to thank the soldier who saved him, only to see a bullet smash through his face, blowing his jaw off and crumpling him to the ground.

"Reloading!" Richardson screamed. He pulled open the feed tray on the top of the machine gun and was lining up another belt of ammunition when a short alien appeared in front of him. Richardson quickly unsheathed his bayonet from his belt and jammed it into the alien's face, just below its wide-set eyes. The alien stumbled back and fired a round from its pistol before falling off the ridge.

The shot blew the feed cover off Richardson's machine gun, rendering it useless. Cursing, Richardson turned and picked up a rifle off a dead soldier. Another soldier dropped, screaming next to Vincent. He didn't bother to look. If any of the soldiers on the ridge stopped firing, there was a good chance they were going to be overwhelmed. There was no time to help anyone.

Somewhere next to Vincent, Fiona screamed in anger and lashed out with her bayonet. She stuck a short alien just below its bellowing mouth with her rifle-mounted bayonet. The alien gurgled and twitched, dark blood sputtering from its mouth. She fired a round point-blank into the alien's face, blowing an ugly wound through its head and sending its brightly colored helmet spinning.

Vincent's rifle clicked with an empty magazine. He hit the small button next to the trigger that dropped the magazine. He fumbled around with a screaming man's ammunition belt when two crescent-moon-shaped jets doubled back toward them. They dropped low beneath the clouds and roared a few feet over the heads of the alien soldiers.

"Get down!" Vincent tried to yell over the deafening din of the surrounding combat.

Almost in slow motion, two light puffs of smoke appeared in front of the jets, and the shape of rockets tore toward the ridgeline. After a bright flash of light, Vincent was swallowed by darkness.

CHAPTER FIFTEEN

Vincent awoke on his back, staring up into the sickly yellow sky. His head pounded so hard it felt like it had been split in half. He had the copper taste of blood in his mouth. His body was racked by so much pain he could hardly lift his head. He could hear little over the high-pitched ringing in his ears.

"I'm alive," he mouthed. He looked around the ridgeline. Wisps of black smoke rose from where he and his squad had defended the ridge, but he was several hundred feet away from the last place he remembered being.

Vincent rolled over onto his stomach and pain surged through his legs. He was too afraid to look down at the possible damage. He inched his way forward. With every bit of effort, he winced at the ceaseless burning in his lower extremities.

The ridgeline was thoroughly scorched and nothing remained alive. The charred remains of soldiers lay twisted and seared to the rocks. There he saw his friend Richardson, surrounded by the enemy's dead. His rifle was fused to his mangled, burnt body. Vincent hoped his death was painless.

He looked around the scoured killing grounds for Fiona, but he couldn't find her. Vincent finally crawled to the lip of the ridgeline, where he and the rest of the soldiers made their failed last stand, and looked down on to the hilltop.

Alien soldiers were still picking up their wounded but leaving their dead, of which there were hundreds, maybe even thousands. When they finally rushed the hilltop, there were perhaps only fifty Defense Forces soldiers left. They made the Alliance pay dearly for the hill.

One of the giant armored hulks kicked over a soldier's body. This monster, unlike the others, wore dark crimson armor decorated with alien designs. Strips of cloth hung from its shoulders.

The soldier, to Vincent's surprise, was still alive. Wounded and trying to play dead when the giant crimson monster kicked him over, now he was screaming in fear. The soldier begged and pleaded with the monster to let him live. Vincent wasn't sure if the alien understood the soldier or not, but either way, his pleas went unheeded. The monster brought a single metal foot down on the soldier's face, silencing his cries.

When the monster turned around, Vincent could see it was wearing a sort of necklace around its armored chest. When he squinted, he could make out several skulls—human skulls—dangling by a beaded rope.

A wave of lightheadedness suddenly overcame Vincent, and he laid his head against the burned rocks of the ridgeline. Among the burned and destroyed remains of his friends and enemies, he slipped back into unconsciousness.

CHAPTER SIXTEEN

Vincent jolted awake to the feeling of something grabbing him. He locked eyes with a strange alien, which jumped back in shock. It was one of the short, stocky aliens. It was wearing neither the plated armor of the soldiers nor the face paint. Instead, it stood there wearing something resembling a cloth bathrobe. A large ornate pistol was holstered on its side.

Vincent panicked and reached down to his belt where his bayonet was supposed to be. It was gone. He felt around on the burned rock for anything to defend himself, and he ended up grabbing a piece of rock. The alien didn't reach for its pistol. Instead, it slowly raised its stubby, tan-colored, three-fingered hands.

It had wide bright red eyes and a sloping forehead. Its thin mouth appeared permanently stuck in a frown, and its rough tan skin had the consistency of the soil, like it was born from the rocks themselves.

"Stay away from me!" Vincent gasped. He tried to look strong, but he was in so much pain that, even if he wanted to, he couldn't have used the rock he was holding to defend himself.

"Vincent?" screamed out a voice from somewhere behind him. Fiona crawled up onto the ridgeline. In her hand was a pistol. Her face was covered in blood, and she was wincing in pain. She raised her pistol in a trembling hand and pointed it at the alien. "Back off!"

The alien took a step back, its hands still out in front of it. A tall, rail-thin alien appeared behind it. Though it appeared unarmed, it was carrying a heavy bag. Its head was barely wider than its neck, and its four-fingered hand look liked it sprouted straight from its thin arm with no hint of a wrist. Vincent recognized it as the same kind of alien that scouted the soldiers before the battle.

"Please!" the tall alien said in a harsh whisper. Both Vincent and Fiona's eyes went wide with shock. "Alliance soldiers are nearby. You must be quiet."

"You're not Alliance?" Vincent stuttered.

"No," the alien whispered.

"You speak Earth Standard?" Vincent asked, still in shock.

"Yes. Him, not so much." The tall alien motioned to the short alien.

"Then what the hell are you doing here?" Fiona said in a pained voice. Her gun was still raised.

"We are . . ." The alien stopped to think about what to say next. "We are taking what is no longer needed." Fiona glanced down at the bag in the skinny alien's grey hand.

"You're stealing from the dead?" Fiona frowned. The alien shrugged.

"What is no longer needed," it repeated. "If you are not quiet, the Alliance will find and kill us both."

Fiona pushed herself to a sitting position; blood soaked through her shirt. "Well, we seem to be at a damn impasse, don't we?"

"You . . . you need medical attention, do you not?" the alien asked.

"Maybe a little." Vincent grimaced as he tried to push himself up. His legs burned with pain.

"Come with us. We can treat you on our ship." The alien nodded. Its mouth smiled a toothless smile.

"Why would we ever go with you?" Fiona spat.

"What other choice do we have?" Vincent asked. "What's the difference between them murdering us or the Alliance murdering us?"

"Ugh, fine," Fiona relented, lowering her gun.

The short alien waddled over and picked Vincent up and placed him on his shoulder. Vincent cried in pain as he was moved and saw the puddle of blood he left on the rocks as the alien cradled him onto its shoulders.

Though he had been thrown clear of the blast, Vincent's legs had been peppered with shrapnel and bits of rock. They hurt worse than anything he'd ever felt, but he was just happy they were still attached. Fiona forced herself to her feet and struggled to steady her legs. She grimaced in pain and stuffed the pistol into her waist band.

"I don't need your help," she growled when the tall alien stepped forward to offer her help. It was skinny and frail, and Vincent didn't see any way that it could help her.

The skinny alien led them down the backside of the ridge toward the Razor Rocks. The aliens shot flittering glances as they walked. The short alien had one stubby arm on Vincent and the other on the curved handle of its large pistol.

Up ahead, a small grey ship was parked where the rocks began jutting up from the earth. The ship looked almost handmade. Much like the jets that had dive-bombed the soldiers on the ridgeline, it resembled little more than pieces of sheet metal bolted together with oversized jet engines slapped on the back.

"Is that thing even going to fly?" asked an exasperated Fiona. The thin alien looked back.

"Of course," it answered. The alien didn't seem to be expressing any kind of emotion in its slightly high-pitched voice. It said something to the other alien in a different language, and the short one shook and grunted. Vincent interpreted it as laughter.

"Hey!" Fiona barked. "What are you two talking about?"

"No offense was meant, human female," the lanky alien said curtly. Fiona frowned.

The small ship's door creaked and dropped open. The skinny alien had to duck down to fit through the door. The short alien fit through fine, but it seemed to have forgotten that it was carrying Vincent and smacked his head on the side of the door.

Inside, the ship was surprisingly large. The front had what looked like several mismatched computers fused together to create some sort of cockpit. A wooden stick came up from the floor in front of a torn chair, and Vincent assumed that was how they controlled the craft.

The rear of the ship had a long table flanked by some cushions on the floor. Several trunks and boxes were stacked precariously alongside the wall. The short alien deposited Vincent onto the table, which creaked in protest.

"How the hell are we going to get medical treatment in this thing?" Fiona snapped, looking around at the cramped and dirty ship.

"I will conduct the treatment," smiled the skinny alien.

"Have you ever treated a human before?" Vincent asked nervously.

"I have never seen a human before today," it answered. "You are bleeding. I assume I must stop that bleeding."

"Alien medical school must suck," Fiona joked.

"You are the alien, human female," it nodded.

"My name is Fiona!"

"You are called Fiona," it repeated.

"And what are you called?" Vincent asked.

"I am called Nox." It pointed at itself. "That is Zinvor." Nox pointed at the short alien who was playing with the computers in the cockpit. Nox opened a box and started fumbling around inside of it.

"You said you weren't Alliance soldiers. So what are you?" Fiona asked.

"We do not follow the Alliance," Nox said. Zinvor yelled something from the front of the ship. "He says the Alliance is the slaves of the Anarchs."

"What is an Anarch?" Vincent asked.

"The metal ones," Nox answered curtly. He pulled something from the box. It looked like a torch of some kind, and Nox started fumbling with the controls.

"The really big guys?" Fiona asked.

"Yes." Nox nodded and blue flames erupted from the end of the torch.

"What are you doing with that?" Just as Vincent finished his question, Nox pushed the torch into the worst of the shrapnel wounds, just above his knee. Vincent screamed in pain and wildly flailed, trying to push Nox away.

"What the hell are you doing?" Fiona screamed and reached for her gun. Before she could pull it out, Nox stopped burning Vincent.

"Bleeding has stopped." Nox nodded and turned the torch off. Vincent lay on his back on the table, screaming and holding his leg.

"You are next, yes, Fiona?"

"Umm." Fiona looked down at the torch. "Actually, I'm feeling okay now."

The ship started to shake and rattle as the jet engines wound up. The searing pain in Vincent's legs began to fade, though he still couldn't support himself. He lay helplessly on the table as Fiona sat, with her gun drawn, on a cushion on the floor next to him. She had ripped the cover off another cushion and wrapped it around her midsection to stop up whatever wound she had been bleeding from.

"So where are we going?" Fiona asked. The two aliens conversed and Nox turned back to her.

"The Hive. The city on this planet," Nox answered.

"Why?" Vincent asked.

"We must bring back the items we found. Then we will talk." The ship angrily rattled more, like it was trying to fight the idea of flight.

"Can we get back to Earth?" Vincent groaned. Fiona gave him a look of concern. Nox turned his head and looked at the two humans.

"That is asking much," he said, pondering the correct words to say. "We will find out more in the Hive."

CHAPTER SEVENTEEN

The small ship finally landed after what was probably the roughest ride of Vincent's life.

"Listen," Nox said. "You are the only humans on the entire planet. You cannot be seen." Hearing that made Vincent cringe. Only a day before, over one million humans were on the planet. Now, there were just the two of them.

Nox rummaged around in another trunk and pulled out two ratty and torn grey robes, much like his and Zinvor's. Vincent wrapped himself up in the cloth and tied it closed. Fiona did the same, found the hood, and pulled it over her head. Vincent struggled to reach over his head and cover his face with his hood.

Vincent pushed himself off the table. He gingerly put one foot on the ground, and then the other, and pain surged through his legs. He gritted his teeth and balanced himself.

"Do I look like an alien?" Vincent gave a painful smile.

"Yes," nodded Nox.

"I mean one of you."

"No, you are unattractive for my race," Nox said. The dull, flat tone of his voice made Vincent question if he was cracking a joke or not.

The door to the ship opened with a metallic groan. The city that lay before them was massive. Brown structures, made from bricks on the bottom and alloys and composites further up, littered the landscape. It was like someone had built a modern city right on top of an ancient one. The streets were crowded with throngs of different aliens, densely packed together on dirt roads with buildings encroaching on either side.

Unlike his hometown, where everything was arranged in a painfully organized grid pattern and every house was identical, the Hive apparently had no central planning at all. Every building was of a different shape, size, and material. None were lined up to create what on Earth would be a functional road network.

Instead, they bent inward on each other and swallowed up what little room the foot traffic had to squeeze through.

While the aliens on the ground level of the city were pushing or pulling wheeled carts, farther up in the sky were personal-sized jets, sleek alien versions of Earth's aero cars, flying back and forth between raised roadways and building entrances. To Vincent, it looked like the city grew more modern with increased elevation. Gleaming skyscrapers were built on top of the squalid buildings below them.

The air was thick with the scent of pollution, food, spices, and the musty smell of countless living things packed together in close quarters. Trash from the higher levels cascaded down and splashed on the dirt path. Aliens walked back and forth, bumping into one another without exchanging glances, and none seemed to have a concept of personal space. Most importantly, no one seemed to notice the poorly disguised humans in their midst.

Fiona and Vincent limped along, trying to follow Zinvor and Nox. Fiona was in much better shape than Vincent and did what she could to help him along. The two aliens cut down so many alleys and up and down so many different flights of stairs that it didn't take long for Vincent and Fiona to lose their sense of direction. Not that it would have mattered—nowhere did Vincent see a sign or anything passing as an address. To get around the Hive, one simply had to know where they were going.

They ducked through a low doorway and went down several more flights of stairs. Vincent began noticing the absence of sunlight. Instead, the alleyways and stairways were lit with a series of dim orb lights attached to the walls.

Each time Vincent took a step down, he let out a whimper of pain. Fiona was no longer helping him, but rather cautiously peering around every corner. Her eyes ceaselessly darted from one place to another, and her hand remained on the butt of her pistol.

Soon, they entered a dank basement. The air was clouded with acrid smoke and stunk of mold. A group of aliens sat on an array of cushions around a low table, where they played a sort of board game and smoked from long pipes. Nox greeted them in an unfamiliar language, but the aliens at the table didn't seem happy to see him.

Their short exchange sounded like an argument, and Nox dropped the bag of items he'd stolen from the battlefield. The aliens at the table, three short waddling figures like Zinvor, stood up and walked over to the bag. They inspected it and tossed it against the wall, throwing their arms up in disgust.

Nox backed away from the angry group, slowly raised his hand, and pointed at Fiona and Vincent. After a brief exchange, the three aliens' attention shifted to the two humans.

Fiona went rigid. Her hand slowly retreated into her robe, behind her back.

"What's going on?" Vincent whispered to Fiona.

"I don't know, but I don't like it," she muttered.

Nox waived his hands and yelled something at Zinvor, who shoved him aside, knocking Nox to the ground.

The three aliens walked toward Fiona and Vincent. Fiona stepped in front of Vincent and drew her pistol, but before she could fire, a deafening boom filled the tiny room. Fiona and Vincent were spattered with the blood and viscera of the nearest alien. Vincent's ears rang so loudly he couldn't hear anything else.

The other two aliens panicked and began drawing pistols. Fiona fired a round that missed its target and slammed into the wall next to Nox, sending up a small puff of dust. She fired again, and this time, her round found purchase into one of the alien's heads. It blew out the back of its sloping skull and splattered Zinvor.

Fiona fired again and dropped the last alien where it stood. She didn't drop her pistol but instead kept it leveled on Zinvor and Nox. Zinvor stood across from the two humans; his large pistol had a thin trail of smoke whirling up from its barrel.

"Wait!" Vincent yelled at Fiona.

"What? These assholes almost got us killed!" she shot back.

"The short one shot first! He could have killed us and he didn't!" Vincent screamed. Fiona looked down at Zinvor's weapon. Even though she had a gun pointed right at him, he pulled a small red cloth from his holster, wiped his pistol off once, and gently placed it back in its holster.

"That skinny bastard didn't, though!" she cursed and shifted her aim over to Nox. Nox, who cowered on the ground during the shooting, stood up and straightened his robe. He yelled something at Zinvor, who crossed his arms in protest.

"Tell us what's happening!" Fiona yelled at Nox.

"Nothing!" Nox yelped, finally showing some emotion in his speech. Fiona fired her weapon and hit Nox in the leg. He howled with pain, rocking back and forth while holding the wound. It oozed blood onto the dusty floor of the basement room. To the surprise of everyone, Zinvor did nothing but stand and watch.

"Okay!" Nox yelped in pain. "We owed them money. The things we took from the battlefield weren't enough to cover our debt. There is a large bounty on live humans to sell to the Anarchs."

"You were going to sell us?!" Fiona barked. She trained the gun up to Nox's face. Again, Zinvor stood and watched.

"Is this true?!" Vincent yelled, limping over and picking up a large pistol from one of the dead aliens on the ground. The weight of the gun in his hand was shocking. He could hardly hold it with one hand, so he cradled it in his arms like a rifle.

"Not me," groaned the deep grumbling voice of Zinvor. "Is dishonorable."

"You weren't going to sell us?" Vincent asked Zinvor.

"No. Take you home," Zinvor nodded. "Mawr no lie."

"Mawr?" Fiona asked.

"Me." Zinvor thumped his chest in pride with a giant three fingered hand.

"It's true! He had no idea!" Nox whined. "I knew they would kill us if we could not pay them this time."

"I don't give a shit," Fiona growled.

"Fiona, wait!" Vincent pushed Fiona's pistol down. "Can you really get us home?" Vincent directed the question at Zinvor.

"I not know." Zinvor shook his head. "I try."

"Okay." Vincent said. "If he tries to sell us or betray us in anyway, will you kill him?"

"Yes," Zinvor nodded. "Nox untrustworthy."

"You stupid noble cave creature!" Nox cursed. "You'll get us killed!"

"Why?" Fiona asked.

"Those smugglers you killed control this whole area! You do not think they heard those shots? We will be dead before we can leave the Hive!"

"We better get going then," Vincent said. Zinvor bent down and picked up the frail, bleeding form of Nox and gently placed him on his wide shoulders. He held his pistol out in front of him. He then began sprinting up the stairs and out of the dingy basement.

At the top of the stairs, several skinny aliens were waiting, pistols in hand, and looking down the stairway in confusion. Zinvor leveled his gun and fired a shot into the crowd, blowing one of the alien's heads off at the shoulders.

Fiona fired and hit one in the leg. It twisted around and screamed in pain as it fell to the ground. Vincent leveled his stolen pistol and fired it, but the recoil was devastating. It roared and kicked Vincent back so hard that he nearly fell down the stairs. The shot tore off the last alien's right arm at the elbow, and it stumbled back and collapsed with a shriek.

The group shoved its way through the crowded streets. Several aliens gave chase, firing weapons at them wildly. Fiona turned to fire her pistol back but heard nothing but a dull click. Vincent turned, dropped to one knee, and fired at them. The shot slammed off the ground and exploded out a shop window. Several attackers dove for cover.

Vincent, Fiona, and the two aliens crashed through the small door to the rickety ship, which rocked on its risers and nearly tipped over. Gunshots slapped off the metallic hull and rang out like an angry hailstorm. Vincent fired again, this time blowing a hand off an attacker. He fell back against the wall and shook his wrist; firing the alien hand cannon had made his whole arm go numb.

Slowly, the jets rumbled to life and the ship shook and fought as it lifted into the air. Shots clanged off the exterior and warning lights blinked and screamed loud, angry noises at Zinvor as he sat behind the controls.

"Where are we going?" Fiona asked over the deafening noise inside of the cramped ship. Zinvor looked back at her, smiled, and shrugged.

CHAPTER EIGHTEEN

"**N**o, really, where are we going?" Vincent asked.

"Elysian. A small planet nearby. We know some smugglers on the planet who make the run to human space. They are our best bet." Nox winced as Vincent tightened down a rag over his bullet wound.

"Tell me. What are you exactly?" Fiona cut in. "You know we are humans, and you seem to know a lot about us. But we don't know anything about you."

"Zinvor is Mawr, like he told you. I am Rhai."

"Then who are the Anarchs?" Vincent asked. "The Metal Ones?"

"Yes," Nox nodded. "They are the Alliance."

"Wait. What do you mean?" Fiona asked. "I thought you were all the Alliance."

"No." Nox shook his head. Something that Vincent understood as despair overtook the normally blank expression on Nox's long, skinny face. "They are the … strongest," Nox corrected himself. "They try to force us under their control. Many of us refuse."

A loud bang interrupted the conversation as Zinvor slammed a wide fist on the dashboard.

"Anarchs!" he grunted. "Demons!"

"Did they take over his planet, too?" Fiona asked.

"No, the Anarchs did not have the numbers to fight the United Clans of the Mawr. So they destroyed their planet. Only the few Mawr who were off-planet at the time survived." Nox's voice waived a bit.

"What?" Vincent noticed he was getting upset. "Why?"

"They were the only ones strong enough to reject them. After the Great Culling, most of the Mawr off-world submitted to the Anarchs to ensure their race survived."

"So the soldiers we were fighting …" Fiona trailed off.

"Forced to fight," Nox said.

"They were like us," Vincent gasped.

"You were also forced to fight?" Nox tilted his head.

"Yes," Vincent nodded. "We didn't have a choice."

"This war. I do not see the meaning of it." Nox shook his head.

"I saw an Anarch wearing all red. What does that mean?" Vincent asked. Zinvor slowly turned back from the cockpit and made eye contact with Vincent. The alien's red eyes burned into Vincent's with a hatred that crossed star systems.

"Red King," he grunted.

"The Commander of all the Anarch armies in this sector. You did not see him, did you?" Nox asked.

"Yeah," Vincent said, remembering the titanic figure in crimson with his necklace of skulls clattering around as he kicked over and executed wounded humans.

"You are lucky to still be walking the plain of the living then, friend. They say facing the Red King in battle dooms a being to death." Vincent shuddered and tried to push the memories from his head. He dropped the hulking, decorative pistol on the table.

"Why do all of Zinvor's race carry these?" he asked, changing the subject.

"Riten!" growled Zinvor. He stood up from his seat at the cockpit, marched over to where Vincent was sitting on the floor cushions, and grabbed the pistol from the table.

"They are called Riten." Nox nodded at his stocky, angry friend. "They are handcrafted by the individual Mawr clans for their warrior caste once they ascend to the ranks of the warriors. It is considered a great honor to kill a clan enemy with it."

"You no Mawr," spat Zinvor. He carried the pistol back up to the cockpit with him. "No use Riten!"

Vincent recalled how odd it was when he saw Zinvor's race dropping their rifles and charging through machine-gun fire to kill Defense Forces soldiers with their handguns.

"Their planet was destroyed?" Fiona asked.

"Yes," Nox responded.

"Why wasn't yours?" she countered.

"Simple." Nox waved the question off with his hand. "We did not fight."

"Rhai. Cowards," Zinvor grunted.

"Yes," Nox thought for a moment about what to say next. "We are not known for our combat abilities."

The tiny ship rocked violently, and trunks and crates were thrown across the cramped space, sending everyone diving for cover from the ship's innards. As the trunks burst open, guns of various shapes and clothes flew through the ship.

"What the hell was that?" screamed Fiona. Nox limped to his feet and hobbled into the cockpit.

"Alliance!" Nox yelped. As the ship rocked again, Vincent was thrown over the small table and landed in a pile of discarded storage trunks.

"Can this ship outrun them?" Fiona yelled, trying to steady herself against the table.

"Not a chance," Nox answered. Vincent righted himself, pushing several of the crates off his battered legs.

"Can we slow them down?" Vincent asked.

"It is a possibility," Nox nodded. "The garbage chute. If we throw out some of our trunks, it could slow them down."

"Would that actually work?" Fiona asked.

"Probably not," Nox said in a matter-of-fact tone. He limped toward the main door of the ship. A small discolored button was on the wall next to it. "I forget. Can humans breathe in space?" Nox asked with a frown.

"No!" Fiona cried.

"Then try not to breathe." Nox slammed the button. A small circular hole opened next to the door, and a deafening roar filled the cabin, sucking the air from Vincent's lungs. His ears popped and his eyes felt like they were being torn from their sockets. He gritted his teeth and grabbed onto a badly riveted bulkhead.

Nox grabbed crate after crate and trunk after trunk and shoved them through the hole. After a few minutes, he hit the button again, and the chute closed. The pressure in the ship normalized and the humans gasped for breath and fell to the floor.

Nox, followed by Vincent and Fiona, limped up to the cockpit. They watched as a few of the crates floated harmlessly off into space. A few ruptured into a violent plume of fire. The Alliance ships effortlessly dodged around the explosions, zipping around the fire and debris in seconds.

"Dammit," Fiona cursed.

"What the hell are you guys even carrying in these things?" Vincent asked, looking around at the surrounding crates.

"It is better you do not know," said Nox.

It surprised Vincent to not see the dull, unfinished-looking metal ships that had attacked his position on the hilltop. These ships were as black as space itself, and they were cut at such an angle as to resemble a bladed weapon. He reasoned that the Anarchs must have been pursuing them.

The ship shook violently. The engines, always emitting a whirling noise, shuddered and died out. The inside of the ship went deathly silent, and Zinvor slammed a button on the dashboard. The ship vibrated and felt like it was coming apart at the seams. Vincent braced himself on the cockpit doors.

Something that sounded like a wind tunnel spun to life. Bolts clattered to the floor from the overhead bulkheads. Zinvor slammed the ship's control stick to the ground, and the ship lurched and dove. Vincent and Fiona were sent through the air and slammed into the back wall. Nox shifted his bodyweight slightly and didn't budge from where he was standing.

"What's happening?" Fiona cried, finding herself pinned to the back wall.

"Are we dying yet?" Vincent screamed, the force pinning him and Fiona to the wall as the ship built up speed and started diving.

"No," said Nox calmly. The ship lurched again, and Vincent swore he could see the ship's dashboard actually shake and move across the floor as bolts ripped free. "We are landing."

Zinvor's flight stick snapped off from the floor and he tossed it across the inside of the cabin in anger.

"That's not what this feels like!" snapped Fiona.

"We are landing with urgency," Nox added.

A bright orange light filled the ship, and the shaking and rattling of the ship worsened. Vincent, still pinned against the wall, could only see a billowing orange wall of flame out of the rear door's tiny window. He assumed that the Alliance had landed a shot and that their death was imminent.

The curtain of fire vanished. When the pressure forcing Vincent and Fiona to the back wall ceased, Vincent ran to the cockpit and saw they weren't crashing; they were in fact landing. Zinvor had managed to drop to the floor and control the careening ship with the broken stump of his flight stick.

The tiny ship had fought through the outer atmospheres of an unknown world, revealing a massive, seemingly planet-sized city. As far as Vincent could see, from one horizon to another, was a sprawling metropolis. From so high in the planet's stratosphere, the whole thing looked like an enormous dirt-colored smear.

A deafening explosion thudded against the small ship. The last engine sputtered and died out, and the ship fell from beneath Vincent's feet. Warning lights blinked and screamed as black smoke filled the small space.

"Now," Nox started, looking back Fiona and Vincent. "Now we are crashing."

Zinvor fought with what was left of the control stick, slowly bringing up the ship's nose to stop the freefall. The ship jumped and shook while it cut through the sky at supersonic speed. Nox calmly sat down in a small chair next to Zinvor and clipped on a seatbelt.

Fiona sat on the floor next to Vincent, who wrapped his arms around her.

"Good idea," she said, putting her arms around him. "We might stop each other from flying around when we crash!"

"That isn't why I'm hugging you!" screamed Vincent in frustration.

"Oh, right." She forced a smile despite the situation. Vincent still wasn't sure if she was being serious or not.

The once distant brown smear suddenly became close. The damaged and smoking ship crashed through neon signs and low-hanging wires before blasting through a building, skipping down a dirt road, and flipping over as it slid to a stop.

Zinvor unbuckled his seatbelt and climbed down from his inverted seat. He stepped over the two humans, who were still huddled together, and placed his two giant hands on the handle to the back door. With a grunt and a shove, he forced the door open and flooded the inside of the ship with light.

Vincent and Fiona struggled to their feet, their legs wobbling under them as they righted themselves and tried to regain their balance. Fiona coughed and tried to wave away the spiraling dust cloud that swirled around them.

"We just crashed from outer fucking space. And lived," she laughed nervously.

"Can't say that every day," Vincent laughed with her.

An explosive shot erupted the dirt in front of the ship's door.

"Anarchs!" roared Zinvor, unholstering his Riten and thumbing its hammer back.

"We don't have any weapons!" contested Fiona.

"Yeah! Give me that Riten back!" Vincent demanded. Zinvor shot him an angry look.

"Skinny pink creature is no warrior," Zinvor spat.

"No argument there, but do you have any other weapons?" asked Fiona.

Nox pulled the last remaining trunk off the ship and slid it in front of Vincent and Fiona. Fiona opened it, and inside was an array of unfamiliar weapons.

From the pile, Vincent picked up a pistol—the most normal-looking weapon he could find. Instead of the usual pistol grip, however, it extended straight out. When he held it out to aim, it felt more like trying to use a pointer at school than a weapon.

Fiona picked up an ugly, crude weapon that looked like nothing more than a few haphazardly welded pipes with a sliding handle under the barrel. Although it was small, she still had to hold it with both hands.

An explosive round punched through the ship's hull and tore through the opposite side before exploding somewhere in the city. Zinvor roared something in his guttural language and stormed out of the ship.

"I guess we're doing this!" cried Vincent, running after Zinvor with Fiona at his heels. His heart leapt into his throat when he saw the sharp jet-black ship of their Alliance attackers.

Two doors, one on each flank of the ship, opened, and two armored Anarchs leaned out, firing their arm cannons. Cannon fire shredded the damaged ship to ribbons and exploded the ground around it. The rounds flying past Vincent's ear sounded like incoming artillery.

Zinvor blasted a shot from his Riten. It impacted the right Anarch's armor, just below its head. The shot scored a large dent, kicking up a shower of sparks, and sent the Anarch tumbling out of the ship. Vincent grabbed where the trigger on his new gun should have been, but he didn't find one. Instead, there was a small push button on the top. He pressed it down with his thumb.

A green laser blast ripped from the end of the barrel, thumped off the side of the Alliance ship, and fizzled harmlessly. Pulling the sliding handle back, Fiona fired a shot from her gun and sent an empty red shell flittering to the dirt. She fired again and painted the prone Anarch's armor with a multitude of small impact marks.

"We have to get out of here!" Fiona screamed, working the slide on her gun.

"Yes!" grunted Zinvor.

"Let's go!" Nox took off running away from the ship, and everyone else had to catch up. As they ran, cannon shots cut through the air around them, exploded off the surrounding buildings, and coated the fleeing group with a fine layer of dust.

Vincent's legs felt like tenderized meat as he ran. His lungs burned with the harsh alien air as he sprinted down the abandoned streets of Elysian.

Nox led the way through twisting alleyways, up and down stairs, and through multiple levels of a city that seemingly had no end. Scared eyes of various shapes and sizes stared out from windows and doorways as the strange group ran past. The Anarchs, forced to dismount from their ship, gave chase, firing their cannons indiscriminately in the cramped alleyways.

Vincent, Fiona, and the two aliens ducked into a store front and cut through a confused crowd of aliens. Pushing through the back door and spilling out into another alley, Vincent wondered if Nox had any idea where he was going or if he was simply fleeing in terror. Alternatively, he could have been leading them into another trap. Vincent didn't trust the shifty alien, but he and Zinvor were the only two aliens he'd met that weren't actively trying to murder him and Fiona. They really had no choice but to follow him.

Nox burst through another door and went down a flight of stairs. He waited at the door for everyone to make it through before slamming it behind them. A lock somewhere in the door whirled with a click. The group found itself in what passed for an apartment in the alien city. There were cushions on the floor and a roll-out bed in the corner, which looked more like the Defense Forces-issued sleeping bag than any bed Vincent had ever seen. There were stacks of trunks and crates like those on their now doomed ship.

"We will be safe here," Nox nodded.

"Is this where you live?" Fiona asked huffing and puffing. She was sweating through her borrowed alien hooded dress.

"Sometimes," he said. "What is the word? It is a hideout."

"What a dump," Fiona said as she examined the room.

"Makes sense," Vincent frowned, cursing his luck that the aliens who happened to be the only ones not trying to murder him were nothing more than common criminals. "What do we do now?"

"We wait. Anarchs leave, and we find our connection. It is our only option," Nox nodded.

"If we are waiting, I would kill for something to eat," Fiona groaned. It dawned on Vincent that they hadn't had anything to eat since before the battle on the hilltop. He wasn't even sure how long ago that was anymore.

"And a shower," Vincent grimaced.

Nox recoiled in horror. "No need to kill for such things. I will give them to you." Neither Fiona nor Vincent bothered trying to explain that they didn't mean it literally.

Nox gave them each a small packet. Vincent twisted the top of his, and it hissed as pressure was released.

"Is this going to kill me?" Vincent asked. His supposed food bubbled like a can of soda.

"Unlikely," said Nox, sitting down on a cushion that just about swallowed his thin frame.

"Good odds," smirked Fiona. She slammed the packet back and sucked it down. She grimaced and swallowed. "It tastes like burning." Vincent shrugged and forced his down. It felt like he had upended an entire bottle of hot sauce. Without success, he tried to shake the taste out of his mouth.

Nox smiled broadly. "Good, no?"

"You were right about the second part," Vincent frowned.

"So how do you . . . clean yourselves?" Fiona asked, not sure how to ask such a question.

"The bathing chamber, of course. Follow me." Nox pulled himself out of his cushion and walked over to an unmarked wall. Nox tapped a small touch panel on the wall about the size of his skinny hand. A previously unseen door popped and slid open.

Inside was a remarkably clean chrome room about the size of Vincent's closet back home. Vincent couldn't see anything resembling a shower.

"How does it work?" he asked. Nox's thin, featureless black eyes did something akin to a human rolling their eyes in annoyance. He tapped the touch pad again, and water shot out of tiny openings in the ceiling and walls.

"Shall we?" Fiona motioned to Vincent with a smile. They started to walk into the shower but stopped. "Hey, how do you close this door?"

"I assure you, no Anarchs will find us here. No need to hide further," Nox informed them bluntly.

"What? No, I don't want you to see us naked, you skinny freak!" Fiona stammered in shock.

"Naked?" Nox tilted his head. "I am unfamiliar with this word."

"It means no clothes!" Fiona yelled.

"I am unaware of the problem this would cause," Nox frowned. It was then that Vincent noticed Zinvor had sat down on a cushion next to Nox, but not before removing his robe and holster.

"Wait, if you guys are cool with being naked all the time, why do you wear clothes?" Vincent asked.

"To protect us from the elements, of course."

"Ugh, I give up. Just close the damned door when we go in." Fiona rolled her eyes in defeat.

"Your race is strange, but I will do as you wish."

Vincent and Fiona walked into the steam-clouded chrome closet of water jets. Nox closed the door as they asked. They stripped off their dirty robes, and for the first time since before planetfall, moved into each other's embrace.

CHAPTER NINETEEN

Vincent and Fiona slipped off into a night of fitful sleep. The events of the last few days rushed into Vincent's nightmares, and no matter what he did, he could not chase them away.

He saw the fields of dead and wounded, the ones he couldn't help as he watched the Anarchs execute them. Suddenly, he was under a ceaseless barrage of plasma artillery, his friends being melted around him by the searing blue lights. Vincent recalled the scorched and mutilated body of Richardson, his rifle fused to his hands.

Vincent rolled and kicked in his sleep. He awoke as Fiona's arms tightly wrapped around him and he felt the warmth of her skin against his. His eyes darted back and forth in the dark room as the blasted and burning battlefield vanished from his mind. He rolled over and kissed Fiona on her pale forehead before slipping back off to sleep.

*****

After sleeping for a few hours, Vincent and Fiona were woken up by the smiling, still naked Nox, who stared down at them. They were wrapped up together on the roll-out bed with several robes pulled over them.

"It is time to meet our connection."

"Ugh, why are you still naked?" Fiona groaned, stretching and sitting up.

"I do not understand. Are you cold?" Nox asked. "You are warming each other, are you not? I thought I read somewhere you humans were warm blooded . . ." He trailed off in thought.

"Um, something like that." Vincent rubbed his eyes. He and Fiona climbed off the bed roll and wrapped themselves in their alien robes. Vincent found his pistol and hid it along his belt line. Fiona slung her gun around her back and hid its bulky form inside her robe. She did a poor job, and its bulge was obvious.

The group made its way up the stairs and out into the bustling streets. The various different sights and sounds of the city assaulted Vincent's senses. He pulled his hood low over his face, but he anticipated no one on the streets would have noticed if he didn't.

Vincent froze when he saw a black Anarch ship on the side of the road. Then another. Then another. The hulking armored forms of the Anarch soldiers stood on street corners. Their featureless armored heads scanned back and forth, looking over the throng of life pushing past them.

"What the hell is going on?" Vincent whispered harshly.

"It looks like we pissed them off," Fiona whispered back.

"It looks like they are conducting a sweep of some kind," Nox answered from the front of the group. "Must be looking for us," he added. Zinvor growled something in his language that Vincent was reasonably sure was a curse word.

"Not secure here. We must go faster," whispered Nox, picking up the pace of his lanky walk. As he picked up his pace, he swayed back and forth, almost like his torso was trying to keep up with his long legs, and his arms swung limply as he went.

The group ducked through a short door and entered a busy, dank room. The air was a thick cloud of irritating smoke. A rail-thin Rhai wearing a dingy brown robe staffed the counter. It was pouring a bright liquid into an array of broken and chipped mugs. Variously different colored bottles lined the wall behind it. The rest of the room was packed full of aliens sitting around low tables on the floor. Their loud conversations came to a halt as soon as the group stepped through the door. The gathering of aliens eyed them with suspicion.

"He brought us to a bar?" Vincent looked around.

"No, he brought us to a shitty bar." Fiona wrinkled her nose. "Reminds me of home, actually."

"Isn't that a good thing?"

"Not if you're from where I am." Fiona shook her head. Most of the aliens in the bar were openly wearing pistols. On the tables were some guns that resembled the one Fiona was carrying under her robe. Every alien in the bar was a Rhai. They stared daggers at the group as it went.

Nox led them to a table that sat six other aliens. The dark blue Rhai, its thin face full of scars, appeared to be in charge. It sat at the head of the table and wore far more elaborate clothing than the rags Nox had given Vincent and Fiona. It wore a tactical vest, loaded down to bear with ammunition, grenades, and a knife, over its black shirt. On its hip was the unmistakable shape of a human-made pistol. Nox chatted with him in a fast, high-pitched language that Vincent hadn't heard him speak yet.

Nox exchanged nervous glances back and forth across the bar and slid a small bag across the table. The blue Rhai opened the bag, nodded, and handed it to his bodyguard on the left.

"Nox!" Fiona hissed from under her hood. "What's going on?"

"He agrees. He can take us to the human colony on Titan tonight. That is as close as he can come with the recent military activity."

"Titan?" Vincent gasped. "That's nowhere close to home!"

"It's better than outrunning Anarch patrols until the damn war is over," said Fiona. "I'll take it."

"Fine," Vincent conceded. Nox turned and exchanged words with the blue Rhai once again.

"He wants us to go back into hiding until he calls for us this evening. We must go quickly. He is afraid that you humans are being tracked." Nox nodded to the blue Rhai and quickly stood up. They made their way back out of the bar without another word.

They pushed through the crowded streets back toward Nox's basement hideout. The number of Anarch soldiers on the streets had increased along with what Nox had called their "auxiliaries"—the Rhai and Mawr aliens pressed into Alliance military service. These auxiliaries comprised most of the troops that Delta Troop had faced back on the hilltop.

"Is all of this because of us?" asked Vincent, looking at the military force from underneath his hood.

"No. Cannot be," Nox answered. "Something else is happening."

"Fidayi," grunted Zinvor.

Fiona raised an eyebrow. "What?"

"The Fidayi. They are the fools who believe they can fight the Anarchs and break the Alliance."

"You mean other aliens?" Fiona looked at Zinvor, who nodded.

"Yes," Nox answered. "They believe the Anarchs are little more than slave masters and are trying to break their hold on the other races."

"So, Zinvor," Vincent began. "If the Anarchs destroyed your planet, why are so many of your race fighting for them?" Zinvor gave an angry grunt.

"After the attack, many of the surviving clans quickly pledged their loyalty to the Anarchs. They saw it was either kneel or become extinct," said Nox. "The clans who refused created the Fidayi, named such because they see themselves as one free clan. A few Rhai colonies also joined them."

"Suddenly, I'm happy the Earth only steals our firstborn." Fiona shook her head.

"What does that mean?" Nox's attention turned to Fiona. "Are the humans not united?"

"Only by force," frowned Fiona. "The Earthlings, they are our Anarchs."

"And you, Vincent, where are you from?" asked Nox.

"Earth," Vincent said, feeling suddenly guilty of his birthplace.

"I do not understand," Nox tilted his head.

"Back when humans established colonies in the system, Earth wasn't unified like it is now," Fiona said. "During the Chairman's 'Revolution for the Greater Good,'"—she made quote symbols with her fingers —"Mars, the Moon, and Titan all sat on the sidelines. Our people had become so much different since the original colonization we had almost nothing in common with the Earthlings anymore. We didn't see it as our fight. Once the Chairman and his followers won, they tried to unify human space colonies as well. The Moon quickly joined, but we Martians resisted. The Earthlings had no mercy and sent in the Defense Forces to force us into the fold. Afterward, Titan went along quietly."

"That is sad," Nox said, devoid of emotion.

"We tried to fight them again ten years ago and lost even worse. Ever since, they've forced Martian families to give the Defense Forces their firstborn child."

"Humans only have one offspring at a time?" Nox rubbed his chin. "How strange."

The group ducked back into the small basement hideout.

"Can we trust this guy?" Fiona asked Nox.

"Probably not," Nox said. His tone of voice made it sound almost obvious. Fiona's eyes went wide.

"I guess the better question is, do we have any other options?" Vincent revised.

"No." Nox shook his head. "I know no other with the ship needed to make it to human space."

"Do you think he's actually going to bring us to Titan?" Fiona asked, her eyebrow raised.

"No," Nox said. "Yoruba is a deceitful and corrupt being. We could not pay him more than you are worth to the Alliance, dead or alive. He will betray us."

"What?!" Vincent screamed. "Why weren't you going to tell us?"

"I thought this fact was obvious," Nox answered flatly. "Our secondary plan is to kill him and take his ship." Zinvor nodded in agreement at Nox's words. A smirk spread across his sloped, stony face. Vincent had a feeling that was Zinvor's first and only plan in most situations.

"Oh," Fiona pondered. "I guess that works, too. You're pretty cold-blooded, Nox."

"False. I am a warm-blooded being."

"Ugh, never mind." Fiona rolled her eyes.

*****

Curled up on the roll-out bed, Vincent and Fiona drifted off to sleep before being awoken by a beeping noise. Vincent sat up, rubbing his eyes, and saw Nox talking into a small handheld device. After a few quick exchanges in the same high-pitched language he spoke earlier, Nox hit a button and set the device down.

"Yoruba is ready," Nox addressed the room. He slipped a tiny pistol into his robes. It was the first time Vincent had seen Nox arm himself—and that put him on edge.

Zinvor strapped on his ornate holster, and his Riten swung back and forth as he clipped it on. He also slipped a savage, hooked dagger into his belt. Vincent slid his pistol into his robe, and Fiona concealed hers inside of her clothes as they set out through the door.

The dark streets of Elysian were lit only by the bright stars shining overhead. It amazed Vincent how millions of aliens could be pushing and shoving their way through the cramped streets of the city during the day, but at night, it was totally barren. He couldn't fight the feeling that someone was watching them while they made their way through the empty streets.

Zinvor's Riten slid from its holster; the metallic click of its ugly wrought metal hammer sounded deafening in the silent darkness. He dropped to one stubby knee, prompting the rest of the group to into a defensive posture. Fiona drew her gun out and pulled its handle back.

Out of the darkness came the dark blue Rhai, Yoruba, and a dozen of his comrades. They were all armed with sleek black rifles and chest harnesses that Vincent had no doubt carried thousands of rounds of ammunition. They looked ready for war.

Their armored dresses covered their whole bodies down to their bare feet. They made the Alliance soldiers Vincent had fought on the hilltop look ill-equipped by comparison.

"Are you ready?" came the slightly high-pitched voice of Yoruba. Vincent and Fiona exchanged glances of concern.

"Why are you so heavily armed?" Vincent asked across the pitch darkness.

"Have you not seen the Alliance on the streets? It is a . . . precaution." Vincent didn't like what he was looking at, but like he and Fiona had discussed, they had no other options. Slowly, the group stood back up and followed the heavily armed aliens. None of them put their weapons away.

They followed them through the darkness and saw no sign of the military force deployed into the city over the last few days. A few minutes too late, Vincent noticed that two heavily armed aliens on either flank slowed down and repositioned themselves behind the group. Very casually, Vincent, Fiona, Nox, and Zinvor had ended up surrounded.

Yoruba, leading the group from the front, turned down an alleyway and walked through the unmarked door of a towering building. The group stomped up a flight of narrow stairs and through a rooftop door. On the other side were a dozen more armed aliens and a ship that looked identical to the sleek, black jets that the Anarchs had used to blow Vincent and Fiona out of space only a few days before.

"He brought his own goddamn army," Fiona whispered to Vincent.

"We've fought bigger." He stared ahead at the jet, trying to conceal the fear in his voice.

"We should probably stop making this a thing," she smirked, her voice hard.

The jet's door clicked and slid open, and bright white light flooded out from the inside. Yoruba walked up the metal steps, followed by the others. The aliens standing around the ship vanished into the night as the jet's door slammed closed.

Inside looked much like the dropship in which Fiona and Vincent had rocketed to the battlefield's surface what seemed like forever ago. Opposite Vincent, seats with very little room in between lined the ship. Zinvor had made sure he, Nox, Vincent, and Fiona all sat on one side of the ship so as not to be split up.

The aliens across from them sat with their rifles across their laps and stared straight ahead at them through their featureless black helmets. Seeing the aliens heavily armed, armored, and wearing full ammo harnesses made Vincent feel naked. Wearing nothing but his Defense Forces-issued boots and a borrowed alien robe that barely stretched past his knees, he felt and probably looked ridiculous.

Yoruba stood in the area between the two aisles as the ship rumbled to life and took flight. Unlike Nox and Zinvor's ship, which felt like it was coming apart at the seams whenever it left the ground, this ship gently cut through the smog of Elysian.

"How long is the flight to Titan?" Fiona asked. A grin spread across Yoruba's thin face.

"Sorry, human, the flight to Titan has been cancelled."

"Traitor," growled Zinvor.

"Shut your mouth you backward barbarian," Yoruba cursed. "You Mawr are always droning on and on about honor. Look where it has gotten you."

"We had a deal!" Vincent said.

"Be silent!" Yoruba hissed. "The Anarchs will still pay me for your carcasses. Remember that." Yoruba turned to walk back into the cockpit of the jet. "The Anarch command ship is moored a few miles away above the city. Do not worry. The trip will not be long." A strange clicking sound erupted from his throat. Vincent knew he was laughing.

The ship was deathly silent as it cruised over the city-planet. The two sides methodically sized each other up. Both sides gripped their weapons with white, tense knuckles. Vincent wondered why they hadn't been disarmed. Perhaps it was because Yoruba knew he had the upper hand. Anyone in their right mind could see fighting in such close quarters would end badly.

Fiona, Vincent discovered, was not in her right mind. She drew up her gun against the alien sitting directly across from her.

"I'm not getting sold to anyone!" she screamed. The blast from her weapon inside the small space was deafening. At close range, the alien's armor didn't stand a chance. Fiona's shot tore through its chest and blew out its back. It coated the inside of the small space in a fine mist of black blood.

The effect of the gunshot inside the ship was not instantaneous. The rest of the inhabitants of the small space sat in shock and coated in gore. Vincent struggled to process what was happening when Zinvor roared and flashed his hooked dagger through the air into the neck or head—Vincent wasn't sure if there was a difference—of the Rhai sitting across from him. A thin trail of blood ruptured from the wound and sprayed across the ship.

The heavily armed alien sitting across from Vincent attempted to raise its rifle in a panic. The long barrel was difficult to manipulate in such a close space. Vincent knew he had to act before he was shot dead in his seat. He took advantage of the alien's speed and lunged across the aisle separating the two sides. He batted aside the barrel of the alien's rifle, and it cracked off a few shots that slammed harmlessly into the wall of the ship.

Vincent grabbed ahold of the alien's helmet and tore it off. The dark slits of the Rhai's exposed eyes widened in fear as Vincent reeled back with the helmet and struck it down into the alien's thin face. Multiple bones inside the alien crumpled and broke under his assault. The rest of its body went limp, and the rifle clattered to the ground. Himmelstoss had taught Vincent something useful after all.

The force from a wayward strike sent Vincent to the floor face-first. He landed with a crash, his face slamming into the metal and sliding across a thick, dark ooze of blood that had pooled on the ship's floor.

The copper taste of blood filled his mouth, and tears flowed uncontrollably from his eyes. He scrambled to his knees, grabbed the downed rifle, spun around, and squeezed off a shot.

It struck the side of an alien that was about to shoot Nox—who was surprisingly still seated like nothing was going on. It screamed and crumpled down on top of Nox.

Fiona racked another round into her gun and blasted a hole through the chest of an alien that was trying to shoot Zinvor in the back. Zinvor wrapped his giant hand around the neck of another alien and jerked it to the side. A sickening pop filled the air as the struggling form went limp.

The sudden madness of battle in the cramped ship sent the pilot into a frenzy. As wild, misplaced gunshots and blood streaked into the cockpit, it dove and spun to still rendezvous with the Anarch command ship.

Finally, Yoruba exited the cockpit. He held out his human-made pistol and fired a shot that hit Vincent's rifle, blowing it out of his hands. Vincent stumbled and fell backward. Yoruba closed in on him and fired another round, which slammed into the floor next to Vincent's head. Vincent sprung to his feet and rushed Yoruba.

He channeled a technique that his physical education teacher in school had drilled into his head while teaching them about rugby. He drove his shoulder into the skinny alien's midsection, wrapped his arms around the back of his thin legs, lifted him up, and slammed him into the ground. Yoruba let out a grunt of air as Vincent's shoulder drilled into its target.

Yoruba's pistol tumbled from his hand and slid back into the cockpit. Vincent, now sitting on top of the alien's chest, started raining down punches onto his face. Yoruba parried the blows expertly, grabbed Vincent's wrist, bucked his hips up, and rolled Vincent to his side. Now on top of Vincent, Yoruba drew out a knife from behind his back.

Yoruba plunged the knife down with both hands, but Vincent managed to catch his skinny wrists and slow him down. The point of the knife hovered dangerously close to his chest. Gritting his teeth, Vincent heaved his lower extremities up as hard as he could. Yoruba was thrown off and flew back. The alien landed face-down on the metal floor. Vincent scrambled to his feet and pinned the alien down.

"Filthy creature!" Yoruba hissed, struggling to get Vincent off him. Vincent grabbed the back of Yoruba's head and slammed his face into the floor. Yoruba flailed his arms around in a vain attempt fight Vincent off. After repeated blows, Yoruba's curses and screams turned to gurgles and finally silence. Blood pooled around the alien's head.

Zinvor stomped into the cockpit and ripped the pilot from the seat. The small screaming Rhai tumbled to a stop among the carnage of the passenger compartment. Fiona dispatched him with point-blank shot from her gun.

"What now?" Vincent asked, his ears ringing from the close-quarters combat.

"Must run!" Zinvor yelled. "Anarchs!"

They were closer than Vincent imagined. Out of the wide, blood-stained windows of the ship's cockpit, Vincent saw a massive structure. A multitiered ship nearly the size of the Victory stretched out in front of them and blacked out most of the sky.

Zinvor didn't wait. He jammed down on the controls and brought the ship into a critical dive back toward the surface of Elysian. The Anarch ship responded in kind. Bright red jets of light cut past the front of the ship as it dove. Explosions erupted all around as the ship was battered by shrapnel in the sky.

Fiona and Vincent tripped over the dead bodies in the back of the ship as they sprinted back to the seats and buckled in. The blood sloshed around at their feet, and the mangled corpses of their enemies rolled back and forth as the ship ducked and dodged around the incoming fire.

"Dammit. Can't we stay in the air for more than five fucking minutes?!" Fiona screamed, digging her fingers into her seat. Her pale Martian skin was spattered with blackish blood and her bright blue eyes were wild.

Nox shoved a body out of the way and emerged from the depths of the gore. He stood up and attempted in vain to brush away the new stains on his robes before joining Zinvor in the cockpit. Even though the ship was diving straight down and forcing Vincent and Fiona back into their seats, Nox strode through the ship like nothing was happening.

The ship impacted the ground with terrifying force. It slid across the ground and, after what seemed like miles, mercifully came to a stop. Zinvor slammed a fist onto the control panel of the ship. Nothing happened. After a few attempts, the damaged but still functioning door creaked open, and the survivors ran out.

CHAPTER TWENTY

Vincent and Fiona sat on one of the several cushions ringing the small basement apartment. On a small data screen, Nox and Zinvor watched what reminded Vincent of an evening news broadcast back home. An alien with tentacles jabbered away incomprehensibly on the screen. Various other languages scrolled underneath him as he talked.

While Nox and Zinvor showed no signs of concern, Vincent and Fiona were suffering through silent panic attacks. For the second time in as many days, they had been shot out of the sky while crashing into an alien world. Yoruba, or at least his ship, was their best hope for making it back to even the fringes of human-controlled space. Both things they thought would bring them home were in a smoking crater somewhere in Elysian.

For the first time since he met her, Fiona seemed concerned. During planetfall and during the massacre on the hilltop, she had a strange aura of calm around her—or at the very least an aura of indifference. Even during their claustrophobic fight onboard Yoruba's ship, she seemed somehow at peace. Now, she stared dead ahead at the featureless wall as a cigarette burned low toward her fingers.

"What else can we do?" Fiona asked.

"I don't know."

"There is nothing we can do." Nox piped in from across the room.

"There's always something we can do." Fiona shook her head. "We just have to think."

"We would need a ship, at a minimum. A good ship," Vincent shrugged. "And even then, we would just get shot down again with that Anarch command ship hanging out over the city." He reached over and grabbed Fiona's cigarette and took a drag. "What are we going to do? Chase it off?" He gave a futile laugh.

"Well, yeah," Fiona answered. "Why not?"

"You are truly mad." Nox shook his head.

"Hey, last time I checked, all of your ideas either got us all nearly killed or sold, and one of them was both of those things. So shut your stupid little mouth," she snapped at Nox. He recoiled at her harshness.

"Alright, so how do we do it?" Vincent said, playing along.

"Hell, I don't know. There's no way we can do it alone, though." She crossed her arms and leaned back against the wall.

"We need to find the only other idiots in the universe who are willing to go to war against the Anarchs." Vincent laughed, handing the cigarette back to Fiona.

"The Fidayi!" grunted Zinvor.

"Absolutely not!" Nox cried. "The only thing on Elysian with a shorter lifespan than a human is a fool who fights next to the Fidayi."

"Sorry, Nox. While I'm thankful for your hospitality, your attempt to sell us aside, I'd rather die fighting to get back home than live out my life in your apartment." Fiona oozed sarcasm. Vincent couldn't argue with anything she said.

"I agree. But how in the hell do we find a group that the Anarchs can't even find?" Vincent asked.

"Easy," snorted Zinvor. "My broodmate. She is warlord."

"His sister is the warlord of the Fidayi," Nox clarified.

"But he said broodmate?" Vincent questioned.

"Yes. His race is born in broods. A female from his brood is clan warlord."

"And a brood is?" Fiona asked again.

"What is the human word for this . . ." Nox thought, rubbing his slender neck. "Group?" he wondered.

"The Mawr are born in litters?" Fiona twisted up her face. "Gross."

"And a warlord is?" Vincent raised his eyebrow.

"Both military and political leader of a Clan of Mawr as voted on by the rest of the Clan." Nox informed. He saw Vincent was about to ask another question. "A clan is the combined familial group that the Mawr live and fight in. Once, there were thousands of clans, all ruled by their own warlords."

"And now?" Fiona asked.

"Technically, there is just the Fidayi now. The Anarchs outlawed the clan system when they took over what was left of the Mawr. The current Fidayi warlord had to change their customs by combining what was left of the race into one free clan." Vincent and Fiona stared at Nox in confusion.

Zinvor grunted something in his deep voice to Nox, who reluctantly nodded in response. Zinvor stood up, strapped on his Riten's holster, and marched out of the basement into the city.

"Wait. Where's he going?" Fiona asked.

"His sister is very suspicious. She also strongly dislikes Zinvor," Nox informed them.

"Why?" Vincent asked.

"When she created the Fidayi, she asked her broodmates to fight with her to avenge their planet's death. Zinvor refused for reasons he does not talk about. She believes he is a dishonor to the clan. There is a very good chance she will kill him when they meet again." Nox didn't seem to be bothered by this.

Vincent thought back to the hatred he once had for his little brother, who always did better in school, social circles, and sports. He would tell on Vincent whenever he caught him stepping out of bounds or trying to skip school. Suddenly, all the problems he had with him seemed trivial—or at least not serious enough to kill him over.

"Jeez," Fiona sighed. "I thought I hated my siblings." Vincent's eyes widened.

"You have siblings?" Vincent asked. She had never talked about her family before.

"Of course," she nodded. "Once someone has a kid on Mars they kind of have to have more. Otherwise you hand over your only kid to the loving embrace of the Committee." She laughed sarcastically. "Once you're old enough to register with the draft office, they kick you to the street and try for a kid they can actually keep."

"How old were you?" Vincent asked.

"Four."

"Fiona, I'm so sorry." Vincent put his hand on her shoulder.

"It's just life there. All of the street kids are firstborn." She brushed away Vincent's hand. "We get our revenge by robbing those high-born assholes," she laughed. "Our little way of reminding them we still exist."

"Man," Vincent grimaced. "I thought my kid brother telling on me when I skipped school was bad."

"You got to go to school?" Fiona smirked. "Must have been nice."

"Way to make me feel guilty about getting an education. Like it mattered in the end," Vincent laughed. "We're both sitting on some alien's bed millions of miles away from home, aren't we?"

"Fair enough," she laughed with him.

"And you know what?" Vincent asked with a smile.

"What?"

"I wouldn't change it for the world," he grinned.

"Ugh, you're so lame," she said as she pushed him away.

*****

The sun went down, and Vincent drifted off into a restless sleep in the basement apartment. In the morning, Vincent was shaken awake by Fiona. She was sitting bolt upright in bed, looking around frantically.

"Huh?" Vincent's eye flickered as they opened.

"He never came back!" Fiona shook him again. "Zinvor never came back! If he dies, we have no chance. We have to go get him."

"Go get him?" Vincent sat up. "We have no idea where he went. We don't speak the language. Oh yeah, and we're human!"

"We don't have a choice!" she yelled. Nox walked back into the apartment; Vincent hadn't even noticed he was gone.

"You humans certainly sleep a lot." He took off his robe and set it by a hook near the door.

"Where's Zinvor?" Fiona asked.

"I am afraid if he never returned, his sister must have killed him."

"And you're okay with that?" Fiona screamed.

"We cannot undo that which has already been done." Nox shook his head.

"Screw that!" cried Fiona. "We have to go get him!" Nox's eyes went wide.

"You wish to confront a Mawr warlord?" Nox asked.

"Did I stutter?" she snarled. "We would leave you behind, but we don't speak his language."

"I want no part in your suicide mission." Nox crossed his arms. Fiona picked up her gun from the foot of the bed roll.

"You say that like I'm giving you a choice." She charged her gun's pump action to make sure Nox understood. "Remember when you tried to sell us to the Anarchs? Well, you owe us one, and I'm calling in the debt."

"Fine, fine." Nox waved his hands downward, trying to get Fiona to put her gun away.

"Tell us everything you know about the Fidayi," Vincent demanded.

"On Elysian, they are everywhere, but not the Mawr themselves," Nox began.

"Not Mawr?" Fiona raised an eyebrow.

"No, if too many Mawr got together in one place, the Anarchs would know something is going to happen. The clan has its own auxiliaries that they use as spies and lookouts."

"If the Alliance has it out for the Fidayi like they do, who would work with them?" asked Fiona.

"The ones with no other choice: Rhai who are conscripted into the Alliance and flee from their terrible lives. The Fidayi promises them protection from the Anarchs if they help them in their struggle."

"Why would they run away from the Alliance only to join another army?" Vincent frowned. "That doesn't make any sense."

"Not every Rhai does this. Only those that have nowhere else to go. If the Alliance finds them, it will be a fate worse than death." Nox shook his head.

"So we have to find one of these auxiliaries so they can lead us back to the Fidayi?" Fiona asked.

"That is the only way I see this working. So yes," Nox nodded.

"I can't believe he ran off and didn't tell you where he was going," Vincent said.

"He probably assumed his own sister would not kill him." Nox shrugged, throwing his robe back around his shoulders. "Like you, he was wrong."

"We don't know he's dead," Fiona barked.

"How are we going to make contact with one of these auxiliaries?" Vincent asked.

"I do not know," he shrugged.

"I would imagine they're normally watching the Anarch patrols, aren't they?" Fiona asked. "We follow those patrols and look for the shady-looking guys watching them."

"That's actually a really good idea," Vincent nodded.

"You humans are not healthy in the head," Nox observed, almost in pity.

"For once, Nox, you're correct," Vincent laughed. He slipped his new human-made pistol behind his back. Some of Yoruba's blood was still on the handle.

After leaving the basement hideout in the middle of the night, Nox led the group to the tallest building in the district and up a twisting spiral staircase. The staircase was barely wide enough for Vincent and Fiona to squeeze through. Nox slid through with room to spare.

The smoggy haze that coated Eylsian like a thick blanket felt like it was only a few feet above Vincent's head. The cold, polluted air stung his skin and eyes while he gazed out over the city. As always, the streets were empty at night. It amazed

Vincent that a city of presumably billions could empty out as soon as the sun dropped from the sky.

"Why does no one ever go out at night?" Fiona asked.

"It is not safe. Too many get caught between the Fidayi and the Alliance. When the sun goes down, only the brave—" He exchanged glances with Fiona. "Or the stupid move about the night."

Vincent and Fiona had pilfered through Yoruba's possessions after taking over his doomed ship the day before. They outfitted themselves with their rifles and ammunition harnesses. Vincent had tried to steal their thick black armor, but the Rhai's frames made the fit impossible.

Vincent had never thought about what to do if a fight erupted. Fiona rarely seemed to make a plan before taking action. She was so stubborn that Nox and Vincent couldn't stop her from running out and trying to do it by herself. In a way, she forced them to go along with her. Vincent was certain that improvisation was actually her real plan anyway. He wasn't sure if he was giving her too much credit—or not enough.

Fiona stared intently through a pair of binoculars she had taken from Nox's hideout. They were old but had a crude version of night vision. One of the eye pieces was shattered, forcing her to use them like a telescope. She cupped her cigarette in the palm of her hand so as to not let the light from its tip betray their hiding spot. The night was cold and silent, with no hint of anything moving through the city district below them.

After several hours of fighting back fatigue, Fiona's eyes widened and she jumped up from where she was sitting. She rubbed her eyes to make sure she wasn't hallucinating and slapped Vincent on the shoulder.

"Alliance!" Fiona whispered, handing him her broken binoculars. He looked off into the darkness, the binoculars' night vision turning the pitch darkness into a sickly green color. A long file of Alliance auxiliaries was making its way down a street.

"What do we do now?" he whispered back.

"Umm." Fiona looked around at the thousands of rooftops around them. They climbed so high into the murky air that their tops weren't even visible. Everywhere he looked, there were a thousand places the Fidayi could be hiding and they would be none the wiser. "Look for other people like us watching them?"

"Have I said how bad this plan is yet?" Nox asked flatly.

"Shut the hell up or I'll throw you off the roof," Fiona growled. Nox frowned his lipless mouth at her.

Vincent glanced around through the binoculars.

"I don't see anyone else." Fiona snatched the binoculars back and peered through them.

"Shit," she cursed. "We have to move with the auxiliaries or we'll lose them."

"And how are we going to do that?" Vincent asked sarcastically. Without another word, Fiona leapt the small gap between the two rooftops. "You got to be kidding me!" Vincent whined. He stood up and chased after her. He landed with a thud on the other side of the gap, fell awkwardly forward, and rolled back to his feet. Nox landed softly behind him.

Fiona was already a few rooftops ahead of them, leaping effortlessly from building to building. Vincent sprinted after her, ducking under thick strands of wires and cables strung along the rooftops. Breathing deeply and struggling to keep up with her, he looked over and saw Nox striding along next to him.

A bright orange flash lit up the night. A deafening boom sent a shockwave through the city and made Vincent wince. A plume of fire erupted from the street level and cut into the sky. Vincent instinctively dove to the floor and curled up into a ball on the rooftop.

The deep rumbling chug chug chug of machine-gun fire interspersed with the pops and cracks of countless personal rifles came from somewhere below. Vincent, still trying to stay low, crawled across the rooftop toward Fiona. Up ahead, she lay on her side, peaking out over the rooftop.

"I think we found the Fidayi!" she yelled over the gunfire.

"Hurray." Vincent faked enthusiasm. "What the hell do we do now?"

"I don't think that far ahead." Fiona shook her head.

"That's kind of what I figured." Vincent said. Errant shots ripped past them and slammed into the building's overhang.

The thundering boom of a cannon shook the building they were lying on. Vincent pulled himself up and looked over the building's parapet. A building had erupted in a plume of fire and its outer wall collapsed into the street.

The Alliance had brought in the same type of hovering tank used at the hilltop battle. Instead of a laser on its turret, though, it had a short, stubby cannon. Wisps of blue smoke curled up from its fat barrel.

The cannon fired again, and a blue streak cut down the street and slammed into the façade of another building. It exploded and the walls above it collapsed down onto the first floor.

"Dammit!" We can't meet with the Fidayi if they all get killed!"

"What are we supposed to do?" Vincent screamed. "Blow up a tank?" Fiona's eyes lit up. "Wait! That wasn't a suggestion!" he screamed at her.

It was too late. Fiona was already running through the roof access door and down the stairs toward the street level. Vincent was back on his feet and chasing after her. He squeezed through the cramped stairwell, his shoulders scraping against the walls on either side of him.

Fiona stopped at the bottom of the stairs, where four Rhai sat on a floor cushion, curled up to protect themselves from the chaos outside.

"Ready?" Fiona asked.

"No, not at all." Before he could ask Fiona if she had a plan yet, she kicked open the door into the middle of a warzone.

Thick black smoke covered the street like a blanket. The area was devastated by combat. The façade of every building was destroyed or crumbling. Blasted and torn bodies of auxiliary soldiers littered the street. The surviving members of the Alliance patrol were hunkered down in alleys and tried in vain to shoot back at the hidden Fidayi fighters. The deafening boom of the tank's cannon made everyone duck. The floor of a far-off building exploded and sent out a cloud of debris and fire.

Fiona snapped off two quick shots at the nearest soldier. The skinny Rhai twitched and fell. She ran down the street toward the tank, firing her rifle as she went. Firing blindly, Vincent ran after her into the dark street.

The scene was chaotic. Blue, red, and green lights streaked by Vincent and slammed into unseen targets. Aliens speaking an incomprehensible language screamed back and forth to each other. The air buzzed and popped with the angry flying slugs of the Fidayi's heavy machine gun. Alliance soldiers ran back and forth as they tried to coordinate the failing defense of their patrol.

Gunfire stitched up the street in front of Vincent, and he dove for cover into an alleyway. Landing softly in a pile of fetid garbage, he panicked and rolled way. Before he could shake the stinging smell, he came face to face with a cowering Alliance soldier. The thin Rhai was sitting on the ground and hiding from the fight; its rifle lay on the ground next to it.

The soldier saw Vincent and tried to back away. Vincent leveled his rifle at it. He looked around and saw no one else, so he slowly lowered his weapon. He then backed away from the Rhai and made his way into the street.

The towering Alliance tank was just up ahead. Fiona zigged and zagged up the road without a care. Laser blasts and slugs cracked into the street around her feet, sending clouds of dust up as she went. Vincent tried to keep up with her but was driven behind cover by bursts of well-aimed gunfire. Bright green flashes scorched the wall next to his head and sent him scurrying.

Each time he tried to charge out into the street after Fiona, every fiber in his being told him not to. His heart raced as he froze in place. He had to catch up with her; without him, she would get herself killed. Without her, he would get himself killed just as fast.

Vincent took a few deep breaths and rushed into the street. He fired his rifle at a soldier trying to take aim at him. The area around the soldier erupted with impacts, and it dove for cover. Vincent ran as hard and as fast as he could, but he couldn't see Fiona anywhere.

"Come down here and fight me like a man!" he heard Fiona cry out from somewhere in the darkness. He heard the high-pitched language of a Rhai scream something back in response.

A dead Alliance soldier was half out of a hatch at the front of the tank, its almost neon red blood a stark contrast against the tank's black armor. Fiona was locked in a firefight with a second alien on top of the tank, but neither could hit the other, so they resorted to slinging insults in between badly aimed shots instead.

"Stick your neck out you skinny weirdo!" Fiona hissed as her shots went wide of her target. Sticking its head out of the tank, the Rhai screeched something in return and fired a few shots in return.

Vincent dropped to one knee and fired a long burst from his rifle. Red streaks scored up the tank's turret and around the soldier, but he didn't hit his target. The Rhai noticed Vincent and returned fired. Seeing an opportunity, Fiona stepped out from the side of the tank and fired a few shots up at the soldier. It twitched and fell back into the tank.

"I thought you died!" Fiona panted, sweat pouring down her face. Vincent noticed she had a small smirk across her face.

"Wouldn't that be so upsetting?" Vincent joked and leaned heavily against the side of the tank, trying to catch his breath. "So now what?"

"The Fidayi welcome us like the conquering heroes we are?" She shrugged.

Disciplined columns of Mawr soldiers filed down to the street from their fighting positions. Clad in dark grey plate armor, the aliens stared out with angry, painted faces from behind variously colored helmets. They carried rough guns that looked like they had been built by hand. On each of their hips hung a Riten.

"They don't look very happy," Vincent pointed out.

"You might be right," Fiona sighed.

Looking no worse for wear, Nox appeared for the first time since the battle began. He grunted out several sentences in what Vincent assumed was the Mawr language. The Mawr didn't answer back but marched silently on. A few soldiers stopped and kicked some of the fallen Alliance troops to make sure they were dead.

A Mawr soldier, his helmet and face paint a dark orange, slapped Nox with an outstretched palm. Nox skipped across the street and landed against the side of a destroyed building.

"Put your gun down," Vincent whispered to Fiona.

"What?" Fiona gasped. "Screw that!"

"Just do it!" Vincent snapped. "I really don't feel like dying right now!" Vincent dropped his weapon and raised his hands in the air. He wasn't sure if that meant the same thing to the Mawr as it did to humans, but he seriously hoped so.

A muscular Mawr closed in on Vincent.

"I'm a friend of Zinvor," Vincent mumbled out. He knew they didn't understand what he was saying, but he assumed they would understand Zinvor's name if he was as important as Nox said he was. The Mawr's thick fist slammed into Vincent's face, knocking him out.

CHAPTER TWENTY-ONE

Vincent woke up on a cold concrete floor. His head pounded and his mouth was filled with the taste of blood. He shook his head to get his bearings and sat up. There was a thick chain around his waist that snaked back to the cracked brown wall, where it was secured with several large bolts.

He spat out a glob of blood and saliva and ran his tongue around his mouth to ensure he hadn't lost any teeth. The crumpled forms of Fiona and Nox lay on the ground. They, too, were chained to the wall.

"Hey!" he screamed at them. Fiona stirred.

"Ugh, what happened?" Fiona moaned.

"It turns out they didn't welcome us like conquering heroes," he answered.

"Mawr do not like outsiders." Nox piped up as he woke.

"Well, we are as outsider as it comes." Fiona scratched her head.

"Yes," Nox nodded. "They will undoubtedly kill you two."

"Has anyone ever told you that you're a wonderfully optimistic person?" Fiona spat onto the dusty floor.

"I am not a person," Nox added.

"Ugh, shut up."

The thick metal door to the cell slammed open and an armored Mawr warrior stepped inside. It did not carry a weapon, though it didn't seem to need one. After feeling that punch, Vincent was more than certain the Mawr could handle everyone in that room with its bare hands.

The Mawr grunted to Nox, who said something in response.

"What did he say?" Fiona asked. The Mawr sneered at Fiona and gave her a smack with its giant hand. Her head bounced off the wall, and she slumped back to the floor. Vincent leapt to his feet, his fists balled. He cocked his arm back and blasted the Mawr in the face as hard as he could, throwing his entire body into the blow.

The Mawr didn't flinch, despite the dark blood seeping down from a cut above its eyes. It grunted in laughter as Vincent squared up with it. While Vincent was a full head taller than the stocky alien, his lean frame did nothing to frighten it.

The Mawr's fist slammed into Vincent's stomach and brought him to his knees. Vincent couldn't breathe. It felt like the punch had sent his lungs up into his throat and crushed his internal organs.

"Aw," Fiona coughed, blood leaking from her lip. "You tried to defend my honor."

"Shut up. I think I'm bleeding inside of my chest."

"Don't worry. That is where the blood is supposed to be. What did he say, Nox?" Fiona asked.

"That he will take you to see the warlord now."

"Then why did he punch me in the damn face?" Fiona spat.

"He says he does not like you."

"Oh, well I can understand that," she shrugged, wiping away the blood on her face with her sleeve.

"Me too," Vincent coughed.

Two more Mawr soldiers came into the room and unlocked the wall shackles. Vincent and Fiona were led at gunpoint down a series of damaged hallways. There were no windows, and the passageways were dimly lit with orange orbs hanging from the low ceiling. Civilians and armed Fidayi watched the prisoners with intense interest. The scene was so different it was like Vincent had been transported to a new planet—one that wasn't under Alliance control.

Eventually they found themselves in a large domed room that, with its rows of bench seating, resembled an auditorium. On the stage sat a Mawr with dark, nearly blood-red face paint. It wore plate armor adorned with colorful ribbons and brutal-looking spikes on its shoulders. On its hip was the largest Riten that Vincent had seen. Soldiers stood unmoving on guard, flanking the seated Mawr and watched the three visitors approach.

"You must be the humans," croaked the deep voice of the Mawr on what seemed to be a throne.

"Yes," Vincent nodded.

"I am the warlord of the Fidayi Clan, Arai." Arai stood up from her seat. "Your . . . slave?" —Arai fought to find the words — "told my retainers that you wanted to speak to me."

"Slave?" Vincent asked, his eyebrow raised.

"That one," Arai pointed to Nox. Fiona stifled a laugh.

"We are friends of Zinvor," Vincent said. Arai frowned at the sound of the name.

"My brother." Arai shook her head. "Dishonorable warrior." Vincent saw no difference between Arai and Zinvor, though he knew now that Arai must be his sister.

"He is not dishonorable!" Fiona yelled. "He risked his life to save ours."

"Hm." Arai crossed her thick armored arms. "He did not pick up arms to defend his clan against the Anarchs." She rose from her throne and walked toward the group.

"Maybe not, but he went to war against them for us," Vincent said.

"He would risk his life for some humans, but not his own clan. That is questionable." Arai paced back and forth. "And you went to battle against the Alliance for him?"

"And we would do it again," Vincent frowned. "Did you kill him?"

"No. He yet lives." Vincent sighed in relief. "It leads me to ask you one thing: why does he devote himself to you?"

"He promised he would get us home," Fiona answered. "After this skinny back-stabbing asshole tried to sell us to the Anarchs." She pointed at Nox, who tried to back away.

"A dubious promise," Arai grunted. "It is impossible."

"We've done a lot of shit over the last few weeks that should have been impossible." Fiona shook her head. "I think we are past the point of caring about the meaning of that word."

"You." Arai closed in on Fiona. "I like you." A smile creased across the Mawr warlord's rough, rocky features.

"So why is it impossible?" Vincent asked.

"You no doubt saw the Anarch destroyer sitting above our city."

"Yeah, you could say we've had a run-in with it," Fiona frowned.

"They discovered we were active on Elysian and came looking for a fight. They are shooting down anything leaving the planet," Arai said. "As long as it is above us, we will remain below. The Alliance cannot fight us in our tunnels, and we cannot fight it in the sky."

"Tunnels?" Fiona asked. "Wait. Are we underground?"

"Yes," nodded Arai. "In order to take away their fleet strength, we Fidayi retreated into Elysian's vast underground tunnel system. We stay here until the destroyer leaves us."

"So," Vincent began. "Let's get rid of it."

Fiona gave him a look of shock.

"What? You're the one that said 'impossible' doesn't mean anything to us anymore. Why should things like 'sane' and 'insane'?" he shrugged. "We'll die on this planet eventually anyway."

"Might as well die facing your enemies," Arai nodded.

"I prefer to, you know, live and win, but yeah, sure," he retorted. Arai ignored his comment, walking past them and out of the auditorium. Vincent and Fiona ran to catch up.

"So what is going to happen to Zinvor?" asked Vincent. Though Arai's legs were significantly shorter than those of a human, she was outpacing Vincent and Fiona.

"His fate rests in the hands of the Military Council, not mine alone."

"His fate?" Fiona gasped.

"He abandoned his clan during a time of war. It is a serious offence. I will lodge your complaints with the council this evening when we meet. Until that time, you are to be confined." Vincent and Fiona shot each other looks. "I do not mean to say you are my prisoners. I cannot have the only two humans on Elysian drawing attention to my clan." Arai nodded to two Rhai soldiers clad in their normal chain armor dresses. They each had one of the ugly Fidayi rifles slung across their backs. The soldiers guided Fiona and Vincent through a set of double doors and into what looked like a small apartment similar to Nox's.

"Hey, where's Nox?" Fiona asked.

"He is being held separately." Arai looked around the small apartment. "In much more austere quarters."

"He might be an asshole, but we need him," Vincent reminded her.

"I understand." Arai folded her arms. "But unlike you two, we cannot be sure he is not an Alliance spy. He is being investigated."

"That's fair," Fiona shrugged. Vincent didn't argue. He'd hardly be surprised if Nox turned out to be a spy. Arai turned and left the room, leaving the two Rhai guards behind.

The apartment was windowless and small. The brown walls were cracked either from old age or Alliance attacks— Vincent wasn't sure which. Two bed rolls lay in the middle of the room, and the small shower closet's door was open. Unlike Nox's apartment, everything had a fine layer of dust on it. A musty smell permeated the room and caused Vincent's nose to wrinkle.

"Better than the cell we just came from, I guess," he shrugged.

"Slightly shittier than Nox's hideout, though," Fiona said.

"That is kind of the theme for our adventure, isn't it?" Vincent stifled a laugh.

"What do you mean?"

"Slightly shittier than the day before," he smiled. Fiona laughed and rifled through her pockets. She pulled out a crinkled cigarette pack and fished out her last one. It was bent and twisted. She placed it between her lips and lit it with a match.

They climbed into the shower and washed off the night's fight, though neither of them tried to make a move on one another. Fiona rubbed a hand across Vincent's face. "You need to shave."

"What?" He grinned. "You don't like the rugged mountain-man look?"

"No, it's not that. It's that I don't like the thirteen-year-old-boy's-first-peach-fuzz look." He frowned and felt his face. He'd never been able to grow out facial hair before; it simply wasn't allowed back on Earth. The fuzzy, light brown hair had started to grow down his neck as well. He laughed at the thought that he must have looked the opposite of his school's rigidly-enforced Patriotic Standard of Citizen Grooming.

"I don't think I'll find any razors around here. Haven't seen any aliens with hair yet. Have you?" Vincent asked, laughing.

"Here," she said, pulling his hair back and tying it off. "Now that your hair isn't in your face, you might be able to hit something when you shoot."

"Doubtful."

"Yeah, you're pretty worthless with a gun," Fiona smirked. "Good thing you're pretty."

"We all have our strengths."

*****

Fiona curled up next to Vincent and slipped off into a deep sleep. He couldn't do the same, however. His mind raced over what could be happening with the Fidayi's council. He hoped it was more lenient than the Human Central Committee. Surely, it wouldn't think twice about killing Nox, as shifty as he was. Even Vincent wouldn't think twice about killing Nox.

Without those two aliens, Fiona and Vincent were doomed, and Vincent knew it. They had nothing the Fidayi could want and knew entirely too much about them to be allowed to leave alive. For the first time since he and Fiona were jettisoned from the Victory, their fates were in someone else's hands. He felt helpless.

Just as Vincent started to drift off to sleep, the doors to their apartment-turned-holding-cell slid open, and two Mawr warriors, clad in grey armor and red helmets with Ritens on their hips, stepped inside. They clearly spoke no Earth Standard, because they started motioning with their hands for Vincent and Fiona to get up.

Vincent slipped his bare feet into his tattered black boots. He had discarded his torn socks weeks before. Fiona didn't bother tying her boots and pulled her messy hair into a pony tail. The Mawr warriors grunted with displeasure as the humans readied themselves.

One of the warriors walked in front and the other behind Vincent and Fiona as they were hurried down the hallway. The lead warrior stopped before a set of double doors. Two more Mawr warriors, standing abreast the door, bowed deeply and opened the doors.

Inside, there was a large table that stood only a foot or two off the ground. Around it sat six Mawr warriors with their legs crossed on cushions. They all had their Ritens out and on the table. Arai was among them, and Zinvor was standing at the other end of the table. Zinvor was naked, without his Riten or armor.

Across the back wall hung a red banner adorned with an image of a silver Riten crossed with what looked like a saber. On either side of the banner stood Mawr warriors armed with rifles. Maps and diagrams lay on the table.

"It is good that you are here." Arai nodded to the humans. "We have made our ruling." Zinvor dropped to his knee and bowed his head. His thick hands curled into fists as they touched the brown, cracked floor.

A Mawr on the other end of Arai climbed to its feet. It was wearing yellow armor; cloths covered with inscriptions draped down from its pauldrons. Its suit, though bright and colorful, was scarred with signs of battle. The Mawr began to speak, the other

Mawr at the table nodding along with him. Arai turned to the two humans.

"That is Cohort Master Gawf, one of my commanders," she addressed. "He says that though Warrior Zinvor abandoned the clan's formation during a time of war, he did not abandon the war against the enemy as a whole—as shown by the survival of you two, sworn enemies of the Anarchs."

Vincent exhaled a sigh of relief. Zinvor was going to live.

"That being said," Arai continued, translating the rough grunts of Gawf. "He still abandoned his kin in a time of dire need." Vincent's heart sank. Zinvor didn't budge as his fate was read out to him. "Which is a serious loss of honor. As such, his sentence is to regain his honor." The other warriors at the table stood and joined Gawf.

Another Mawr warrior, pushing a rickety cart, entered the room. On it was a set of jet-black armor and a long cloth emblazed with words Vincent could not read.

"Warrior Zinvor, you are hereby sentenced to spend the rest of your life cloaked in the black of the Tsarra." Vincent and Fiona exchanged confused looks.

"What the hell does that mean?" Fiona interrupted. The council turned and looked at her. Arai frowned.

"It means his life is now tied to one mission. If he fails the mission, he must keep living on as a Tsarra, one without honor," Arai pointed out. "Should he complete his mission, he will be buried in the Hall of Honor with our legendary heroes." A smile crept across Arai's rigid face.

"Buried?" Vincent asked. "Wait. He has to die?" Vincent gasped.

"Of course," Arai nodded. "A life full of dishonor can only be fixed with a glorious and honorable death. A warrior's death."

"What's his mission?" Fiona spat at the council.

"A warrior is bound by his word. And this council cannot order him to break his word even if we do not see the value in such a mission," Arai said.

"What the hell does that mean?"

Gawf, though unable to understand what she was saying, seemed particularly bothered by Fiona's constant questioning. "He must fulfill the promise he made to you two by ensuring you find your way back home."

CHAPTER TWENTY-TWO

Vincent and Fiona were speechless. Zinvor was doomed to death while escorting them home.

"Even you said we would never get home!" Fiona cursed at Arai. "You gave him an impossible mission!"

"You have not let us get to that part yet, rude human," Arai growled. She grunted something to the other council members, and they nodded their heads. "This plan will require you."

"How?" Vincent raised an eyebrow.

"We cannot hope to shoot the destroyer out of our sky. What we can do is destroy it from within," Arai said. She nodded to one of the warriors standing guard, who opened the double doors and escorted in Nox.

"He wasn't a spy?" Vincent asked.

"No," Arai replied. "He is—what words did you use—an asshole?" She smiled. "Also very useful to us. The Alliance know him to be a smuggler of various goods. He is our key into that demon ship."

"I did not have a choice in this plan," Nox squeaked from the back of the room. Gawf slammed the table with his fists, and Nox stopped speaking.

"How would he get us inside?" Fiona asked.

"The Anarchs would very much like to get their hands on the two humans who crashed into Elysian, would they not?" Arai smiled.

"Dammit," Vincent sighed. "We're bait."

"Again," Fiona frowned.

"Yes," Arai nodded. We will trick the Alliance into thinking that Nox is delivering the two humans. We will instead hide an entire cohort of my warriors inside."

"Will that be enough to take over the ship?" Vincent asked. He thought back to how many soldiers were onboard the Victory.

"No, but it will be enough to surprise them and gain control of the bridge temporarily. We need enough time to detonate the munitions hold."

"What exactly do we have to do?" Fiona asked.

"You will be captured by Alliance soldiers," Arai started. "After you are taken, we will launch our attack once they are distracted."

"What if they just kill us?" Vincent shouted. "You'll be too late!"

"Are you not willing to die for the greater good of the mission, for the good of the people?" Arai questioned. "It would be a glorious death."

"I'd rather have a glorious life," Vincent sighed.

"I think you were just accidently deep there for a second." Fiona smiled at Vincent.

Arai grunted something to the other warriors on the council, and they grunted something back.

"They say human warriors are strange," Arai laughed. Vincent felt a little pride swell inside him at being called a warrior by a Mawr. To him, they seemed like a race bred for nothing other than war and fighting. Up until a few months ago, he was bred for nothing other than skipping school and getting in trouble.

"So what's our next step?" Fiona asked with her arms crossed.

"We pick our best warriors and prepare for battle. It will be at least one more night. Tomorrow morning, we will go. Prepare yourself accordingly," Arai nodded.

The group walked back down the hallway, this time without any escorts. Nox and Zinvor, now clad in the black armor of the Tsarra, had rejoined them. He hadn't spoken to the group since his sentence was passed down. As Zinvor passed by other Mawr warriors, they bowed to him, and Zinvor would reach down and touch their armor as he passed.

"Why are they bowing to him?" Fiona asked Nox.

"Being a Tsarra is a great honor," Nox said. "They are jealous that he is able to commit his entire life toward his mission. They are asking for his blessing as they go to war tomorrow."

Fiona gasped. "Asking for a blessing? He has a death sentence. How is that something to admire?"

"To the Mawr, a Tsarra is a spirit of their war god sent down to the plain of the living to have one single, final mission. When he falls in battle, they do not see it as Zinvor dying; they see it as the spirit simply going back to the war god's realm." Vincent thought he could hear something like sadness in Nox's high-pitched voice.

"Zinvor, you can't believe this shit, can you?" Fiona asked harshly. Zinvor lifted is head and acknowledged what they were talking about for the first time.

"I am vessel for Paterazm," he grunted. "The most high."

"Um, Paterazm?" Vincent asked.

"Their war god," Nox informed. "It is the highest of all of the Mawr's gods. Don't bother asking how many gods they have. I do not think even they know anymore."

"You don't have to die for us, Zinvor," Fiona chided.

"I bring you home," Zinvor said. Vincent was sure he didn't care about their protests.

They walked back into the small apartment. Someone had cleaned the place up, and there was no longer dust covering every surface, though it still smelled musty. On the bed roll were two compact pistols. They had the gun-metal-grey color and rough welds of the Mawr's weapons.

Fiona held the small gun in her hand; it was barely bigger than her palm. She pulled back the slide and looked down into its chamber.

"It feels like a damn toy," she laughed.

"Small enough to fit in our boot." Vincent looked at his gun, sliding it down his ankle and next to his foot.

"You're not going to run away, are you?" Fiona spat at Nox, who was taken aback at being addressed.

"No." He shook his thin head. "I fear if I did, Arai would skin me alive."

"Whatever motivates you," Vincent shrugged.

*****

Once again, Fiona was the only one to sleep that night. She curled up against Vincent, her small toy-like pistol next to her head while she snored away. Vincent brushed back her tangled blonde hair and wondered how, no matter the situation, she could sleep like a baby. He was nervous enough for the both of them.

Zinvor took apart his Riten and laid it out on a red cloth. Piece by piece, he cleaned it and put it back together. He repeated the process dozens of times throughout the night as Nox watched silently from across the room. The otherwise quiet room was interrupted every few seconds by the metallic clacking and grinding noises of Zinvor's Riten being assembled and reassembled.

The door to the apartment creaked opened sometime in the morning, and Arai walked in, flanked by warriors on either side. In addition to their regular armor and Ritens, they now wore across their bellies rifles and harnesses of ammunition and grenades. For all the craftsmanship of their Ritens and armor, their sewing skills were seriously lacking: their ammunition harnesses were barely being held together by a stitch.

"Are you ready?" Arai asked. Everyone minus Fiona was already awake. She sat up in bed and stretched widely. Her tattered brown Defense Forces-issued bra strained to hold together at the shoulder.

"I am the picture of readiness," she said half asleep and rummaging through her pockets before she remembered she was out of cigarettes. "Can't believe I'm going into battle without any smokes," she groaned. Nox reached into a small brown bag he was carrying and tossed her a single crinkled cigarette. "How did you get your weird-ass fingers on this?" she asked.

"I have my connections," Nox nodded. Fiona lit a match and took a deep drag.

"Oh yeah, that's the stuff," she smiled. Arai coughed and waved away the growing cloud of smoke that filled the room.

"I do not understand what this smoke is for," Arai coughed. Fiona smiled and passed the cigarette over to Arai, who took it awkwardly between two of her thick brown fingers. She raised the cigarette up to her wide, lipless mouth and breathed in deep. She hacked and coughed, giving the cigarette back to Fiona. "That is foul!" She struggled to catch her breath.

"I know. Isn't it wonderful?" Fiona smiled and took another deep pull.

They followed Arai out of the apartment, down the hallway, and through countless twists and turns as they went deeper into the Fidayi's network of tunnels and passageways. Eventually, she led them to a massive underground room. In the middle of the room, a huge transport ship was parked. It had seen better days. Its cockpit windscreen was shattered and blown out, and the ship was bolted together mostly with random bits of scrap metal. A whirling jet engine hung off the back.

As Vincent approached, the ship loomed over them. Its scratched and damaged grey exterior fit right in next to the legions of Fidayi warriors and their rifles. He was curious if everything the Mawr built looked so slapdash and ugly. He couldn't imagine what their cities looked like before they were destroyed by the Anarchs' plasma fire storm. When they saw Arai, the group of warriors stood ramrod straight and snapped downward into a bow in unison.

"Is this thing going to make the flight?" Fiona looked sideways at the rough cargo ship.

"It does not have to go far," Arai noted.

"Just all the way to the scene of the crash," Vincent frowned.

"It is sufficient for the task at hand, I assure you." Arai furrowed her brow.

"Either way, you should seriously fire your mechanic." Fiona grimaced at the ship's exterior.

The loading ramp of the ship creaked and groaned in protest as two Rhai lowered it to the ground with ropes attached to the end.

"Comforting," Vincent muttered.

The orderly files of Mawr warriors turned on their heels and marched onto the ship. Their thick, armored feet, which resembled hooves more than feet, shook the ground as they went. The ship's decking objected to the sudden introduction of the weight by cracking underfoot.

Zinvor fell in line with the group of warriors. Nox, Vincent, and Fiona were the last ones to board. Inside, row after row of empty crates hid the mass of waiting Mawr warriors. They stood, unmoving, shoulder to shoulder, waiting for their turn to disembark and go to war high above the surface of Elysian.

The ship shook and rattled as the rusted and beaten engines wound up. It felt like the ground had refused to let it leave by reaching up and grabbing the ship. The shaking made the stacks of crates dance and tumble onto the ground. The Mawr warriors barely moved as everything came down around them.

Finally, the ship fought its way into the air. Through the tiny porthole window, Vincent could see the ship passing through a hole in the ground and into the city above them. Level after level of the Fidayi's underground hideout slid past the window. It was as if they had created their own underground Elysian in which to live, free from the Alliance on the surface.

The hallways and passages of the underground city were crawling with Rhai and Mawr, like ants scurrying through a colony. Seeing the surprising power of the Fidayi gave Vincent a little more confidence, though only a fraction of that power would be being used against the Alliance destroyer in the sky. He hoped it was enough to at least pull he and Fiona to safety before everything came down around them.

Once the ship exited the underground city and floated above the surface of Elysian, it took little time for the Alliance to notice. Once it did, its sharp black ships were quickly on them and flying circles around the cargo ship.

"Shit!" Fiona cursed "They're going to shoot us down!"

"No." Arai shook her head. "We have made contact with them as smugglers. They know we are coming. You can thank your friend for that."

"How are you so sure?" Vincent asked in a shaky voice.

"If we had not, they would have shot us down already," Arai pointed out.

With a pair of black attack ships on either side, the cargo ship lifted through the dark yellow clouds. The light that once beamed through the ship's tiny portholes was snuffed out as the Alliance destroyer took over the sky.

"You nervous?" Fiona asked Vincent. Her wry, near-constant smirk smiled back at him.

"Being used as bait for the aliens that killed all of our friends by other aliens to facilitate some galactic civil war? What ever could I be nervous about?" Vincent forced a laugh. Fiona slowly wrapped her hand around his. "Another day at the office."

"At this point," Fiona began. "You're almost not even being sarcastic anymore."

"Almost." Vincent gripped her hand a little more tightly.

The ship shook and came to a stop. Nox stepped forward in front of Vincent and Fiona, and Arai vanished from view behind the wall of empty crates with the rest of her warriors. A Rhai slowly lowered the ship's door.

A blinding light flooded the inside of the cargo ship. Vincent turned away to shield his eyes from it, but he felt himself being pulled away by several small angry hands and quickly slammed to the ground. As his eyes adjusted to the light, he began to take in the scene around him.

Rhai soldiers in white one-piece jumpsuits stood in the landing bay. Each had a rifle in its hands, and each rifle was trained at the broken and dented door of the ship.

The landing bay of the destroyer couldn't have been more different than the inside of the Victory. Instead of an ugly, unfinished grey with giant protruding bulkheads, the inside of the Alliance destroyer was a near seamless, gleaming white and appeared obsessively clean and sterile. Vincent's arms were forced behind his back and restrained. The restraints, clearly designed for the much thinner Rhai, cut into Vincent's wrists, which seared with pain.

"Ugh!" Fiona screamed as the small cuffs were latched around her wrists. "I'm going to snap your skinny ass in half!" she cursed. Two Rhai soldiers moved to either side of Vincent, grabbed him by the crooks of his elbows, and dragged him forward. Vincent couldn't understand them, but he detected strain in their voices as they dragged his comparatively heavy bulk into the hanger.

After a few minutes of gasping and straining, the two aliens dumped Vincent on the floor of another sterile room. Fiona hit the floor next to him. The aliens turned and left the room, and a door silently slid closed behind them.

"Shit," Fiona cursed as she rolled herself over onto her backside and sat herself up against a flawless white wall.

"I think my hands are dying," Vincent gasped into the floor.

"The pain lets you know they're still attached," Fiona joked.

Vincent couldn't help but smile. "You never fail to lift my spirits."

The door to the room slid back open, and Nox was thrown inside. Black blood oozed from his skinny face as he landed backward on the ground next to Vincent.

"You gonna die?" Fiona asked. The tone of her voice made it seem like she didn't care.

"I will not die. I am injured," Nox chirped matter-of-factly. Two Rhai soldiers stepped into the room and began delivering kicks to the prone, bleeding, Nox. Nox curled up and tried in vain to protect himself.

Fiona, as always, seized the initiative. She rocked up to her knees and launched herself forward. She flew across the small room head-first and slammed right into the midsection of one of the aliens. The Rhai crumpled under her assault, and she landed on top of it. She stood and straddled the downed alien. She continued driving her head down into the alien's face, which crunched and collapsed under the assault.

The other Rhai turned and cracked Fiona in the head with its rifle. She fell onto her side, and blood trickled down her pale face. She rolled onto her back and flailed wild kicks up at the attacking alien. The Rhai exchanged high-pitched clicks with its injured comrade. They pushed past Fiona's kicks and through the door, closing it behind them.

"Stop trying to get yourself killed!" Vincent cursed at her.

"Hey!" Fiona snapped back. "That skinny asshole dies, we can't talk to anyone!" She propped herself back up into a sitting position. "I doubt Arai sticks around and translates for us full time if this prick dies."

"This name you have given me does not make sense," Nox coughed as blood ran out of his mouth.

"Are you trying to get beaten to death?" Fiona spat at the prone alien. "A 'thank you Fiona for stopping my weird skinny cousins from stomping a hole in my ass' will do just fine." Nox did not respond. Instead, he dabbed blood away from his face with a sleeve.

"Did they say how long we would be waiting in this damn closet?" Vincent asked.

"I believe this is a detainment cell," Nox corrected. "I see no garments."

"I swear I'm going to shoot you again," Vincent snapped. "I swear he knows what he's saying is stupid."

"What I am saying is factual," Nox wheezed, and blood came out of his thin mouth.

"Now I see why they beat your ass," Vincent cursed. "Next time I'm going to help."

The door to the cell slid back open. The Rhai Fiona had attacked returned with his wounds bandaged, and looked angry. This time, it brought five other soldiers with it, each having left their rifles behind in favor of metal batons. At the end of each baton, blue energy crackled in little twisted arcs, wrapping around the end of the thin rod.

The injured Rhai, its face covered in blood-soaked bandages, cocked back its baton and delivered a sickening blow to the side of Fiona's head, opening a deep cut across her forehead. She collapsed onto her side. The soldiers chuckled to themselves as they closed in around her.

Vincent dove at them. He knocked one to the ground with his shoulder and kicked another in the stomach, sending it doubling over. The Rhai fought back and slammed a rod into Vincent's midsection. It sent a jolt of electricity through his body. Vincent suddenly felt like every inch of his body was on fire. He tried to scream, but his mouth was clamped shut by the electrical current surging through him.

He collapsed to the ground. A soldier stood over him and rained down blow after blow with its blue crackling rod. Every blow sent Vincent contorting and twisting with electricity-driven pain. When the Rhai were satisfied that Vincent was done fighting, they went back to Fiona. She still lay motionless on her side in a pool of blood.

Vincent rolled over when his hands suddenly came free: his restraints had broken under the Rhai's assault. The surging pain faded from his muscles, and he pushed himself to his back. He slipped a hand down into his boot and withdrew his concealed pistol.

The sudden burst of pressure from the pistol's report made Vincent wince. The back of the nearest soldier exploded in a cloud of black gore, and it collapsed onto Fiona. Vincent leveled his pistol on the next Rhai and fired again. The tiny pistol's recoil nearly shattered his wrist. The bullet slammed into the shoulder of the soldier and exploded it outward, spraying blood across the once white walls.

The other two soldiers panicked and ran out of the room, leaving their dead behind.

"Fiona!" Vincent screamed. Fiona pushed a mangled body off her with her legs and slowly lifted her head.

"Ugh," she groaned as blood streamed down the side of her face. "I had them right where I wanted them."

"Turn around. I got to get you out of those things. They're going to be coming back." Vincent crawled over to Fiona and slammed her restraints with the butt of his pistol. When they gave way, Fiona pulled her pistol from her boot, her restraints still dangling from her wrists.

"I hope Arai hurries the hell up," Fiona cursed. She spat out a mouthful of blood onto the floor. The dull thump of footsteps echoed down the hallway and approached the cell.

"I think they're going to be late." Vincent pointed his pistol at the closed door.

The door silently slid open, revealing several Alliance Rhai soldiers with their weapons out. Before Vincent could pull the trigger, he was staring down the barrel of a dozen weapons.

"Well shit," Fiona frowned.

"What do we do?" Vincent said. "They aren't shooting."

"We're worth way more alive. I say let's make them earn it."

"Good idea."

The Rhai screamed at them in high-pitched shrieks, never moving their weapons away from their targets. At that range, even the most nervous soldier couldn't miss. It was obvious from Fiona's unsteady gun that she was thinking the same thing. It didn't matter how much they were worth. If either one of them fired, the Rhai would kill them where they stood.

"So scary!" Fiona yelled at them "You look like a bunch of school girls with eating disorders and sound like yappy-ass dogs!" she laughed in their faces.

The roar of gunfire filled the room. Fiona and Vincent instinctively dove to the ground. Gleaming white panels shattered and blew off the wall as a torrent of gunfire ripped the cell apart.

The burning stench of gunpowder filled Vincent's nose. He opened his eyes and stood up. The doorway was cluttered with the corpses of the Alliance soldiers who, only seconds ago, were threatening to kill them.

Zinvor, clad in his jet-black armor, stepped in front of the door, and the hidden Fidayi cohort rushed down the hallway past him. The barrel of Zinvor's rifle still had smoke twirling upward from its barrel.

"Sorry I late," he grinned.

"Damn right you were!" Fiona pushed herself to her feet.

"How did you know you weren't going to hit us?" Vincent asked. Zinvor looked around the room and shrugged, letting out a small grunt.

"How comforting," Vincent sighed. The sound of gunfire came from where the other Fidayi had run to.

"We must go." Zinvor motioned down the hallway. Without another word Fiona, Vincent, and Nox hurried after him.

The previously pristine white hallways were slick with thick black blood. Rhai soldiers of the Alliance were strewn about and crumpled dead. It was clear from the wounds that many of them were shot down as they tried to flee the rushing Fidayi warriors.

Up ahead, Fidayi warriors fired their rifles around corners and down two snaking hallways. The deafening blasts from their rifles assaulted Fiona's and Vincent's ears. Zinvor took up a position behind one of the warriors.

"Where are we going now?" Vincent yelled over the gunfire.

"Bridge." Zinvor pointed up ahead. "They go to weapons bay." He pointed to the other group of warriors. "Big boom!" he grinned. Zinvor smacked the two leading warriors on the back, and with a guttural roar, they charged down the hallway.

Blue lasers snapped by their heads and slammed into the walls, scouring the wall with burn marks.

Fiona, caught up in the moment, screamed and ran after them. Vincent chased after her, lasers ripping past him as he ran. He felt naked with only the small pistol to protect himself. Fiona bent down and grabbed a long, sleek black rifle from one of the dead Rhai. Vincent followed suit, pillaging through the remains of a dead enemy.

The Fidayi cleared the way in only a few minutes. The Alliance soldiers were too busy fleeing for their lives to put up much resistance, and the Fidayi methodically cleared the way forward. They made it to a set of massive metal doors. A few of the warriors tried pulling on them, but they were locked tight. Zinvor grunted something to one of the warriors, who dropped to one knee, unslung a leather bag from its shoulder, and rummaged through it.

It attached a small box to the center of the doors and unspooled wires from a small roll. The crowd of warriors stepped back and came to a stop. Zinvor grunted an order. In response, the warriors all dropped to a knee and protectively turned their heads away from the door. Fiona and Vincent followed suit.

The blast shook the ship under Vincent's feet and blew the reinforced doors inward. The bomb curtained the hallway in a thick cloud of black smoke. Shortly after the blast, laser fire tore through the smoke and ripped into the warriors in the hallway.

A warrior to the left of Vincent let out a deep, painful roar and collapsed to the floor after being struck by several laser bolts. Vincent dove for cover. Only once he was lying on the ground did he notice there was no cover to be found in the blasted and destroyed hallway. Lying prone, he was stranded out in the open. He crawled, arm over arm, until he got behind the body of the fallen Fidayi warrior. He heard the dull thump of shots as they slammed into the body in front of him. The warrior's dark blood pooled out of his wounds and soaked Vincent.

He rolled over, brought his stolen rifle up to his eye, and opened fired. Blue lasers shot from the barrel. The Fidayi warriors up ahead jumped to the side of the ruined door, the jagged metal barely giving them cover from the now increasing flood of blue lasers.

Then Vincent heard a familiar noise—the deep-throated thunk and whoosh of an Anarch's cannon. It exploded in the middle of the huddling Fidayi warriors. They were blown backward into the hallway, a few of them being torn to shreds by the fusillade of laser fire.

One of their bodies landed next to Vincent. The warrior had a leather sash across its thick, armored midsection. The sash held several softball-sized devices covered in spikes attached to a small handle. Vincent recalled a similar device being hurled at him during the fight on the hilltop. More importantly, he remembered how much damage they could do.

He tore the sash from the warrior's body, rolled over, and tied it around himself. He was much thinner than the dead warrior, and it required several wraps to get it tight. Another cannon shot blasted a wounded Fidayi warrior to pieces. It covered the survivors in the hallway with a fine mist of gore.

Zinvor stepped out into the oncoming fire. He unholstered his Riten, reached into his leather sash, and pulled out a spiked grenade. He fired his Riten through the rolling black smoke and roared. His furious scream could be heard over the din of combat, and the rest of the Fidayi joined him.

Zinvor rushed forward through the smoke with his warriors behind him. To Vincent's surprise, Fiona was on their heels. Vincent pushed himself to his feet and ran off after them. As he tripped and stumbled over the dead and wounded warriors in the hallway, a laser shot struck his rifle, blasting it from his hands.

Empty-handed, Vincent leapt through the destroyed double doors. Finally, through all the smoke, he saw a massive control room lined with a multitude of screens and computers and walled with a giant arching window that overlooked the never-ending city of Elysian.

The control room comprised three levels, the lowest of which the Alliance had abandoned to the Fidayi. Alliance soldiers were firing down on the Fidayi from the levels above, taking cover behind stacks of computers and large digital screens.

Vincent stood exposed. The other side of the door was the vast open first floor with nothing to hide behind. The exposure gave the shrinking number of warriors no choice but to press the attack. They rushed forward and started fighting their way into the second level.

Vincent grabbed another rifle from the ground and took hastily aimed shots up the stairwell into the second level's defenders. He was a bad shot with a human rifle; with the strange Rhai technology, he knew he wasn't going to hit anything. The attackers made their way onto the second level, and most of the Rhai fled up the stairs to the third level. Many of them were cut down during their flight, their bodies tumbling back down the stairs.

An Anarch cannon shell slammed into the ground in front of Zinvor, raking him with shrapnel. Zinvor stumbled back, slammed his fists against his heavily armored chest, and rushed forward up the next flight of stairs. His blinding rage fueled the rest of his warriors to keep pushing forward.

Fiona fired at the Alliance soldiers on the third level. Her well-aimed shots sent little spouts of black blood and shattered helmets into the air almost every time she pulled the trigger. She would pop off a few shots, get up and run to a new position, and do it again. A cannon shot blew apart her cover only seconds after she had moved on to a new position.

Vincent gave up aiming. For only a few seconds at a time, he poked out from behind cover and held down the trigger of his alien rifle. It kicked into fully automatic fire, and he swept it back and forth along the Alliance positions. The alien gun didn't recoil like any gun Vincent had ever used before. If it wasn't for the high-pitched crack that it made whenever he pulled the trigger, he would have hardly noticed it was firing at all.

Zinvor tossed a spiked grenade in an arc up the stairs, and it detonated with a dull crump. The incoming fire slackened and gave the Fidayi an opening to charge up to the third level. The warriors shoved Vincent and Fiona to the back of the line as they made their way up the stairs. The thick red-armored warrior in front of Vincent grunted as laser shots struck it. Pieces of its armor broke away under the assault. Despite the leaking of bright, almost neon red blood from underneath its broken armor, the warrior pushed forward.

Once at the top of the stairs, the bleeding warrior finally collapsed dead. Vincent and Fiona vaulted over it and stepped onto the third level of the bridge. The surviving Alliance soldiers had nowhere left to run. The incoming fire intensified, and the mostly-wounded Fidayi struggled to find cover.

The trapped and desperate Rhai soldiers of the Alliance poured laser fire into the warriors as they hunkered down behind desks. Ritens boomed and the Rhai were blown to pieces. Fiona shot a soldier down, leapt over a column of digital displays, and cracked another soldier in the head with her rifle like it was a baseball bat. The Rhai's helmet cracked and its head splattered against the white floor.

Vincent followed her, firing his weapon wildly from his hip. A streak of blue lasers ripped in between Fiona and Vincent. Vincent turned and returned fire with an erratic burst. The defender twisted around in pain, spraying black blood across a bright computer screen.

Standing in front of a curved panoramic window that stretched from one side of the cockpit to the other was the hulking armored form of an Anarch warrior. The armored monster turned, and red scrolls swayed back and forth from its wide shoulders. Through its featureless helmet, it stared out into the battlefield and raised its deadly cannon.

An explosion tore through the middle of the rushing horde of Fidayi warriors. Vincent attempted to fire at the Anarch, but his weapon let out a dull hiss. He smacked the gun with the palm of his hand, but again, nothing happened. He tossed it aside and pulled his small pistol from his boot.

"You okay?" Vincent yelled over to Fiona. The blood from the cut on her head had dried, giving her blonde hair a crusted brown look. She smiled at him.

"I think I should be asking you that," she joked back, looking down at his gun. "How the hell did you make it this far and still not know how to shoot?"

"Pure luck!" he grinned. A blue laser seared by Vincent's face, burning a wound across his cheek. He winced away and reached up to find it wasn't bleeding—the laser had cauterized the wound. "Okay." Vincent shot Fiona a panicked look. "I have whatever one step below pure luck is."

"Clearly."

Their conversation ended abruptly when an Anarch shell exploded against the control panel they were hiding behind. They were thrown across the control room and nearly fell off the side. Vincent crashed into a guard rail, his pistol flying from his hand.

He coughed, pain surging through his midsection. His vision was blurred and he pawed around on the ground looking for a weapon. He found nothing. He blinked, his eyes trying to regain focus.

"Ugh, Vincent, you okay?" Fiona called. Vincent looked over and could make out Fiona pulling herself to her feet. Like him, she was unarmed.

"Yeah," he groaned. He couldn't see the battle unfolding only a few feet away; the Anarch's cannon had covered the area with thick smoke, the sting of which made Vincent's eyes water as he climbed to his feet.

Vincent's ears rang and his head pounded. The smoke dissipated, and the battle was all but over.

The Anarch warrior, flanked by the surviving Rhai soldiers, advanced on the lone remaining Fidayi: Zinvor. He was taking cover behind a battered and shot-up computer column. Neon blood oozed out from Zinvor's legs. Several chunks of his armor were blown away, revealing ragged wounds. He fumbled with his Riten as he reloaded it with his unwounded hand.

Vincent was determined to do something—anything—to save Zinvor. Apparently, Fiona came to the same conclusion. She reached down and grabbed a fallen Fidayi's rifle. She raised it to her shoulder and fired off several heavy shots. The recoil nearly knocked her over.

Vincent sprinted forward, reached down, and grabbed a grenade in each hand. The Alliance soldiers' fire slackened under the assault as they attempt to move behind cover. Fiona's shots dropped the remaining Rhai soldiers before they could act, leaving only the towering Anarch. Fiona landed a shot perfectly in the middle of the Anarch's featureless grey helmet. The shot ricocheted off it with a sharp ping.

Vincent cocked his arm back and pitched a grenade at the Anarch. To his surprise, the spiked grenade stuck to the pauldron of the giant and detonated. The Anarch's arm blew off, sending its cannon and a surge of bright orange blood flying into the air. The Anarch let out a deafening roar. Its anguished voice sounded as metallic as its armor.

The Anarch, now lacking its cannon, charged at Vincent. Its horrible wound gushed blood as it lunged forward. Vincent tossed his other grenade and dove to safety amidst the wreckage of a nearby control station. The grenade stuck to the Anarch's chest and erupted into a ball of flames.

The Anarch's chest was blown out, sending jagged pieces of fractured armor and orange innards across the control room. The Anarch stumbled a few more steps, its synthetic roars turning into pained gurgles and groans before it collapsed, helmet first, into the ground. Orange gore flooded out onto the white floor.

CHAPTER TWENTY-THREE

nly a few minutes after the Anarch died, the rest of the Fidayi assault force made its way into the destroyer's control room. Arai led a group of Fidayi Rhai technicians to start going through the few control stations in the room not destroyed in the fighting.

"We must go," Arai ordered Vincent and Fiona.

"What?" Fiona shook her head. "I thought we won?"

"No," Arai frowned. "We control a few quarters of the ship, but the Anarch reinforcements are coming from within. We cannot face them all."

"We leave," winced the wounded Zinvor. The sight of such a strong warrior in pain unsettled Vincent. "Big boom," he nodded.

"Yes," Arai confirmed. "We broke into their weapons bay and rigged it to explode. The Alliance is not long for Elysian."

The Fidayi turned and walked out of the control room. The wounded were left behind if they could not walk. The dead were also left behind, but their Ritens were taken from their holsters and brought back with the assault force. Many of the wounded were reluctant to part with their cherished pistols.

"Why aren't you helping your wounded?" Vincent asked Arai harshly.

"If they cannot stand, they cannot fight." Arai shook her head. "A Mawr that cannot fight is a Mawr that cannot live. A warrior for Paterazm's cohorts, not mine."

"Damn, that's cold blooded," Fiona said. "I thought Martians were harsh."

The survivors pushed themselves back into their rickety cargo ship. There were far fewer Fidayi warriors for the return trip. The ones that were still standing sported several ugly open wounds apiece—all of them except Arai, who was unharmed.

The ship shuddered and broke free from the destroyer's grasp. The Rhai pilot turned the craft and sent it flying back toward Elysian's surface. Vincent wasn't sure if the pilot was purposely flying away from the destroyer as fast as the ship could go or if the ship had finally broken down and was in free fall back to the planet below them.

Fiona and Vincent sat against the wall of empty crates.

"You killed an Anarch." Fiona nudged him with her elbow.

"Yeah, I guess I did," Vincent sighed. He was still trying to absorb everything that had happened. "That was a really stupid thing I did." He started to laugh.

"Yeah, I thought you were dead for sure." Fiona laughed and put her arm around him.

"I'm still not entirely sure I'm not," Vincent said through his nervous laughter.

"Well, the way this shit bucket is rattling, you might still have a chance at dying," Fiona laughed, patting the unfinished grey wall of the ship.

"Lucky me. I thought I was done with that for the day."

The ship slammed into the ground, its engines trying to arrest its landing the best they could. Everyone in the stricken craft got to their feet once the ship came to a rest. This time, the ropes securing it finally quit, and the ship's door rattled and fell off.

The assault force's survivors slowly climbed out and into the hazy Elysian air. Arai stood, her arms crossed, staring up at the destroyer.

"Shouldn't we go back into the hideout?" Vincent asked. He was expecting to see swarms of the Alliance's black ships racing after them.

"No," Arai responded. "It is over." Before Vincent could ask what she meant, columns of fire erupted from the belly of the massive Alliance destroyer.

Black smoke vomited from the jagged hole. Explosions, first small but growing in size and intensity, raced in a line toward the head of the ship, toward the control room that Vincent, Fiona, and Zinvor had fought so viciously over. Before long, the bridge window exploded outward.

The destroyer listed to its side and fell to the surface. Debris cascaded onto the city as the ship disappeared over the horizon. The ground shook, and the sky's normally dark yellow haze lit up like dawn on Earth.

Fiona and Vincent cheered and hugged. Fiona spat curses at the distant fireball and held up two middle fingers as it faded.

"Is that some kind of human salute?" Arai asked, confused.

"No," Vincent laughed, shaking his head. "Do you know any human insults?"

"Some, yes," Arai confirmed.

"It means go fuck yourself," Fiona grinned.

"You wish the Alliance would fornicate with itself?" Arai frowned, not really understanding.

"Umm, it's supposed to be funny," Vincent shrugged.

"Yes. Quite humorous," Arai nodded, not laughing or smiling. He wondered if Mawr could actually laugh in the first place.

"So," Vincent started. "What happens now?"

"We wait for the rest of the Fidayi fleet to reach us. Then we can leave this planet."

"We can go home?" Fiona asked with hope in her voice.

Arai nodded. "It is possible."

"How possible?" Vincent asked.

"What is it this one said once before . . ." Arai began. She scratched her chin deep in thought. "Impossible doesn't mean anything to you?" Arai turned and started marching off. "It is good you believe this. You will need it."

CHAPTER TWENTY-FOUR

The city of Elysian was alive with wild cheers and throngs of aliens waving Fidayi Clan flags. Legions of Fidayi warriors stood rigid and lined the streets as the survivors of the assault force walked through. As they did, the waiting warriors bowed deeply. No one seemed to bat an eye at the fact that most of the warriors were wounded and bleeding. When the partiers in the street saw Arai approach, they fell silent. They climbed down to their knees and pronated themselves onto the ground.

Vincent was left in awe at the sight. Rhai, Mawr, and other aliens as far as he could see were down on their knees. They were all muttering something he could not understand.

"Nox," Vincent whispered. "What are they saying?" Nox, who had all but vanished during the fight on the destroyer, popped out from behind a Mawr warrior.

"Hail Arai, the savior of Elysian," Nox informed him.

"Wow. Do they really all like her that much?" Fiona asked.

"It is doubtful." Nox shook his head. "They are as afraid of the Fidayi as they were of the Alliance."

"Well, that's significantly less heartwarming," Vincent sighed.

"Nothing wrong with people being so terrified of you they just submit." Fiona shrugged. "That's how we elect our governor on Mars."

"I'd expect nothing less," Vincent said. "I figured you guys selected your leader based on some kind of bracket-style death match tournament," he laughed.

"Oh, shut up," she said. "So if they are just cowed under the Fidayi like they were under the Alliance, is the Fidayi really any better?" Fiona asked.

"I would say yes," Nox nodded. "They claim that once the war is over, they will leave the planets to rule themselves. Their past conduct has proven this to be true. They do not force the population into their ranks like the Alliance do, either. They promise anyone who serves in their cohorts a warm meal, which is more than some have in Anarch-controlled space. Though just being around the Fidayi makes the odds of being annihilated via Alliance orbital weapons systems increase significantly."

"Take the good with the bad I suppose," Vincent frowned.

The returning assault force made its way back to the underground headquarters. While they had no reason to hide from the looming destroyer any longer, it seemed to Vincent that they had come to see the miles of underground tunnels as their home.

The Fidayi left Fiona and Vincent on their own, and they retired to their musty apartment. Fiona turned the water on and winced as it hit the gash on her head.

"I think I might need stitches," she winced, dabbing at the cut gently with her shirt. Their door creaked open and a Rhai entered.

The skinny alien pushed a rusted metal cart, on which were neatly folded clean clothes, a few of the familiar alien food packets, and some thread with a needle. The alien bowed to them, turned, and left the room. Fiona picked up the needle and thread.

"Lovely," she groaned.

"Wait, you're not going to ..."

"Have any other ideas? You saw the wonderful medical care the Fidayi offered their wounded." She walked over to the shower. "There's no mirror. I'm going to need your help."

"You're kidding. I don't know how to give someone stitches!"

"What do they teach you kids on Earth?" She pinched her gashed skin together and stabbed in the needle, thread dangling off the end of it. She gritted her teeth and slowly went to work.

"Damn," Vincent grimaced.

"Girl of your dreams, yeah?" She forced a laugh as blood flowed freely out of the wound. When the sewing was done, she collapsed back onto one of the floor cushions and closed her eyes. "How does it look?" she gasped. Vincent walked over to where she was sitting and looked down at her fresh stitches. To his surprise, they actually looked well done.

"Not bad actually. Wait. This wasn't the first time you did that, was it?" He frowned. She leaned up and kissed him. He could smell the blood still coating her hair and face.

"Of course not," she smiled.

CHAPTER TWENTY-FIVE

Vincent and Fiona awoke when Arai, Zinvor, and Nox slammed their apartment door open. They sat up and rubbed the sleep from their eyes.

"Do you find your quarters too cold?" Arai asked.

"No," Nox pointed out helpfully. "Humans sleep in pairs for security."

"No we don't!" Vincent spat. "That isn't what's happening right now!"

"Yes, they are mates," Nox corrected. He clearly considered himself an expert on the human race.

"Strange." Arai crossed her thick armored arms. "I did not know they were of different sex."

"You couldn't tell that we're different?" Vincent yelled.

"You do have the same haircut as me now," Fiona joked, tussling Vincent's long hair.

"You're not helping!"

"I am sorry to have disturbed your mating, but the council would like to meet with you two," Arai interrupted.

"We weren't mating!" Fiona yelled.

"Why else would you share your chambers with the weaker sex?" Arai frowned.

"You know, that's actually a good question." Fiona looked sideways at Vincent.

"That part isn't even worth arguing, is it?" Vincent asked.

"You're learning," Fiona grinned.

After getting dressed in their new clothes, Vincent and Fiona made their way to the council chambers. The same group of angry-looking Mawr warriors sat on the floor behind a low table, same as before. This time, Rhai soldiers milled about in the background on various computer terminals. They looked like they had been ripped straight from the destroyer they had just attacked.

"I hope this is good news," Fiona said quietly to Vincent.

"You will not be disappointed then," Arai said, sitting down on her cushion behind the table. Fiona bristled, surprised that she could hear her. "Our technicians have combed through the Anarchs' computers that we captured from the control room of the destroyer. We have learned many things."

"Why do I not like where this is going?" Vincent raised his eyebrows.

"According to the Anarchs, your human military is launching a counterattack after its recent defeat that you were a part of."

"Good," Fiona frowned. Vincent was glad to hear that the Defense Forces were out for revenge after what happened on the hilltop, even if that battle felt like a whole lifetime ago now.

"No." Arai shook her head. "The Anarchs have infiltrated your military's intelligence networks. They know exactly what is going to happen. The Earth's military will undoubtedly be crushed."

"Shit," Vincent sighed.

"The Anarchs also have plans to do to your people what they did to ours," Arai said quietly. For the first time since they had met, Vincent could hear some real emotion in her voice.

"What do you mean?" Fiona frowned.

"Didn't they destroy your planet?" Vincent gasped. "The plasma fire storm?"

"Yes." Arai nodded solemnly. "According to the information on the destroyer, they already have their new weapons stations built and are in the process of charging their plasma reservoirs to strike."

"So it's over?" Vincent's heart sank. "No way." Fiona put her arm around him. He knew she really didn't care what happened to Earth, and in all probability, the destruction of Earth could only help her people. Without Vincent and everything he grew up around, she would never have been abandoned on the streets and doomed to a life of fighting wars in places she'd never heard of.

"There is a chance," Arai said. "Though not a good one." One of the other high-ranking Mawr at the table, a fat older alien with a deep scar over one of its eyes, grunted something at Arai.

"What?" Vincent asked desperately.

"We know where the Anarchs are preparing their charging stations. If we launched an attack on the planet, we would almost certainly be routed." Arai folded her thick hands together on the table.

"So we can't even try?" Vincent said.

"Wait. Hold on," Fiona interrupted. "You have the Anarchs' computers, and the Anarchs had total access to the Defense Forces systems. Why can't you just warn them?"

The council erupted into a cacophony of deep throated grunts. More than one of them pounded its huge fist onto the table.

"We are not allies of the humans," Arai said. "Do not think our kindness toward you to extends to your entire race."

"You don't have to be allies," Fiona said. "Do you think you can beat the Anarchs if millions of them aren't off fighting our Defense Forces?" Fiona walked toward the council as they frowned at her. "Because I know what I saw in that control room. One Anarch nearly killed us all. It sure the hell tore up some of your warriors without breaking a sweat!" Arai jumped to her feet.

"You dare insult my clan?" she growled.

"No!" Fiona screamed back. "Look, I hate Earth more than anyone in this room, but if you let the Anarchs destroy it, nothing is going to be left to distract them from your little uprising out here and they'll steamroll your clan just like they did to your damn planet! We obviously need each other!"

"Get out!" Arai ordered, pounding her thick fist on the table. Before Fiona could argue any further, she and Vincent were dragged out of the council by warriors and escorted back to their apartment. This time, though, Vincent heard a distinct locking sound from the outside. Once again, they were back in a cell.

"Did you have to start an argument with them?" Vincent found himself taking his frustrations out on Fiona.

"Yes, I did." She closed in on him and got in his face. "Those overly honorable shitheads are going to get your planet destroyed. One of us has to care about that lump of worthless rock." She backed away from Vincent and crossed her arms. "They know I'm right. They just don't want to admit it."

"Why do you even care?" Vincent shook his head. "You hate Earth, the Central Committee. You hate it all."

"Do you really think once the Anarchs burn down your planet they'll just leave mine alone?" Fiona paced around and finally sat down on one of the cushions against the wall. "We'll end up just like we are now. Look at the Rhai: they aren't in charge of anything; forced to do one thing or another. Or the Mawr; either submit or live the rest of your life in tunnels, telling yourself that you're waging some glorious war. At least with the system we have right now, your entire family doesn't get burned alive." Vincent was taken aback that she was worried about his family—people she had never met.

"What if it works?" Vincent sat down next to her. "We somehow convince these assholes that they need to save Earth. Then somehow we get back home. Then what do we do?"

"I don't know," Fiona shrugged. "I'll worry about that if I'm still alive."

"I won't let anything happen to you." Vincent wrapped an arm around her.

"Gonna protect me with those sweet shooting skills?" She laughed and pushed him away.

"You're such an ass!" Vincent cursed.

*****

The door to their room swung open and Arai and several of her warriors stepped in.

"You." She pointed at Fiona.

"This should be good," Fiona muttered and stood up. The way Fiona squared her shoulders toward Arai made Vincent think she expected a fight. Regardless of how tough Fiona was, Vincent doubted she could do much against Arai in a fist fight.

"You come into my council meeting and start demanding things. Demanding changes to our military policy. You are very brash."

"I've been called a lot of things before, but nothing so nice," Fiona smirked.

"It is apparently what was needed." Arai crossed her arms. "I knew what you said to be true, even if it is distasteful. We cannot stand alone against the Anarchs. The elders, the cohort masters—they are set in their ways and cannot see our new reality. Your actions on the destroyer . . ." She nodded to Vincent. "And your outburst . . ." She looked at Fiona. "Seem to have swayed their minds to helping your people."

"Wait. You mean . . ." Vincent stood up.

"We have contacted the human military and informed it of the Anarchs' plans." Arai crossed her thick arms. "Any action against the Anarch fortress planet will require all of our forces to launch a joint attack. It will take time to rally the cohorts."

"Can't you just order them to do what you want?" Fiona raised an eyebrow.

"While I am the warlord of the clan's cohorts, the cohort masters sometimes forget they are not truly the ones in charge and must be reminded." The implication was clear to Vincent.

"How long do we have?" Vincent asked.

"Not long enough." Arai turned and began walking out of the room. "We will launch the attack regardless of readiness. We have no choice. We must act before the stations are finished charging."

"This sounds like a suicide mission," Vincent moaned and sat back down on the bedroll.

"Seems to be a reoccurring theme with us, doesn't it?" Fiona forced a smile and sat down next to him. "What's one more for the road?"

"We really need to think of a different way to spend time together." Vincent laughed and leaned his head on her shoulder.

"I don't mind," Fiona smiled.

"You don't mind nearly dying every other day?" Vincent asked sarcastically.

"We wouldn't have met any other way," Fiona shrugged. "And you're pretty alright." She smiled her crooked smile.

"Hey, you never know," he started. "I almost volunteered to work on Mars as part of the rebuilding effort. We could have met."

"Those idiots," Fiona laughed. "They show up waiving about their little flags and handing out books about how great your Chairman is. Reading never filled any bellies, and try as they might, loyalty to some asshole on an entirely different planet never kept any of us warm during the winter."

"Excuse me, but that is our Chairman," Vincent pointed out sarcastically.

"Pfft." She dismissed him. "The only thing those zealots were good for was beating up and stealing their wallets."

"You would have mugged me?" he laughed.

"Oh, honey." Fiona grabbed him by the chin. "I would have had my way with you."

CHAPTER TWENTY-SIX

few days passed, and it seemed like nothing had changed. Even though Arai had talked to them about the need for urgency, the Fidayi warriors in the underground hallways and patrolling the newly won streets of Elysian didn't seem to be in a rush to do anything.

In fact, they seemed to be doing the exact opposite. When the warriors weren't on the surface patrolling their newly conquered planet, they spent most of their time below ground cleaning their Ritens in the same ritualistic way Vincent had seen Zinvor do or sitting in groups as one member read verses of something from a data display. It reminded Vincent of when he was in grade school. The ethics professor would stand in the middle of a circle of kids and have story time. He would always be interested until the professor started talking about "the glory of the Chairman," and he would have to fight off falling asleep.

Vincent and Fiona also started to learn the Mawr's deep, growling language. At first, he felt ridiculous trying to grunt clumsy words to passing warriors, but after several attempts, some of them returned his badly mispronounced greetings. They seemed to be amused at his attempts at their language.

Vincent sat in on some of the group readings, mostly out of boredom, but also because he was curious. He thought it was strange that this race of warriors—which was apparently so terrifying that instead of fighting them, the Anarchs scorched their planet with plasma fire—sat around in reading circles like human children.

He couldn't understand much of what was being said. Eventually, Arai got word of the strange human who kept bothering her warriors and came out to the readings. She sat down next to him on an empty cushion.

"I hear you are learning our language?" she asked quietly.

"Trying. Badly, may I add," he smiled.

"Can you understand what my warrior is reading?"

"One or two words. How did you end up learning our language?" Vincent asked.

"It is a warrior's duty to constantly expand their knowledge. Most study the arts. I chose to learn the tongues of the other races." Vincent was taken aback. The Mawr always seemed like a backward race only obsessed with battle.

"Do not be so surprised," Arai smiled. "My kin and I did not always live underground," she said. "Our home world was lush and bountiful with wonderful places of learning for warriors of all of the clans to further their knowledge." Vincent could hear the anger welling up in the warlord's voice. "Until the Anarchs decided to create that infernal Alliance."

"Why did they do that?" he asked.

"A simple method of controlling the other races without having to risk any of their own. You see, while the Anarchs are incredibly powerful, they are also very few in number. Their technological advances allowed them to project their power much further than their numbers originally allowed. The battle suits that they wear are second to none."

"What do they look like outside of the suits?" Vincent asked.

"I do not know," she said. "I have never seen them outside of combat. We know nothing of their civil life."

"But they knew enough about you to know that in a stand-up fight you would eventually win." Vincent saw the hard expression on Arai face dissolve.

"Yes, when my ancestors rejected their demand for an alliance, they attacked. We rebuffed their attacks time and time again. It was then that they unleashed those demonic weapons on our home world. Everything on the surface was destroyed." Arai's deep growling voice faded away.

"The plasma fire storm?" he asked. "How did any of your race survive?"

"Yes, waves of blue flames descended from the sky and washed away all that lived. At the time of their attack, several of our cohorts were off-planet engaging the Anarchs on several of their outpost worlds. The clans were destroyed and thrown into chaos." She dropped her head. "Many of the surviving cohorts saw no other way and joined the Alliance. Hundreds of others refused, and eventually a cohort warlord unified the scattered warriors into a new clan: the Fidayi. That warrior was my father."

"How long ago did you become a warlord?"

"Only a few years ago." Vincent could tell it was a sore subject for the strong warrior. "I was chosen by the people to be warlord, and many of the cohort masters did not approve. They believed my brother would make a much better leader. I had to prove myself time and time again."

"Because you're a female?" Vincent asked.

"Of course not." Arai shook her head. "Because I am younger. Zinvor is the elder of our family. He is also a much more talented warrior."

"They didn't seem to mind sentencing him to death," Vincent frowned.

"Being declared a Tsarra is an honor. I understand it is difficult for an outsider to understand." Arai cast her glace away.

"You're forcing him to go on a suicide mission," Vincent snapped.

"Forcing?" Arai looked shocked. "You misunderstand. Zinvor chose to don the black armor of the Tsarra and to become a tool of our glorious Paterazm."

"Why would he do that? He said he didn't want to fight anymore!" Vincent asked.

"Because if he had chosen another option, he would have had to leave your side. He could not accept that." Arai's voice was filled with sadness. "My brother and I disagree on a great many things, Vincent, but it pained me to see him place that armor on his shoulders, blessing or no."

"I'm sorry." Vincent's head dropped.

"Tell me of your battle against the Alliance," said Arai.

"Fiona and I were dropped from a huge ship onto the surface of a planet we'd never heard of. We had no idea what we were up against." Vincent's voice lowered as he remembered the Alliance's artillery crash down from the sky and burn several hundred soldiers alive. "We fought the best we could, but Fiona and I were the only ones who survived." He thought back to the Anarch in red armor crushing the helpless wounded.

"Your comrades died an honorable and glorious death, Vincent." Arai put one of her large hands on his shoulder. The strength of her grip was breathtaking.

"No." Vincent shook his head. "They just died."

The reader of the group began to loudly spout off another passage, and the other warriors in the group bowed their heads, deep in thought.

"What are they reading?" Vincent tried to change the subject.

"Their affirmations. They do these daily," Arai said. "It is a way to prime our warrior spirit in between battles. I will have that Rhai you brought translate a version into your tongue for you."

"Thank you," Vincent nodded. "What's he saying?" he asked as the reader began another passage.

"Even if it seems certain that you will lose a battle, retaliate. Neither wisdom nor technique has a place in this. A true warrior does not think of victory or defeat. A warrior plunges recklessly toward an irrational death." She continued translating. "Single-mindedness is all-powerful," she finished, her eyes closed.

"Reminds me of home," Vincent smiled slightly.

"How so?" Arai asked.

"We had a book that we had to read from a lot in school. It was called the Book of Ethics. Our professors acted like it was the most important thing in the world."

"What was in this book?"

"Ways that we can serve the Chairman." Vincent saw the look of confusion on Arai's face. "He's our warlord, I guess. By serving him, we serve humanity. Or so it said." He shrugged.

"You served him by becoming a human warrior, no?"

"No." Vincent let out a little laugh. "I'm no warrior. I broke the law and my punishment was to be a soldier for a few years."

"And what law did you break?"

"You know that book I was just talking about?" Vincent smiled.

"Yes."

"I drew in it," he laughed.

"That is all?" Arai grunted a deep throated laugh. "The man who wrote this book must know his words are meaningless." She patted Vincent on the shoulder. "This . . . Chairman, was it? He seems like a very vain, weak man," Arai said. She made a point, and Vincent couldn't help but agree. Arai stood up and began to walk away.

"Is your book not important?" Vincent asked her.

"No, the book itself is just another vessel for the words. Those words can be passed down through the tongue if need be. The book is just a tool. Tools can be discarded or broken. The words are the only important thing."

"I never thought of it like that. Maybe he made the book so important because he knew his words themselves were meaningless." Vincent wondered out loud. If he had been overheard saying that sentence on Earth, he would have been shot.

"You survived battle with the Alliance, outran Anarch patrols, and helped destroy an Alliance destroyer," Arai said. "You killed an Anarch warrior in one-on-one combat. You may not have been born of warrior blood, but I certainly see a warrior sitting before me right now." Arai patted Vincent on the shoulder again. Even acting casually, Arai's strength was frightfully apparent. She stood up, and to his surprise, bowed slightly to Vincent. She turned and marched off, her guards on her heels.

*****

True to her word, there was soon a small black data display delivered to the lone human apartment on Elysian. Fiona sat on a floor cushion and read some of it out loud.

"Live every day as if your body is already dead." She frowned down at the little display. "You know, for a book that talks about dying all the time, there is a lot of stuff about poetry and gardening. I thought I saw something in there about the importance of flowers."

"Yeah, it turns out the Mawr aren't just armored, toad-looking killing machines. I mean, they are all of those things, but they're also apparently deep as hell, too." Vincent sat down next to Fiona.

"Eh, I don't know. I think I liked them better that way. I'm not so sure about all of this artsy crap." Fiona furrowed her brow.

"It's weird. I think this is how they get ready for battle." He pointed to the book. "We figured it would look something like what we were doing on the Victory, but they've been training their whole lives. This stuff psyches them up or something, though you couldn't tell by looking at them."

"I don't know about all this reading crap, but I think I liked the get-hammered-and-have-sex-all-night technique we used on the Victory," she smirked.

"Oh, I am all about that. In every way." He tossed the small display behind him.

CHAPTER TWENTY-SEVEN

Vincent was sitting in on another one of the group readings with Fiona when Arai approached them.

"How are the language lessons coming?" Arai asked.

"Good. I understand almost twenty words of it now," Vincent smiled nervously.

"I can't understand a damn thing," Fiona complained. "It sounds like you guys are having a long, drawn-out burping contest."

"I do not want to interrupt your affirmations, but can I see you two in the council chambers?" Arai asked. Vincent and Fiona nodded and stood up, following after her.

The inside of the council chambers was not populated by the panel of alien generals as it had been before. The council table was a mess of maps and overhead photos.

"Before we get started, I must first ask you a question. What do your names mean in your language?" Vincent and Fiona exchanged glances, surprised by the question.

"Their meaning?" Vincent shrugged. "After I was born, my dad picked it out of the list of approved names that the Committee put out."

"It means nothing?" Arai asked, shocked. "And you?" She glanced at Fiona.

"It's the name of a bar," she shrugged. "I picked it because I liked the way it sounded."

"Wait. What?" Vincent asked.

"No one names their kids that the state is going to take. Waste of energy. When they kicked me out, I fell in with a group of kids who lived behind Fiona's Tavern. I thought it sounded nice."

"And Olympus? Did you pick the last name, too?" Vincent asked.

"No, the draft office did. I'm draftee Fiona from Olympus. Therefore, I'm Fiona Olympus to them."

"I know that shouldn't surprise me at this point," Vincent said, rubbing his forehead. "And the Mawr?" he asked Arai. "How do you get your names?"

"A Mawr must wait until their tenth year of birth and their elders bestow a name they have earned during their first years," she nodded. "Arai means 'bold and steady.' They say I was meant to become warlord."

"You have to earn it?" Fiona asked. "What if you don't earn anything?"

"They would be cast out as a shame to their clan."

Fiona gave a little laugh. "Damn, that's rough."

"Says the person who named herself after a bar," Vincent laughed.

"And what does Zinvor mean?" Fiona asked, ignoring Vincent.

"Holy warrior," Arai answered. "He was the pride of our father for his feats on the hunting grounds. Arai walked over to the low table, where she sifted through the maps and documents for a moment before turning back to Vincent and Fiona.

"What's going on with this stuff?" Fiona asked, pointing to the maps.

"As you know, we have been planning an assault on the Alliance." Arai turned to face the two. "It will be the largest attack my clan has ever launched against those infernal beasts since the death of our sacred home world. I have never in my life seen all of my cohorts in one place, but there is one problem."

"Problem?" asked Fiona. "Did the Defense Forces not listen?"

"No, not that. Though they were very resistant. The problem is that no human soldier has ever been a part of a clan battle formation. I have no intentions of changing that."

"You're going to make us sit on the sidelines?" Fiona gasped.

"No way!" Vincent yelled. "Not after everything we've been through."

Two warriors entered the room, each pushing a tall metal cart. They bowed deeply to Arai and exited the room as quickly as they entered. Arai approached the carts and opened their doors, their hinges squeaking. Inside the carts were suits of warrior armor. One set was dyed a watery blue color, and the other was a rust-colored red. At the foot of the suits were Ritens.

"I will, however, allow the first two warriors of the Human Cohort to fight in my formations." Arai nodded to the armor. "Vincent, your armor is the one on the left." She pointed to the blue set. "It is the color of your home. It also represents water. You can be as docile as a calm sea but as violent and unpredictable as a surging wave when you need to be. Fiona, yours is the one on the right. The red is the color of your home: the color of the blood of your people and the deep anger and hatred you hold in your heart for what has been done to them."

Vincent and Fiona stepped toward the sets of armor. Vincent reached out and touched the shoulder of his suit. What he had thought was some kind of metal this whole time was not. It was made of overlaying scales that felt soft to the touch, almost like a supple leather. He bent down and picked up his Riten. Though still heavier than any human handgun, it was much lighter than the Riten he'd taken from a fallen warrior. Under the Riten was a thick brown holster sewn to an adjustable belt.

Letters and scripts were carved into it, starting at the Riten's curving handle, across its ammunition wheel, and down its barrel. Vincent hadn't even attempted to try to learn the written language of the Mawr, so he had no idea what it said.

"What does it say?" he asked Arai.

"Vincent of Earth, Hero of the Breach. For your actions in ensuring our attack on the destroyer was a success."

"Aw, you got the cool nickname," Fiona moaned.

"Yours says Fiona of Mars, The Fury of Elysian. For your habit of charging forward straight at the enemy with no regard for personal safety."

"Oh, never mind. Mine is awesome." Fiona smiled and picked up her Riten.

"Please, try on your new armor." Arai waved them forward.

Vincent slipped on the armor, and though he always assumed the warriors' armor was heavy, he found it as light as the clothes he was wearing. He wondered how long Arai had her warriors working on the armor, as it was very obviously created just for them. They managed to hand-craft gloves for their much different human hands, not to mention the long pants of armor, as the Mawr themselves were short, stocky, and almost entirely torso.

"Wow, it fits perfectly," Fiona remarked. She slid her Riten into its holster.

"We left the feet open, as you can tell." Arai pointed down to her feet, which still reminded Vincent more of scaly hooves than actual feet. "We do not wear those covers that you do." Their boots were just about the only thing that still survived from their time in the Defense Forces.

"I'm assuming this means the attack is soon," Vincent thought out loud.

"Yes," Arai nodded. "The first phase is already underway."

"What?" Fiona asked, motioning over to the multitude of charts, maps, and pictures.

"Both the human army and my cohorts have already begun operations to secure a landing and control area. The fortification is on the dead world of Grawluck." Arai walked over to a map on the low council table. "A small planet on which it rains nearly constantly. The Anarchs exterminated its inhabitants decades ago when they discovered that they could use the planet's vast energy stores for their plasma charging stations. It is also heavily fortified with the highest concentration of Anarch warriors and auxiliaries outside of their core worlds."

"How many?" Vincent gasped.

"We are expecting three times the size of the force we are able to field," Arai said.

"How the hell are we going to deal with that?" Fiona cried. "One Anarch tore us apart on the destroyer!"

"We are depending on the element of surprise. They would never expect us to know what they are doing there. Paterazm willing, it will be enough."

"Hoping sounds promising," Fiona frowned.

"We do not have a choice." Arai shook her head. "If we wait to gather any other forces, the Anarchs' charging will be complete and the plasma weapons could be deployed against Earth. I cannot plan a battle with forces that I do not have."

"Be honest with me. How good of a chance do we have at succeeding?" Vincent asked.

"A better chance than if we do nothing," Arai nodded.

"I think that's their form of optimism," Fiona laughed. "Screw it. Let's do this." She slapped Vincent on the shoulder.

"We will be landing with the next wave of cohorts. We leave shortly." Arai nodded and marched off.

For the first time in several days, Fiona and Vincent walked through the passageways and made their way back to the surface of Elysian. Like Arai had said, the dark yellow sky was crowded with the telltale black shapes of ships orbiting high above the surface. Unlike a formal military, none of the ships were the same. Vincent saw some unusual sleek black ships that he assumed were captured Anarch vessels. It seemed to Vincent that, much like its underground military operations on Elysian, the Fidayi scraped together whatever they could from everywhere they could to fight the Anarchs.

"It looks like they pressed every ship they could into service. Comforting." Fiona crossed her arms, looking up at the crowded sky.

"Still better than the one we used to attack the destroyer in," Vincent said.

"What the hell is a cohort anyway?"

"It's like a troop, but they're all related in some way," Vincent shrugged. "Brothers, sisters, cousins. Their commanders control them like a king of some kind instead of just an officer. Kind like how District Committees rule over their areas back home and only have to listen to the Central Committee."

"You've really caught on with the language, eh?" Fiona glanced sideways at him.

"Understanding, yeah. Speaking, not at all," he laughed. "I sound like a brain-damaged cave person when I try to speak to them."

"To be fair, you sound like that to me all the time," she grinned.

"Why are we friends again?" Vincent sighed.

"Because you love my winning personality."

"Clearly," he said. Fiona slapped him on the butt, and her palm made a loud crack sound off his armor.

"I know why I keep you around," she smirked.

A black ship burst through the yellow clouds and swooped low over the irregular brown buildings of Elysian. It hovered overhead for a few seconds before landing a few feet in front of them. The side doors of the ship let out a hiss and slid open. Inside, at least twenty warriors sat on seats facing out toward the sliding doors.

Zinvor, Arai, and her bodyguards walked up behind Vincent and Fiona. Trailing some ways behind the bodyguards was Nox, who looked tiny in comparison.

"Get in," Arai smiled. Even though this was hardly the first time he'd climbed aboard a ship fully expecting to die, this time it was different. He didn't have the normal feelings of pre-combat nervousness come over him. Before, his heart would attempt to break through his chest and the saliva in his mouth would dry up. He wasn't sure if charging into combat—something so insane that he'd never dreamt of it before—had simply become old hat or if it was something else.

Vincent sat down between Fiona and a hulking Mawr warrior that carried a belt-fed machine gun nearly the size of

Vincent. The slugs that dangled from a leather ammunition belt were nearly as big as one of his fingers. The ship's door slid closed, and the craft silently floated toward the sky.

"Why is Nox coming?" Fiona asked. "He's not exactly useful."

"He is joining the Rhai technicians I am sending in to hopefully shut down the charging stations." Arai nodded at Nox, who was shaking in fear.

"He doesn't seem like the technician type," Vincent laughed. What started as a simple chuckle grew into uncontrollable laughter, and Vincent doubled over in his seat. The Mawr in the tightly packed space gave him odd looks.

"Did you finally snap?" Fiona looked sideways at him.

"No," Vincent laughed, having to wipe away tears. "This shit is just so stupid."

"Huh?"

"Did you ever think that in Earth's most dire moments, its rescue party would be a criminal, a Martian, and thousands of aliens?" He fought to breathe through his fits of laughter. "There isn't a single person—" —he looked at the Mawr "Or alien in this ship they wouldn't find a reason to line up against a wall and shoot, but here we go, off to save their asses from other aliens they wish they could kill." He threw his hands up in the air in mock outrage. "It's just so damn stupid."

"The Defense Forces are coming too, though," Fiona shrugged. "Tons of them."

"Yes, but they do not know why they are coming," Arai added.

"Wait, what?" Vincent asked. His nervous laughter faded away.

"We did not tell them about the Anarchs' weapons or their abilities." She shook her head. "They think the Alliance force gathering on Grawluck is an invasion force for the human home cluster. They know nothing of the plasma fire weapons."

"That seems like a pretty important part to leave out!" Fiona blurted out.

"From what I have heard, and seen, if these weapons fell into the hands of your military, they would simply use them against the Anarchs or all of the outer worlds. Your leaders cannot be trusted. I thought if anyone understood it would be you two. The weapons must be destroyed." From the tone of her voice, that decision was not up for debate.

Vincent nodded. "Actually, that is a good call."

"She understands the Central Committee better than the Earthlings do," Fiona laughed.

"Why won't you use the weapons?" asked Vincent. "You want to get revenge on the Anarchs for destroying your home world, don't you?"

"Of course I do. The temptation to use them against their creators certainly crossed my mind. But such weapons are an abomination. They kill without discriminating between warriors and non-combatants and salt the soil so nothing will ever live there again. To use them is to drain the charging planet dry of its energy resources so it can never be used as a cradle of life again." Arai bowed her head. "No matter how deep my hatred is for those armored demons, I cannot dishonor myself by doing the same thing to them as they did to us."

"So you hope by smashing their weapons and giving the humans a victory, they might back down?" Vincent asked.

"Yes, a loss at Grawluck would not defeat the Anarchs. Their military reach is vast. But it would deplete their forces outside their home cluster. If it is a decisive victory, we may be able to bring the fight to their homes for the first time."

Arai reached into a pouch on her hip, pulled out a data display, and turned it on. A detailed hologram popped up showing various battle positions, enemy forces, and friendly forces. "The stations are inside these large buildings, in silos underground. Before we can destroy them, we must fight our way through these strong points." Arai pointed to a ring of fortifications arrayed in the shape of a large star. "Each point is connected to the others through trenches. If we attempt to fly over these positions, Alliance guns will undoubtedly shoot us down, so we must assault them on foot. The first phase has advanced through the first several lines of trenches and established a safe zone for us to reinforce the attack."

"What have the Defense Forces been doing?" asked Fiona.

"They have been assaulting from the west. I am sorry to tell you we did not inform them of the fortifications they would be assaulting." Arai's voice disclosed a tinge of sadness.

"What?" Vincent asked. "They'll be cut to pieces!"

"If the Defense Forces do not prepare for what lies ahead, they will be slowed down significantly more. It will give us more time to break through in the east and get to the weapons stations first." Arai saw Vincent's facial expression. "I am sorry. I did not mean to deceive you."

"Wait," Fiona said. "Are we going to see any of the Defense Forces?"

"We are being transported to the joint command area, so yes," Arai nodded. "Did you think I was going to let you run into battle without me? You two are to stay at my side."

"Well, that should be an interesting conversation," Fiona said.

"Are you not happy to see your kin?" Arai looked confused.

"I know I should be." Vincent's voice fell. "Going home just means a few more years in the Defense Forces." He forced a smile. "Our experience so far hasn't been the best."

Fiona frowned. "Hey, at least you get to go home for real at some point."

"But you hate your home," Vincent joked.

"I like that red ball of dirt better than the inside of dank spaceships for the rest of my life," she spat.

Through the windows of the ship, Vincent saw a small dark brown planet come into view. The number of ships above Gawluck dumfounded Vincent. They were so numerous that they formed a dark curtain across much of the planet.

He could see the long, ugly industrial forms of Defense Forces capital ships, much like the Victory. Orange plumes flashed all around them, sending an untold number of artillery shells down at a target he could not yet see. The small black shapes of dropships raced toward the planet in a never-ending stream.

Arcing blue lights, which Vincent knew were Alliance artillery, streaked up from the planet's surface. Several of the small dropships vanished in fiery explosions before they could reach the battlefield. These losses didn't stem the oncoming wave of human soldiers, though. Dropships flooded out of the Defense Forces vessels like a cloud of angry insects.

The Mawr ship descended through the planet's atmosphere. Vincent's stomach tightened as the engines wound up. He clenched his fists on his lap and closed his eyes to steady himself. He felt Fiona's hand tighten over his and managed to force his eyes open long enough to look over at her. She sat in her seat, ramrod straight, with her eyes slammed shut. His momentary relief vanished at the sight of her nervousness.

He distracted himself by glancing over at the warriors who seemed indifferent to the fact they were descending into a warzone. Most stared at their data displays; bright red symbols jumped up into the air as they scanned through their affirmations. Other warriors fidgeted with the ammunition wheels of their Ritens, filling the inside of the ship with metallic clicking noises.

Vincent grabbed a dented, rusty rifle from a weapons rack bolted to the hull of the ship. It was one of the homemade rifles that the Fidayi built. They appeared rough and neglected. Vincent assumed that the Mawr spent so much time cleaning their Ritens that they had no time to maintain any other weapons.

Fiona also grabbed a rifle. She wrapped her fist around the bulky charging handle and tried to pull it back, but it wouldn't budge. She heaved a few times. It cracked as the rust broke free and slammed to the back, loading the rifle.

"Someone needs to put a couple of passages about cleaning your damn rifles in those affirmations of yours," Fiona cursed at Arai.

"Our long guns are of no importance," she said. "They are simply tools until we can get in close and dispatch our enemies with our Ritens."

"No thanks," Vincent laughed. "I'd rather use a rifle. Or better yet, be far away in an artillery unit. That would have been sweet."

"They all died, too, you know." Fiona smirked at him.

"Artillery?" Arai gasped. "That is a job for the Rhai, not warriors."

"Is that who operates the Fidayi's big guns?" Fiona asked.

"Our artillery, armor, and ship fleet, yes," Arai nodded.

"They might be twitchy, backstabbing, skinny pricks, but damn they got a sweet deal," Fiona laughed.

The ship shook as it broke through the planet's atmosphere. Dark clouds obscured the planet below, and lightning flashed through the sky. The engines whirled, slowing the ship down as it cut through the clouds and into the curtain of rain. Even though it was supposed to be the middle of the day, the planet was cloaked in darkness.

The light from thousands of exploding artillery shells illuminated the darkness in quick flashes. Vincent saw the familiar box shape of Reapers swooping back and forth, their way lit by the explosions of their rockets. Thousands of flashing lights, going opposite ways, tore through the night at one another. To Vincent, it seemed like the entire planet was exploding below him.

"Holy shit," Fiona gasped as she pressed her face against the window.

"Can we go back up now?" Vincent said, only half joking.

"Below is the battle that will decide the fate of the galaxy," Arai smiled. "You should feel honored for being blessed with the chance to take part in such a glorious conquest."

"She sounds like a poster from my school's auditorium," Vincent sighed.

"Is this a good thing?" Arai asked.

"Nope. Not even slightly," Vincent said.

The ship rocked as an explosion lit up the night in front of it. The Rhai pilot pulled the ship hard to one side before bringing it back on course. Vincent and Fiona were slammed back into their seats and reached out for each other as the ship rocked.

The warriors didn't acknowledge they were nearly blown out of the sky. A fireball exploded a few hundred feet in front of them as the gunners on the surface found their mark. The lead ship in their group was atomized before their eyes. The debris from what was left of the ship and its occupants rained down on the battlefield below.

The pat pat of rain on the ship's hull was replaced with the high-pitched twang of bullets and lasers striking its tough metal skin. The pilot deftly swung the ship to safety, but a nearby craft wasn't so lucky. The concussion from it exploding shook the inhabitants of Vincent's ship back and forth in their seats. Another erupting blue plasma plume lit up the sky in front of them, rattling the ship so hard even the warriors couldn't ignore it. They looked around and shifted uncomfortably in their seats.

"We are close," Arai said.

"You think?" Fiona screamed.

CHAPTER TWENTY-EIGHT

Just as quickly as it accelerated, the ship came to a screeching halt, throwing everyone forward.

"Get your shit together, man!" Vincent cursed.

"He is supposed to do that," Arai said calmly. "It makes it harder for the enemy to shoot us down." Outside, the unrelenting downpour of rain had transformed the surface into a churning sea of mud.

Vincent stepped out of the ship and expected to be soaked through. While his head and hair were unprotected, their tight-fitting armor kept him entirely dry. Unfortunately, the one human piece of clothing he'd kept—his boots—were flooded with water. The rain was piercing and cold, and soon Vincent began to lose feeling in his feet.

Arai stepped out into the mud and moved to the head of the new column. She marched through the darkness and stinging rain toward a bustling command area. Tents and small boxy dropship-like craft were sunk into the mud. Warriors rushed back and forth out of the craft, and the wounded hobbled into tents. Like on the destroyer, none of them were receiving medical attention.

Then a sight Vincent was sure he'd never see again walked in front of the group: a human soldier. The soldier was part of a stretcher team carrying an injured soldier into an adjoining tent. Soldiers cloaked in cape-like rain slickers busily walked through the command area. Their grey uniforms were stained dark brown with mud.

In the distance were lines of huge artillery pieces. The artillery's human crew busily scrambled around to ready the guns. All at once, the long line of artillery fired. The force of the guns was bone-shaking. Their barrels flashed and hundreds of shells screamed off into the night at an unseen target. The humans and warriors hustling around the command area paid them no attention.

The human soldiers froze when they saw Vincent and Fiona clad in Mawr armor and walking with the alien commander. Vincent tried to ignore them, but he could feel their gaze burning into him.

"You think they noticed?" Fiona laughed nervously. "Take a picture, you pricks!" she yelled at them.

Arai led them into the small craft and closed the door behind them. The inside had been transformed into an ad hoc command center. Wall-sized displays glowed brightly with maps and pictures of the Alliance's battle positions. In the middle of the room was the usual low Mawr table surrounded by cushions. Three of the cushions were occupied by Defense Forces officers. Medals hung heavy from their chests, and they wore tall, grey peaked caps. Unlike the mud-covered soldiers outside, they were spotless.

Vincent did a double take when he saw a face he recognized. Sitting next to a scarred Mawr warrior was the grizzled, sunken old face of Colonel Rostov, the man who forcibly enlisted him in the Defense Forces. The human officers expressed surprise at the presence of Vincent and Fiona with a Mawr commander, but none recognized Vincent.

The human officers stood up to meet Arai and her entourage. Arai, knowing humans as well as she did, extended a hand to the colonel in greeting, but he did not shake it. Rostov looked down at Arai's hand, and Vincent could tell it was a look of disgust.

"Colonel Rostov, Earth Defense Forces." He greeted her in his thickly accented voice. Arai dropped her hand and her gaze hardened.

"Warlord Arai, Clan Fidayi," she grunted.

"And who are these two with you?" Rostov asked. Arai began to answer him when Fiona cut her off.

"Fiona Olympus. That is Vincent Solaris." She pointed over at Vincent.

"Hmm. And how did you end up in such dress?" he asked as he looked the two up and down.

"We survived the Victory," Vincent mumbled.

"Survived the Victory? Do you mean to say you two were on the ESS Victory?" Rostov repeated. Vincent could tell from the tone of Rostov's voice that he didn't believe the story.

"Yeah," Fiona reinforced. "We did what we had to do."

"We should really get to the offensive, Colonel," Arai interrupted.

"Yes," Rostov agreed. "Of course." Though he addressed Arai, his eyes never left Vincent and Fiona.

"As you can tell, our forces are engaging the Alliance forces all along the eastern line here." Rostov pointed up at the illuminated map. "We have yet to break through, but we expect to shortly, after which time we will drive through the enemy's center. This cursed atmosphere is totally frying our communications equipment, though. Our forward units cannot communicate with one another, our fleet above, or our fire support base here. We have resorted to using message runners to deliver orders to the front. It is making the advance very difficult."

Arai stood slowly, looking at the map. "You have not taken the strong points yet, Colonel?" she asked.

"No, they are significantly stronger than we originally anticipated. Our armor regiments are churning those scum into the mud, though. The death blow will be dealt soon."

"Good," Arai nodded. "My cohorts have taken the two western-most strong points." Arai pointed at the map. "And we are assaulting their trenches as we speak. I hope for this to be over with by the end of the cycle."

"The what?" Rostov asked.

"The week," Vincent cut in. Rostov shot an angry look back at him but said nothing.

"Good. Then the bombardment will stay on target for now." Rostov crossed his arms. "After we smash their lines, what then?" he asked. "Why does your clan," —he frowned saying the name— "want to help our Chairman?"

"I do not care about your Chairman. I only care about defeating the Anarchs, Colonel," Arai said matter-of-factly. "As should you. They are the ones who attacked your people on your Moon."

"Right," Rostov growled. "That is what you say." He turned to walk out of the craft. He flipped his slicker's hood over his high peaked cap before turning to Vincent and Fiona.

"Would you like to join my staff and I in my quarters? I would like to hear the story of your supposed survival," Rostov said with his eyebrow raised.

"You got some smokes?" Fiona asked. Try as she might, she could never find Earth brand cigarettes on Elysian despite its large population of smugglers. She had managed to barter with Nox for scraps of tobacco of unknown origin, but it was far from the same thing. She had tried to smoke with the Mawr, but whatever plant matter they were smoking in their pipes did not agree with the human respiratory tract.

"Of course," Rostov answered. "And drinks. I know I could use one after dealing with such beasts."

"I'm sold," Fiona smirked. "Let's go, Vincent." Vincent and Fiona followed Rostov out of the craft. Arai shifted uncomfortably behind them but said nothing. Zinvor, who'd been standing silently behind his sister, started to follow them but was stopped by Arai before he could leave the craft. She said something Vincent couldn't understand and Zinvor nodded.

They walked back out into the driving rain and sloshed through the mud. They exited the Mawr side of the camp, which other than the hospital tent and command craft, was devoid of equipment. Warriors sat out in the rain, waiting for orders or laying asleep in the mud.

The human side of the command center comprised a small village of tents that were barely able to stay staked into the ground in the mud while the rain and wind tried its best to tear them down. Outside one tent, bloody bandages, scraps of uniforms, and body parts were discarded in a pile. The screams of the wounded came from inside. Next to the tent there was a trench full of the water-logged dead, discarded out of the hospital tent like garbage.

Rostov walked past the scene without stopping while Fiona and Vincent took in the full scope of the horror. Vincent questioned Arai's scheme of keeping the Defense Forces in the dark about the mission's objective. He wondered how many Richardsons, Collins, or Ikaris were dying out in the mud because of it.

Fiona pushed Vincent forward. They passed a few more tents. Lines of cots filled with dead-eyed, tired soldiers stared back out at them. All of their stone-grey uniforms were stained with mud and blood. The only parts of them that stuck out were their eyes, the whites of which shone like lamps in the darkness.

Rostov pushed the door open to a Reaper that had landed in the mud and was converted into his personal quarters. The inside of the ship had been gutted of its seats. Instead, there was a real bed, including a mattress, and a large metal table covered in maps and charts. It was surrounded with chairs, all but one filled with Defense Forces officers. They looked at Fiona and Vincent with an equal mixture of disgust and confusion.

"Pour these two a drink," Rostov ordered. A young captain handed them two glasses filled with a brown liquid. Fiona slammed hers back in one gulp and winced. Vincent took a sip and the fluid burned its way down his throat.

"So you say you two survived the Victory," Rostov questioned.

"Absurd!" cursed one of the officers. Vincent noticed he was a major. "The Victory was destroyed before it even got to the battlefield!"

"Shot from the stars!" cursed the captain. "The Chairman said so himself!"

"Wait. What?" Vincent gasped. "You think we never landed on Ryklar?" he stammered. "Are you serious? Do you think a ship that size just up and vanished?"

"Ryklar?" laughed Rostov. "That disgusting alien dirt ball was destroyed by the Victory's guns shortly before the vile alien fleet ambushed her."

"Your lies dishonor the martyrs of the Chairman," the Captain said.

"Rostov, your last place of duty before this mission was Area Six, wasn't it?" Vincent asked, sneering at the group of officers.

Rostov's face sunk. "How did you know that?"

"You enlisted me." Vincent crossed his arms.

"Solaris." Rostov thought back, scratching his chin. He frowned after a few seconds. "A sentenced soldier."

"How else would you have put me on that ship and me not be dead!" Vincent spat.

"We fought on that damn planet for weeks!" Fiona said, indignant.

"And just how did the Victory's glorious army lose on the field of battle? And its only survivors are a criminal and a Red? The idea is laughable."

"Badly," Vincent snapped. "I have the scars to prove it." He slammed back what was left of his drink. Fiona stomped forward and grabbed a cigarette from the table the officers were sitting at. Without asking, she put it in her lips and lit it.

"Some smugglers found us among the dead and took us in." Fiona exhaled a big cloud of smoke.

"We had to fight the Anarchs a few times, but the Fidayi protected us. We would be dead without them." Vincent poured himself another drink.

"That sure is some tale," Rostov grumbled. "And how is their war against these Anarchs going?" he asked.

"Not well. They can't win a fight against the Alliance unless you're involved." Fiona crossed her arms.

"You talk like you're not one of us, girl," Rostov frowned.

"That's because I'm not," she sneered.

"Well, your journey is over." Rostov finally sat down. "You're back with the Defense Forces now and away from those vile things. We will get you a fresh uniform shortly."

Even though that was the moment Fiona and Vincent had been waiting for, nothing about it looked or felt right. He could tell Fiona was uneasy, too.

"So why did the Defense Forces agree to help the Fidayi?" Vincent asked.

Rostov pounded back a drink and laughed. "We have our reasons. And it's not to help those frog creatures either."

"To finally crush an Anarch army?" Fiona piped in.

"That is just an added bonus." Rostov poured himself another drink. "We want that weapon they're aiming at us."

Vincent's heart sank. They knew. Arai had done her best to hide this information from the Defense Forces, but they still found out. Even worse, Arai didn't know.

"Those stupid animals next door thought they could hide that from us," he laughed. "Probably planned on using them on us themselves. Once we take those positions, it won't take us long to wipe them out." Rostov read the expression on Vincent's face and placed his glass on the table.

"You knew about them," he growled. "You knew those creatures were leading us with lies!"

"No!" Vincent stuttered. "I mean yes! But we were trying to help."

Fiona moved quicker than Vincent. She reached for her Riten, but before she could pull it from its holster, a rifle butt struck her in the head, and she crumpled to the ground.

"You bastards!" Vincent screamed. A hand reached over and ripped his Riten away from him.

"In on those monsters' plans, eh?" Rostov stood up and walked over to them. "Race traitor!" he barked while delivering a kick to Vincent's midsection. His armor cushioned the blow, but it still brought him to his knees. "Put these two in the brig!" Rostov ordered. "Make sure they don't get back to their precious aliens to tell them anything." Vincent struggled to stay upright as the soldiers forced his arms behind his back. He glared up at Rostov, his eyes burning with hate. Rostov smiled as they were taken away.

CHAPTER TWENTY-NINE

The soldiers dragged Fiona and Vincent out of the Reaper and through the mud. Fiona hung limp, unconscious from the blow to her head.

"Yell for help and I'll shoot your whore in the face," growled one of the soldiers, shoving Vincent forward. The barrel of the soldier's gun touched Fiona's back. Vincent wasn't sure how tough the Mawr's armor was, but he was certain at that range it didn't matter. The small craft that Zinvor and Arai were in was only a few feet away, but it grew smaller as they were escorted through the rain and deeper into the Defense Forces side of the camp.

Soldiers hurled insults at them as they moved through the camp.

"Traitors!" screamed one.

"Shoot them!" screamed another. A soldier stomped out of a tent and delivered a punch to Vincent's face. Vincent saw stars and tasted blood. He wasn't sure if he was crying or if it was just rain running down his face. Fiona woke up, her eyes wild as she saw Vincent being assailed.

"Piece of alien-loving trash!" cursed his assailant.

"Hey!" screamed one of the soldiers escorting them. "Calm down. You'll all get your chance with these pieces of shit."

"Give me a few minutes with that Red!" hooted a voice from a tent.

"Try it and I'll skin you alive!" growled Fiona. She flailed a kick back at the soldier escorting her but missed. He grabbed Fiona by her hair and slammed her face into the mud.

"Let her go!" Vincent screamed. The soldier laughed as he kicked Fiona in the back. She tried to fight back, but with her hands restrained, there wasn't much she could do.

The soldier escorting Vincent slammed him in the stomach with his rifle. The armor protected him enough, but he still doubled over in pain. The soldier then grabbed him by his bindings and dragged him toward another Reaper. The doors slid open and Vincent was dropped inside. Fiona came crashing in a few minutes later. Her stitches had reopened, and blood mixed with the mud and dirt on her face. Her blue eyes burned with rage.

"They're going to stab Arai in the back," she gasped, spitting out a mouthful of dirty water. "We have to stop them."

"How do you suppose we do that?" Vincent sighed. "That piece of shit is going to have us shot before we have a chance." The ship shook as artillery crashed and exploded nearby. "Or we get blown up first."

"Should have known better than to trust them." Fiona shook her head. "This is my fault."

"What?" Vincent asked. "No, it's not. Your idea made perfect sense. It's not your fault they found out about the Anarchs' plans."

"How did they find out? I thought Arai was hiding it from them."

"She was," Vincent said. "Since the Anarchs were hacking into the Defense Forces systems, they must have found where it was coming from and put two and two together. They knew that the weapons existed; they used one on the Moon. The Defense Forces might be assholes, but they aren't stupid."

Fiona struggled a bit and got to her feet. Dripping wet and covered in mud, she walked over and kicked the ship's door.

"Let me the hell out of here!" she screamed. Her heavy boots clanged off the ship's door. "I won't need a Riten for what I plan on doing to you!"

"Save your energy," Vincent said.

"I will." She stopped kicking. "Only so I can rip them apart with my bare hands when they give me a chance." She sat down back on the cold metal floor next to Vincent.

*****

The hours that passed felt like an eternity. Vincent's cold and wet feet had turned him into little more than a shivering shell of his formerly defiant self. He and Fiona leaned in close to one another, but he was still freezing.

"Shit. I wish they would just shoot us and get it over with," Vincent said.

Fiona laughed, her voice quivering. "Quitter." She managed a smirk.

The door slid open and two soldiers holding trays of food stepped in. Without a word, they dropped them on the ground. The contents slopped around, turning the food into a strange brown slurry.

"Mind cutting off the ropes so we can eat?" Vincent asked.

"You want to join those animals, you can eat like one," one of the soldiers sneered.

"Why don't you shoot us and be done with it?" Fiona said.

"We will once the field marshal passes judgment on you. But not before we have a little fun." The other soldier smiled. "It would be a shame for such a pretty girl to go to waste, even if you probably screwed a couple aliens."

"Not half as many as your mom did," Fiona smirked. The soldier kicked her hard in the face. The blow threw Fiona back and smacked her into the wall. Blood dripped from her mouth. Vincent assumed she would have been knocked out cold, but she gurgled laughter in response. She spat a mouthful of blood straight up at the soldier and it splashed him in the face. He recoiled in disgust.

"You don't know where I've been," she growled with rage, blood dripping down her chin. The soldiers back-peddled out of the ship, slamming the door behind them.

"Holy shit. Are you okay?" Vincent slid across the floor to get a closer look at Fiona.

"Yeah, they hit like pussies." She spat out some more blood, and Vincent started laughing.

"Did you see that guy's face? I think you made him shit himself," he laughed. Fiona started laughing with him. "But seriously, you scare me sometimes."

"Good," she smirked. "Can't have you wandering on me." She leaned in and kissed him on the forehead.

*****

Fiona fell fast asleep from the head trauma, exhaustion, or the fact that she could sleep in almost any circumstance. Vincent remained wide awake and stared straight ahead at the door. Through the night, the never-ending rumble of artillery explosions shook the cold floor under him. Soldiers screamed as they were carried into the first aid tent. The other soldiers drank, laughed, and joked.

At one point, they burst into song. Their words were slurred from hours of drinking, but Vincent could hear it clearly.

"The Defense Forces marches in enemy land,
And sings a devil's song.
A rifleman stands in alien land strong,
And silently hums along.
We care about nothing around us,
And the whole galaxy can see
The Chairman leads us forward,
Toward eternal victory."

At the end of the song, the soldiers started cheering, which woke Fiona up.

"Don't they have anything better to do than sing stupid-ass songs all night?" she moaned, half asleep.

"I guess not. I can't feel my damn feet." Vincent tried kicking the heels of his boots on the ground to get some feeling back, but nothing worked.

"Me either, and my head is killing me."

"I wonder why. You've only had your head bounced off twenty different things in the last few days."

"About as often as we get our asses kicked and locked in different jails," Fiona laughed.

"Yeah, we really need to work on that. It's a stupid habit," he laughed with her.

"Nah," she laughed. "It's our thing now."

"Can I ask you something?" he asked as his laughter died away.

"Shoot."

"What the hell do we do now?"

"Get out of this damn ship. Kill everything we see. Save Arai," Fiona said like her plan was just that simple.

"Okay, I'll bite." Vincent laughed sarcastically. "What then?"

"No idea," she shrugged. "We've been through this. I don't think that far ahead."

"Well, our career paths just narrowed pretty significantly." Vincent leaned forward, trying to take the pressure off his wrists. The soldiers purposely tied his rope tight.

"What do you mean?"

"The Defense Forces want to shoot us," he sighed. "I guess we can't go back."

"I'm heartbroken."

"I'm serious!" Vincent cried. "Our lives are over!"

"Vincent, when are you going to notice something that I noticed when I was ten?"

"What?" Vincent asked, half screaming. "What am I missing?"

"Our lives suck!" she screamed at him. Vincent's eyes went wide. "Face it! You were thrown in jail for drawing in a book, and the only thing that stopped you from being executed was serving in that stupid-ass military singing out there in the mud." She paused to kick the door in anger. "They abandoned your ass on Ryklar to die. And when you didn't, they apparently just told everyone the battle never happened!"

"But I'll never see my family or my friends," Vincent stammered, trying to gather his thoughts.

"Your family hates you and your friends sold you out to the damn cops!" Fiona screamed in his face. "The best thing that ever happened to you was getting left to die on that godforsaken hilltop."

"The best thing that happened to me was you," Vincent said suddenly. Fiona's pale face turned a slight red and her eyes went wide.

"Shut up," she cursed. "You're being an idiot."

"Without you I would've been dead a hundred times over by now. And I—" Fiona cut him off.

"I said stop it, dammit," she frowned. "Getting emotional isn't going to get us out of this situation."

The argument led them into hours of silence. Fiona stared straight ahead at the door, not moving. Vincent wasn't sure if she was so angry at him that she couldn't even look at him or if she was trying to think of a way out of the situation. To his own surprise, Vincent's mind was quiet. He wasn't thinking about how he could never go home or how, in all likelihood, he would never get out of this damn ship.

He was thinking about how, the next time that door opened, he'd be led out and shot in a flooded trench somewhere. After everything they had been through it would all end with them being left out to rot. It would be the last time he would see Fiona alive, either because one or both of them were dead. Vincent hoped the only thing they would do was shoot them. He was scared what those mentally broken soldiers might do to them.

If his unit hadn't been slaughtered on Ryklar and they survived the meat grinder of war for a little bit longer, would they have turned into animals like the ones outside? He had already done so many things he never thought he was capable of.

The door slid open, revealing Rostov and another man. The other man was tall and rail thin. His face was sunken and looked nearly skeletal. A rain slicker was tied around his shoulders and a full chest of medals shone through it. His grey pants had a red stripe going down the side, and on his waist hung a bright silver sword.

"On your feet," Rostov growled.

"Fuck off, we aren't yours to order around anymore," Fiona snarled back. The old man's eyes went wide at the open disobedience.

"Excuse me?"

She glared at them. "You're going to kill us both anyway. Why should I show you any damn respect?"

"Do you know who this is?" Rostov closed in on Fiona, who rose to her feet to meet him even though her arms were still tied behind her back. "This is Field Marshal Molke. He will be the one sentencing you."

"I wonder what the sentence is," Vincent said. "Or do you have more than one sentence?"

"You are the two who say they survived a battle on Ryklar, is that right?" Molke asked. "I don't know how that's possible. The Chairman himself said the Victory was lost with all hands." Molke scratched his chin. "They say they were on the Victory?" he asked Rostov.

Rostov nodded. "Yes, sir. The boy I gave to the Area Six Replacement Unit myself. That whole unit was loaded on the Victory before its departure for Ryklar."

"And the Red?" Molke asked.

"I don't know where she came from. Probably from one of the annual Martian roundups the recruiters there do." Rostov glanced down at a data display. "But the manifests put them both onboard when it left Earth."

"Hmmm." Molke paced around the small ship. "Then how did they get off?"

"They must have deserted during a port call during the journey." Rostov glared at them. "No other way they would have survived. Unless we believe this tale about a full Defense Forces army being wiped from the field of battle by these monsters."

"Yes, a million man battle simply being ignored is ridiculous," Molke nodded. "We don't have time to deliberate on this right now." Vincent picked his head up, and for a moment it sounded like they weren't going to be killed. "Just have them strung up in the morning. Traitors do not deserve the firing squad," Molke said curtly before turning and walking out of the ship.

"Yes, sir."

"A million men on Ryklar. Another million here. What's two more, right, asshole?" Vincent stared at the ground, shaking his head. Molke turned to face Vincent one last time.

"Soldiers are born to die." He frowned and walked out. The door slammed behind him.

"The execution team will be here in the morning," Rostov told them, turning on his heels.

"Don't have the balls to do it yourself?" Fiona smirked "Can pass the sentence but can't carry it out?" Rostov turned and kicked her in the chest, his metal replacement leg dropping her to the ground.

"If it was up to me, I would beat you both to death with my bare hands," he growled. "The field marshal wishes to see you hung. Don't worry. I'll make sure it'll be very slow."

"I don't know how . . . or when . . ." Fiona spat out more blood. "But I'm going to fucking kill you." Fiona's words were little more than a guttural, animalistic growl. Even though she was tied up and crumpled in pain, Vincent swore he saw a glimmer of fear in Rostov's cold, dead eyes. The colonel turned and walked out of the ship without another word.

"Shit." Vincent dropped his head. "I can't believe after everything this is how it ends."

"No," Fiona said.

"No? No what?"

"It's not over. I don't know how, but it's not." Her voice wavered. It sounded like she was trying to convince herself more than him. Vincent didn't say anything; he didn't know what more to say. After everything they had tried, they were going to end hanging at the end of a rope.

*****

Neither of them slept that night. They lay close together on the floor, their hands still tightly tied together behind their backs. Vincent had his face buried in Fiona's dirty blonde hair. It was matted with blood, mud, and dirt, but it didn't stop him. He knew that it was going to be the last night he was ever going to spend with her.

He wasn't sure how he expected their adventure to end. He wasn't even sure how Fiona actually felt about him. He wanted to tell her for so long now but figured she would just blow him off. There was no point of holding it back anymore, though; it just didn't matter at this point.

"I love you," he whispered.

"Stop being so damn lame," she responded, though Vincent saw her smile slightly. She wiggled a bit and struggled to get into a position to face him. She leaned in and kissed him. Her ever-present smirk pulled the corner of her mouth back.

"I'm sorry it's ending like this," Vincent said, fighting back tears as his eyes started to burn.

"How else was it going to end?" Fiona sighed. "Were you going to take me home to meet your parents and live in one of those hideous committee-issued houses?" She laughed slightly. "Praising the Chairman in the morning before going off to our committee-issued jobs?"

"My dad would hate you so much," Vincent laughed.

"I'd say we move to Mars. Get a piece of land outside of Olympus and just tell the whole universe to fuck off."

"Titan. As far away from Earth as we can be."

"That sounds perfect." She kissed him again. "Maybe in another lifetime."

"Yeah."

"That would be a sweet lifetime, though," Fiona grinned. Vincent noticed her eyes were welling up, too.

"Don't cry," he smiled. "It ruins your tough chick persona."

The Reaper's door flew open and a group of soldiers stood over them.

"Did we ruin a moment?" sneered the lead soldier. Sergeant stripes adorned his dirty collar.

"Just plotting your death is all," Fiona smiled.

"Cute," the sergeant spat. "Let's see how much lip you have in you when you're hanging from a rope."

The two were pulled to their feet and pushed out of the ship. Vincent splashed through the mud. His feet had been numb for so long he didn't notice the cold anymore. He saw that none of the soldiers carried any weapons on them. He assumed it was a precaution in case he or Fiona managed to get loose; they would have nothing to arm themselves with.

They were led behind the array of command tents and landed Reapers to a small clearing. A pole was driven into the ground, and it was bent at the top. From the bent hook hung a chain, looped at one end. Vincent wondered how many soldiers Molke had sent here to die—to spend their last few minutes in this universe struggling for air as their necks were crushed by a repurposed utility chain.

Vincent was kicked to his knees. He saw Fiona forced to do the same. She was staring straight down at the muddy ground. There was something unsettling watching her sit brooding in silence. Even in the worst situations, she had some quip, something smart-ass to say during it all. Not now, though. Vincent wasn't sure if the drips coming off the end of her chin were rain or tears.

"What should we do with you?" He kneeled down in front of Vincent. The smell of his breath assaulted Vincent's nose. The sergeant's rotting teeth stuck out at odd angles and were every color other than white. "A traitor and a Red," he smiled. "It's times like these that make me glad I volunteered for this detail."

"Too afraid to fight the Anarchs so you volunteered to kill people who can't defend themselves. How brave of you." Vincent spat in the sergeant's face. A wad of phlegm slapped the sergeant on the bridge of the nose and dripped down with the rain. The sergeant responded by punching Vincent in the mouth. Vincent saw stars but he fought to stay upright. He didn't want to give the bastard the satisfaction of knocking him out.

"Me first," Fiona said quietly.

"What was that?" questioned the sergeant.

"Hang me first," she said. Vincent had never heard her speak like that before. Her voice was defeated and deflated.

"What?!" Vincent screamed.

"I can't watch you die," she sobbed.

"Isn't that heartwarming," laughed the sergeant. He picked up Vincent and pushed him toward the chain. "Guess I know who is going first now."

The sergeant grabbed the chain and pulled it down. The metal was ice cold on Vincent's neck, and his skin was pinched between the links of the chain as the sergeant tightened it. Vincent gasped as his windpipe was crushed. He felt the ground slip away from him.

Fiona launched to her feet, head-butting her guard in the nose and rupturing it with a crack. Her hands were still tied behind her back, making it hard for her to keep her balance, but she pressed her attack. The guard stumbled back and fell into the mud. She spun and kicked her other guard in the side of the neck. He fought to stay on his feet but went down face-first into the mud. Fiona walked over and stomped the back of the soldier's neck. The soldier twitched in the mud before going limp.

The other soldier climbed back to his feet, blood pouring down from his mangled nose. He lunged at Fiona. She ducked and dodged, kicking him wildly when she could. She back-peddled as the soldier closed in and landed a few more strikes.

Vincent began to flail, his toes just barely touching the mud. It wasn't enough to relieve the pressure on his neck. His eyes bulged, and he felt himself gagging as he fought to breathe. It felt like his head was going to explode as his vision began to narrow and turn fuzzy.

Fiona kicked out at the sergeant. He unsheathed a knife and slashed out at her. Fiona spun away from his attacks but was blindsided by a punch from the other soldier. She spun and fell helplessly into the mud.

The deafening boom of a Riten blew the sergeant's chest open, and a second shot tore Fiona's attacker's head clean off. The black form of Zinvor rushed forward and released Vincent from the noose. Vincent collapsed into the mud, coughing and gasping for air.

Fiona ran to Vincent and cut his bindings. Fiona's face was bleeding from several cuts from her fight with her two guards.

"Are you okay?" she asked frantically.

"What?" Vincent began, his mind cloudy. "What's going on?" He looked around.

"I told you I couldn't watch you die!" Fiona cried. She leaned in and kissed him.

"We must go soon," Zinvor grunted.

Fiona shook her head. "We have some business to attend to."

"Hm?" Zinvor frowned.

"I promised someone something. I have to see it through." Fiona stood up, helping Vincent to his feet.

"Where is Riten?" Zinvor asked them.

"These assholes took them. We're getting them back," Fiona cursed. "Do you have grenades?" Zinvor didn't answer; he simply dug a free hand into a leather pouch and handed her two of the spiked Mawr grenades.

"Time to clean house." She handed one to Vincent.

The group marched back through the mud toward the command area.

"What happened back there?" Vincent asked.

"Zinvor saved our asses," Fiona said.

"Arai think you went back to humans. I know this not true. I look for you," Zinvor smiled.

"Zinvor, they know about the weapons. They're going to betray the Fidayi. We have to warn her," Vincent said.

Zinvor nodded his agreement.

Fiona approached the first tent, kneeling in the mud near the opening. The soldiers, wrapped up in their rain slickers, were fast asleep on their cots. They were far enough from the front line that they assumed they didn't need to leave anyone awake to guard them.

"You take the other one." Fiona pointed to the second tent. "On the count of three." Vincent sloshed across the mud as quickly and quietly as he could, taking his place next to the tent's door.

"One . . . two . . ." Fiona began. She thumbed the arming switching on her grenade and Vincent did the same. "Three!" she yelled. Vincent stood up and pivoted to throw his grenade through the tent when he came face to face with a lone awake soldier sitting on his cot. The soldier's pale blue eyes and blonde hair stood out from the dirt and mud that caked his uniform.

Vincent froze, unsure what to do. The soldier leapt from his cot and tackled Vincent. Right before Vincent hit the ground, he tossed the grenade over the attacker's shoulder, and it tumbled through the tent.

The soldier landed on top of Vincent, throwing wild punches. Vincent covered his face with his arms, and the soldier's blows deflected harmlessly off his armor. The two dull thumps of the grenades exploded, and screams filled the air. Vincent punched the soldier in the face and rolled off him, holding his nose. The giant hoof of Zinvor slammed down on top of the soldier's face and he went limp.

Fiona walked into the burning tent, grabbed two rifles, and threw one to Vincent. She went through the pockets of one of the dead. She pulled out a pack of cigarettes and a lighter and stuffed them into her ammunition harness.

The three stalked toward the Reaper acting as the Defense Forces command center. Vincent's anger bubbled as he recalled the officers sitting around their table and cursing him and Fiona—calling them liars and frauds for claiming they survived a battle that they insisted never actually happened.

The thought deeply bothered Vincent. When bad things happened, like an entire army being destroyed, the Committee would just cover it up. They couldn't possibly allow the Committee, or especially the Chairman, to ever look weak. They certainly couldn't acknowledge a failure like the Defense Force's assault on Ryklar. It was better to say the Victory was destroyed before it had the chance to send its glorious army into the field than to tell the truth: that the Defense Forces were annihilated in battle and that the military they had spent an endless number of words glorifying had been soundly defeated.

How many horrible things had happened during Vincent's life that the Central Committee just decided that no one needed to know? He shuddered to think about what happened during the Mars rebellion. Were the rebels there as bad as the Committee said they were? He didn't know what to think anymore.

They came to the door of the Reaper. Zinvor stomped up to the door, grabbed hold of its long handle, and heaved back. The locked door sprang free as it was torn from its tracks. Inside, three officers awoke and shot upright from their beds. Vincent scanned the interior of the small ship, but saw neither Molke nor Rostov.

"Where is Rostov and Molke?" Fiona screamed at them.

"And where's the stuff you took from us?" Vincent yelled after her.

The officers mumbled but couldn't get their words out. Fiona fired one shot right into the face of the captain who had grilled them the day before. The back of his head exploded, covering the wall and the other officers with gore.

"Rostov went to the front!" screamed the major. "Something about being close to the objective!"

"And Molke?" Fiona growled at him.

"He has his own quarters not far from here. I'll show you!" the major cried. Vincent went through the trunks and boxes that filled one side of the ship. He found one Riten—Fiona's—and their belts of grenades. He strapped on the leather belt and handed Fiona her belongings.

"No sign of your Riten?" Fiona asked.

"No," Vincent replied. "One of the bastards must have taken it."

"We'll find it," she nodded. "You, let's go." She pointed to the major. He crawled out from underneath his covers and stood barefoot in nothing but his Defense Forces-issued tan underwear. Fiona motioned with her rifle for him to step outside. Once he was outside, she turned and shot the other officer and he collapsed back onto his bed.

The major folded his arms in a vain attempt to keep himself warm. He walked through the driving rain with his head down. Soon they arrived at another Reaper. A rain- and wind-tattered red flag hung from next to the Reaper's door. It showed the rank of a field marshal.

"The Chairman would be so disappointed in you," Fiona quipped, shooting the major. His half naked body dropped into the mud. Zinvor stepped forward and tore the door of the Reaper off its rails.

Inside, Molke was awake and still in full dress uniform. He studied maps on a display, their neon green holograms dancing around in front of his face. He shot to his feet in disbelief that anyone would dare disturb him.

"You!" he said in a hollow voice.

"That's right. Me," Fiona grinned.

"Where's my gun you prick?" Vincent cursed at him.

"I have nothing of yours, boy," Molke said calmly. He sat behind his desk once again. "Do what you will. It will not change anything."

"What this mean?" Zinvor questioned.

"It means they're almost to where the weapons are," Fiona frowned.

"You and your vile creatures can do nothing to stop us," Molke grinned. "The eagle and star will hang over the entire universe. Anything that defies us will be put to the torch."

Fiona slid her Riten out of her holster and leveled it at Molke's head. The old man's eyes went wide. The look of fear that spread across his wrinkled face made Vincent smile.

"Don't worry," Fiona smirked. "Soldiers are born to die." She pulled the trigger and reached over to the other side of the table. After a few seconds of fumbling with something, she pulled off Molke's sword belt. She strapped the sword around her waist. "We need to find Arai." Fiona looked at Zinvor.

"She went to command final attack." He struggled with the words.

"She went to the front, too?" Vincent said. "Zinvor, do you have a radio that we can use to contact her?"

"No." He pointed into the sky and shook his head.

"Remember Rostov said something about the atmosphere killing all the communications systems," Fiona cursed.

"She's caught right in the middle of it!" Vincent said.

Fiona nodded. "Let's go find her."

CHAPTER THIRTY

Zinvor, Vincent, and Fiona stalked through the dark command camp. They made it to the small craft used by the Fidayi as a command post and opened the door. Inside were several dead warriors still seated on floor cushions around the center table. Two Defense Forces soldiers rummaged through crates and boxes stacked at the back of the room. Fiona and Vincent shot them in the back before they had a chance to turn around.

"It's already started," Fiona cursed.

"Shit. We've got to go." Vincent tried hurrying out the door but was stopped by Fiona.

"We need to find a map or something so we know where we're going," she chided him. The three searched the room. After going through the dead's various pouches and pockets, Zinvor found what they were looking for.

"Here," Zinvor said. He held up a printed map, stained bright red with the blood of a dead warrior.

"Can you read this?" Vincent asked Zinvor. The Mawr's symbols and written language were completely lost on him.

"Yes," he nodded.

"Let's go find Arai," Fiona ordered.

"Wait. So who are we fighting right now?" Vincent scratched his head.

"Everyone that isn't a Mawr I guess," Fiona shrugged. "If someone looks at you wrong, put them in the ground."

"Alright, let's do this."

The group made its way out of the camp. Every few seconds, an exploding artillery shell would drop to the ground and light up the darkness. Once the darkness fell again they would move forward at a crouch.

It didn't take long for them to stumble upon the terrible price of the ongoing battle. The carpet of the dead and dying

Defense Forces soldiers was so thick that they could have walked across them and not touched the mud. Intertwined with them were the skinny bodies of the Alliance Rhai soldiers.

A Defense Forces tank was stuck, belly down, in the mud. A giant gaping hole was torn in its frontal armor, and tongues of flame flickered out into the rain. Nearby was the first of the Anarch bodies, surrounded by dead soldiers.

The Alliance had deep trenches dug into the muddy ground and reinforced with metal and beams of wood to prevent them from collapsing. The Defense Forces had paid dearly for every single trench they managed to take. The trenches were full of Rhai and Anarch dead. Their bodies were sloshing back and forth in the long-since flooded trenches.

The trenches were just narrow enough that Fiona and Vincent could jump across them, slipping and splashing in the mud on the other side. They would then turn and catch Zinvor as he launched himself over, because his short, stocky legs were unable to give him enough lift.

Several wounded soldiers wandered around the blasted muddy landscape. They were so shell-shocked and crazed that they stumbled past the group without even noticing it. A few of them fell face-first into the trenches below and did not get back up.

"Holy shit," Vincent whispered.

"Where the hell is everyone?" Fiona asked, stepping on the back of a dead Rhai.

"They must have pushed to the central positions, like Rostov was talking about," Vincent said. "Or died trying."

"A whole lot of the died-trying it looks like," Fiona said, disgusted as her boot slipped into the viscera that had spilled out of one of the dead bodies.

The constant booming of artillery gradually died away, and soon, the only sound in the night was the screaming of the abandoned wounded and the distant sound of incessant gunfire.

"Why would they stop shelling them?" Vincent asked, his eyes darting back and forth in the dark. Because of the non-stop flash of artillery explosions, they had never actually adjusted to Grawluck's never-ending dusk.

"I can think of two reasons," Fiona thought. "One: they ran out of shells, which seems impossible. Or two: they're so close to the central positions they're afraid they would hit their own men."

"Shit," Vincent whispered a little too loudly. "We don't have much time."

"We don't have any time. At this rate, we will be there to pick up the pieces."

A rifle shot snapped past Vincent's head and they all dropped, belly down, into the ground, splashing in the mud.

"Hey!" a voice screamed out. "Who's there?"

"Don't you think you should have asked that before you shot?" Fiona screamed back.

"Uh," the voice thought for a second. "Sorry! I thought you might be some of those Fidayi or whatever they're called trying to sneak around us!" Fiona simply stood up and walked toward the voice. Vincent followed her, and Zinvor crawled forward through the mud, trying to conceal himself.

"What are you guarding?" Fiona asked, walking calmly toward them.

"Oh, we're the rear guard. We've been out here for hours. Are you guys our relief?" the tired voice asked. As Vincent and Fiona got closer, he saw it was just two soldiers. They were standing in one of the captured and flooded Alliance trenches. They had a belt-fed machine gun and rifle between them. All around their feet were the water-logged corpses of humans, Rhai, Anarchs, and Mawr alike. They didn't seem to be bothered by the charnel house they found themselves guarding.

Vincent assumed that he and Fiona were covered with enough mud that it obscured their armor and that the soldiers simply mistook them for regular Defense Forces troops.

"The main force is right over there then?" Vincent asked.

"Yeah."

"I thought we were working with those Fidayi guys. What happened?" Fiona asked them.

"Oh yeah," the soldier laughed. "About two hours ago, Rostov gave the order to start shooting them. They're holed up in some building about a mile that way. Stupid monsters didn't even see it coming," he cackled. "These idiots here didn't even have time to draw their weapons before we took 'em out." He kicked one of the dead Mawr at his feet. As he did, his chest was blown open as Fiona shot him with her Riten at nearly point-blank range. Vincent shot the other soldier dead before he could reach for the machine gun.

"We're too late," Vincent cursed.

"No, he said they were hunkered down and defending themselves. They're still alive," Fiona said. "Let's go."

With their cover blown, the group took off at a slow jog. They would have run faster but Zinvor's short legs did not allow him to keep up with the humans. During the run, they passed several stretcher teams carrying the wounded back from the raging battle up ahead. Scattered in between the stretcher teams were the walking wounded shuffling their feet through the mud. Their eyes were wide, but it was clear they saw nothing. Vincent watched as several of them fell into shell craters among the countless dead.

The soldiers of the Defense Forces must have been so confident in their victory that they assumed anything alive was on their side. Even the squat, armored form of Zinvor didn't raise any questions as they passed.

"We gotta take them out!" Fiona whispered harshly.

"No!" Vincent nudged her with his elbow. "Let them pass. We can't fight everyone!"

"Fine, but if one of them so much as sneezes at me wrong, I'm going to shoot him in the face," she snarled at a passing stretcher team. A soldier with no legs writhed back and forth on the stretcher, bouncing with every step his carriers took.

The sounds of gunfire got closer. They could see the burning tracers from human machine guns and the bright lasers from the Alliance rifles streaking back and forth in the darkness.

"I have a question," Vincent whispered. The group stopped, took a knee, and looked down a steep hill. The mass of fighting men, tracers, and lasers was astounding. In the tangle of fighting below them, they couldn't tell where one side began and another one ended, or even who was fighting who.

"What the hell do we do now?" Vincent asked.

"Shit. It's chaos down there." Fiona scratched her dirty face.

"If we walk into that, we're going to die quickly and pointlessly," Vincent sighed.

"You can drive this?" came a deep throated question from Zinvor. They turned to see what he was talking about. He was standing next to a utility vehicle, or UV. The UV was a four-seater armored aero truck. It had a driver's seat like a normal truck, though its thick bulletproof windshield was half the size of a regular one. The truck's bed, however, was an enclosed armored cab with a hatch on its roof that opened to a massive belt-fed machine gun.

"I never have before," Vincent conceded. "And I think it's busted. Why else would they have abandoned it?" The UV, which normally hovered a foot off the ground, was stuck in mud. "I don't think its engine can start if its bogged down like that."

"I fix." Zinvor pounded his chest and stomped through the mud over to the stranded UV. He bent down and placed his two big hands on the rear of the cab and started lifting.

"There's no way," Fiona uttered as she watched the spectacle. "There's no way, right?" She looked over at Vincent.

"That thing has got to way a couple tons," Vincent added. The rear of the UV started lifting up out of the mud. Zinvor's face remained calm as he hefted the UV up and shifted it slightly out of the hole. He stepped back and dropped it on top of a damaged alloy bunker.

"I can't believe I just watched that happen," Vincent gasped.

"Let's figure out how to drive, I guess," Fiona laughed.

Fiona climbed up the side of the cab and opened one of the hatches. The cab was empty other than a few empty ration packs and cigarette butts.

"Jackpot!" Fiona screamed and dove head-first through the hatch. She popped back up a few seconds later holding a wrinkled, battered pack of cigarettes; one was already dangling between her mud- and blood-covered lips.

"Focus," Vincent said.

"So are you saying you don't want one?" She teased him by dangling the pack in front of him.

"Of course I do." He snatched the pack, placed one between his lips, and lit it with her lighter.

"You want to drive?" she asked.

"I've never driven a car before. What makes you think I can drive their armored truck thing?" He made a face at her.

"You're saying that like I was giving you an option." She smirked and dropped back inside of the turret. Vincent walked around to the truck's driver-side door and heaved it open. The armored door hissed as air rods released and expanded, pushing the door open for him.

The cramped space was walled with different data displays, controls, and dials. A steering wheel came up from the floor with pedals on either side of it.

"Hey!" He heard the muffled voice of Fiona from the cab. "Put on the headset!" He looked around and found a headset. It had two cushioned ear cups and a microphone that bent down near his mouth.

"Can you hear me?" he asked through it.

"Yeah, turn this hunk of crap on," she ordered.

"I don't see any button labeled 'on' anywhere," he cursed. "I'm just hitting everything."

"Well, hit it faster!" she said. Vincent looked around and pressed the one button he hadn't yet touched. The UV rumbled, and he heard the engines under him sputter. It lifted off the ground before dying and slamming back onto the bunker.

"What the hell was that?" Fiona asked.

"Piece of shit isn't starting!" Vincent complained. He hit the button again. The engines crackled, sputtered, and finally whirled to life. The UV popped back into the air and stayed there this time. "I think that did it," Vincent cheered over the headset.

"Let's go!" she yelled. Zinvor, a rifle in his hands, climbed into the cab with Fiona, squeezing up through the hatch with her.

Vincent looked through the tiny window, but it was caked in mud. He found a lever on one side of the UV's windshield. He pushed it up, and the armored windshield popped free and swung out of the way. Mud and rain lashed into the open hole and onto Vincent's face as he hammered the gas.

"Zinvor!" Fiona shouted into the headset. "Hand me some ammo!" She grabbed the huge machine gun in both hands and opened up the feed tray. Zinvor pushed a crate of ammo into the holder next to the gun and passed her the belt. She took the first bullet, which was about the size of her palm, in her hand.

"I've never used this thing before, so if I accidently kill us all, my bad," Fiona laughed.

"Let's not do that," Vincent sighed. The battle was coming closer and closer and the mass of combatants was growing larger and larger. Jutting out of the mud like an obelisk was a square building. In contrast to the unending sea of mud and driving rain, the white building stuck out like a blinding light.

The Defense Forces had been unable to fight their way inside because the battle was still raging all around. A deep trench was cut around it, and whichever army was inside was putting up one hell of a fight. Soldiers as far as he could see were charging the trench and building complexes but were being forced back. Vincent hoped the Fidayi were down there somewhere.

"I think it's an entire regiment!" Vincent screamed as mud flew up and slapped him in the face.

"Who are they shooting at? The Fidayi or the Alliance?"

"I have no idea!" he shouted.

"Shit, I have to do something!" Fiona yelled.

"Either way, if the Alliance is down there or not, the Defense Forces have to be stopped!" Vincent yelled at her.

"You're right!" She slammed down the feed tray of her gun and grabbed the duel charging handles on either side. With a grunt, she pulled them both back, loading the bullets with a loud clack.

Fiona squeezed the trigger and the gun came to life. Vincent didn't know what to expect from the weapon, but with every shot, it sent out a round that exploded into the ground. The sheer power of the gun shook the entire UV and Fiona's aim was going wild.

"Stop the damn truck. I can't hit anything!" she screamed over the gunfire. Vincent slammed on the brakes. With her aim steady, she unleashed hell on the swarm of Defense Forces soldiers.

She pulled the trigger. Thud, thud, thud. The gun rocked the UV and an entire line of soldiers exploded mid-sprint as Fiona's fire raked through them. Thud, thud, thud. The UV rocked again, and this time her shots hit a bunker in which a squad of soldiers was taking cover. It vanished in a flash of mud.

Several soldiers made their way up the hill. At first, Vincent assumed they were making their way to the rear, but it quickly became clear that they were curious about the sudden ambush.

"Shit. Fiona, I think they noticed us." Vincent lowered his head back into the driver's compartment.

"And here I thought we were being so sneaky!" she laughed. The soldiers opened fire on the UV, their slugs slamming off the front of the vehicle and sending Vincent ducking for cover. Fiona and Zinvor dropped down into the cab, and the storm of slugs raked across the top of the UV.

"Damn, that was close!" Fiona said. Vincent peered out of the hole and saw a group of ten soldiers advancing on the UV while another group lay prone in the mud, giving them suppressing fire.

"Shit!" he screamed and leaned over and grabbed his rifle, sticking it out of the hole where the windshield once was and blindly firing at the advancing troops. "Fiona, get on the gun!" A slug slammed into the armor next to Vincent's head and peppered his face with shrapnel.

"I'm trying!" She squeezed off a stream of shots that impacted only a few feet in front of the UV. The exploding rounds violently shook the truck and sent a cascade of mud and blood into the driver's area.

"Aw, come on!" Vincent whined. A grenade bounced off the edge of the windshield hole and landed in his lap. A small wisp of smoke curled off it and floated into Vincent's face. He stared wide-eyed at the grenade as it cooked off. "Grenade!" he screamed. He grabbed it and pitched it back out of the hole. Vincent ducked for cover as the grenade exploded just outside the UV, curtaining the area with a fire ball.

"You alive down there?" Fiona screamed, her voice barely audible over the sound of she and Zinvor's outgoing gunfire. Vincent picked up his head and tried to wave away the smoke filling the driver's area.

"I think so," he coughed.

Slugs still snapped and cracked off of the UV's armor. Vincent reached into his pouch, pulled out a grenade, and tossed it out the window. He transitioned back to his rifle, this time building up enough bravery to peek his head up and aim. As his eyes looked over the top, he saw an obscure form creeping through the mud a few hundred feet in front of them. He thought the shape looked familiar, but he couldn't place it. It turned, and he saw the silhouette of a long barrel.

"Tank!" Vincent screamed at the top of his lungs. An explosion ripped the ground apart only a few feet in front of the UV, nearly knocking it out of the air.

"Go! Go!" Fiona yelled back. Vincent slammed on the gas as another tank round hit the ground beside them. Fiona fired round after round at the tank. Small orange explosions impacted the tank's turret, but Fiona's gun didn't so much as scratch the tank's armor. The cannon erupted again, and the shell tore through the air over the UV so close to Vincent's head that he heard it whistle past.

"We have to do something!" Fiona yelled in between bursts of gunfire. "That damn thing is going to hit us soon!"

"Drive me closer!" Zinvor roared.

"Are you insane?" Vincent screamed.

"Do it!"

Vincent floored the UV and turned right into the path of the tank. A hail of bullets and slugs rained down onto the UV as it drove over the attacking soldiers, sending them diving for safety.

"This is so damn stupid!" Fiona exclaimed. The UV rocked as a rocket struck its side. The back of the vehicle swung out, and its rear end dipped, skipping across the mud as the engines struggled to hold it up.

"Dammit!" Fiona yelled. "Hold it together!"

"Where the hell did that come from?" Vincent fought with the steering wheel as smoke poured from the UV's undercarriage.

"I don't know, but we can't take another one!" Fiona yelled.

The tank was nearly on top of them as Zinvor climbed on top of the UV, his Riten unholstered.

"What the hell is your plan?" Vincent asked, looking back at him.

"Bring me closer," he grunted.

"Whatever you say." The enemy tank tried to escape from the charge of their damaged and smoking UV. It crept away in reverse and poured fire onto the UV with its machine guns. Zinvor ducked as bullets impacted around him. Fiona dove into the cab for cover, and Vincent hid below the edge of the windshield hole, driving blind.

The tank was only a few feet away from them. He yanked on the steering wheel, dodging it at the last minute, and the UV hit the side of the tank, their armor grinding against each other with an ear-piercing screech. Without a word, Zinvor leapt off the UV and onto the front slope of the tank.

"What the hell is he doing?" Fiona screamed. She tried in vain to get back to her position but was forced back by enemy gunfire.

"Drive!" Zinvor roared as he climbed up the tank. Enemy soldiers trickled over to the area to aid the tank, the operators of which had undoubtedly called in support.

"Screw that!" Fiona yelled back. She grabbed onto the trigger of the gun and swept it across the advancing soldiers. "Give Zinvor cover fire!" she ordered.

"On it!" Vincent called back. He peeked out of the windshield hole and burned through his magazine as fast as his finger could pull the trigger.

Zinvor bounded up to the top of the tank and was met by the tank commander, who was leaning out of his hatch and attempting to reload his heavy machine gun. Zinvor blew the man's head off with a single shot from his Riten. The tank commander's body fell back into the turret, covering the turret's roof in blood.

Zinvor dropped onto his stomach and fired several times into the tank's open hatch until his Riten ran dry. He rolled onto his back, unhooked his grenade pouch from his armor, and dropped the whole thing into the hatch. He then sprang to his feet and leapt off the turret, landing with a splash in the mud below, surrounded by soldiers.

"Shit! That tank is going to blow!" Fiona cried. "Go!"

"I'm trying!" Vincent stomped on the gas, but the UV struggled as it belched smoke and fire from its undercarriage. The UV raced around the stricken tank, sending several soldiers diving for cover. Outside, Zinvor reloaded his Riten and dropped several attacking soldiers.

A soldier appeared in Zinvor's blind spot, his rifle up and ready. Before he had a chance to shoot the raging Mawr warrior, Vincent crushed him under the burning engine of the UV.

"Get in, you psycho!" Vincent yelled. Without hesitation, Zinvor dove and grabbed onto the side of the UV, and Vincent sped off. A few seconds later, the tank exploded behind them, sending a mushroom cloud of burning debris into the air and momentarily transforming the dusk into day. The UV was slapped hard by the shockwave, and Vincent struggled to keep it on course.

"I can't believe that worked!"

"Me either!" Fiona laughed, slapping Zinvor triumphantly on the armored shoulder.

"I always know," Zinvor nodded. Vincent and Fiona laughed harder at the alien. Up ahead was a small smoke trail cutting through the air, and it took Vincent a second to remember what it was.

"Shit! Rocket!" he screamed. The rocket dove downward at the last second and detonated right under the UV, which was thrown into the air and came crashing down into the mud.

"I got him!" Fiona called out, her gun coming to life for a quick burst. Rifle slugs began to hit the side of the struggling UV as more soldiers closed in. "Get us out of here!"

"I'm trying!" Vincent kicked and stomped on the gas, but the engine sputtered and coughed. A slug slammed off the steering wheel in between Vincent's hands and he ducked for cover. "Give me some cover, dammit!"

"Yeah, yeah!" Fiona yelled back sarcastically in between long bursts of gunfire. Mercifully, the UV engine cranked back up. The bullet-riddled and smoking hulk rose above the mud, its engines streaming black smoke under it.

"We're back in business!" Vincent cheered and hit the gas.

As they closed in on the weapons building, they took fire from the warriors defending it. They clearly mistook the UV for a Defense Forces vehicle. Vincent just hoped they didn't have any anti-tank weapons aimed in their direction.

"Slow down!" Fiona yelled at him. Vincent pressed on the brake and nothing happened.

"It isn't working!" he screamed. "The shot we took must have taken out the brakes!" Vincent slammed the brakes again, but nothing happened. The UV, still charging forward at full speed, skipped across the top of a trench, this one full of fighting Fidayi warriors who dove out of their way. They crashed and burst halfway into the side of the building.

Vincent climbed out from the driver's seat, his head foggy, as warriors rushed forward to confront them. He held his hands up as he stared down the barrels of their rifles. They lowered their guns once they recognized his armor.

"Arai?" he asked them, and they pointed further into the building. He tried to shake the stars from his eyes after their violent crash.

"Fiona!" he yelled out at her. The cab portion of the UV had not come bursting through the building, so she had to climb down and through the hole in the wall.

"Yeah?"

"She's down there. Let's go." He nodded and they ran off through the building.

The building, once a large research facility, was now a war zone. Dead Rhai and Anarchs, mixed up with dead and dying Fidayi and Defense Forces soldiers, lay all over. Other warriors ferried ammunition to the fighting positions and piled captured weapons and Ritens together. Even the severely wounded were still fighting in one way or another. Only the dead Fidayi were out of the fight.

A warrior led them to Arai, who was directing several other warriors toward a staircase that presumably led underground.

"You are here!" Arai exclaimed. It had to have been the most emotion Vincent had ever heard her use in speech. "I thought you went back with them."

"No," Vincent clarified. "Arai, they knew about your plan with the weapons the whole time."

"Yes, it seems that way. We thought we were fooling them, and they were using us the whole time." Arai lowered her head. "All is not lost, though. We control the building and the weapons are below us."

"Really?" Fiona gasped. "Let's blow them up!"

"The Alliance still controls the bottom levels of the building. We are trying to clear them out, but they are holding fast."

"Can we win this?" Vincent asked.

"Our fleet is fighting its battle above us as we speak," Arai nodded. "We have only our battle to worry about. Everything else is out of our hands. I have sent a Rhai technician team to break into the charging stations. We must secure it for them."

"So where do you need us?" Vincent asked.

"You can join me in our assault to take the control room downstairs," Arai said. She walked toward the stairway. Its white walls were stained with the bright red blood of the Mawr, and several dead warriors slumped around the large archway door. Vincent could hear the loud thudding of the warrior's rifles and the sharp snaps of Rhai laser fire below.

Arai turned back and looked at him. "Why did you come back to us?"

"They were going to betray you, Arai. We had to tell you," Vincent said, hanging his head.

"Your goal was to go home, was it not?" she asked.

"I don't know if I have a home anymore. I found out a lot of things that made me question what home actually is. You treated us more like one of your own than they ever did. Like family even."

"And no one fucks with family," Fiona said, nodding. Vincent swore he could see a smile creep across the tough, hard face of Arai.

"Where is your Riten?" she asked Vincent.

"When they captured us, it was taken from me by a man named Rostov. I will get it back."

Arai nodded. "Yes, you will have me to contend with over who gets to end that human's life." Her features hardened. "And their warlord, von Molke."

"Oh, we took care of the old bastard," Fiona chuckled. "Do you want his sword?" She pointed to the sword dangling from her hip.

Arai smiled. "No, it is rightfully yours." She turned toward the archway. More warriors rushed past her and down the stairs. "It is time." She walked down the steps, unholstered her Riten, and thumbed back its hammer. She let out an unintelligible and thunderous roar, and the warriors below answered her in kind. Their war cry shook the walls of the stairwell and they stormed forward.

Like the control room on the destroyer, this one comprised several different terraced platforms stretching deeper and deeper underground. Unlike the ground level, there were no laboratory facilities, only row after row of computers and giant data displays the size of the wall with maps of the planets of the galaxy. Mars, the Moon, Titan, and Earth were labeled with red circles. The Moon had a large red hash mark through it. Another screen showed the fractured defensive lines around the facility. Everything other than the facility was colored red.

The first terrace was full of Rhai dead and a few twisted armored corpses of the Anarchs. The wall near the next flight of stairs exploded with an Anarch cannon round and sent several warriors flying. A few warriors charging down the stairs were ripped apart by heavy machine-gun fire.

Vincent and Fiona took cover behind a wall of computers and peeked over and down onto the next level. Below, a phalanx of Anarch soldiers stood shoulder to shoulder, firing their armor-mounted cannons and machine guns up at the advancing warriors. Their armor was covered in dents and cracks from the torrent of Mawr fire, but they still held strong.

Behind the wall of walking armor, Rhai soldiers took cover. They peeked out from behind the towering Anarchs and fired well-aimed shots from their rifles before ducking away behind their living wall. As the Anarchs advanced, the Rhai inched up behind them.

A warrior with a massive machine gun came down the stairs and onto the terrace with Arai and the others. He advanced toward Fiona and Vincent, only to be torn in half by a burst of well-aimed Anarch machine-gun fire. The gun tumbled from his dead hands and landed in front of Fiona. She leaned out and grabbed it, handing it to Vincent.

"You were always good with one of these," she said. Vincent looked down at the huge gun. It was easily twice the size of the machine gun he'd used in the Defense Forces.

"With a human gun!" he exclaimed. "This thing is a damn cannon. It'll break my shoulder."

"I think those assholes down there are going to do a lot worse than break your shoulder," Fiona said, pushing the gun into his arms.

He sighed and propped the gun on the ledge of the computers, pushed the butt stock into his armored shoulder, and let loose a burst down at the Anarchs.

The gun sent a punishing recoil through his body. It hurt so badly that most of his bursts of fire went far from his intended targets. His arm tingled and his hand went numb. The Anarchs saw their attacker and fired, sending Fiona and Vincent ducking for cover.

"Try aiming!" she yelled. Vincent peeked his head over again and aimed at the feet of one of the Anarchs. He squeezed the trigger, and the gun recoiled wildly. The first bullet punched into the Anarch's leg armor. The recoil of the gun made the rest of the burst shoot upward. The bullets stitched a straight line through the Anarch's armor, and bright orange blood oozed out of the wounds. It buckled and fell face-down onto the white floor.

Without hesitation, the rest of the Anarch horde closed the gap. Each soldier shifted over, shoving aside the bleeding armored body. Their firing swept across the top terrace, killing several warriors and sending the rest diving for cover. Fiona and Vincent dropped onto their stomachs as their cover was destroyed by incoming fire.

Arai armed a grenade and tossed it in a wide arc over the stairs and onto the terrace below. It detonated at the feet of the Anarch phalanx. Pieces of debris and broken armor were thrown into the air, and an Anarch soldier stumbled and fell onto its back. The rest of the Anarchs shifted into a single-file line, and in an orderly fashion, withdrew down another set of stairs to the level below.

Arai and her warriors had to climb over piles of their own dead and wounded as they rushed forward and down the stairs.

"Arai, how far until we get to the weapons?" Vincent called out, struggling to make it down the stairs with the massive gun held across his shoulders.

"Ground floor." She pointed ahead. "Not far now." A blue laser slammed into Arai's chest and she stumbled back, a smoking hole bored into her armor.

A wave of Rhai soldiers rushed up the stairs, their rifles blazing wildly. Arai shot one down with her Riten; the warriors were caught by surprise by their sudden desperate charge. Several warriors lashed out at the Rhai with their bare hands, and many of the Mawr were shot down by the charging Alliance soldiers.

Vincent fumbled with his heavy gun and dropped it from his shoulder to the ground. He leapt behind it and started firing powerful bursts into the line of soldiers charging at them. The impact of the bullets was devastating. The skinny, mostly unarmored Rhai were blown apart as if hit by an explosive. After a few long bursts from his weapon, there was little left standing. Some Rhai fled back down the stairs, leaving behind dozens, if not hundreds, of their dead.

"Arai!" Fiona cried. "Are you okay?" Arai looked down at the hole in her chest armor. Bright red blood leaked through it.

"Is nothing of consequence," she claimed. "We must finish this." She took the heavy machine gun from Vincent and handed it to one of her surviving warriors, who gave Vincent its beaten and dented rifle in return. She reached back to the warrior and drew a knife from a scabbard and handed it to Vincent. "For your long gun," she nodded.

He slipped the knife's mounting ring around the barrel of his rifle and it locked into place. Arai rushed down the last flight of stairs, her warriors following with Fiona and Vincent at their heels. The stairs were clogged with piles of Rhai corpses. They slowed the advance, and soon, the defenders on the ground floor were shooting at Vincent and the others caught together on the staircase.

Warriors bailed over the side of the stairs and fell to the ground below. They landed with a sickening thud before getting to their feet.

"We have to jump!" Fiona yelled over the gunfire.

"We aren't one of them!" Vincent screamed. "We'll break our damn legs!"

"Better broken legs than getting shot." Fiona grabbed Vincent by the shoulder. "Tuck and roll!" she shouted before pushing him over the edge and jumping after him. As they fell, an Anarch cannon round slammed into the stairs. The explosion sent warriors, debris, and bodies flying.

Vincent landed hard, rolling a little too late and coming to rest on his back. Fiona hit the ground like it was well practiced, rolling up into a kneeling position. Vincent sat up and saw that maybe only half of the warriors on the stairs had made it down alive.

Arai rushed forward, firing her Riten into the few surviving Rhai, with her warriors close behind. Clearly shaken, the Rhai dropped their weapons and ran, but they had nowhere to go. The armored phalanx of Anarch soldiers had reformed and returned fire. Alliance and Fidayi alike were caught up in the gunfire.

The warriors pushed forward toward the Anarchs, getting so close as to render their cannons useless. Ritens fired at point-blank range, gouging huge bloody holes in the Anarchs' armor. The Anarchs slammed into the warriors with their iron-clad arms, sending them skipping across the battered floor.

With her Riten in one hand, Fiona drew her stolen officer's sword with the other. Vincent chased after her, feeling naked in the middle of a battle full of armored monsters. He fired off two powerful rounds from his rifle, which kicked hard against his shoulder. One round slammed into an Anarch's armor, leaving a scorched dent, but the other shot went wide.

The Anarch charged at Vincent, swinging its arms. Vincent backpedaled, firing in full automatic mode. As the rounds impacted, the Anarch was slowed down. Dents and cracks formed all over its wide torso. A giant arm slammed into Vincent's right side. He felt the crunch of several ribs giving way. He howled with pain and flew across the room. He crashed into a data display screen. His rifle tumbled from his grip, and his entire right side burned with agony.

The Anarch closed in on him. Its arms came up over its armored helmet, winding up for the killing blow. Suddenly, it buckled with an impact, and orange blood foamed from under its helmet. Fiona stood behind it, her Riten outstretched and smoke curling up from its barrel. Even with her arm outstretched, she only came up to the beast's waist.

The Anarch spun and slammed an arm into Fiona's stomach. Her Riten and sword fell out of her hands, and she was sent backward, end over end. Orange blood poured out of a jagged wound at the back of the Anarch's head, but it didn't seem to be deterred by it. It stomped toward Fiona, who struggled to get back up.

Vincent pulled himself out of the debris pile and stumbled forward. It felt like every rib in his chest was broken, and every breath brought tears to his eyes. He fought to put one foot in front of the other and winced as he bent down to pick up Fiona's Riten.

He steadied his aim and fired a powerful blast into the Anarch's back. Its armor cracked, and a second shot blew straight through. The Anarch stumbled and fell to its knees, its blood staining the charcoal grey armor with neon orange. Vincent walked a few steps forward and fired again. The Anarch's helmet ruptured and blew apart. The armored monster twitched and fell limp to the ground.

Fiona pushed herself to her feet and limped over to Vincent, taking her Riten back.

"You okay?" he winced.

"I should be asking you the same thing." She forced a smile.

The room shook with an explosion as a warrior detonated a grenade, blowing itself and an Anarch soldier apart in a cloud of smoke and blood. Just as the battle seemed to be turning in their favor, two large bay doors slid open and in stepped something Vincent hadn't seen since the battle on the hilltop: an Anarch clad in rust red armor scarred from years of conflict. Its chained necklace of skulls swung back and forth as it stomped into the room. Vincent remembered its name from the hushed tones that Nox had told him.

"The Red King!" he screamed. The Red King's right arm rose up, anda rush of burning crimson flame erupted from a tube mounted on its wrist. The flame washed over a group of warriors. Instead of screaming and running away, they rushed the Red King, firing their Ritens and throwing grenades.

The Red King's armor was peppered with damage from his attackers, but they were eventually consumed by the flames. The other warriors pressed the assault before being driven to cover as the Red King's other arm went up and fired a stream of blue lasers at them.

Warriors charged headlong at the Red King, firing and throwing grenades before being cut down by a combination of flames and laser fire. The Red King marched forward, its armor cracked and scarred, but it was not slowed. Arai fired a point-blank blast into its midsection, tearing open an ugly wound.

The Red King slapped her away with a swing of its laser arm. She slammed hard into the wall and went limp, blood bubbling from her mouth. Riten, rifle, and machine-gun fire impacted the Red King from all sides. It swung its bulk in every direction, shooting flames and laser bursts. The flaming warriors flung themselves forward, weighing the Red King down with their burning bodies in a vain attempt to slow its advance.

The Red King, now bleeding, slogged forward with its armor ablaze. Fiona fired her Riten, and the shot slammed off its massive shoulder. The Red King set the ground on fire behind her as she ran for her life. Vincent grabbed one of the dead warrior's rifles and sprayed the contents of its magazine at the burning monster. Rounds impacted all over it but did little more than draw its attention to Vincent.

Vincent's weapon made a dull click as it ran dry. He cursed, taking the empty magazine out of the rifle and throwing it uselessly at the Red King. He turned and ran as fire burned across the ground. Fiona fired into its back, and the Red King stumbled forward.

"Shoot his damn flame thrower!" Vincent screamed, flames rushing out and burning at his heels. The Red King stomped forward after him.

Fiona fired again and again. The Red King spun, the huge bore of its flame thrower pointing right at Fiona's head. She winced and fired. The round traveled up the barrel and exploded. Flames rushed wildly up the Red King's arm and engulfed its armor. Fiona dove out of the way as the Red King erupted with flames.

The dark crimson metal bulged and cracked, vomiting smoke and fire. The laser cannon on its other arm twisted with pressure and exploded with blinding blue light. Brilliantly ablaze with pieces of armor exploding outward, the Red King kept attacking. A flaming arm slammed into a charging warrior, setting it on fire and sending it tumbling across the floor.

Fiona fired again, blowing the Red King's pauldron off. Instead of blood coming from the wound, fire ruptured out of the hole in its armor. The Red King stumbled, swinging its flaming appendages recklessly. The attacks against the burning monstrosity were starting to take their toll.

Arai was back on her feet and firing. Her shots stitched up the Red King's back, fire and smoke bursting out of the wounds. A loud, ear-piercing, guttural roar filled the control room.

Vincent advanced, a fresh magazine loaded into his rifle, and fired bursts of shots only a few feet away from the Red King.

Each time the rifle kicked back against his shoulder, the Red King recoiled with pain. The surviving warriors, struggling from various wounds, closed in on the injured Red King and pumped round after round into the burning husk of armor. Finally, the Red King fell to its broken knees. It tried to lash out one last time, but its movements were so slow that the warriors were able to dodge its attacks with ease.

The Red King fell face down on the once-white floor. The raging fire that had engulfed it finally fizzled out. An acrid, foul-smelling black smoke twisted up into the air from the countless holes in its armor. Cautiously, the warriors approached the motionless Red King, their weapons still raised and trained on the fallen monster. Arai limped over and ripped the chain of skulls from around its shoulders and tossed it aside. She grabbed a jagged edge of the King's helmet and tore it free. Vincent saw several lights and displays inside of the helmet flicker and go dark.

CHAPTER THIRTY-ONE

Arai held the severed helmet up above her head triumphantly, and the warriors cheered. They punched their Ritens into the air and roared.

"The weapons," Vincent panted. "What about the weapons?"

"Our technicians are working on them as we speak. They must stop the charging process before they can be destroyed. The process will also destroy what is left of this dead rock." Arai winced and she limped toward him. "We must hold the facility until they are complete. It should not take long."

A large group of warriors rushed down the stairs and into the command room's upper terrace. Zinvor was in the lead. He carried the massive mounted machine gun from their stolen UV.

"What's going on?" Fiona yelled at them. Zinvor grunted something to Arai, and the warlord's eyes went wide.

"Our line has broken. The humans are coming. I thought we had more time."

"They have to take the control room from us." Fiona crossed her arms. "Let's make that a bad idea for them."

"Start centralizing the ammunition from the fallen. We will need it," Arai ordered. Zinvor nodded and marched off. "We can hold them off. Frail and afraid things, those humans," Arai frowned, her wounds causing her obvious pain.

"I'm out of ammo." Vincent looked down at his weathered rifle. It was now tinged black from the Red King's fire-wielding assault.

"We do not have enough to fend them off," Arai confirmed. Vincent saw blood bubble from a hole in her armor as she spoke. "We will have to set some kind of trap."

"Rostov is bound to think he's won," Fiona said, frowning.

"We could hold our fire until they're close." Vincent pointed at the last flight of stairs that led down to where they were standing. "Hide down here until they funnel down the stairs." Fiona smiled broadly. "Close enough for a Riten."

"You claimed you were not a warrior, but you are certainly thinking like one." Arai walked over to a limping warrior with a deeply scarred face and burnt orange armor. Arai grunted an order, and he bowed deeply, struggling off afterward to spread the order around. "We will ambush them on the stairs. Once we are out of ammunition, we will close in on them."

"Close in on them?" Vincent raised his eyebrow. Fiona smacked his arm and he realized what Arai had meant. "Oh. Oh."

"How close are your technicians to shutting down the charging process?" Fiona asked.

"I do not know. But I do know if we cannot hold them off, it will not matter," Arai said grimly.

The warriors carefully set themselves into the wreckage of the control room. Several small groups of warriors lay down on the ground and others concealed themselves with bodies and debris. Vincent and Fiona pulled one of the many displays and computers away from the bullet-marked walls and slid in behind it.

Vincent had managed to find one half-empty magazine of ammunition. He assumed it only had about fifteen shots in it. Fiona had a pilfered Rhai laser in her hands with an unknown amount of energy left in its stores. She had set her Riten on the ground next to her and her sword next to it. Vincent could see only three rounds left in the Riten's wheel.

Vincent laughed. "How many last stands are we going to have?" He took a deep drag of a cigarette and passed it over to Fiona.

"Most people only get one. Consider yourself lucky," she smirked, the cigarette clenched between her teeth.

*****

The damaged double doors slid open. The sound of them rattling across their tracks was deafening in the deathly silent control room. The sharp clack clack clack of the lead Defense Forces soldiers' boots snapping on the floor echoed in the cavernous space.

"Spread out!" commanded a loud voice. The voice was thickly accented, and at its command, the sound of footsteps broke into that of a run. From his hiding spot, Vincent saw the tired, hollow-eyed, and filthy soldiers, numbering at least two troops—around three hundred men—spread out and make their way down the first flight of stairs to the middle terrace. Every few steps, they would stop and kick one of the dead Mawr, Rhai, or Anarchs or start rifling through their gear for war prizes.

Having encountered nothing but a sea of corpses, the soldiers relaxed and let down their guard. An older officer in his long rain slicker and peaked cap led the way down the second flight of stairs. His rifle was slung across his back, and most of his soldiers followed his example, throwing their rifles over their shoulders like they were backpacks.

A warrior, hidden under several Anarch dead, lay in waiting at the foot of the stairs. He had the huge belt-fed machine gun nestled against the pauldron of his armor and was staring down its crooked, damaged sights. Next to him was Zinvor, with his salvaged UV machine gun. Vincent grimaced at the thought of what its exploding rounds would do inside such an enclosed space. Neither Zinvor nor the other warrior had much ammunition left, but at that range, Vincent was sure it didn't matter.

The two machine guns roared to life. The concealed warriors behind them joined in with their guns and grenades. The soldiers on the stairs were dead before they noticed they were under attack. It all happened so quickly that Vincent and Fiona didn't even have the opportunity to open fire. The soldiers on the second floor panicked and ran, trying to get back up the first flight of stairs and out of the control room.

The warriors in hiding advanced up the stairs, trampling what was left of the dead and wounded soldiers underfoot, and ran forward firing. The soldiers were cut down as they fled for their lives. Fiona and Vincent came out from their hiding spot, rushing up the stairs with the warriors.

As the warriors swept through the soldiers, the few survivors who had managed to escape the ambush on the stairs and make it to the upper terrace began to fire down on the advancing Fidayi, even though dozens of their comrades were still trapped between them. Warriors and soldiers alike were caught in the hail of gunfire.

Fiona and Vincent dove to the ground as the air above them was transformed into a storm of steel. The warriors disregarded such things, charging into the storm. Their armor splintered and flew apart as the bullets tore through their ranks. The warriors pushed their wounded and dying forward as they closed the gap between them and the soldiers. Their limited Riten slugs punched massive ragged holes in the soldiers and sometimes took out two at a time. When their weapons ran dry, they set upon the soldiers with anything and everything, including their bare hands.

Vincent and Fiona joined the fray. The swarming melee of Fidayi warriors crashed through the once disciplined firing ranks of Defense Forces soldiers. Vincent slashed a soldier across the stomach with his bayonet and fired a round from his rifle at point-blank range. He tore the bayonet free just in time to parry an incoming blow from another soldier and doubled him back with a kick to the midsection. He fired a pair of rounds into the soldier's chest; his body armor could not stop them at such close range.

Fiona hacked and slashed with her stolen sword, taking down a soldier who was leveling his rifle to take a shot at Vincent. Before he could thank her, he shot down a soldier charging up from behind her with a bayonet aimed at her lower back. A warrior was stabbed repeatedly in his chest and brought to its knees by a group of three soldiers. Vincent ran forward, firing his rifle on automatic, and dropped the three attackers. The wounded warrior struggled to its feet, bright blood oozing down its armored chest.

The tide was turning in the Fidayi's favor. The Defense Forces soldiers were tired, scared, and leaderless. Those not caught up in the path of the warriors' attacks had already broken and fled out of the control room, leaving their comrades behind to be slaughtered.

Vincent was caught up in the high of combat, screaming alongside his new Fidayi comrades as they crushed the soldiers. He slashed and stabbed his way forward, shoulder to shoulder with Fiona and the warriors.

He panted heavily and looked around for more targets when he saw the soldiers had been driven from the control room entirely. He dropped to a knee next to one of the fallen soldiers and started rummaging through his ammunition carrier. He unbuckled the tattered cloth harness heavy with full magazines and strapped it around his chest. He grabbed the dead man's rifle, leaving behind his blood-soaked Mawr rifle, and walked to where Fiona and Arai were standing.

"How much longer?" Vincent asked.

"I do not know." Arai shook her head. "They should be done."

"How far away are they?" Fiona asked.

"Not far. This is simply the control room. The charging stations themselves are not far from here." Arai holstered her Riten. "We must go."

Arai, moving visibly slower because of her wounds, walked back down the terraces of the control room and to the door on the ground floor. The door had been badly damaged in the fighting and would no longer open on its own. Zinvor stepped forward, gripped a twisted and bent edge, and pulled it back. It peeled open in such a way that reminded Vincent of opening a Defense Forces ration pack.

Stepping through the door, Vincent saw a long tunnel. It was built in the same fashion as the control room—a flawless, seamless white. It looked like the hallways onboard the destroyer above Elysian. The bloody, dirty, and exhausted warriors in the corridor looked out of place in such a sterile environment.

Soon, the calm of the corridor began to fade. The white surfaces ahead were coated in the same gore as the control room.

"There was not supposed to be any enemy here," Arai cursed, unholstering her Riten.

"If they knew the plan . . ." Vincent thought out loud.

"They knew where the charging stations were," Fiona finished.

The group cautiously made its way down the hallway, weapons raised. They came to another door flanked by the slumped corpse of a Mawr warrior.

"They must be inside," Arai nodded to Zinvor. He stepped forward, and with a hard kick, the door buckled in on itself. A second kick took it down completely.

Inside was another control room, the floor littered with the skinny corpses of Rhai. Judging by their dress, Vincent assumed they were the technicians sent in by Arai. Standing at a data display was a group of humans, their own handheld devices plugged into the computer terminals.

One of the flawless white walls was broken by the form of a huge window that looked out into a silo. Tubes, cables, and chords snaked up either side. At the bottom of the silo, what looked like a turbine spun rapidly, emitting a dull hum. Bright green particles floated around above the turbine. As Vincent watched, the green particles began to glow brighter and grow in number.

"You creatures thought you could hide this from us!" barked the familiar voice of Rostov. He walked into the room, hands on his hips in triumph. His soldiers raised their weapons as they walked through the door at his heels. Rostov's eyes went wide when he saw Fiona and Vincent standing among the warriors. "But how?"

"Your executioners suck," Fiona smirked. "And your field marshal didn't even put up a fight." She put her hand on the hilt of the stolen sword.

"Traitors," Rostov spat.

"Regardless of your feelings about my kin, you do not know what you are doing!" Arai shouted.

Rostov furrowed his brow at the short warlord. "These weapons will allow us to wipe the galaxy clean from your vile kind."

"You killed the only people who knew how to stop them, you idiot!" Vincent screamed, pointing down at the dead Rhai at their feet.

"Stop them?" Rostov gave Vincent a hateful look.

"You have no idea what you just walked into the middle of, do you?" Vincent asked, incredulous.

"It is not my job to ask questions, traitor. The Chairman wants these aliens' weapons, so I shall deliver."

"We were doing all of this to save Earth, you idiot!" Vincent tossed his hands in the air. "Your blind obedience just killed everything we know!"

"You were just keeping this power from us!" Rostov screamed.

Fiona frowned. "You can steal whatever you want now. It won't make any difference."

"You lie!" Rostov yelled. The ground began to shake. The dull hum grew into a roar. The floating green particles flashed into a blinding green light. "You did this! May the Chairman curse you!"

"By the looks of it," Fiona laughed, "there isn't going to be a Chairman for much longer."

"You Red whore!" Rostov drew a pistol faster than Fiona could react and fired. Vincent saw it coming. He leapt forward and pushed Fiona out of the way. Rostov's bullet slammed into Vincent's shoulder. He twisted awkwardly and landed face-down on the cold, blood-stained ground.

Vincent's head swam and his shoulder burned with pain. His entire right arm was numb and he couldn't move it. The air above him erupted with a burst of close-quarters gunfire. After a few violent seconds, it was over. He pushed himself to his knees. His head was foggy, and everything seemed to be moving in slow motion.

He looked around and saw a warrior he knew as Masa dead on the floor, his face caved in by a close-range slug. Zinvor's hand was mangled, and he cradled his Riten awkwardly in his other hand. Fiona furiously kicked and punched one of the downed soldiers. None of the other soldiers were left standing.

Vincent stood up, and the feeling slowly came back to his arm, first as a tingling pain and then back to normal. Vincent felt the spot where Rostov's bullet had impacted, just above his heart. His dark blue armor had a small gouge taken out of it, and the top several layers had broken away, but it did not penetrate.

Vincent walked over to where Fiona was viciously beating a man he now saw was Rostov.

"Is he dead?" he coughed. Fiona turned and was shocked to see Vincent standing there. She jumped up and kissed him.

"I thought you were dead, you asshole." She pushed him. "Why the hell did you try to be a damn hero?"

"I thought it would have been terribly ungentlemanly of me to just let you get shot." He forced a smile. Vincent knelt down next to Rostov, who to his surprise was still breathing. He started patting him down and felt along the wounded man's belt line. He felt the bulky shape of his Riten holstered there, drew it out, and strapped it on his waist.

"Do it," Rostov muttered. His teeth were broken at odd angles and blood oozed from his mouth. He was hard to understand. "Just kill me, traitorous scum."

"Oh I will," Fiona spat.

"Not yet." Vincent waved her off. "I want you to watch what you did first." Vincent fought for breath through his painfully broken ribs. "I want you to watch our world burn."

The ground began to shake violently as the deep, rumbling roar of the plasma charger reached its maximum. The bright, swirling green light erupted upward and out of the silo. For several minutes, the blinding light surged from the spinning turbine and tore up through the dark sky above. The torrent of light slowed and then finally stopped. The turbine returned to his previous dull hum as the remaining particles of green light flickered and died away.

Vincent saw tears welling up in Rostov's eyes, though he wasn't sure if they were from Fiona's beating or the sight of a doomsday weapon hurtling toward his home. Vincent unholstered his Riten and fired a shot into the crying man's chest. The tears stopped flowing from his lifeless eyes.

Vincent and Fiona approached the window and glanced up through the open silo. The darkness of Grawluck's sky was gone and was instead replaced by a sickening shade of green. Somewhere out above them, the burning plasma would strike Vincent's home and burn away everything he had ever known in a sea of fire.

"I am sorry." Arai's head dropped. "I have failed."

"No." Vincent shook his head. "You tried harder to save my planet than my own people did. What happens now?"

"I do not know. Maybe your planet will survive the coming attack. Perhaps your people will become like mine." As Arai walked through the carnage in the room, she approached the door that Rostov and his men had snuck into and pushed it open. She was greeted by the driving rain and cold.

Arai's legion of Fidayi warriors had clawed their way out of the muddy, flooded trenches and greeted her with sharp bows. Most were badly injured, and all of them were so filthy that they looked like clumps of living mud. It was as if Grawluck itself had risen to join the vast slaughter taking place on its surface.

Defense Forces soldiers were still hunkered down in the blasted landscape. Vincent could see their wild eyes glowing in the green light. They were peeking out from behind their crumbling parapet walls. They had obviously been expecting Rostov to walk out that door. Vincent was sure that, upon seeing Arai, they knew that they had lost. The Fidayi stood shoulder to shoulder, their hands on their Ritens. Vincent was unsure how many of them even had ammunition left.

Arai marched forward, and although she was wounded, she did not show pain or slow down. Vincent and Fiona walked next to her, treading carefully on the lips of several massive shell craters. The bottoms were filled with water, and in them floated the bloated corpses of two of perhaps many thousands of dead humans who now rested in the cold embrace of Grawluck.

A shaking soldier brought his rifle's sights up to his eye and aimed at them.

"It's over!" Fiona yelled at him. The soldier lowered his rifle, shocked that he was being yelled at in his language. "Go home! If it even still exists," she called.

Every step Vincent took, his face throbbed with pain and his shoulder burned. He was certain one of the terrified and exhausted soldiers would shoot them down. Strangely, the soldiers started climbing out of their trenches and, unsure of where to go, began following after the Fidayi.

"What do you think they'll do?" Vincent asked.

"Ask someone who cares."

"It's not their fault they listened to orders. We would have done the same thing," Vincent pointed out. "Hell, we did do that."

"They can find refuge on Elysian if they so choose," Arai interrupted. "Or if they want to go home, we will not attack their ships."

"But they just tried to kill you," Fiona said.

"They are not the first to try to kill me or my kin. My war is not with them. And you humans have bigger worries now," she began. "Speaking of which, what will you do now? Come back to Elysian with my clan. We can seek vengeance on the Anarchs together."

"Thank you, but I'm going to have to say no. I'm not so good at this war thing." He pointed to the bullet-sized dent in his shoulder armor and black and blue face. "I think I'll sit the rest of this whole thing out."

"It is a shame. And you, Fiona?"

"As much as I'd like to burn down the galaxy with you, I kind of like this idiot, so I'm going with him," she smirked, putting a filthy arm around Vincent.

"Where will you go?" Arai asked.

"I don't know," Vincent shrugged. "Nothing for us on Earth anymore."

"I hear Titan is nice this time of year," Fiona said, smiling.

Vincent smiled back. "It's a date."

"Ugh, I can't believe I love you."

"So you do love me?" He raised an eyebrow.

"Of course I do, stupid."

"Ugh, you're so lame," he joked.

Fiona smirked, gave him a kiss on his bloody, mud-covered cheek, and slapped him on his armored butt. They said their goodbyes and made their way across the blasted landscape as the green glowing hue faded back to black.

MEET THE AUTHOR

Joseph Kassabian served 8 years in the US Army and multiple tours in support of the Global War On Terror. After he got tired of getting yelled at for wearing the wrong hat, he exited the Army to pursue a career in writing. He has used the bitter, jaded, and sarcastic sense of humor that he learned in the ranks and turned it into books, articles, and a podcast. Joe spends his time with his dog in the Great Moist Northwest while screaming at a laptop screen.

A mysterious woman hires Vera Shadow, Private Detective, to find a missing college student. The trail leads Vera from the dormitory of Dorwich Institute of Magic to a seedy nightclub, an upscale penthouse and the docks. Little does she know the rabbit hole goes deeper than she thinks.

CPSIA information can be obtained
at www.ICGtesting.com
Printed in the USA
BVHW040822170519
548603BV00011B/86/P